P9-DBO-843

Highest Praise for Gregg Olsen

Heart of Ice

"Gregg Olsen will scare you—and you'll love every moment of it."
—**Lee Child**

"Olsen deftly juggles multiple plotlines."
—*Publishers Weekly*

"Compelling, engrossing . . . an absorbing, enjoyable read."
—*Romantic Times*

"Fiercely entertaining, fascinating . . . Olsen offers a unique background view into the very real world of crime . . . and that makes his novels ring true and accurate."
—*Dark Scribe*

A Cold Dark Place

"A great thriller that grabs you by the throat and takes you into the dark, scary places of the heart and soul."
—**Kay Hooper**

"You'll sleep with the lights on after reading Gregg Olsen's dark, atmospheric, page-turning suspense . . . if you can sleep at all."
—**Allison Brennan**

"A stunning thriller—a brutally dark story with a compelling, intricate plot."
—**Alex Kava**

A Cold Dark Place

"A page-turner . . . a work of dark, gripping suspense."
—**Anne Frasier**

"This stunning thriller is the love child of Thomas Harris and Laura Lippman, with all the thrills and the sheer glued-to-the-page artistry of both."
—**Ken Bruen**

"Olsen keeps the tension taut and pages turning."
—*Publishers Weekly*

A Wicked Snow

"Real narrative drive, a great setup, a gruesome crime, fine characters."
—**Lee Child**

"A taut thriller."
—*Seattle Post-Intelligencer*

"Wickedly clever! A finely crafted, genuinely twisted tale of one mother's capacity for murder and one daughter's search for the truth."
—**Lisa Gardner**

"Tightly plotted, gripping . . . an outstanding addition to the suspense genre."
—**Allison Brennan**

"An irresistible page-turner."
—**Kevin O'Brien**

"Complex mystery, crackling authenticity . . . will keep fans of crime fiction hooked."
—*Publishers Weekly*

"A top-notch thriller . . . a powerhouse of a book."
—**Donna Anders**

"Vivid, powerful, action-packed . . . a terrific, tense thriller that grips the reader."
—*Midwest Book Review*

"Keeps the reader guessing and gulping from the very first page."
—**Jay Bonansinga**

"Tight plotting, nerve-wracking suspense, and a wonderful climax make this debut a winner."
—*Crimespree* **magazine**

"Wonderful . . . compelling and horrifyingly real."
—**Seattle Mystery Bookshop**

"Olsen writes a real grabber of a book. If you're smart, you'll grab this one!"
—**Linda Lael Miller**

"A compelling story, tightly woven, that kept me riveted to the final page."
—**Susan R. Sloan**

"*A Wicked Snow*'s plot—about a CSI investigator who's repressed a horrific crime from her childhood until it comes back to haunt her—moves at a satisfyingly fast clip."
—*Seattle Times*

Also by Gregg Olsen

GREGG OLSEN

VICTIM SIX

PINNACLE BOOKS
Kensington Publishing Corp.
www.kensingtonbooks.com

PINNACLE BOOKS are published by

Kensington Publishing Corp.
119 West 40th Street
New York, NY 10018

Copyright © 2010 Gregg Olsen

All rights reserved. No part of this book may be reproduced in any form or by any means without the prior written consent of the publisher, excepting brief quotes used in reviews.

If you purchased this book without a cover, you should be aware that this book is stolen property. It was reported as "unsold and destroyed" to the publisher, and neither the author nor the publisher has received any payment for this "stripped book."

All Kensington titles, imprints, and distributed lines are available at special quantity discounts for bulk purchases for sales promotions, premiums, fund-raising, educational, or institutional use. Special book excerpts or customized printings can also be created to fit specific needs. For details, write or phone the office of the Kensington special sales manager: Kensington Publishing Corp., 119 West 40th Street, New York, NY 10018, attn: Special Sales Department; phone 1-800-221-2647.

This book is a work of fiction. Names, characters, businesses, organizations, places, events, and incidents either are the product of the author's imagination or are used fictitiously. Any resemblance to actual persons, living or dead, events, or locales is entirely coincidental.

PINNACLE BOOKS and the Pinnacle logo are Reg. U.S. Pat. & TM Off.

ISBN-13: 978-0-7860-2044-7
ISBN-10: 0-7860-2044-X

First printing: February 2010

10 9 8 7 6 5 4 3 2 1

Printed in the United States of America

For Rita Ticen Burns

Prologue

"Quiet, bitch," he said. "Be a good girl and do as I say."

His words came at her with the smell of sweat and motor oil. They were delivered in a strangely calm, almost soothing, cadence.

The young woman was terrified, her body, her very presence, shrinking under his power.

"Don't!" she said, the words falling from her trembling lips.

"Good girl," he repeated.

Tears rolled. A coppery flavor filled her mouth. It was as if she tasted spare change, yet her mouth was empty. She was bleeding where he had struck her.

And her pleas for help were called out only in her head, *God, help me!*

No answer. Just a slow fade. A curtain pulled. A moon eclipsed. Then absolutely nothing at all.

That was before. Just how long ago, she couldn't be sure.

Her memories were a mosaic. They came to her, not the seamless movie reel she had imagined people saw in their mind's eye when their final moments came and their life flashed before their eyes, but in tiny shards and splinters: Her high school graduation. How she and her best friend Danita had bought a bottle of screw-top wine from a mini-mart near the Tacoma Dome, where the ceremonies were held. They'd guzzled it in Danita's old car. Real tough, she'd thought. The only bad thing she'd ever done in a childhood of helping her mother raise her siblings, making solid-B grades, and working part-time jobs when she could fit them in between her household chores.

What did I do to deserve this? she asked herself in a blip of lucidity.

Her mind jumped to how her mother had sat her, her brother, and her sister in a neat row on the old floral davenport that faced the relic that was their TV. Mom snapped off a soap opera and fought back tears. The other kids were younger, but she knew right away before she opened her mouth what this little family meeting was about.

"Your papa and I . . ."

Another splinter drove into her. She recalled how she'd stolen a handful of candy corn from a bin in the produce section in the market when she was seven. She never told anyone that she'd done so, but to that very day the sight of the triangular orange, yellow, and white Halloween confection made her stomach churn with guilt. She never stole anything again, never broke any law. One time when she was stopped by a state trooper, she cried because she thought she'd been speeding and was going to get a ticket. Instead, the affable cop with a soup strainer of a mustache told her that her taillight was out, flashed a smile, and waved her on to the nearest repair shop.

"Need to be safe," he said. "Have a daughter of my own and wouldn't want her driving with a winking tail light."

Some thoughts materialized as if underscored by the divine, reminding her not to steal, that parents don't always stay together, that there are good men out there too. Some were more random. Things that came to her that felt like filler, a recap of moments that had never been important. She lost her car keys the week before. She threw up on a merry-go-round when she was four. She hated ravioli from the can and could remember the slap she got from her aunt when she told her so at the dinner table.

Shutting her eyes did nothing. The images still bombarded her.

Stop, she thought. *Think. Think. You don't want to die. Not here, not in this place.*

The man on the other side of the wall that separated them had his own flood of recollections. He steadied himself by leaning against the small doorway. The rumble of an old refrigerator's ice machine soothed him like one of those cheap motels with Magic Fingers attached to the bed frame. Drop in a quarter, ride the pulsating massage. Feel good. He thought of her begging for mercy.

"Don't do this. You don't want to do this!"

But he did want to. So very, very much.

He remembered how, after that, everything had been about the killing.

Even when he'd watch TV and a potato chip commercial would come on, he'd rewrite the familiar tagline in his head: *Nobody can kill just one.*

In the shadows, the young woman was growing a little stronger, a touch more coherent. She felt the rumbling of something outside the space that held her prisoner. She was on her stomach. Her hands had been bound by tape. Her feet too.

She realized that she was breathing hard. Fast, out of fear. She told herself to slow down. She didn't want to pass out. Not like before.

She remembered his hand reaching around her as he held her from behind. He'd had what looked like a dirty T-shirt balled up in his fist. At that moment she had known she was probably going to die.

He had pinched her neck and pressed the fetid cloth to her mouth and nose. Tequila? Cleaning fluid? Acetone? She felt the wooziness that comes with too much to drink and maybe too little sleep. She felt her knees starting to bend, although she commanded them to stay locked. The world around her started to grow faint. She couldn't even hear his breathing, at once so labored and hot against the back of her neck.

I don't want to die. Why are you doing this to me? Who . . . what are you?

Of course, no words came from her bruised and bloodied lips. Her interior monologue was screamed through the fear in her eyes only. She was falling. The lights were going out.

Help me. Please, someone.

Then nothing.

Her last thoughts were the darkest that had ever gone through her mind.

I hope he only rapes me. Yes, only rapes me.

Her wits were nearly gone, but she knew the ridiculousness of her thoughts. She had a friend who'd been raped in a restaurant parking lot. It was nothing to wish for, but in that moment it was the only hope that she had.

She wanted to live.

PART ONE
Celesta

Doing what I do is hard enough. . . .
Finding the right girl, the one who knows her place,
that's damn near impossible these days.

—FROM AN E-MAIL RECOVERED FROM THE
SUSPECT'S COMPUTER

Chapter One

March 29, 8 a.m.
Near Sunnyslope, west of Port Orchard, Washington

The early mornings in the woods of Kitsap County, Washington, were wrapped in a shiver, no matter the season. The job required layers and tools. The smartest and best-prepared brush pickers started with an undershirt, another shirt on top of that, a sweater or sweatshirt, and a jacket. Gloves were essential too. Some were fashioned with a sewn-in cutting hook to expedite the cutting of thinner-stemmed plants like ferns. A sharp knife or a pair of good-quality loppers made easier the business of cutting woody stems like evergreen huckleberry, salal, and in the Christmas-wreath season, fir and cedar boughs. As the day wore on, pickers shed their clothing, a layer at a time. Picking was hard work, and a good picker was a blur, cutting, fanning, and bundling, before bagging floral gleanings in thick plastic bags.

Instead of garbage in those bags, of course, there was money.

Pickers often left indicators they'd been through an area.

Empty bags of chips emblazoned with Spanish words that touted the snack's flavor. Sometimes they left torn gloves or leaky boots in the forest. Some left nothing at all.

Sunday morning Celesta Delgado—along with her boyfriend, Tulio Pena, and his two younger brothers, Leon and Reno—left the mobile home they were renting in Kitsap West, a mobile home park outside the city limits of Port Orchard, just before first light. Behind the wheel of their silver-and-green 1987 Chevy Astro van, Tulio drove northeast toward state-owned property near Sunnyslope where they held permits for brush picking. Celesta and Tulio also worked at a Mexican restaurant in Bremerton, but this being Sunday, they had the time to earn—they hoped—about $60 apiece for a day's work in the woods. The center seats of the van had been excised so they'd be able to haul their gleanings back to the brush shed, or processing plant, off the highway to Belfair. The two younger ones sat in the backseat amid supplies and the cooler that held lunch.

Celesta, at just five feet tall, was a fine-boned woman with sculpted cheeks and wavy black hair that she wore parted down the middle and, only at the restaurant, clipped back because it was required. She adored Tulio and tolerated his younger brothers with the kind of teasing repartee that comes with both love and annoyance.

"You boys are lazy! Help your brother fix the van."

"Hey, Celesta, you take longer with your hair than Shakira!"

At twenty-seven, Tulio was five years older than the love of his life. He was a compact man with the kind of symmetrical muscular build that suggested he worked out to look good, rather than worked hard with his body. The opposite, of course, was the truth.

Tulio parked the van adjacent to a little crease of pathway into the forest, the entrance to Washington State Department of Natural Resources land that had been cleared by loggers in the 1970s. The second growth provided the ideal growing conditions for the foliage that serves as filler for market bouquets. Anyone who's ever purchased a bunch of flowers from a grocer has held in his hands the gleanings of dark green to accent gerbera daisies, tulips, delphinium, and other floral showstoppers. They've held the work of those who labor in the forests of Washington and Oregon.

The small group all put on thick-soled rubber boots and retrieved their cutting tools, rubber bands, and hauling bags from the back of the van. Then the quartet started out, their Forest Service tags flapping from their jacket zippers. They could hear the voices of Vietnamese pickers, so they turned in the opposite direction and followed a creek to a narrow valley. Stumps of massive trees long since turned into houses, fences, and barns protruded from mounds of dark, glossy greens. The area had not been over-picked, which was good. It was getting harder to find places that didn't require a three-hour hike. Tulio had been assured that the area was regulated and in good condition. It was good, though, not to have been misled. He valued their permits and foraged with care rather than with the bushwhacker mentality that denuded sections of the forest. Tulio saw it as a renewable resource—that is, renewing and filling the usually empty fold of his wallet.

"Don't cut all the moss, bros," Tulio told Leon and Reno. "There won't be any to come back and get later."

"*Sí!*" they chimed back, looking at Celesta.

Celesta shrugged a sly grin. She'd been the one who over-harvested the moss from the trunk of a big-leaf maple the last time they went out to work in the forest.

Fog shrouded patches of the valley as the four fanned out to cut and bundle. They set to work. Celesta was the slowest of the four because she sought out sprigs that were of a higher quality. No wormholes. No torn edges. Just beautiful shiny leaves that were often mistaken for lemon leaves by those who didn't know botany and sought a more romantic origin for their floral displays than the sodden forests of the Pacific Northwest. Bunches of salal were pressed flat and stacked before being bagged.

The morning moved toward the afternoon, with three trips to the van and then back into the woods. No one saw the Vietnamese pickers they'd heard talking in the woods at the beginning of the day. At the van, Reno and Leon heard the sound of car doors slamming somewhere nearby. They assumed more competitors were on the way, but they never saw anyone.

Around 2 P.M., Celesta decided she had to use the bathroom. She loathed squatting in the woods. She told Tulio she was going back in the direction of the van, where she'd seen the remnants of a shed that would provide some kind of privacy.

"All right," he said. "Two more loads, and the day is done."

"Good, because I'm tired." Celesta lugged her latest batch of greens over her petite shoulder and disappeared down the same deer trail they had followed into the clearing.

Even in the midst of a spring or summer's day with a cloudless sky marred only by the contrails of a jet overhead, the woods of Kitsap County were always blindfold dark. It had been more than eighty years since the region was first logged by lumberjacks culling the forest for income; now it was developers who were clearing land for new tracts of ticky-tacky homes. *Quiet. Dark. Secluded.* The woods heaved quietly in a darkness that hid the fawn or the old refrigerator that someone had unceremoniously discarded. Patches of soil were so heavy with moisture that a person stepping off the nearly imperceptible pathway would feel his shoes being nearly sucked from his feet.

The woods were full of dark secrets, which is exactly what had attracted him in the first place. He'd noticed the brush pickers when he'd been out on the hunt several weeks before, when he had an urge to do *something*. A crammed-full station wagon was parked on the side of the road as close to the edge as possible without going into the ditch. They poured from their vehicle, talking and laughing, as if what they were about to do was some kind of fun adventure.

He sized up the women.

Most were small.

Good.

Most were thin, reasonably pretty, and young.

Also good.

Some didn't know English—at least not enough to speak it with any real fluency.

He took it to mean that they were likely illegals.

Excellent. Who would care if one of those went missing?

A few days later, he returned to the place where he knew more of them would come. From across the road, he watched the pretty dark-haired girl get out of the van, flanked by three young men.

A challenge.

He liked that too.

Later, when he felt her body go limp in his arms, he smiled.

Good girl, he thought. *Give yourself to me.*

A half hour or more passed, and Tulio wondered why Celesta hadn't returned. The air had warmed up considerably, and he'd stripped down to a sleeveless T-shirt. He called out for his brothers, and the three of them gathered up their impressive haul of cuttings.

"She must be waiting back at the van," he said.

An hour had elapsed by the time they made it to the clearing.

"Celesta?"

No answer.

Tulio put his bag down and unlocked the Astro van.

"Where are you?"

Leon, the youngest, hurried over to the vehicle, waving a pair of gloves and a cutter that were obviously Celesta's because she'd used pink nail polish to apply her initials and a tiny rendering of a daisy.

"Look, I found these. She left them there," he said, indicating an area of gravel near the path into the woods.

Tulio took the gloves and stared into his brother's worried eyes. "What happened? This doesn't make sense. Something's wrong. Something has happened to Celesta."

Chapter Two

"Now, that's attractive," she thought.

Kendall Stark sat in her white Ford SUV in the school parking lot and fumbled in her purse for a toothpick. *Nothing.* She checked the glove box. *Again nada.* A sesame seed from a morning bagel had lodged between her front teeth. Coming up empty-handed, she used the corner of one of her Kitsap County sheriff's detective business cards. Tacky as she knew it was, *mission accomplished.* She reset her rearview mirror and got out of her car, proceeding toward the front office of South Colby Elementary School. She said hello to Mattie Jonas, the school secretary, who in turn handed her a clipboard with a signup sheet.

Son's spring conference, she wrote for the reason of her visit.

Mattie nodded. "You know the drill. Gun-free zone. No exceptions, even for Kitsap County's finest."

With her mind on the meeting, Kendall had forgotten to

remove and store her Glock in her car's gun safe, something procedure called her to do. While the school secretary looked on, she removed the magazine, set the safety, and put the gun into a metal lockbox that the secretary had provided for that purpose.

"We don't worry about you," Mattie said, locking the box with a key she kept on a chain around her slender wrists. "I mean, you and the other cops are on the side of right, but a rule's a rule."

"Of course," Kendall said.

"How's your mom?"

Kendall sighed. "Good days and bad days. More bad days lately, I'm afraid."

Mattie didn't press for details. It was clear Kendall didn't want to go into it. It was a question that came at least once a day. Most people in town knew her mother. Port Orchard was small enough that on any given day, paths would cross with those who shared histories. Mattie had been an assistant in Kendall's mother's fifth-grade classroom many years ago. Mrs. Maguire—never Ms.—was a favorite of anyone who had her. Bettina Maguire was a marmalade-colored redhead who taught her pupils with the fervor of a preacher and the kind of self-deprecating humor that made other teachers standoffish and jealous.

Kendall walked the familiar corridor to Classroom 18 and turned the knob, her heart beating a little faster as she went inside. Lori Bertram's classroom was a riot of construction-paper cutouts and the smells of all things that seven-year-olds live for: Paste. Sour green-apple candy. Guinea pigs. Lori Bertram had been teaching at South Colby for the past six years, but she still carried the enthusiasm of a first-year teacher. Ms. Bertram was a brunette with pointed features and a splatter of freckles over the bridge of her nose. A charm bracelet with all fifty states, something she used as a teaching tool, jangled whenever she moved her arm.

"Good afternoon, Ms. Stark," she said, motioning toward

one of those impossibly small chairs. Green eyes sparkled through wireless frames.

Kendall Stark was there about her son Cody, an autistic boy who was easy to love but a challenge nonetheless. He was blond-haired and blue-eyed, like his mother. His head was like a small pumpkin, so round and perfect. In photographs, he was the ideal. A cherub. The Gerber baby. The image of the child that young women always dreamed would find their way into a perfectly appointed nursery. He was almost one when the doctors first diagnosed the possibility of "delayed development." *If only.* At two, the autism was confirmed. The diagnosis, at first, was a torpedo speeding toward every dream Kendall had for her son. It would never change her love, of course, but in her darkest hours she knew that her son was born to suffer in some way. It broke her heart.

To outsiders, at least, it appeared to take longer for Steven Stark to come to terms with the idea that their son was "different from the others." An advertising salesman for a hunting and fishing magazine out of Seattle, Steven used to be the kind of man who was all biceps and bravado. Snowboarding. Bungee jumping. Driving fast cars. He was drawn to whatever gave him a challenge, a rush. He had assumed that when he became a father, he'd be able to relive the excitement of the things that didn't seem to be in the dignified realm of adulthood. He loved his son too. But the cruelty of autism was a chasm between father and son. Steven's love, it seemed, was seldom returned. There would be no playing catch. No baseball games. No deer hunting.

"This may not be the son you've dreamed of," Kendall said on the way home from one of their first consultations with an autism specialist. "But in time you'll see. He will be the boy of your dreams."

Steven put on his game face. "I'm sure you're right, babe."

"God gave us a special son because we're the right parents for him."

"I know," he said, his tone more rueful than he'd wanted.

Later, when she played back the conversation, she wondered who had said what.

Kendall Stark knew no speeches could change what Lori Bertram was about to tell her. She knew that the second-grade teacher cared for her little boy. She'd said so many, many times. She'd arranged for special testing, more hours from the support staff than were required to help him stay in the same class as the kids he'd known since preschool.

"Kendall," the teacher she said, lowering her glasses to view a printout, "I'm sorry to report that things aren't working out for Cody here at South Colby as we'd all hoped."

The words were not a surprise. Ms. Bertram had sent several missives home, as had the special education teacher, Ms. Dawson. All seemed to agree that Cody was not a candidate for mainstreaming.

"Cody's needs and challenges are too great for a standard classroom," she said.

As a detective, Kendall knew the kinds of questions to ask in order to get the kind of result she wanted. But not now. She was powerless.

"I can get him more help," Kendall said. "Another specialist."

The teacher looked away. The moment was awkward. "Look, you already have. You have done an exemplary job, and I know whatever avenue you choose to pursue will be the right one. But the truth is, having him in the classroom is too disruptive to the education process."

Kendall thought about fighting back. She wanted to tell the teacher that what was best for Cody was that he'd stay with the other children. But she held her tongue. There had been enough warning that this was coming.

"I've told Inverness about Cody," Ms. Bertram went on. "They might have room for him in the fall."

"I see," was all Kendall could come up with. The teacher's words were meant to offer hope, but they stung.

The Inverness School was in Bremerton. Reviews on the institution were mixed. Some kids were boarded there, which Kendall considered no better than warehousing the disabled. The school itself earned decent marks from educational advocates for the disabled. It was probably the best place for Cody in Kitsap County.

The only place.

"Can I see him before I leave?" Kendall asked.

Ms. Bertram nodded. "He's in music now. Follow me."

The two women walked down a polished-aggregate corridor to a small classroom filled with the sound of children singing "Baby Beluga." Only one little boy remained silent, the flicker of recognition that something was going on around him barely discernible. Yet, like a flipped switch, when he saw his mother, he rushed over, nearly knocking down a little girl.

"Mama!"

She scooped him up and gave him a loving embrace, kissing the top of his beautiful blond head.

"I was here to see your teacher," she told him.

She gave him another peck on his forehead and told him she'd see him at home after school.

"I love you!" the boy said.

Cody was a child who didn't say much. Unsurprisingly, the words he did utter went straight to his mother's soul.

"I love you, Cody."

Her gun secure in her holster, Kendall returned to her car feeling the heaviness of her son's complicated future on her shoulders. Steven was at home, asleep—his routine on the day back from a three-day trip to a sportsmen's show in Louisville. She could feel the tears start to come, but she willed them to stop. The tears were for Cody.

Inside, she knew that Cody's heart would be broken when he found out that he'd have to leave the children that he'd known until now. Kendall recognized that he had some understanding that he was different than his friends, Adam and Tristan. She saw his frustration when he tried to play a video game. He saw how the others could read. He saw that the monkey bars at school were for those with the dexterity to hold on tight and swing. Kendall and Steven had vowed they'd raise their son with the advantages of knowing that, while he was indeed different than others, his future was full of promise. They knew there might someday be a day of reckoning.

Which just came in the form of the conference with Ms. Bertram.

Kendall turned on her cell and noticed that there'd been a call from Josh Anderson, one of the nine others who carried a gold Kitsap County sheriff's detective star.

"Kendall, the lieutenant wants us to work a missing brush picker's case. Don't ask me why. She probably ran back to wherever the hell she came from. Celesta Delgado's the name. Hope things went well with Cody's teacher. Get your ass in here so we can get to work."

In the room made just for her misery, Celesta Delgado woke once more. By then she'd figured out that she was not in a car trunk, as she first had imagined. There would be no way she could fiddle with the emergency latch as she'd seen a young woman do on the *Today* show when she reenacted her own escape from a would-be rapist.

Or a killer.

Her eyes traced a pinprick of light that bored through the wall, which was weeping with condensation.

Celesta wriggled some more, panting, pushing, trying to break the tape that kept her strong body constricted. She did not want to be raped. She wanted to get the hell out of there. She twisted with all of her strength and somehow rolled herself on her side, her hands still behind her back. She wanted to scream from the pain emanating from her shoulders, but it wouldn't matter.

Her mouth was bound too.

Again she followed the light. She could see better now, both eyes in play.

If only she could shout. At no time in her life did she ever think she would die like this. Die—yes, die. No rape. No way out.

Tears rolled down her sticky cheeks. Celesta needed to pull herself up and get out of there.

The door swung open, and a blast of light came at her all at once. A shadowy figure moved toward where she'd pinned herself against the wall, screw tips clawing at her back. She pushed away from him as he moved forward.

Yet, there was nowhere to go.

"Please, God," she said. "Can't you hear me?"

Chapter Three

All the offices that dispense and manage justice for Kitsap County hunker on a hillside in Port Orchard overlooking Sinclair Inlet, a blue-gray swath of Puget Sound that breathes in and out with the tide like the last warbling spasms of an emphysema patient. The current runs mostly on the surface, leaving a deep layer of muddy oil from the naval shipyard that occupies the north side of the inlet. At night the shipyard twinkles like a kid's dream of a military holiday: tiny white lights on aircraft carriers and naval tugs. Contiguous with the courthouse and jail, the Kitsap County Sheriff's Office was an office-space planner's version of hell. Outside, the building was a jumble of concrete, glass, bricks, and the occasional spray of ivy. It appeared ordered and well maintained. Inside, however, past a lobby decorated with a sheriff's star fashioned from dozens of silver CDs ("The same artist did one of a fish for Fish and Wildlife, and it looks even better. The CDs look like fish scales!" was a receptionist's familiar refrain) and the requisite display of confiscated weapons and pot pipes, was the entrance to a warren of offices connected by passageways that rivaled the circuitous schematics of the Winchester Mystery House. Go down the hall, around the corner, double back, turn another corner, and a visitor could easily lose his or her way. Drop bread crumbs. Carry a cell phone. Pay attention. The hodgepodge was the result of making do as the always cash-poor county grew in size.

Kendall breathed a sigh of relief when she found a parking space behind the building—something she wouldn't have even attempted if she'd arrived first thing in the morning. The expansion of the county jail a few years prior had consumed much of the on-site parking for Sheriff's Office employees. But it was 10 A.M., and she knew that coming in that time of day was occasionally rewarded with a spot vacated by someone off to a meeting or out on a call.

The fifteen-minute drive from her son's parent-teacher conference had been full of introspection, soul-searching, and heartache. It was partially, Kendall felt, the same battle other working mothers waged every day. *Do I do enough for my child?* It was a conflict that she was sure should have been resolved with her mother's generation. Yet it was a debate that still plunged a hot needle into her skin. No mom could ever really think she'd done enough—especially if she did *anything* for herself. That included pursuing a meaningful career, of course. Anyone without a special-needs child is always at the ready to tell those who have one what they ought to do.

At thirty-one, Kendall Stark had been in law enforcement for a decade, having started as a reserve officer for Kitsap. Next had come a three-year stretch as a Washington State Patrol trooper assigned to her home region. She returned to the Kitsap Sheriff's Office to live and work in a community she loved. She'd moved up to detective after only six years, the result, she felt, of PR-motivated affirmative action by the previous sheriff, who ran for office with the pledge to see more women in higher positions. She was smart, attractive, and a very good investigator. She was the poster girl for the future of an office that had battled an "old-boys' network" image that rankled the Democratic base of a county in search of change.

Kendall told herself over and over that how she had gotten there, how she leapfrogged over a couple of other candidates, didn't matter. Ultimately, she'd proven herself and won the respect of most of the Sheriff's Office. The sole exception was a small cadre of women: a pair from the records department and an icy brunette who ran the supply functions for the detectives unit. Those three seldom gave Kendall a break. The week before, she overheard them bashing her when she slipped into the break room, the sound of the old microwave popping corn masking her presence.

"She obviously hasn't put her son first. What kind of woman would work these hours when her little one is in such need? I know it isn't PC, but it says a lot about a woman who doesn't nurture her own."

Kendall pretended that she hadn't heard a word.

"Hi, ladies," she said. "You know you shouldn't be making popcorn, unless you make some for everyone." Her smile was frozen.

"Oh, hi, Detective," said the one who'd been talking. She always said "detective" with a slight coating of sarcasm, as if Kendall should be behind a keyboard doing administrative work rather than out in the field dealing with the worst crimes committed against human beings.

"Blame Deb," the other chimed, her face suddenly scarlet. "I'm on Weight Watchers, and I can't even have this stuff. Movie-butter style, no less!"

Kendall took a Dr Pepper from the machine. "Tell me about it."

She left the women in the break room that afternoon and

took the longest, most serpentine route back to her desk in her dank, windowless office. She needed every moment to compose herself, to deflect the intentional cruelty of the "Witches of Kitsap," as her husband liked to call them. Kendall would fight for Cody's future with all that she possessed, but ultimately she knew that there likely was no magical fix for her seven-year-old. It left a hole in her heart. She saw her detective's gold star as a means to fill it by doing something worthwhile. To stop pain elsewhere. And in Kitsap County, there had been more than enough.

Some cases never left her. The baby that had been dropped on his head by his Bremerton shipyard worker father, the little girl who'd been offered up for sex to an online predator by her Port Gamble mother. The young man from Seabeck who'd been in and out of the county jail so often he thought he'd be able to leave some belongings behind for his next stretch of incarceration.

That Monday morning she'd resisted the urge to go home and tell Steven face-to-face what the teacher had said. Having their son in a regular classroom for most of the day had fueled hope that he'd be able to live as others did when he was grown, when they were gone. That had faded, and she couldn't break the news to Steven in person and see in his eyes the pain of the loss of hope once more.

Before collecting her things and locking her car, Kendall punched the speed-dial number for Steven. When he didn't pick up, as she knew he wouldn't, she left a message:

"Honey, bad news. We'll need to check out Inverness for Cody. Ms. Bertram was very nice, but they just can't help him there. Not the kind of help he needs. I'm not angry. Just sad. See you tonight."

Rain started to fall. She looked up and regarded the crack in the gray sky. It was spring, and the weather had—in typical Pacific Northwest fashion—forgotten the season. The wind kicked up a little, sweeping maple-tree pollen in a pale orange swirl over car windshields and against the curb. Across the parking lot, under the overhang where a couple of corrections officers had left a pair of plastic office chairs, she saw Josh Anderson and the glow of a cigarette.

"You really should quit, Detective," she said as she approached him.

He nodded. "I would if I could, but I blame the county. They used to let us smoke at our desks, you know."

"So I've heard. They used to let you shoot seagulls at the dump too."

Josh crushed out his smoke. "Those were the good old days."

Kendall smiled. "Let's go inside."

At fifty, Kitsap County Sheriff's Detective Josh Anderson had turned the corner. Every day that he looked in the mirror he could see that he was no longer the man that he used to be. Lines now creased what had been an exceedingly interesting, if not handsome, face. It had been the kind of visage that telegraphed sexuality and vitality. A look. A wink. A smile. Yet that was fading, and fading fast. His black hair was snowy at the temples, and his hairline was marching backward. His nose seemed longer at the tip. The hooded eyelids that had once given women sighs of desire were now the slightly fleshy bags of a man growing older.

Josh had been married and divorced three times. The last time, to a county deputy prosecutor, ended in a bitter and very public sideshow nine years earlier. Although Washington was a no-fault divorce state and his peccadilloes were therefore irrelevant, they did matter when his wife sued for sole custody of their son, Drew. Everyone in the Kitsap County Sheriff's Office knew he couldn't keep his trousers zipped, but the public soon found out. The local paper latched on to the story, and when Josh Anderson went down, it was with a resounding thud. He lost his position as president of the Deputy Sheriffs Guild, or union, and did a two-year stretch as a civil deputy before crawling back to detective. He acted as though he was unrepentant. His ex-wife was a "bitch and a ballbuster." He used to joke that he was a serial philanderer or that women were like items on a buffet line just waiting for him to sample.

"I can't help myself . . . and, apparently, they can't, either," he once told Kendall in a revealing bit of introspection.

This guy's ego is ten times the size of the brain in his pants, she had thought, almost saying it aloud.

As the years ticked by, Josh Anderson felt the kind of niggling self-loathing that told him he was a "three-time loser."

What a difference a decade made.

Anyone passing by the adjacent offices occupied by Kendall Stark and Josh Anderson could see the distinct differences in the two detectives' personalities and habits. There was a wall between them, but with Josh's office first and Kendall's next, it was almost like some bizarre "before and after" HGTV makeover show. Josh's office was a maelstrom of paperwork and coffee cups—ceramic and paper. If he had a filing system of any kind, it was beyond the ability of anyone short of Einstein to figure it out. In reality, he figured that if Kendall had everything in order, why should he? He could saunter over anytime and pull a file or notebook without so much as a sigh from his exceedingly organized partner. His desk drawers were crammed with office supplies he didn't need: He had more Post-it notes than the supply cabinet. He had a stress ball in the shape of a globe and loved "squeezing the life out of the world." No houseplants, of course, unless the island of green mold floating in one of those cups counted as such.

"Science project," he laughed when Kendall once told

him that if he didn't watch it, "the blob you're growing over there will overtake this office."

Next door, Kendall's desk was in order. A framed photo of her husband and son, a ruffled pink and white African violet that defied the odds and never stopped blooming under a banker's lamp with a green glass shade, and a small Roseville pottery vase that her mother had given her for a pen and pencil holder commanded a pristine work surface. Her notebooks were color coded and filed in alphabetical order. A desk drawer was stocked with PowerBars, green tea, and low-sodium ramen for the days when she was too busy, too absorbed with a case, to leave for a bite.

"Missing brush picker?" Kendall said as she hung her coat on the hook behind the door.

Josh nodded. "Yup. Only in Kitsap."

Kendall continued looking through a small stack of messages. "What's the story?"

"Missing since early yesterday. Boyfriend's here. Let's chat him up."

She'd been his favorite thus far. She'd been passive at first, as he commanded her to be.

"Like you're dead. Okay? No fight. Or I'll kill you. Just that simple. Easy to understand, right?"

"Please don't hurt me. Please, I'll do what you want."

"You're a good girl," he said as he tightened the leather straps around her wrists.

"You're hurting me!"

"Are you going to keep talking? I told you to shut up."

"But it hurts."

He took a spool of duct tape and scraped at it with a pocketknife, searching for the start of the roll.

"More than a thousand uses for this stuff," he said, finally pulling a long piece. "Bet the makers don't know about this one."

Her eyes flooded with tears, and she struggled on the mattress that he'd offered her. Pinpricks in the wall allowed a sprinkling of light to fall over the room, the dank place where she was being held captive.

On the floor next to the mattress were a green blouse, blue jeans, and a brand-new box cutter, still wrapped in its Home Depot cello bag. All ready to go.

Chapter Four

With a jacket over his restaurant uniform, Tulio Pena sat quietly in the secured area adjacent to the detective's offices, next to a pasty-faced young man holding a large plastic bag marked with his name in large letters. After seven months as a guest of the county jail, the man with the bag was waiting for his mother to take him home. Tulio, nervous and beside himself with worry, tried to make small talk with the just-released inmate.

"My girlfriend's missing. That's why I'm here."

The young man fidgeted. "Bummer. I'm sorry."

Tulio nodded.

"I'm starting over again."

"Good luck."

"Thanks."

The Kitsap detectives emerged from the hallway.

"Mr. Pena?" Kendall asked.

Tulio jumped to his feet so quickly that it startled the young man on the seat next to him. He dropped his bag.

"I'm Tulio Pena. Please help me."

Kendall nodded understandingly. "That's why we're here. Let's go somewhere we can talk."

The trio found space in a small interview room. Kendall offered the young man coffee or a soda, but he declined. He only wanted one thing.

Celesta.

Tulio's dark, almost-black eyes were bloodshot. It had been almost a full day since his Celesta vanished from the woods. When he first reported her missing, he was told that little could be done for twenty-four hours. It didn't seem right, but he understood it. He and his brothers scoured the woods the rest of the day and that morning. When twenty-four hours had elapsed, on the dot, he was in the interview room.

"Something has happened to my girlfriend Celesta," he began.

Kendall reviewed the reporting deputy's report. "We're here to help, Mr. Pena. It says she, you, and your brothers were harvesting brush out near Sunnyslope?"

"*Sí*," he said, before quickly correcting himself. "Yes."

"Were you licensed to pick there?" Josh asked. "You legal here?"

Kendall wanted to kick Josh under the table. The question would have to be asked, of course, but not right then and not with an accusatory tone. It had nothing to do with the fact that a young woman was missing. At least, not in any way she could imagine.

"Yes. Yes, we are, and yes, we had permits." There was a flicker of indignation in the young man's eyes.

Kendall soothed him, or at least tried to. The last thing the county needed was a complaint that could spiral into a lawsuit.

"I think what my colleague is getting at is, was Celesta familiar with the woods? The area?"

Tulio focused on Kendall. "Oh. Yes. She had been there before. She didn't get lost. She couldn't have gotten lost. She made it back to the van. We found her stuff."

Again Josh pushed. "Your girlfriend and you, did you have a fight?"

Tulio shook his head. "No, never."

"Was she angry about going out there to pick brush?"

"No. She liked to help. We were sending the money back to her family in El Salvador. Here's her picture, taken last month. You will put it on TV and in the papers, right?"

He slid a photo across the table.

"She's very pretty," Kendall said, looking at the image of a smiling Celesta Delgado. Glossy dark hair. White teeth. Lips that were generous and brown eyes that sparkled. *Beguiling eyes*, she thought.

"Once we determine if she's missing, we'll do a media release. No guarantees that anyone will run her picture," Josh said. "A dozen people go missing every day. Most come home when they are good and ready to."

The young man's eyes pooled. "She's missing. She's in trouble."

The detectives took down Celesta's description and noted that her brush bag was found just inside the trailhead, heavy with neatly bundled salal.

"You go to work, now," Josh said, his tone condescending. "We'll call you at work if we need more information. Understand?"

Tulio stood. His hands trembled a little, and he put them in his jacket pockets, in an attempt to steady himself. "I have a cell phone."

Kendall looked at Josh, a cold stare to indicate that he had stepped over the line.

"Good," she said. "Keep it with you. I'll walk you out."

* * *

Kendall found Josh back behind his messy desk, sipping a cup of coffee and looking online at Craigslist.

"I need a new pressure washer," he said.

She ignored him. "What was that all about? You treated that guy like garbage."

Josh set down his cup. "I'm just irritated. These brush pickers are scavengers. They come around the county stripping away whatever they think they can sell, and then they move on. They're raping the woods, that's what they're doing."

"Don't tell me that you're now concerned about the environment," she said.

Josh turned back toward the computer. "No. I'm just sick of our resources being used up by transients. The whole goddamn county is being overrun by meth-heads, brush pickers, Navy pukes, and others who have no vested interest in doing things the way they ought to be done. This girl's like the rest of them. She got what she wanted and split."

Kendall looked at her watch. "Awfully early for you to be in such a foul mood."

"I'm always in a foul mood."

"Tell me about it."

"Look, Kendall, you work the Delgado case. I'll juggle the backlog."

The "backlog" was a stack of drug and gun cases that he could work in his sleep.

"Fine," she said, looking at her notes. "Maybe Celesta did leave for home, as you seem to think. But maybe something happened to her. Good luck with finding your pressure washer."

Kendall walked across Division Street into the new Kitsap County Administration Building, where a commanding view of the Olympic Mountains and Sinclair Inlet filled the floor-to-ceiling windows. It was a luminous beauty of a building that looked as if it had been plucked out of Seattle or some other city of means and planted on the hill across from the courthouse. Kendall smiled to a records clerk she knew and continued across the gleaming floors to a hole-in-the-wall coffee shop. The barista waved at her and started making her usual midday pick-me-up, a Tuxedo Mocha: white *and* dark chocolate. Cup in hand, she returned to her SUV and drove out to Sunnyslope, to the pathway off the highway where Tulio Pena said he'd parked the van the day before.

A jogger stopped to catch his breath as she got out of the SUV. "Hi," he said, squatting a little, his elbows pinned to his sides.

Kendall said hello and identified herself.

"Looking for that renegade bear again?" the jogger asked. He was referring to an incident the prior month when a man riding his mountain bike through the woods had been attacked by a black bear. It seemed that his dogs had spooked the mom defending her cubs, and the man, hapless and ill-prepared, was caught in her crosshairs. She ripped off his ear and tore out his cheek. Local animal lovers sided with the bear, saying that the animal "was just doing what a mama bear does" and that "the bike rider shouldn't have brought his dogs."

Kendall shook her head. "No bear. Looking for a missing brush picker."

"Oh," he said. "That's good. I mean, that it isn't a bear. They can be pretty scary. Seen a couple around here in the past year."

The detective held out the photograph of Celesta Delgado.

"She's pretty," the man said.

"Yeah, she is. She went missing yesterday. You live around here?"

"Up the road in Sunnyslope."

"Seen her or her crew out here?"

The man shook his head. "We get pickers around here all the time. I don't pay 'em much attention. Sometimes they leave a bunch of trash in the woods, and that pisses me off."

"How's that?"

"Most of us who live out here live here for a reason. We don't want to live in town next to Wal-Mart, and we don't want people tramping around here with carts and bags thinking the forest is their personal convenience store."

Kendall had heard that sentiment a hundred if not a thousand times before on Kitsap County calls. Kidnap County, as some called it, could be the kind of place where people had gates, dogs, guns, and an attitude that said "back off!" in no uncertain terms.

It was, she reflected, a good place to hide out and be alone.

"If you see her, call us. Okay?"

He took her business card and put it in his back pocket. "Sure. Will do."

Kendall looked around and noticed the weave of various car and truck wheel treads in the muddy parking area. She walked toward the woods, an archway of ocean spray marking its entrance. She found some remnants of salal cuttings, a bundle of rubber bands, and the muddy footprints of at least a dozen people and a few dogs. Sunlight sifted through the maples and cedars, sending globes of light to the damp forest floor. She walked about a hundred yards before something pink caught her eye: a cellophane wrapper emblazoned with a depiction of a smiling shrimp and Asian characters.

Kendall bent down, her heels digging into the muddy soil, and wondered if it was evidence or carelessness. She bagged the wrapper, just in case, and got back into her car as a deer wandered into the parking lot. The scene was breathtaking in its incongruity.

The forest is so beautiful, yet so dangerous.

She got back in her car and started back to Port Orchard. The sky had darkened. She turned on her headlights and wipers as rain began to splatter on the windshield. Many of Kitsap County's rural roads have no edges, no borders, as they wind through forests of Douglas fir and western red cedars. Tree trunks along rural roadways are thickly collared with salal, huckleberry, and the spires of the native sword fern. Some roads follow old deer trails from Puget Sound inland to valleys fed by a network of streams.

The woods were lush and lucrative.

And, just maybe, Kendall Stark thought, *deadly*.

Celesta Delgado was naked, shivering, on a sheet of plastic when she awoke. It was so dark in the room that she reached for her face, struggling to see if her own black hair had blocked the light. She couldn't reach. She rolled back the moments as best she could. She'd been out in the woods. But where was she now? Had she passed out? Why couldn't she move her arms? She tried to sit up, but her legs were paralyzed too.

Had she been in an accident?

Nothing in her memory suggested an accident, and the realization that her predicament was intentional came over her. Fear consumed her. If she'd been hurt and was in the hospital, would she be nude? She'd never been hospitalized before, yet she knew that every patient was allowed the dignity of some covering. She shivered again as cool air moved over her body.

A fan?

She wanted to call out, but her voice failed her too.

What is happening to me?

There was nothing to do but wait and cry tears that simply oozed into the fabric of the blindfold over her eyes.

She lay there, frozen and terrified, in the dark until a harsh voice was directed at her.

"Your hands and feet are no longer tied. Get up."

Celesta heard the commands; nevertheless, she was unsure how to maneuver in order to perform them. She knew she was on her back, of course, but she had no idea how to pull herself upright. She was still blindfolded and confused about how to orient herself from the plastic sheeting that

held her. She was so cold by then that her buttocks felt stuck
to the sheeting. It was as if she were bound in plastic like a
half-frozen roast.

"I know you can't see, bitch, but you can hear. Now, get
up. Roll over. On your knees."

Celesta couldn't cry out, although inside her head she'd
screamed Tulio's name over and over.

Tulio, please help! Tulio, save me!

The man in the dark grabbed her ankles. Celesta winced
in pain as his callused hands scraped her skin. He pulled her
down the plastic sheeting, now wet with her own urine.

"You're going to do as I say or you're going to die."

She nodded, her cheeks now wet.

Tulio! Tulio!

He spread her legs and started to rub against her buttocks.
She could feel the hair on his stomach and the hardness of
his penis as he grunted and rubbed.

"Now, don't move while I do you, bitch. You move, you
die."

Please no!

She tightened her thighs as he raped her.

"I said don't move, bitch." He slammed a fist into her kid-
ney. "Don't budge!"

A sharp pain worse than she'd ever known tormented every
nerve in her torso. It was like an electric shock running from
the base of her spine to her brain. She felt the man's sticky-
hot semen roll down her inner thighs.

She'd been praying for rescue. Now she wished for death.

"You ready?"

For what? What more could you do to me?

But the man wasn't talking to Celesta. She heard another
person moving in the room, coming closer but not speaking.
The hands that grabbed her this time were smaller.

"No lube needed, I just primed the pump," the man said.

Everything that was happening to Celesta was beyond

wrong, but what was happening now was beyond her comprehension. She screamed out in pain.

"Shut up, bitch!" said the man who had raped her first.

The other remained silent while violating Celesta with some kind of a cylindrical device. It was rigid, cool, not made of flesh.

The first man started to laugh. "You have to get better at this."

Celesta vomited blood.

God, take me from here. Jesus, take me home.

Just as darkness cascaded over her, she thought she saw the face of an angel. From a small slit in the tape across her eyes and head, she caught a glimpse of a divine figure. Yes, she was sure of it. She was small and beautiful, with a smile that brought a sense of peace.

"Help me," she whispered.

Chapter Five

March 30, evening
South Colby

Steven and Kendall Stark lived in a gray and white 1920s bungalow above Yukon Harbor in South Colby, a few miles outside Port Orchard on the way to the Southworth ferry landing. Since her childhood in nearby Harper, Kendall had admired the house and how it sat on an incline backed with an impressive grove of moss-covered maples and silver-barked alders. It didn't take any convincing to get her husband to share her dream. In fact, when the house went on the market five years into their marriage, it was Steven who surprised his wife with an open-house flyer and a promise "to make this happen for you, babe."

A stone-edged walkway led from the street to wide front steps and a covered porch that seldom saw a summer evening without the presence of someone kicking back with a beer or a soda, watching the bay turn from blue to ink. It was a home that felt instantly comfortable, like those favorite brown leather slippers some dads wear for decades until they split at the toes. The place had been remodeled in the 1980s by a couple who likely didn't realize the benefits of restoring a vintage home to its original charm. Wall-to-wall carpeting was easy enough to remove to expose original fir floors, but layers of mauve and kelly green paint over the rest of the woodwork was a daunting challenge. It took Steven and Kendall almost a year to scrape, sand, and re-stain the doors and trim. In the end, the house was any young couple's vision of the perfect first home—enough room for children, a lawn that rolled from the front door to the main road, and a view of Blake Island and the harbor interrupted only by a few power lines and the frontage road.

Steven destroyed the kitchen making his specialty for dinner, lasagna layered with roasted red bell peppers and sweet apple sausage. Between sales calls, he picked up a loaf of French bread at the Albertsons on Mile Hill Road and slathered it with garlic butter—Cody's favorite.

By the time Kendall made it home, the house smelled like an Italian restaurant. And a pretty good one at that. If she was stuck with the dishes ("You cook, I'll clean"), the deal seemed fair enough.

"Where's the wine?" she asked, setting down her things and taking off her coat.

"Uncorked and breathing." He went for the glasses, the last pair that matched from their wedding stemware. "Cody's in his room."

The words were familiar. Cody's way of coping was isolation.

"We have to talk," she said.

"I know."

Kendall nuzzled the back of her husband's neck as he poured the wine, a dark, almost syrupy cabernet that infused the glasses with the glow of a glass full of rubies.

"We can't pretend he's going to be okay," she said.

"I stopped pretending a long time ago."

She took a sip of her wine and thought carefully. "You know

what I mean. We're going to have to reconsider Inverness or something like it. He's got his whole life ahead of him, and we have to find out what is best for him."

Steven's eyes narrowed on his wife. The year before she'd cut her medium-length blond bob to a shorter cut. Sometimes when she hastily ran the hair product through her hair in the mornings, she ended up with an almost spiky do. It suited her. It made her deep blue eyes more pronounced and more of a mirror of what she was thinking.

"He's not living there, and you know that," he said.

Kendall set her wineglass on the still-mauve laminate kitchen countertop.

"We have to do what's best," she said. "I just wish I knew what that was." A tear threatened to roll down her cheek, and she wiped it away.

There would be plenty of time for crying later. Her husband was more certain about the future, taking a kind of optimistic approach that she'd abandoned. Partly it was because of her job, but also because her dreams for her little boy had faded over time too.

"I'm going to check on Cody," she said, heading down the hallway to Cody's room with its captain's bed, orca wallpaper, and array of toys that would be the envy of any child his age, or maybe a little younger. He was playing with a puzzle that he liked to put together, wrong side up.

Kendall let her mind wander back to the first moment she had any inkling that something was different about Cody. She never allowed the words *wrong* and *aberrant* to find their way into her thoughts. Even the euphemisms like *special* or *challenged* were banished from her vocabulary when she replayed any of the instances in which her beautiful boy seemed, well, *different*. He was three months old, a bundle of pink skin and downy blond hair swathed in a pale blue blanket. The cat had jumped up on the coffee table and knocked over a tippy vase of daffodils, sending it crashing to the floor. The noise startled Kendall but not Cody. Not at all.

He just stayed still, a slight smile on his rosebud lips, his blue eyes fixed on the table lamp. Kendall worried that Cody's lack of response could indicate hearing impairment. She snapped her fingers in his face.

Again nothing. A trip to the pediatrician the next day confirmed that his hearing was fine.

It was more serious than mere deafness.

"It's too early to say, of course," the doctor said, "but this kind of intent, uninterruptible gaze can sometimes foretell autism."

Kendall felt the air rush from her lungs.

"Are you sure?"

"Look, Kendall, I've been a pediatrician long enough to see the early warnings. Testing will need to be done, certainly. But the truest indicator will be time itself."

"But he might outgrow it, right?"

"Some do. Most don't. And, dear, remember, there are varying degrees of severity. Maybe we'll be lucky here."

The word luck always stuck in her mind. Kendall Stark was not a believer in the concept. She felt that all people, good and bad, had a role in the outcome of their lives. As a cop and as a mother, she had to think so. Otherwise, the world was too random of a place for order.

Order was what she craved.

She stood quietly watching Cody as he worked the puzzle on the braided rug that covered the old fir floor of his bedroom. He never turned the pieces to make them fit. He just knew where they snapped into place. She wondered what other strange talents her special son might have. Autism was heartbreaking beyond comprehension, she knew, but there was a bit of magic in the disorder too. Some children could work numbers in a way that an MIT graduate couldn't; some were artists whose inspiration was otherworldly.

And yet, she had prayed for a miracle since the day of his diagnosis. That there would be something that would bring her son back to what she and Steven had dreamed their child would be. Kendall put on a brave face with Steven, because she had to. And no matter the future—a gifted child or one who stared forever into space—Cody Stark would always be her beautiful boy.

Later that evening, after Cody was asleep, the story of the missing brush picker and the harsh reality of the teacher's conference no longer fighting for her awareness, Kendall and Steven took a moment just to hold each other. It was not a mechanical embrace or a kind of attempt by one to guide the other to the bedroom. It was something deeper, the kind of gesture that confirmed that no matter what they faced, they would always face it together. The spring evening was warm enough for a sweater, and the couple went outside on the porch with the last of their cabernet. Miles away, across Puget Sound, they could see a portion of the Seattle skyline, including the iconic spire of the Space Needle.

Lights flickered on a few boats that moved silently through the waters. Some carried freight destined for the ports of Seattle or Tacoma. Some held partiers who'd had too much to drink, fisherman who were disappointed by what they hadn't caught, marine biologists who wondered where a missing member of a local pod of orcas had gone.

One carried a dark specter of depravity that no other human being could imagine.

He tucked a Camel straight between his lips and looked out over the water as a trio of harbor seals bobbed in the wake of another boat, now all but a pinprick on the horizon. She'd been the perfect victim. Her terror was a rush, a vibration that stimulated. She was, in fact, his Magic Fingers. She was what he considered a lucky catch, a girl just begging to be a victim because of her trusting nature. He preferred those who fought a little harder or wore their skepticism like a shield.

His cigarette dangling, his fingertip rubbed across the silver Crossfire lighter that felt so good in his palm as he let the cool evening air pour over his handsome face.

She was looking at the Seattle skyline.

He imagined a conversation:

Everything all right, baby? she asked, her eyes a mix of worry and fear.

No problems I can't fix, he answered into the wind.

Need any help?

He shook his head and went to cut the boat's engine.

No. You've done enough.

Kendall crawled under the covers and nuzzled her husband. Steven was asleep, snoring softly in the manner she found more charming than irritating. The regular rhythm of his slumber was something that she could always count on, and it comforted her just then. She found herself thinking of how her life might have gone if they'd stayed apart. She remembered how lost she'd been that lonely, dark time years ago.

His voice on the phone still reverberated in her memory.

"Kendall, I don't really know what's going on."

"I don't, either."

"But you do," Steven said.

"I need more time to sort out things."

"I'm begging you," he said, his voice a quiet rasp. "Please."

Chapter Six

Tulio Pena had left two voice messages on Kendall's office phone. Both were colored by the anguish of a man frightened to death. In the background, Kendall could hear the sounds of piped-in mariachi music and the clatter of dishes being cleared.

"Do you know anything? Did you find anything?"

She knew he worked a late shift, so she didn't call back with the non-answer she'd have to give. Families of the missing always hungered for any tidbit of information offered up by anyone in a position to know anything: first, by investigators, then by reporters, and lastly, if the period of time elapsed had become too long to foster hope, by a psychic. Most cops working a missing-persons case have felt the wrath of a family in search of answers.

"We're doing all that we can," she'd said more than once.

"All that you can? It seems like nothing! Nothing at all!"

"We can't give you visibility for every detail of our investigation."

That last line choked in her throat whenever she had used it. Sometimes it was more posturing than a real reflection of what was going on in the offices of the in investigative body.

Her sesame-seed bagel at the ready, Kendall went about some background research. She knew about the brush industry, of course. She'd been raised in Kitsap, a region with NO BRUSH PICKING signs as commonplace as GARAGE SALE placards. She booted up her PC and started the search for crimes on LINX, a regional criminal database. She used the key words: brush, floral industry, violence. From her open doorway, she saw Josh Anderson in the hall trying to work his vanishing charms on a pretty young temp.

He'll never change. And he'll never get her to go out with him, she thought.

She clicked on a couple of hits on the subject in a law enforcement database. In Oregon, two men had been killed over a cache of cinnamon-scented mushrooms that brought an astonishingly high price in Japan's epicurean industry. A Filipino woman in Thurston County was mutilated by a rival picker when she was caught working his territory.

He cut off both her thumbs.

"You bitch, you steal no more," he'd said over and over as she ran holding her severed thumbs to her chest, screaming out of the woods. The man was eventually arrested and convicted and was serving ten years in Walla Walla.

A report indicated that violence had escalated along with the demand for floral greens. It seemed that more and more illegal immigrants were taking up the trade as the land, in some places, became overworked. She learned that Sheriff's Office stats indicated that over the past two years the number of complaints made by private landowners had doubled.

The complaint made by Brett Matthews of Olalla in the very southernmost part of Kitsap County was typical of what Kendall found in the reports:

You should see the noble fir my dad planted twenty
years ago. They've skinned the branches up to the
tiptop. Hope someone's enjoying that Christmas
wreath at my expense. What's with these people?
Why don't they stay off my land? Next time I'll shoot
anyone who comes to rustle what's mine.

Kendall checked Mr. Matthews' tax records to make sure
he didn't own any property in the Sunnyslope area.
He didn't.
An article in the mainstream press also caught her eye. It
had appeared in the Olympia paper two years prior. The
writer presented the idea that brushpicking was one of the
last vestiges of the Old West, a kind of job that pitted man
and woman against the elements, literally living off the land,
dodging bullets, and collecting just enough money at the end
of the day to feed the family and do it all over again. They
were floral rustlers. Cowboys fighting over what they felt they
had a right to.
It was after eleven, and Kendall called Tulio, figuring that
no matter how late he'd worked, he'd want to talk to her.
A younger man, who identified himself as Leon Pena, answered.
"One minute. Tulio! The police are on the phone!"
"Detective Stark, do you have news?" His voice was full
of hesitation and hope.
Kendall locked her eyes on Celesta's photo and spoke into
the handset. "I'm afraid not." She refrained from reminding
him that they'd only had the case a day, but she knew that
even an less than savvy observer who watched any TV whatsoever knew that missing-persons cases were solved in hours,
not days. Days of searching usually meant someone was dead
or had run away.
"Tulio, have you had any problems out there with other
pickers?"
"Problems? What do you mean?"

"Did anyone threaten you or cause problems with you where you were picking?"

There was a short pause. "No. No, Detective. We did not want any trouble. We heard some Asians out there that day, but we never saw them. We never talked to them."

"All right. I have one other question, Tulio. This is touchy, difficult. . . ."

She could almost hear him gulp on the other end of the line. She wanted to let him down easy, if there was any possibility that Celesta Delgado had left him for another man, no matter how unlikely the scenario.

"How were you and Celesta getting along? Did you argue?"

"We were in love."

"In love, yes," she said, repeating his words. "But was she happy? Do you think she might have been seeing anyone?"

"No. She loved me. Only me."

Only you, she thought. *Of course, only you.*

She told Tulio that she'd continue working the case and that if she had any more questions she'd call. As she hung up, Josh Anderson appeared in the doorway. For the first time Kendall noticed he was wearing a new suit, a gray chalk-striped outfit with a crisp blue shirt and a raspberry tie.

"How's your day going?" he asked.

"Fine," she said. "In court today or going to your home-coming dance?"

"Funny," he said, sliding into a chair across from her. "I've got some important business to attend to."

"Okay." Kendall looked back down at her work.

"Aren't you going to ask what it is?"

She took out a highlighter and made a yellow trail through some text on the printout. "Nope." She could feel his agitation percolate inside his brand-new suit, and she loved it. She knew that Josh Anderson was the type of man who never missed an opportunity to tell someone—particularly a woman—how smart, how successful, and just how in demand he was. She silently counted to three.

"I'm speaking at Burien today."

Burien was the location of the state's police training facility.

"Really, Josh? I guess you forgot to mention it." She glanced at the whiteboard hanging on the wall adjacent to her desk. In block letters, it read:

JOSH SPEAKING ON INVESTIGATIVE RESOURCES
IN MID-SIZE JURISDICTIONS

She waited a beat. "Of course I remember. Break a leg, Josh. I want to hear all about it. I'll work the Delgado case while you're basking in the glow of your admirers."

He smiled at her. She had his number. And that's why he liked her most of the time.

Those who worked in it called it a brush shed, but Every-Greens of Washington called their processing offices next to the Old Belfair Highway a "dream factory." The sheet-metal-sided building was the size of a mid-century high school gymnasium with faded panels depicting bouquets that celebrated the major holidays: Christmas, Valentine's Day, Mother's Day. Kendall parked next to a row of old cars, many mud-caked with cracked windows and backseats containing baby blankets and Wendy's food wrappers. She figured they were the cars of the processors, mothers who worked there part-time during the week and possibly up in the woods on the weekends as pickers.

Karl Hudson was a round-faced fellow of about sixty, with heavy bags under his eyes, protruding ears, and hairy knuckles that gave him a distinctly simian appearance. He introduced himself to Kendall as the president and chief operating officer of the company that his father and mother had founded in the 1950s. Every-Greens was one of the oldest purveyors of floral greens in the state.

"You said you're here about Celesta Delgado."

"Yes, that's right."

"I don't like surprises," he said. "So I checked. Her residency status was good. She was a good picker. Always had a permit. All our pickers do."

Kendall followed him into a large room with about twenty massive tables. Young and middle-aged women were busy sorting the raw bundles, trimming the stems of leaves that appeared bug-eaten or torn by the move from the forest to the bag.

"That's the moneymaker," he said, indicating a bunch of salal, its dark green, almost leathery leaves glossy with water from a quick rinse. "Lasts for months in cold storage. Can't keep up with the demand. Bet you've had your share of bouquets."

Kendall nodded. "A few."

"When you think about it," he said, "we *are* dream makers here. Our team creates the foundation for wedding arrangements, new baby bouquets, and, yes, even memorial wreaths. Every moment marked by flowers carries a little bit of Kitsap County."

"Was Celesta ever a processor here?"

Karl motioned for Kendall to take a seat in his office, which she did.

"She was here for about a month, until she got the restaurant job. She was a good processor. She figured she could make more waiting tables. I didn't stand in her way. Was glad to have her out in the woods with the Penas. Good people. Good workers."

She knew that was the bottom line for Mr. Hudson.

"Any problems that you know of between Tulio and Celesta?"

"I wouldn't really know. They seemed happy." He looked down at her file.

"You seem hesitant, Mr. Hudson."

"Look, I am concerned. We've had some turf wars. Demand is huge, and we've got people coming up from Mexico and other points south canvassing the woods for any scrap of green they can find. A few years ago, it was impossible to get pickers. Now the woods are overrun with them."

Kendall didn't say so, but she could feel the ugly undercurrent of racism in the way the man referred to those who worked for him—those who made him enough money to buy the Lexus she saw parked out front—as *them*.

She noticed the CELEBRATING 50 YEARS gold sticker that was affixed to the outgoing mail on his desk.

"A lot has changed in fifty years," she said.

"Yes. My father-in-law started this place. He's dead now, and a good thing—he'd go apoplectic if he had to deal with what I do these days. Between you and me, these people don't really want to work. At least, not hard. Not like they did back in the day."

"I see," Kendall said, deciding she'd never buy a supermarket bouquet again.

"I pay the processors a dollar more an hour than minimum wage, and benefits to boot," he said, glancing through his office window, which overlooked the women hovering over tables, sorting salal.

"Celesta and the Delgado brothers at least had the kind of entrepreneurial spirit that made this country great. You know, when it actually *was* great."

When they were finished, the Every-Greens president escorted Kendall back through the work area.

A Mexican woman of no more than twenty-five handed her a single rose flanked by a fan of huckleberry.

"Celesta is a nice girl. I hope you find her," she said.

Before Kendall could say anything, Karl Hudson shot the young woman a cold look.

"Break time isn't for another forty-five, Carmina. Let's get back to work, ladies."

Chapter Seven

March 31, 10 a.m.
Port Orchard

Instinct and intuition often play an important function in police work. Those who deny their crucial roles are likely those who don't possess that something extra that allows an interrogator to home in on the truth when the facts don't always add up: how the flutter of an eyelash indicates a lie, the curl of an upper lip says more than the words coming from the subject. Truth, Kendall Stark knew, was more than the sum of available facts. There was nothing to really back up the belief that Celesta Delgado simply ditched her boyfriend in the middle of cutting brush in Sunnyslope. Nor did she think that the gentle man who'd come into the Sheriff's Office was involved with her disappearance. She drove out to Kitsap West, the ramshackle mobile home park that was best known for a dead baby that had been found the previous year on the other side of the rusted eight-foot wire fence that cordoned off the single- and double-wide mobiles, along with a smattering of travel trailers and fifth wheels.

She parked her SUV in front of space 223, a single-wide Aloha with new steps and decking, and knocked.

A woman of about sixty answered. Although it was past ten, she was still wearing slippers and a bathrobe. As she spoke, the remnants of the cigarette she'd been smoking curled in the still air. And while she had a pleasant face and reasonably warm eyes, everything else about her told Kendall that she was going to be of no help. She barely opened the door, for starters.

A sure sign that the person is hiding something inside: a messy house, maybe a dead body . . .

"I don't need a vacuum or aromatherapy if that's what you're here for," she said.

Kendall offered a smile. "I'm a detective with the Sheriff's Office. I'm Kendall Stark."

"I don't know anything about my nephew."

Kendall suppressed a smile. She could never begin to count the times that someone misunderstood why she was on their front doorstep and offered up a relative or a neighbor as a quick means to save themselves from some hidden concern.

"Ma'am, I'm not here about your nephew. I'm here about the missing woman who lived next door."

The woman widened the door a bit more. "You mean the Mexican?"

"I think they are Salvadoran."

"Same to me." She motioned for Kendall to come inside. "I liked Celesta. Nice girl. What she was doing with those rowdies, I'll never know."

A four-foot patch of linoleum served as the entryway to a living room that was papered in a cheery orange poppy print. A brown sofa, two small chairs, and a TV playing a shopping channel that sold only gems completed the milieu of a person of big dreams and modest means.

"I didn't catch your name," Kendall said, scooting a sheaf of newspapers to one side of the sofa before taking a seat.

"Sally Todd," she said. "Coffee?"

Kendall politely declined. "No, thanks. I'm here about Celesta. You seem to think there was trouble at home. Am I getting that right?"

Sally Todd tightened the knotted belt on her robe, a pale blue flannel garment that needed laundering, and took a seat facing her visitor.

"Look, these days there is always trouble with young people. I know the girl. I know Tulio and his brothers too. They had their music playing at all hours. I called the sheriff on them five times last summer. You can check on that, if you don't believe me."

"Did Celesta ever indicate to you that she wanted out of the relationship? That maybe she wanted to return to El Salvador?"

The older woman looked for her cigarette case and pulled out a More. She flicked on her lighter and pulled air through the slender dark brown cigarette.

"She said that Tulio was no good and she wanted to get away from him. He was too controlling."

This interested Kendall, although she wasn't sure if she believed anything this woman had to say. "Really?" she asked.

"I'm talking out of school," she said, "but I don't care. The girl needed to get away from the lot of them. The Pena brothers have turned this quiet mobile home park into party central. I think one of the boys stole my leaf blower. They denied it. But that's what I think. I called the sheriff on them too."

"I see."

"Yes, and you can verify all of this. The girl finally got some sense. Really, picking brush? What kind of life is that? She could do better than that. Who couldn't?"

Kendall thanked her. She didn't tell her that the county was rife with desperate people who would do just about anything to survive—and stay out of the reach of the law. Picking brush was far from the worst endeavor she could imagine.

With Josh Anderson away at the academy speaking about his experiences investigating rural crimes, detectives' row in the Kitsap County Sheriff's office was far quieter than usual. Almost pin-drop hushed. Two were out in the field, running down drug cases, and a third was working the third murder of the year, the case of a Seabeck woman who'd been arrested for the killing of a woman she and her husband had picked up after a night of partying at the Bethel Saloon. The tavern was a Kitsap classic, a rough-around-the-edges biker-type bar that shared a parking strip with a butcher, Farmer George's, frequently prompting a retort about the two establishments' close proximity:

"Wonder which is the bigger meat market?"

"Judging by the looks of some of those biker babes hanging around the pool tables, I'd say there's more gristle at the Bethel than at Farmer George's."

Kendall Stark had felt genuine concern coming from Tulio Pena when he spoke about Celesta. She'd seen the way a husband or boyfriend can try to emulate devotion or worry by saying the right words. Sometimes they even eke out a tear to punctuate the moment with a display of emotion that is supposed to support their position as a loving partner.

"I don't know why she did this to me."

"I had no idea she was unhappy."

"All I ever did was love her."

Kendall just didn't see a false note when Tulio gave his statement. Even so, something troubled her greatly, and there was no way to really dismiss it. The reporting deputy noted in the initial missing-person report that Celesta Delgado's purse had been left behind in the van.

Inside the purse were the three main indicators of an abduction or a homicide: Celesta's cell phone, keys, and wallet.

No woman running away leaves those things, she thought.

It was around five when Kendall found her husband and son in the plaza of the Kitsap County Administration Building. Steven had a client meeting that evening, and they'd planned on an early dinner. A few clouds had rolled in, obscuring the Olympics and turning what had been a lovely afternoon into what promised to be a cool spring evening.

Cody's face lit up when his mother emerged from the Sheriff's Office walkway. "Mommy! I see you!" he said.

Kendall beamed and ran toward her son with outstretched arms. Some days there were no words, just the rocking of a small body as he looked at her with eyes that seemed empty of recognition.

"Hi, you two," she said.

"Ready for a dinner out?" Steven asked, his broad white smile another salvo to her heart.

"Yes, I am," she said, scooping up Cody. "Pancakes, everyone?"

Cody smiled.

Whenever they went out, they'd have pancakes at the same restaurant, in the same booth.

"Make mine banana pecan," Steven said with a wink.

"Strawberry for me." Kendall shot back.

It was always banana pecan, strawberry, and blueberry. Each member of the Stark family had a prescribed meal, time, and place. To deviate was to cause unease and ruin what was a pleasant dinner—or, in this case, breakfast—out.

"How's your day going?" Steven asked.

"Oh, you know." She set Cody down and gave her husband a quick peck. "Kind of slow."

"Any sign of the missing girl?"

Kendall and Steven talked shop only on the most cursory level. He'd tell her if he closed a big ad sale; she'd mention if a perp had been nailed or a case stymied. But she didn't like to bring her work into their personal lives. They'd agreed to take his car to eat, then drive back to the Sheriff's Office parking lot so Kendall could take Cody home.

"I'm worried about her," she said, sliding into the passenger seat of the nine-year-old red Jeep Wrangler that they'd purchased just slightly used a couple of years after Cody was born. Despite his age and size, Cody was secured in a car seat, behind his parents.

"I thought she bolted. I mean, Jesus, she was working two jobs. I'd leave town too." Steven glanced at Cody in the rearview mirror. He was watching the world slip by his window.

"Josh talked to Celesta's sister in El Salvador. She's as worried as Tulio is."

"Boyfriend troubles, maybe?" he asked, turning onto Sidney Avenue and heading south to Tremont.

Kendall turned on a CD, a Raffi recording that Cody loved. She turned around, hoping to catch a smile, but the little boy just stared out the side window.

"I really don't know. Can we talk about something else?"

"I drove over to Inverness this afternoon," Steven said. "Just to check it out."

Kendall felt his words stab at her, although she knew Steven meant no harm. The idea of the alternative school for their son hadn't really set in yet. She wasn't *ready* for it to set in.

"I thought we'd do that together," she said.

Steven let a sigh pass from his lips. He took his eyes off the road and looked at her.

"I was making a run up to Bainbridge to meet with an advertiser. It was on the way home."

"I see. I guess that makes sense," Kendall said, looking away.

Why are you pushing this? she thought. *Putting him there is one step closer to saying he's never going to get better.*

As much as she loved Steven, there was no doubt there was a wall between them. She knew that some walls can never be scaled. Not even with all the love in the world.

Chapter Eight

April 1, 10 a.m.
East Bremerton, Washington

The Azteca was a quintessential cookie-cutter Mexican restaurant, one of the type that sprouted all over America around the time that salsa overtook ketchup as the country's best-selling condiment. Frothy frozen margaritas in flavors that God (or a decent bartender) had never intended—peach mint, cantaloupe, and blackberry—and tortilla chips warm from the deep fat fryer, served until the meal itself becomes an afterthought.

Kendall took a call from an Azteca busboy named Scott Sawyer, looked at her watch, and decided she'd head north from Port Orchard and time it for lunch. Josh was out pursuing a lead on a drug dealer near Wye Lake, so she drove up alone.

"I have something important to tell you," Scott had said in a voice that cracked in a way that suggested he was barely out of puberty. "It's really important. About the case you're working on."

"Can you give me a hint?" she asked, wanting to find out before she left if the kid had anything worth telling.

"Celesta had something going on here with another waiter. Tulio was so mad I thought he was going to kill her."

That was certainly enough for the drive up the highway to Bremerton.

Peeling off his apron, Scott Sawyer slid into an orange and brown vinyl booth in the back of the restaurant. He was blond, pale, and as lanky as an orchard ladder. He introduced himself and apologized for keeping her waiting. She'd had to tell the server twice she didn't want any more chips, although she'd barely touched her basket. She wondered if anyone ate the red and green chips, a tip of the hat, or rather sombrero, to Mexico's flag.

To Kendall, it always seemed more like a nod to Christmas.

"First off, I just want you to know that everyone here really likes Celesta. She's our best hostess by far. She trained me."

Kendall smiled. "I've heard nice things about her."

"When the boss remodeled the restaurant in Port Orchard, she was the one he selected to hostess the grand reopening."

The waitress brought a taco salad and silently set it in front of her. For a second, Kendall thought she detected the server rolling her eyes slightly. It was subtle and could have been a nervous tic.

"I made the dressing," he said. "Good stuff. Not good for you, but good stuff."

Kendall speared a piece of lettuce and dipped it into the spicy sour cream dressing.

"Anyway," Scott went on, "Celesta liked me. I could tell. I knew that she was hooked up with Tulio, but she just, you know . . ."

"No, I don't *know*."

Scott rested his bony hands on the table. A tattoo across his knuckles spelled out ROCK AND ROLLA.

"She could do better," he said. "Tulio wasn't going anywhere. She didn't like the brush thing. She wanted to move forward here, not run around the woods with a clipper trying to make a buck."

The server—who wore a name tag that said MARIA but, with her green eyes and blond highlights, looked more like a Mary—shook her head as she cleared the table on the other side of the restaurant. She caught Kendall's eye, and the detective made a mental note to speak to her before leaving the restaurant.

"You said on the phone you had some information that could be helpful in finding her," she said to Scott. "Do you know where she went? Did she say anything to you about leaving town?"

Though clearly enjoying the attention, Scott looked a little impatient. He wasn't ready, it seemed, to cut to the chase.

"I'm getting there. I'm getting there, Detective Stark."

"All right. We're trying to find a missing person, Scott."

"You'll find her. But she'll be dead when you do." His words were delivered matter-of-factly.

Kendall felt a chill. "How do you know that?"

Scott flexed his tattooed knuckles and grinned. "Because I bet you money that Tulio killed her. I read the article in the paper. That's why I called. Tulio and his brothers are big liars. They want to act all lovey-dovey and whatnot, but that's a big fat lie."

Now Kendall could see where this was going. "How do you know this, Scott? Is this an opinion or what?"

"No. One time Celesta and I were messing around in the back."

"'Messing around'?"

"Well, not like that. It wasn't messing around. I had a tear in the strap of my apron," he said, picking up the food-spattered white garment that he'd removed before sitting down. "See right here?" He pointed to some black thread. "That's where Celesta sewed it up. I was wearing it at the time, and Tulio came in and saw us. He thought something was going on."

"But nothing was, right?"

"Right, I mean, I wish. But no, nothing. He just lit into her, saying, 'If I ever catch you touching another man, I'll do what they do to whores back in El Salvador!'"

"And what did you take that to mean?" she said.

"I don't know exactly. I went online and looked up what they do to cheats in El Salvador, and I found something about how a woman can go to prison for six years if she gets caught cheating on her husband."

"But Tulio and Celesta weren't married."

His break over, Scott got up to return to the kitchen. "They acted like it. Or at least *he* did."

Maria, who turned out to be Maryanne Jenner, a student at Olympic College in Bremerton, rang up the bill at the cash register by the front door. The recorded mariachi music blared from the bar, and Kendall had to strain to hear the young woman.

"I hope you don't put much faith in what Scott says," she said. "He's had a thing for Celesta, and she wouldn't give him two seconds of an hour."

"Was Tulio the jealous type?"

"Look," the young woman said, "I've never seen it. Not from him. Others, yeah." She handed her the change, and Kendall pushed it back to her.

"Thanks. One more thing, Detective."

"What's that?

"I think she's dead too. She'd never just run off. Celesta wasn't that kind of girl."

All cops know that if Oscars were handed out to workers in any profession other than moviemaking, it would be to homi-

cide detectives, who must approach suspects with an un-
yielding poker face, or ratchet up sincerity to win over those
on the brink, or feign anger to force a meltdown of defenses.
Kendall had liked Tulio Pena and believed him. She did not
believe or like Scott Sawyer, but it was her duty to follow up
on what he had said.

It wasn't going to be a good cop/bad cop scenario when
Kendall and Josh met with Tulio for a follow-up interview
based on the information provided by Scott Sawyer and Maryanne Jenner at the Azteca Restaurant. Josh remained disinterested in the case, sure that Celesta had ditched her
boyfriend for greener pastures.

Or at least where she didn't have to quite literally work
greener pastures.

Kendall told Tulio that they found some evidence and he
needed to come down as soon as possible. He was in the little room within thirty-five minutes of her call, still wearing
the white Mexican wedding shirt that was his restaurant uniform.

"Tell us what you did with Celesta," Kendall said, looking
dead-eyed at Tulio as they sat across from one another in a
small, windowless interrogation room in the Kitsap County
Sheriff's Office.

"What *I* did with her?"

Kendall forced all her emotions to flatline. "Yes. Did you
fight?"

"I don't know what you are saying."

"Did you tell someone that you would make her pay if
she ever left you for another man?"

"She would never."

Josh was snapped back into the moment by the adrenaline
coming from across the table. "We have a witness who says
so."

Tulio was caught completely off guard. He pushed back
his chair. "Who? Your witness is a liar!"

"Look," Kendall said, finding her way back into the interview, "we have a good idea what happened. You argued in the woods, didn't you. She told you she wanted to leave you, correct?"

"She never."

"Did you beat her? Did you choke her?"

His eyes were filling with tears. "I love her." The compact man across from the detectives shrunk before her eyes. "No. I did not."

Josh jabbed an accusing finger at him. "What did you and your brothers do with her body?"

By then Tulio had stood up. "We did nothing."

"It is only a matter of time," Josh said. "We will find out what you've done with her."

Kendall saw genuine emotion in Tulio's eyes, and her instinct was to tell him that everything would be all right. That they'd find her. That they didn't really think he killed her. Tulio got up and went toward the doorway, stopping before passing through.

"You don't believe me. But I am not lying."

Kendall felt a twinge of shame as Tulio made his way out of the building. She *did* believe him, but there was nothing else to go on. Something had happened to the young woman in the woods near Sunnyslope.

For the next two days an angry and confused Tulio did what he'd been told: he waited. He and his brothers returned to Sunnyslope and yelled out Celesta's name. They called the police a couple times a day, but got the same response from the deputy who'd gone out to see them following that first call. So Tulio did what he'd seen others do in cases in which the police stonewalled.

He called the newspaper.

And while Tulio was seeking answers, the man who had them kicked back and enjoyed what made Washington such a lovely place in the spring.

Never too hot.

Never too cool.

He did all of the things that other men did. He drove to work. Drank beer. Barbecued. Went out on his boat in Puget Sound. Hauled in crab pots brimming with Dungeness beauties. He even took his boat up to Hood Canal during the short-lived shrimp season. He considered heading toward the Theler Wetlands in Belfair, where he'd dumped his victim, but he thought better of it.

Mostly, however, he reveled in what he'd done and what he'd do next. He knew the smartest killer would never kill in his own backyard. He likened it to how a dog wouldn't defecate in his own kennel. How a drunk tries his best to get to a toilet rather than vomit anywhere where cleanup would be required. A smart killer doesn't discard a victim too close to home. He'd researched what had been the downfall of others who'd aspired to the kind of greatness that he did. He wasn't sick, just clever. The others hadn't refined the rules as he had.

He wrote them down on a scrap of paper in his office at the shipyard.

Never kill someone who will be missed.
Never tell anyone.
Never kill in close proximity to another kill.
Never kill someone with a child.
Never kill someone in your family.

As he contemplated his next move, the man with the sharp blade knew that at least one of his rules would be violated, but he carelessly dismissed it. Clever as he was, he felt that set of laws he'd adopted served a mighty purpose.

They kept others in line.

Chapter Nine

At twenty-four, Serenity Hutchins knew that her return to Port Orchard to work on the city's weekly newspaper, the *Lighthouse*, was the necessary first step in her media career. A stepping-stone sunk into familiar ground. It wasn't about being a failure when she wasn't hired by a major Northwest daily. Starting at the *Lighthouse* was merely the best she could do for now, especially in an industry floundering in a failing economy. She'd come home, but she was not the same person who had graduated from South Kitsap High. She was no longer the girl who'd squandered her high school years dating a football player who'd claimed that she'd be his bride once he turned pro.

Which, of course, never happened.

Certainly, Rick Silas had a decent college career and was a third-round pick of the Seattle Seahawks, but after a lifetime of promises of undying love, he'd found a new love—a cheerleader, no less.

Life wasn't fair, and Serenity Hutchins knew it. She probably always had.

She could have moved in with her mother in Bremerton; instead she chose to rent an apartment at Mariner's Glen in Port Orchard, one of those hopelessly nautically themed apartments that saw great use for rusty anchors, ratty nets, and heaps of silvery driftwood at its entryway. She lived there with her cat, a black-and-white tabby named Mr. Smith.

Her editor, a heavyset fellow who'd worked at papers in Seattle and San Francisco but had come back to helm the tiny Port Orchard newspaper, lumbered toward her. Charlie Keller could have been Serenity's idol. He'd interviewed a couple of presidents as a part of the *San Francisco Chronicle*'s editorial board. He had been nominated for a Pulitzer Prize twice for spot news reporting. He'd even had a long-running column in the *Seattle Times*. He'd done it all, *had it all*, and then lost it to a gambling habit.

He'd come home to Port Orchard to finish out his career and die.

That will never happen to me, Serenity thought as she watched Charlie maneuver between the newsroom desks, his beefy frame pounding on the hollow flooring of the modular building that was the modest headquarters of the *Lighthouse*. *I'm going to make a name for myself and stay on top for good.*

She smiled at him.

"Hutchins," he said. "Might have something for you."

She liked it when he used her last name. It was so *All the President's Men*. "What's up?"

"Missing brush picker out in Sunnyslope. Probably nothing. Probably more about a homesick girl wanting to go back to El Salvador than anything. You want the story? Remember, nothing much happens around here, and that's pretty much the way they like it."

Serenity was finishing up an article about a beautification project that had languished for years as downtown Port Orchard merchants griped about the cost.

"What makes you say that?" she asked, dropping the story into an electronic file folder for the copydesk.

"Talked to Josh in the Sheriff's Office."

"I'll run it down," she said. "Details?"

Charlie looked over by the front door, where a clean-cut man in a blue sweatshirt and jeans was waiting. He had black hair and the faint tracings of a goatee that had either just started or, if it had been growing a while, he ought to abandon.

"That's the boyfriend," Charlie said. "Tulio Pena is his name. Let's put something in the paper. Okay?"

Serenity took a notepad and pen and went toward Tulio.

"See if you can get a picture, okay?" Charlie called out. "We need art, you know."

"I know," she said, with the resignation that came with the realization that photos and coupons were the primary reason anyone bothered with the *Lighthouse*. Text—no matter how good—was needed only to fill the spaces between art and ads. She thought of it as "word mortar designed to keep the ads from falling off the sheet of newsprint."

The *Lighthouse*'s conference room was furnished with seven ladder-back chairs and an antique mahogany table that, newsroom legend had it, was salvaged from a near-shipwreck around the Cape by one of Port Orchard's first settlers, a sea captain who'd planned on retiring in Seattle but instead settled in Sidney, the forerunner of present-day Port Orchard. The back wall had the framed sheet-metal press plates of some of the biggest stories covered by the paper throughout its history: The stock market crash. World War II. Kennedy's assassination. Neil Armstrong's walk on the moon. By the late seventies, not only had the *Lighthouse* switched to cold-type processing, but several purchases by out-of-state companies had stripped the paper of its pursuit of the big story. In a very real way, the display was a reminder that, outside of a small news hole, the *Lighthouse* was merely a shopper feeding a shrinking gob of income to an out-of-state owner. It was no longer a paper of daily record. It had gone weekly as a cost-cutting move not long after it changed hands.

"I heard what he said," Tulio said, indicating Charlie Keller, as he took a seat across from Serenity. He opened an envelope carrying three photos and slid them across the deep, dark wood surface.

Serenity noticed a slight tremor in his hands.

This guy is scared, she thought.

The images were of Celesta Delgado. One had her in a raspberry cap and gown; another in a Mexican peasant blouse embroidered with holly and poinsettias. The last was of the two of them, taken with a flash as the sun highlighted the tops of the Olympics. She was a lovely girl, not much younger than Serenity.

"She's a high school graduate," he said. "We both are." His eyes fixed on the photo; then he looked up at the reporter, trying to detect a flicker of surprise. He'd met enough people who, because his skin was bronze and his accent could not be masked, assumed that he could not be anything but a migrant. One of the invisible who do the jobs no one else wants.

"South Kitsap?" she asked.

"That's right."

"Any family here? You know, so I can talk to them about Celesta's background."

Tulio shook his head. "Her dad died, and her mom and sister moved back to El Salvador. She's only got me. I am her family. We were going to be married in August."

Serenity pointed to the photo of Celesta in the Christmas blouse, her hair thick and blue-black.

"Taken at work," Tulio said. "She is a restaurant hostess at Azteca. She was employee of the month earlier this year."

"You want us to publish these photos, right?" she asked.

"Yes," he said. "The police are doing nothing. We have to find her. I need help."

Serenity understood. She didn't blame the Sheriff's Office. They were understaffed and overworked just like anyone else. Maybe a little story could help.

"Tell me everything about the day Celesta went missing."

Tulio took a deep breath. "Okay. We left early. . . ."

Within an hour of Tulio Pena's departure, Serenity put the finishing touches on a short article about Celesta Delgado. The photo-imaging guy at the paper had done a reasonably decent job with the scans, holding the detail that would look beautiful online but surely would muddy up on the printing presses. She finished a bottled water with some leftover eggplant parmigiana that had at most one more day of survival in the refrigerator.

Brush Picker Vanishes Near Sunnyslope

A local woman disappeared while harvesting greens for a floral supply warehouse Sunday afternoon.

The Kitsap County Sheriff responded to a call from Celesta Delgado's boyfriend, Tulio Pena, at 3 p.m. just off the Sunnyslope highway fronting DNR land.

Delgado, 22, and Pena, 27, were working as brush pickers, along with Pena's two brothers. All carried permits issued by the state.

"We were having a good day," Pena said in an interview with the *Lighthouse*. "Celesta was taking a bag of salal back to the van, and the next thing we knew, she was gone. Something is wrong."

Kitsap Sheriff Jim McCray says that his office is investigating.

"We are putting resources on it," he said, "but we are concerned that this might be the case of a young woman who got tired of things here, or missed her family and went back home. She did the same thing three months ago."

McCray was referring to reports that Delgado left her job as a hostess at the East Bremerton Azteca Mexican Restaurant without giving any reason. However, a check by the *Lighthouse* indicated that the departure was a misunderstanding. Delgado was rehired by Azteca following a three-week absence.

"Her sister in El Salvador was ill. She did not leave without warning that time," Pena said.

But this time, Pena says, is different.

"Something has happened to Celesta," Pena said. "Please help me find her. I am—we are— very, very worried."

If you've seen Celesta Delgado, please contact the Kitsap County Sheriff's Detective Kendall Stark this newspaper.

Serenity finished the article by writing extensive captions to accompany the photos. By providing the text with the images of Celesta, it would ensure that the overburdened copydesk would publish the pictures, at least online. She'd made a few calls to the numbers that Tulio provided. It seemed that everyone—the police, her employer, and her friends—believed that it was possible she left the country for her mother's home in El Salvador

Everyone considered it an option but Tulio Pena. He complained to his brothers when he read the paper the next morning: "They are treating Celesta like she doesn't matter. Like we don't know her. It is not right. She's lost, or she's been taken."

Or, as he was about to find out, something far worse.

* * *

He looked at the article that Serenity Hutchins had published in the paper. Sure, it was only a small-town paper, but in time he'd see his hobby find a place in the pages of newspapers far bigger. *More important.* Serenity would get something out of that too, and she'd have him to thank for that, of course.

He ran his fingertip over her byline, smudging it into oblivion.

The blood flowed from his heart to his genitals, and his erection throbbed until he could take it no more. He slipped his hand under the waistband of his underwear.

He knew what he liked.

He pulled up Facebook, logged on with a bogus name and e-mail address, and went to the group called "Girls Who Want Adventure."

The young woman who'd posted the day before had taken the bait and answered his e-mail offering a job on a boat in Seattle. She was blond, blue-eyed. She had the kind of all-American-girl good looks that advertisers selling cornflakes and diet soda love to feature. He leaned close to the screen as he ejaculated.

Both a methodical hunt and a surprise ambush had their distinct appeal, but this one would be different.

He'd set a trap.

He reached for a Kleenex to mop up the evidence of his arousal.

Yes, she'd be just fine. But when? Timing, as he knew, was everything.

Chapter Ten

Serenity Hutchins set down her phone and looked at her note-pad. She noticed for the first time that she'd been crying as she wrote down an anonymous caller's deluge of cruelty. Everything he had said in a flat, barely audible voice had revolted her. She was sick to her stomach. Tears had spattered the top sheet of her reporter's notebook, sending the blue ink into a swirling bloom. She took a sheet of paper towel and blotted it. The transfer of ink and tears reminded her of blood.

She dialed her editor's home number.

Charlie Keller was in the middle of a model of a steamship, *Virginia V,* one of the last of the famed Mosquito Fleet that flitted from Sinclair Inlet east to Seattle and points southward too. He'd painstakingly created the model himself, out of balsa and fir. His dining room table had been converted to a mini-shipbuilder's workspace since he'd returned to Port Orchard. It was the only hobby that kept his attention and kept him out of the Indian casinos. His house was a modest one tucked in the ivy-infested woods off Pottery Avenue. It was a three-bedroom with dinged-up wooden floors, a cracked tile countertop in the kitchen, and not a window treatment to be had. Mrs. Keller was missed for many reasons, and the lack of window treatments was somewhere near the bottom on the list of a lonely man. His dog, Andy, a smooth-coated and very overweight dachshund, was curled up on a sofa cushion that Charlie had removed and placed on the floor.

The phone rang, Andy lifted his head, and Charlie got up to answer. It was after ten. As he ambled over to his cell phone on the kitchen counter, he wondered who'd be calling him at this late hour.

It was Serenity.

"Kind of late for a call," Charlie said somewhat gruffly. He slumped back into his chair and rubbed his socked foot over Andy's protruding belly.

"I know. I'm sorry. I mean, I wouldn't have called if I didn't need to know what to do here."

Her voice was shaky. Charlie Keller's annoyance at the intrusion turned to concern.

"You sound stressed. You okay?"

"No. I'm not. I'm scared. Charlie, I just got off the phone with some freak who says he's a killer. He said he killed Celesta Delgado. He also said he had plans for another girl."

Charlie sat down next his model of the Virginia. "Probably a crank. Don't sweat it. I talked to five Zodiac wannabes when I was down in San Francisco."

Serenity didn't think so. "He was so direct about what he did to her. He told me things that he did to the body. Disgusting things."

"I see," Charlie said, adjusting some line that he'd coiled on the deck of the boat model. "I'm not saying, Serenity, that he's absolutely not the killer. But I'd bet this house that it was a crank caller. What exactly did he say?"

"He started by telling me how he subdued her, how she begged him to let her go."

"Who?"

"Celesta, I guess. Maybe another girl. I don't know. He says he held her for three days. He . . ." Serenity looked down at her notes as if she needed to see the words in order to repeat what the caller had said. *As if his words could be erased from her mind.* "He said he penetrated her with a rolling pin. He said he put a vacuum cleaner hose onto her nipples. He said that he choked her while she begged for her life."

Serenity stopped. She was sobbing, and she hated that she'd fallen apart, even if it was just on the phone.

Charlie wanted to say something gruff and inappropriate about the caller being a Martha Stewart hater or something, but he held his tongue. The young reporter was crumbling.

"Kid, it'll be all right," he said, trying to comfort Serenity, and yet glad that he was on the phone with her and not searching for a tissue in his office.

"I guess so," she said, regaining a measure of composure. "What should I do? Call the sheriff?"

"You *could*. But let's hold off until tomorrow. First, you don't know if his info is genuine. Chances are, like I said, it isn't. Let's run down the story tomorrow, first thing."

"I don't know. I mean, are you sure we shouldn't call Detective Stark?"

"Look," he said, "we all have jobs to do. We'll work the story tomorrow."

Serenity didn't want to argue. "If you say so."

"That I do. Now, are you going to be all right?"

"I think so. Good night, Charlie."

"Good night, Hutchins."

He hung up, a slight smile on his face. It wasn't that he

was happy about the fear in her voice. It was the memory of his experiences as a young reporter.

Those days were long gone.

Serenity thought of calling someone else just then, maybe her sister. But she dropped the notion. She was still unnerved by the creepy caller, but her editor was probably right. It had been a crank call. Part of her reasoning was that killers don't often call to brag about what they'd done. But why *her*? There were far bigger newspapers serving the region: Bremerton had one, Seattle had one, Tacoma too. She could understand why he wouldn't call a TV or radio station; those would require audio and video for a story.

But why her?

She decided to make a cup of decaffeinated Market Spice tea and take a book to read in bed. While she set a mug of water in the microwave, she walked through the apartment, checking the windows, the front door, and the slider that led to the small balcony. Everything was locked. The microwave dinged, and she took her drink and the novel she was reading to her bedroom.

Yes, she thought, the caller had to be a fake.

As the crow flies, the man who'd called wasn't far from the Mariner's Glen apartments, where the reporter lived. He emerged from the seldom-used bank of phones in the back of the bar at the China West Restaurant and ordered another beer.

A plump man in his late fifties, dressed in a blue shirt and khaki vest that he couldn't have buttoned if he'd tried, sat on his right, staring straight ahead as the bartender went about her business.

He slipped the prepaid phone card inside his wallet.

"Old lady pissing you off?" the man in the vest asked.

"Huh?"

"You were on the phone. Just figured your old lady was bitching at you like mine does."

The bartender sent down a beer.

"Yeah. Never stops."

"Yeah, I guess I'm in the same boat with you and every other guy. I'd like to shut that bitch up."

The man sipped his beer. He wasn't thinking of his wife just then. He had his mind on another woman.

"Yeah, shutting her up is good," he said. "Sometimes I'd like to shut her up permanently."

"Tell me about it."

The man just smiled. He'd already told someone about it. And that felt really good.

Trey Vedder's father, a prominent Bremerton dentist, thought his son's lack of drive and tepid enthusiasm meant that he'd been given too much too soon. The nineteen-year-old college dropout didn't seem to mind one whit when his grades from Washington State University dipped low enough for the academic watch list. His father thought otherwise and yanked him out "faster than an abscessed tooth" and told him he'd work a year. He had one caveat: "It'll be with your hands and back instead of your brain. You need to see what's out there for those who miss the boat."

Trey took "the boat" literally: he took a job at a Port Orchard marina cleaning the dock, helping the harbormaster, doing whatever needed to get done.

It was late afternoon, and Sinclair Inlet was darkening as the sun moved west toward the Olympics. The foothills faded behind some feathery clouds.

"Need any help?" Trey said, more out of boredom than the desire to be genuinely helpful.

The captain of a thirty-five-foot Sea Ray, the *Saltshaker*, shook his head. "Got it handled, kid," he said.

The teenager held his hand out to catch the line anyway, and the captain gave in and tossed it in his direction.

"How's the fishin'?" Trey asked, securing the blue nylon rope.

The captain cut the motor. "Wasn't fishing."

Trey looked over at a white plastic bucket on the deck. He thought it contained chum used as bait. Inside, red liquid swirled to conceal what, with a little more scrutiny, he made out as a pair of gloves.

"Nope. Just a little redwood stain job in the galley," he said. "I'll dispose of the bucket at the transfer station."

Trey nodded as the man snatched up the bucket. The remark, however, struck him as a little odd. A lot of boats in the harbor had redwood-stained woodwork. But he'd been inside the *Saltshaker*.

It was fiberglass, aluminum, and vinyl.

PART TWO
Marissa

Job interview, Tuesday, shipyard clerk. Daycare poss.

—FOUND IN THE VICTIM'S PURSE, RECOVERED FROM
A DUMPSTER

Chapter Eleven

April 9, afternoon
Bremerton

The car sped along the back roads of Kitsap County, faster than it should. The driver didn't care. Speed on a slippery pavement only ratcheted up the excitement of the hunt. It was as if what he sought to do weren't dangerous enough. It wasn't enough of a rush without the added risk of being stopped by a cop and assuming the affect of a concerned driver pulled over for a routine traffic stop—and not the look of a killer about to be apprehended. That, he was sure, would never happen as long as he paid attention to the rules.

He got on Highway 16 at Tremont Avenue and drove toward Bremerton. He slowed the vehicle in Gorst, the little burg at the tip of Sinclair Inlet. Gorst was always a possibility for what he had in mind. A topless bar and an espresso stand with baristas in pink leather hot pants was the chief draw for those who just might fit what he was looking for.

Something a little different. A little dangerous. Something pretty.

Nothing caught his eye. No need to brake, just keep going. Around the inlet and the off-ramp that led traffic past the row of Navy destroyers, aircraft carriers, and assorted ships awaiting their turn in the scrap heap. It was known as the Mothball Fleet—or, by those who disdained all things military, "tax dollars at work."

It amused him how Bremerton, a decaying Navy town always on the cusp of a renaissance, had never been able to shake the vestiges of seedy tattoo parlors, hookers on the stroll, and druggies lurking in the garages of three-story parking lots. Half-million-dollar condos along a revamped waterfront and a horde of fine restaurants did little to ease the reality that places might change, but people's habits don't.

Except for some daydreaming, he'd never hunted in the place that, out of the entire Kitsap Peninsula, afforded the most chance for success.

The ferry landing was like raw bait swirling in a bucket and cast overboard. It was surefire. It attracted both people with a place to go and those who had no schedule, no clue, no interest in anything but loitering.

Or maybe scoring some heroin or the warm mouth of a hooker.

Before the enormous steel-hulled car ferries were deployed to shuttle people from one side of Puget Sound to the other, a veritable swarm of wooden steamers plowed the cold blue waters. The flotilla, aptly and lovingly called the Mosquito Fleet, had long since gone by the wayside in favor of so-called "superferries." Yet, Port Orchard, a town that never really got the hang of redevelopment, held on to the good idea that had come and gone. The old wooden *Carlisle II* served as a link from Port Orchard's ferry landing to Bremerton's just across Sinclair Inlet.

It was afternoon, and Sunday's second shift of shipyard commuters had long since gone to work. The boat was empty, save for Midnight Cassava and a couple of beleaguered out-of-towners heading over to walk the deck of the USS *Turner Joy*, a retired navy destroyer that had been playing host to tourists and war buffs for more than a decade.

"You know of any good places to eat?" a ruddy-faced fellow with gold chains coiled in the neck of his shirt asked her.

Midnight smiled. "I wish I did." She latched on to the disappointed look on the visitor's face. "Kidding. If you like seafood, try Anthony's. A little pricey but good. There's also a great Belgian beer and fry place not far from the ferry landing."

The man smiled and then looked over at his wife. "A beer sounds good. . . ."

"In a couple of hours it might," snapped the tall woman with close-cropped silver hair that was either stylish or unflattering; Midnight couldn't be sure.

As she looked out across the water pondering her future, tide lines of flotsam and jetsam arced along the steely, flat surface. She knew the job she was doing was a young woman's game and she had responsibilities.

Soon she'd start over.

Midnight Cassava had spent part of the day riding the boat back and forth from Seattle to Bremerton. She was a slim woman, with olive skin, a full mouth, and eyes that were skilled at never registering much interest in anything. Or anyone. She was twenty-seven on her birth certificate, but the miles on her life's odometer put her closer to forty. She didn't like to work late at night: Feeling the chill of the air between her legs in some man's car was far from a pleasant experience. She'd thought that those days of "lingering and loitering" were behind her. She thought she could score the money she needed by using Craigslist to troll for johns. That, however, was before her computer was stolen and her drug habit escalated. Her plans for becoming a dental assistant or a lawyer had vanished. Midnight wanted out. Anything would do. Even a shipyard clerk's position, a job she planned to interview for, would be fine. Until then, she was merely hoping to get through the day.

Working the Washington State Ferries system was a tough gig, but with a little one at home, Midnight needed to be able to turn a trick, get off the boat, feed Tasha, and get back to work. The two-hour ferry ride back and forth worked into a schedule that she could manage.

Morning runs from Seattle to Bremerton were useless for her particular endeavor. Most of the men and women (Midnight would perform a sex act with a woman on rare occasions, and preferred it to having sex with men: it was less invasive) were in too much of a hurry to get to where they were headed. They had jobs to get to. Meetings to prep for. No one was in the mood for sex. That was fine. Midnight liked to sleep in as late as Tasha allowed her. She usually started up the ramp to the car deck around 4 P.M. That ensured she'd catch a couple of blue-collar guys looking for a blow job in the bathroom. She even had a regular, a physician who had a Lexus with black tinted windows. He'd invite her down to his car, and they'd have "around the world" in the backseat. With the noise of the ferry's enormous engines a perfect cover, the doctor would cut loose with the most vile epithets that a woman could ever hear. But he paid well, never coming up short like some of the others who "swore" they had another fifty, but could produce only a twenty-dollar bill.

Midnight hung around the magazine and newspaper rack near the bathrooms. The racks were filled with brochures and flyers for getaways and activities that targeted the interests of the out-of-state traveler. There were also scads of publications with names like *Coastal Homes* and *Saltwater Residences* advertising the good life. Midnight sat across from the racks at a table bolted to the floor, prison-cafeteria style. The tops of her breasts and her pretty eyes were her calling

card. She had the kind of emotional intellect that could determine who wanted to look and who wanted to touch. She
laughed about it with her girlfriends.

"To get a guy, all you have to do is look at his package,
then flick your eyes to theirs," she said. "And bam! If they
look back at you, you've got a shot."

She'd give a nod, and the fellow with the lustful look in
his eyes would slip into the bathroom. Making certain the
room was empty, she'd follow. The stall next to the urinal
trough was ideal. The engines below rumbled as they churned
the water, obscuring the muffled moans of pleasure. She'd
shut the door, turn the lock, and go to work.

Her friends asked her how it was that the ferry crew, the
skipper in particular, didn't bust her or at the very least kick
her off the boat, but she just laughed.

"Who do you think Tasha's daddy is?"

That evening, work done, Midnight sat on a bench on the
plaza near the ferry landing and watched a fountain that she
thought spurted water like ejaculate: one pulse, then another,
weaker one. She put on a pair of walking shoes and slipped the
pumps she wore for most of her "shift" back into her oversize purse.

"You look lonely," a man's voice said.

"You look horny," she shot back, after a quick check of
his crotch.

"I might be."

"You might be a horny cop too. Are you a cop?"

"Nope."

"Then Midnight just might be able to take care of your
problem."

The man flashed a smile, his teeth white and straight. He
was clean-cut, and even from five feet away she could smell
his cologne. He wasn't some dirty, trashy john.

"My car's over there," he said, indicating the parkade.

"All right," she said, glancing at her watch. A half hour

until the last ferry took workers from Bremerton to Port Orchard. "Let's get going. I have things do to."

He showed that big white smile again. "Me too."

Darrin Jones had answered service calls for Otis Elevators for twenty-seven years. It was a business, he unfailingly said whenever anyone inquired about the work he did, that had its "ups and downs."

The Monday morning he was called out to the Bremerton parkade was cool and breezy, with a band of silver clouds heading over the Olympics and on their way to bump into the Cascades. The parkade job was considered a low priority, as there were adequate stairways and reasonable access for disabled drivers on the first level. The call that the elevator had been jammed was ten hours old.

Darrin pulled into the parkade, disturbing a couple of crows that had found the confines of the concrete structure, invited by its debris field of fast-food leavings. He parked his gray panel truck in front of the elevator and looked at his wristwatch. He'd made good enough time that he could kick back and smoke before getting to work, despite signs posted that admonished him not to light up. On the seat next to him was a folder holding the details of a Caribbean cruise that he and his wife, Lynnette, were scheduled to take the following Monday, the day he officially kicked off his retirement.

Five workdays to freedom!

Another car pulled in and drove up to the next level as he crushed out his cigarette and made his way toward the elevator doors. He noticed a thin brown smear two thirds of the way down at the point where the facing doors met one another.

People are pigs, he thought.

For a second his mind flashed on his retirement and how dealing with anyone he didn't want to bother with was almost over.

Darrin pushed the button, but the elevator didn't respond. He checked the fuse box around the corner.

Looks good. Damn thing's just jammed.

And then Darrin did what anyone in his position would do, despite hundreds of hours of training and being told that a "machine should never be forced" by the operator. He punched a slot-head screwdriver between the door gaskets and worked it like a lever. It was jammed, but not so much that he couldn't wrestle it open as he'd done a thousand times before. He widened his stance, tucked his fingers into the opening, and grunted.

The doors slowly moved, but the second he could see inside, Darrin Jones wished he'd bailed on that service call.

The floor had a spray of blood.

"Holy shit," he said under his breath.

He knew that he was required to call the police whenever there was anything suspicious to report. Company policy was precise on it. But he also knew that a call to the police would mean irritating discussion and paperwork.

I'm going to the Caribbean, he thought. *Lynnette and I don't deserve this.*

Darrin looked around. It was quiet. He went back to his van and retrieved some rags and a canister of cleaning fluid. He hated the company. He hated the people who pissed, defecated, or bled in his elevators.

He wasn't going to call it in, and he sure wasn't going to miss the rum punch he'd been dreaming about.

Chapter Twelve

Evil can lodge in the psyche like a *Partridge Family* song that catches a clock radio listener off guard as they wake from a night of steady slumber. The words that spewed from the man who'd called Serenity to detail what he claimed he'd done to the dead woman in the bay were like that. She replayed his words as she showered, brushed her teeth, and dressed in her work uniform: a pair of black jeans and a white sweater. She grabbed her notebook, purse, and car keys. She skipped breakfast, not feeling hungry.

She had a million more questions for the man, and she half hoped he'd call again, although the thought of it made her empty stomach turn. She wondered why he'd called her instead of another reporter for a bigger paper. The timbre of his voice had resonated in a strange way too. It wasn't that he had an accent or anything distinguishable; it was kind of an average voice. Slightly mechanical, maybe.

Charlie Keller met her by the office door.

"I asked Josh Anderson to come up," he said.

Serenity rolled her eyes. "Great, Charlie. He's always hitting on me."

Charlie lowered his voice as he led her into the conference room, "You'll be sorry the day dirty old men *don't* hit on you. But you're too young to know that right now."

Josh was already ensconced in the boardroom/interview room. He had a Seahawks mug of burned-on-the-bottom-of-the-pot newsroom coffee and a rolled-up copy of the *Seattle Times*.

"No mention of any missing girl," he said, thumping the paper on the back of a chair.

"Maybe no one knows she's missing," Serenity said, taking a seat across from the Kitsap County Sheriff's Office detective. He was handsome, confident. Maybe a little too cocky, she thought. Her eyes landed on his open shirt collar, and she wondered why he felt compelled to expose that tuft of slightly graying chest hair.

"Charlie says you got a nasty crank call," he said, eyeing her.

She nodded at the understatement. The call had been nasty indeed.

"If it was a crank," she said.

"Tell the detective what he said to you." Charlie fished a powdered donut from a box that Serenity suspected was left over from the day before, when the ad staff had brought in the fried pastries to kick off their "Donut Make Sense to Advertise" promotion. White confectioner's sugar drifted like snow onto his robin's-egg-blue tie, but Charlie didn't appear to notice.

"Look," she said, "I'm really not comfortable relaying all of the disgusting things that creep said to me."

"I can take it," Josh said. His tone was breezy, almost tauntingly so.

Serenity let out a sigh. "Of course you can."

"Tell him," Charlie finally said, dusting the sugar from his tie.

She took out her notepad and hurled what that man had said to her across the table.

Sex toy.
Kitchen rolling pin.
Duct tape.
Wire restraints.
Slice 'n dice.

The last one caught the detective's attention.

"Sounds like a commercial on late-night cable."

"Yeah, if your channel is Hell TV. Seriously, Detective Anderson—"

"Call me Josh," he said.

He was hitting on her again. Charlie winked at Serenity—at least, she thought he had.

"Okay. *Josh*," she said. "The man was a freak and enjoyed every minute of the call. I wouldn't be surprised if he was masturbating while he talked."

"That wouldn't surprise me, either. Get his number?"

"Do you mean did I write it down so I could call him back for more of his vile talk?"

Josh narrowed his brow. He seemed to almost enjoy making her squirm a little. "No, that's not what I mean. On your cell phone. Did you capture his number?"

"He called my landline. And no, there was no number. 'Private caller' was the designation that came up."

Serenity picked at a cinnamon twist but determined it was beyond stale. *Almost petrified*, she thought.

"Did you notice anything about his voice—anything that might help ID him? You know, while the conversation is fresh."

Serenity thought for a moment while the two men looked on. "His voice was odd."

"Odd?" Josh asked.

"Yes. Kind of bland."

The detective pressed her for details. "Old or young?"

She studied him with a prolonged stare, in a manner that was meant to show she was doing so. "Old. About your age."

Charlie reached for another donut, an attempt to mitigate the tension in the room—or simply because those donuts were pretty tasty. Sugar and all.

Josh's face with a little red, but he tried not to let on that the insult had struck a nerve.

Almost immediately, Serenity amended her answer.

"I didn't mean that he was an old man like you," she said. "I mean *mature*. You know . . . someone middle-aged."

Josh Anderson grinned. The pretty young reporter had challenged him a little, and he liked it. If she was a little sorry that she hurt his feelings, that meant that she was interested.

All the pretty girls were.

"Every time I do this, I sound like Mickey Mouse," Melody said, setting down the voice changer while her husband impatiently looked on. "I just can't do it."

Sam took the device and moved the slide control, modulating timbre and pitch.

"You can. And you will," he said. "It just takes practice. First time I did it, I thought I sounded like Darth Vader." He pushed the headset back at her, and she took it.

"All right," she said. "I'll practice." She dialed Sam's cell number, and he answered.

"Hi," she said.

"Slide the settings," he said.

"Okay. Here I am."

Her voice sounded unsure but more masculine. Not quite an automated digital tone but something less than human.

"Lower," he said. "But just a bit—don't overdo it, babe."

Melody moved the control almost imperceptibly.

"How's this?" she asked in a voice that sounded distinctly completely male.

"Love it," he said. "Now, say what I want you to say."

She looked down at some notes that she'd written to remind her just how she was supposed to play it.

"You're a hot little bitch," she said, hesitating.

"Tell her," he said.

"I like that top you wore the other day. The one that showed off your body."

He looked at her from across the room. One hand was in his pants; the other clamped the phone to his ear.

"Why are you doing this to me?" he asked.

"Because you deserve it, bitch," she said.

"I'm going to hang up right now."

"Hang up on me, bitch, and you die."

He took his phone from his ear and motioned for her to come. Melody took off the headset and started toward him.

"Pull off your panties," he said. "You're a very good student, and you need a reward. I got something for you."

Melody did what she was instructed. It wasn't about being acquiescent or afraid. The fear just gave way to the thrill of what they did together. She didn't think that what her husband was doing to her just then was any kind of a violation. It was a gift. She accepted him and whatever he put into her. She knew deep down what he wanted. He'd told her time and again.

"You're an obedient bitch, but you're not as pretty as she is. And I'll bet she's a whole lot more fun in bed."

"All I want to do is please you," she said, dropping to her knees.

"Then shut up and suck. You talk too much."

Chapter Thirteen

April 13, 4 p.m.
Port Orchard

Donna Solomon did not fit the profile of a mother of a prostitute. She had never had any problems with men, drugs, or the law. To look at her was to see the very image of professionalism and personal accountability. At fifty-two, Donna worked as a charge nurse in the maternity ward of Harrison Medical Center in Bremerton, a job she'd held for more than fifteen years. She was a round presence with stick legs and a slight bulge around her tummy and a butt far bigger than she wanted. Heredity, she figured, thinking of her own mother and the scourge of a large buttocks and piano legs. She worked out four days a week at the Port Orchard Curves, doing a mild weight circuit and twenty-five minutes of cardio to Moby songs. Her butt was always going to be big, but she didn't think it had to get any bigger. And yet despite all the things she tried to do to better herself—Curves, continuing education classes at Olympic College that had nothing to do with nursing and the *New York Times* crossword puzzle on-line every day—she had her hard luck too.

She divorced her husband, Zachary, after their adopted daughter, Marissa, put them through the wringer in ways that no parent could or should endure. Marissa had set a fire in the kitchen when she was six, run away from home at ten. By thirteen there was no more room for pretending that there was anything they could do to be the close family they had desired when they had brought her home in a private adoption from a Russian orphanage.

Donna Solomon rarely spoke of Marissa, although hospital administrators and other nurses at Harrison would happily have lent a sympathetic ear. When Marissa, who stopped using her given name in favor of Midnight Cassava, was arrested in a Bremerton Police Department prostitution sting at a local park, she was given her second chance. It turned out she wasn't the target of the sting, but a Bremerton cop had been. Midnight was one of the chief witnesses in a case and ended up with a lightning-fast plea deal.

What should have been a gift was turned into a sense of invincibility. Midnight had convinced herself that she was able to do whatever she wanted. She continued working the streets, the ferry, wherever she could score a john, partying the money away and doing whatever it was she wanted. It was the ultimate F-U to her mother, of course. Donna accepted that the daughter she chose to love had abandoned her. She could not return any of the love she received. Everything was about money, blame, and the choices others made.

When Midnight was seven months pregnant, she showed up at the nurses' station looking for her mother. It was the first time she'd been to the hospital since she was a teen and was determined, it had seemed, to make her mother's life as miserable as possible. She had left with a physician's bag of drug samples. No charges were pressed because Donna was able to retrieve the missing samples. Donna had been pulling strings for Marissa since the day they brought her home from the agency.

After Midnight's return and the impending pregnancy, however, things started to change. It started with a few phone calls. Mother and daughter met for lunch a couple of times at a drive-through in Navy Yard City, on the edge of downtown Bremerton. By the time Tasha was born, her mother and grandmother had come to an understanding: if the little girl was to have any semblance of a home life, they'd have to work together.

Donna never knew who the father was, and understood that it was probably something her daughter didn't know for sure. She told herself that it didn't matter. No man was needed. She'd help out however she could, and she'd be there whenever Midnight needed her, no matter the conditions. The terms, as she eventually learned, were to watch the baby on weekends and after shifts—but only when asked.

"I'll call you when I need you, Mother. Don't think about interfering with my life or my daughter's. As long as you get that, we'll be fine."

Donna didn't argue. She knew that Midnight had no real job. The money that she used to pay for her apartment over one of Port Orchard's downtown junk shops was from prostitution. Or maybe selling drugs. Whatever it was, it was bad news. Over the first few months of Tasha's life, Donna could see a change in her troubled daughter, and she held out hope that someday things would work out after all.

Not only for the baby but for her own broken heart.

It was Tuesday, and Donna Solomon hadn't heard from her daughter since Saturday. She knew the rules. She knew that trying to involve herself in Tasha's life was a risk. Too much interest might feel like a hard shove to a daughter whose love she wanted more than anything.

After work, she parked her car in the lot behind the aptly named Pack Rat's Hideaway and climbed the stairs to her daughter's apartment and knocked.

No answer.

She pushed the bell.

Again, nothing.

She listened, and she could hear the sounds of a baby crying.

"Tasha?"

No answer.

"Marissa!"

A man wearing oil-soaked blue jeans and a red flannel shirt poked his head out of the apartment next door. His face was the picture of annoyance and anger, a pinched mouth and eyes that told Donna Solomon that a smart person wouldn't mess with him.

"Can you tell that ho to keep her kid quiet?" he asked. "Jesus, some of us have real jobs and need to get some shut-eye. The kid's been crying all night. Day and night. I don't give a shit about the day, but I don't like putting up with some brat squawking when I need to get some sleep. I get up at four a.m. Kid's going all night."

"I'm sorry. I'll tell her," Donna said, defusing the man's anger with complete understanding.

"You better. That's what I say."

"I will. I said so."

"Fine. That bitch is a piece of work, you know."

Donna shot the man a cold stare. "Yes, I know, sir. That bitch, as you call her, is my daughter."

The man, slightly embarrassed, retreated into his apartment.

Donna tilted her head and listened as the sound of a cry emanated from inside the apartment.

"Marissa! Open up!"

She jiggled the doorknob. *Locked.*

The sound of the crying grew louder. With a surge of

adrenaline—the type that turns a frightened mother or grandmother into Wonder Woman—Donna rammed her shoulder
against the hollow-core door with such force she could feel
the frame bend and break.

And she nearly dislocated her shoulder in the process.

"Marissa!"

Once inside, Donna hurried into the expected disorder of
the living room. If Donna kept a spotless home, her long-
troubled daughter was the opposite. Things were never filthy,
but nothing was put where it ought to be. Magazines and
clothes were piled up on the coffee table in front of the TV. A
bouquet of wilting red roses sat on the TV next to a small
framed photo of Tasha.

"Marissa?" Donna's heart was thumping, and the pain in
her shoulder nearly made her cry. Obviously something was
very, very wrong. She hurried to the apartment's sole bedroom, the one that Marissa shared with her daughter.

Tasha was standing in her crib. She'd somehow shredded
her diaper and her little body was smeared with feces and
her bedding soaked in urine. Seeing her grandmother, the little girl let out an even louder wail.

"Oh, baby, it's all right. Grandma's here." Donna scooped
up Tasha, shivering and crying. She didn't think twice about
how filthy the child was. She held her close. "It'll be all
right. It'll be all right."

She spun around the room dreading the bathroom, as it
was the only place in the apartment where her daughter
could be.

The door was open a crack, and she moved it open with
her feet.

"Marissa, are you in here?"

But she wasn't.

It was only her and Tasha. She grabbed a baby blanket
and wrapped it around the crying baby. The stench was nearly
overpowering. The white mattress cover was stained with a
dark pool of urine, nearly the color of strong black tea. Tasha's

lips were dry and cracked. But despite her crying, no tears came to her eyes.

"Oh, my sweet baby, you're dehydrated. How long have you been alone? Why did your mother leave you?"

She looked around for a bottle but found none. She went in to the kitchen and dampened a towel with tap water. She dabbed at Tasha's dry lips, letting some moisture into her mouth.

"Marissa, what did you do? Marissa, where are you?"

She reached for her cell phone and dialed 911, first requesting an ambulance, then a police officer.

Josh Anderson responded to the call to the apartment above Pack Rat's Hideaway, joining officers from the Port Orchard Police Department, who had the jurisdiction for the city limits. The city police and the Sheriff's Office had a long history of cross-training and cooperation. Josh was on the roster to join in that Tuesday. By the time he arrived, child welfare caseworkers had already followed Tasha's ambulance to the hospital. Donna Solomon didn't fuss about it. She needed immediate medical assistance. If Donna hadn't come when she had, the worst possible outcome would have been likely.

A day later, and Tasha might not have survived.

"My daughter has her problems," she told the Kitsap County detective as they stood by his car in the parking lot off Bay Street, "but she wouldn't leave Tasha for any real length of time—never long enough for the baby to be in jeopardy. Something has happened to her."

Josh knew Marissa by reputation and rap sheet. Most local cops did.

"But your daughter does hang out with unsavory types, doesn't she?"

Donna knew he was trying to be kind. He probably knew plenty about her daughter. The distraught mother and grandmother could appreciate his kindness, of course, but she wasn't looking for that just then.

"You know very well that she does," Donna finally said, her voice rising with more emotion than she wanted to reveal. "But it didn't mean she isn't a good mother—that she doesn't love her child. She would never leave her for more than a minute or two."

"Point made. Was the baby's father involved in her life?"

It was clear just then that he knew what kind of life Marissa had. If he didn't, he wouldn't have referred to the "baby's father"; he would have presumed that Marissa had a husband.

"Look, my daughter and I seldom talk about anything of importance, except for Tasha. Not for years. I don't know who the 'man in her life' is, and she never told me. Frankly, I never asked."

"Do you know who her friends are? Maybe someone who knows her better than you do?"

Donna had held it together pretty well. She'd been through tough times, the late-night phone calls from drug dealers demanding to know where Marissa had gone. But the truth hurt. She knew nothing much about her daughter. *Nothing at all.* A single tear rolled down her cheek, but she flicked it away so quickly she hoped that Josh Anderson hadn't seen it.

"She might have been seeing someone," Donna said. "I saw some flowers in a vase. She's not the *Better Homes & Gardens* type to have fresh flowers from the market. But, as I've said, I don't know my daughter very well. Really, you have to believe me: she loves her baby girl. I see the look in her eyes. I see the way she held her. She wouldn't leave her."

"I'm sorry," Josh said. "We'll do our best to find her."

"Do you need me to make a statement or anything? You're treating her as a missing person, right?"

"Yes, we are."

"Fine. Then you'll need this." She reached into her purse, pulled out her wallet, and found a photograph. "This was taken three weeks ago. Look at that mother with her baby. Tell me . . . Tell me . . ." She stopped to compose herself. "You know that she loves her daughter."

Josh looked at the photo. It was a color image printed at Wal-Mart. It showed Midnight Cassava, a.k.a. Marissa Solomon, with Tasha on her lap. They were sitting in a booth at a restaurant. The table had two plates of food. Two cups of coffee. One was positioned in front of Marissa and the baby. The other was in the immediate foreground.

"You take this shot?"

Donna shook her head.

Josh tapped his finger on the photograph, noting the obvious. "I guess your daughter has some friends," he said. "Someone took this picture, right?"

Donna Solomon turned away. She knew nothing about any friends. She was happy, though, that Marissa had any at all. She wondered if being a mother had become too much and Marissa had run off somewhere, but she never said so. She thanked the detective and went with a Port Orchard police officer to give her official statement.

A half hour later, Josh found Kendall in her office.

"How'd it go downtown?"

"A lot of to-do about nothing. Hooker went on a bender or ran off. Feel sorry for her mom, though. Nice lady. Kids are so much work, and you never know what you're going to get."

Kendall turned her attention toward her computer screen.

"You're right about that," she said quietly.

The conference room suddenly felt very uncomfortable as Josh Anderson broached the subject of recording and running a tap on the phone calls Serenity was receiving from

the supposed killer. He conceded that the calls might be untraceable, but it was an option on an investigative list that
was short. *Too short.*

Charlie Keller, however, would have none of it.

"We believe in cooperation, but that's a violation of our
rights to gather news independently. We don't want Big
Brother looking over our shoulders."

"We could get a court order," Josh said.

"We'll fight it," Charlie said. "And we'll win."

Serenity looked at Kendall, but both stayed quiet.

"Maybe," Josh said, raising his voice a little. "But if there
is a serial killer at work around here, your paper will look
like you don't give a crap about anything but your precious
rights."

Charlie's face was red and the veins in his neck, night
crawlers. "They are pretty precious. In this day and age, there's
no doubt that the government has its fingers everywhere they
want to be. Get your disgusting wiretap. Get your court order.
We're not saying yes to anything."

He looked at Serenity, who appeared anxious as she took
in her boss's tirade. She moved her gaze from one person to
the next.

"I'll do whatever Charlie says," she finally said. She knew
that he'd been involved in the Zodiac case in San Francisco,
at least on the periphery. The papers there had been used as a
conduit for messages between the purported killer and the
police. Ultimately, Serenity felt, everyone had looked bad
because the case was never solved.

After Charlie and Serenity filed out, Josh turned and
whispered in Kendall's ear.

"I'll work on her. I'll get her to agree."

Two hours later, Josh showed up in Kendall's office carrying a paper Starbucks coffee cup. He had, apparently, gone
out. He could be a selfish jerk at times, but usually office
protocol dictated that anyone who went out specifically for

lunch or coffee would make the rounds to see if anyone wanted something.

"The girl said she'd do it," he said.

"What girl?"

"Serenity Hutchins said she'd let us run a tap on her line. She had one condition, and I agreed to it."

Kendall set aside the meager case file and studied Josh.

"What agreement?"

"She doesn't want her boss to know. He's a freak about it. She's scared. I said we'd do it."

Kendall hesitated a minute. "When?"

"Tonight. That pervert said he'd call her tonight."

Chapter Fourteen

As she prepared herself for an evening with her husband, Melody Castile climbed into the shower and let the water run over her body. She set aside a pink plastic razor and some shaving foam and spread her legs. While Sam called for her to hurry, she went about the business of shaving her most private areas.

Although, she knew, there was no privacy whatsoever.

It had started with small things.

Melody wore her hair shoulder length when she and Sam Castile first met. He complimented her on the color and style, saying that he'd never seen a woman's hair with such a sheen.

"Like the sun is shining through you."

Three months into their relationship, Melody decided to surprise him with a new look. She had her hair shorn. She thought the haircut was stylish, sophisticated.

Sam hit her. *Hard.* "You're stupid, Melody. You looked so

sexy and hot before. Now you look like some boring chick from Bremerton. Pop out some kids, get fat, and be nothing."

His words hurt, and she never cut her hair again.

Six months into their relationship, Sam asked her to drop the rest of her life and move in with him. He'd bought some property down on the Key Peninsula and was going to build a house. They'd live in a travel trailer down there, with no running water, no cell phone service, and no power.

Melody told her family about it, making it sound as though she and Sam were going to be living off the land as they built their dream house.

"He wants to use the actual logs on the property. Isn't that cool?" she asked, her eyes sparkling with excitement.

Serenity, still at home, caught the disapproving looks of her parents. No one really liked Sam or thought that he was a good match for Melody. Even before they married a full year later, the couple had completely fallen off the family grid. When Serenity was still in junior high, she and her parents drove out to the peninsula to see the new house. They waited in the unfinished living room on lawn furniture for about a half an hour before Melody emerged from the back bedroom. She was so pale and thin that her mother gasped.

"Honey," she said, "are you all right?"

Melody looked at Sam. "I'm fine. Just tired. It's a lot of work to get this place in order. We barely have time to eat and catch our breath around here."

A moment later Sam started the tour, pointing out all that he'd done and chiding his bride for being "Miss Lazy" and not doing enough to help. Melody laughed it off, but Serenity thought that there was no real laughter behind her eyes.

The bedroom was dominated by an enormous four-poster made of alder logs that had been peeled and oiled to a tawny sheen. A stuffed grouse fluttered in a corner; a deer head hung over the back window—trophies testifying to a man's hobby. Serenity caught her mother's eyes riveted to the headboard where two large steel hooks had been sunk into the wood and oily leather straps dangled. Everyone noticed the hooks, but no one remarked on them.

After the tour, Melody served ice tea and sandwiches. The conversation was a bit strained, and then at exactly 2 P.M. she stood up and thanked everyone for coming.

"I have chores to do now. So you'll all have to go."

"We've only been here an hour," her mother said.

"And we've enjoyed every minute," Sam said. "But Mel's right. We've got things to do, and we have to get them done."

Serenity went to embrace her sister good-bye, but Melody pulled back slightly. She'd never been much of a hugger, but it was a cold reaction that seemed in keeping with this strange afternoon visit.

"Something's going on there," she said in the car as they began driving home.

"The only question I have," her mother said, "is why in the world anyone would want to live all the way out here in the middle of nowhere. It seems so remote."

Her husband leaned his head out the window as he backed up, not wanting to hit a pile of lumber crowding the dirt driveway.

"Bingo. You've got the reason."

For the next two nights, Kendall, Josh, and a tech named Porter Jones showed up in Serenity's Mariner's Glen apartment. They'd set up a feed that ran the phone through a listening and recording device. Of course, a tap could have been set up off location, but that would require a judge and there'd be a lot more heat about "freedom" of the press. Serenity didn't seem to care about that right then. While she wanted to advance her career, she wanted to prove that the voice she was hearing was not some kook, but the voice of a killer.

A telemarketer called twice.

Josh looked at her. "You know, you can get on a 'do not call' list."

"Thanks for the tip," she said.

"Serenity," Kendall said, "are you sure you're getting calls on this line?"

Serenity's eyes went cold. "Yes, I'm sure."

"That's what she says," Josh cut in.

Kendall let out a sigh, but held her tongue. It was interesting that Serenity would have some new blog post or article just about every other day. Where was her source? Why hadn't he called?

If he was real at all.

Kendall got up to take a break from the huddle around the dinette table. She stepped over the sleeping tabby cat, Mr. Smith, through the living room to the apartment's sole bathroom. Next to the sink, she noticed an open shaving kit. It didn't take Sherlock Holmes to figure out that Serenity Hutchins probably had a boyfriend.

"I didn't know you were seeing someone," Kendall said. "The shaving kit."

Serenity barely looked at her.

"That's my dad's," she said. "He stayed over last week."

Chapter Fifteen

April 18, 11:15 a.m.
Port Orchard

It was a crystalline morning without the fog that had coated Sunnyslope for the past several days. Certainly the mist burned off by the early afternoon, but for morning people like Trevor Jones, the muslin shroud over the woods was a complete and undeniable downer. He longed for his home in the Midwest, where most mornings—no matter the season—started with a sky patched with blue. It seemed that when it wasn't raining in the Northwest, it was foggy. At least on his days off. He threw a leg over his mountain bike, called for his Labrador, Cindy, and went for a ride. He thought he'd pedal through Sunnyslope, toward the Bremerton Airport, then maybe as far as Belfair, a town along the southern shores of Hood Canal. Cindy would see him only as far as the end of the driveway: The invisible fencing collar that she wore had reminded her that, as much as she'd like to go with Trevor, she had to stop.

"Sorry about the force field, Cindy!" Trevor said as he spun out toward the road.

The dog looked forlornly at him and then turned around.

"Good girl!"

Trevor had twenty bucks in his wallet, a bottle of water, and the conviction that at twenty-nine he was still allowed to take the time for a Saturday ride. He put in long hours in the metal shop at the shipyard, and outside of tipping back a few beers on Friday nights and video games during the week, this was the extent of his fun. His wife, Crystal, was back in their tidy home, sewing a top that she intended to wear to a luncheon at the Central Kitsap School District office, where she worked as an aide.

Trevor pedaled toward the entrance to the woods, then turned down a pathway that looped through part of the forest before joining the road near the airport. His heart was pumping as he went up a little rise, his wheels cutting into the coffee-black soil, his iPod on shuffle mode. He stopped to catch his breath at the top of the rise and took a drink of water. A breeze fanned the beads of sweat on his face.

He noticed a tangle of long dark hair draped over some old deadfall and assumed that horseback riders had been through the area.

As he took another sip, his eyes returned to the clump of hair. It was shiny and fine.

Too fine for horsehair.

He got off his bike to get a closer look.

It was a considerable clump, maybe fifty strands. It looked remarkable not only for its silkiness but also for the violence with which it had been removed. It was held together on one end by what looked like small patch of skin.

Jesus, he thought, recalling the article about the missing brush picker, Celesta Delgado, who had been featured in this latest edition of the newspaper. *That brush picker must have been attacked by a bear. I'm getting the hell out of here.*

But before he did, he took out his cell phone and punched in three digits: 9-1-1.

Kendall Stark looked down at the tuft of hair on the steel table in the center of Kitsap County's mini crime lab, a cinder-block-walled room that had the vibe of a sinister high school chemistry lab. The lab, with both rudimentary and sophisticated forensic science equipment, was the central location where all evidence was processed. On the far wall was an old aquarium used for superglue testing for latent fingerprints; black and infrared lights that could pinpoint the location of blood or semen on a garment; and a series of images that showed various blood-spatter configurations. In the event that something required more refined analysis, it was dispatched to the labs operated by the state in Olympia or even to the FBI.

Kendall turned the clump of hair with her latex-gloved fingertip and reached for a tape measure. The strands were fifteen inches long and held together by a tag of human skin that had dried to pliable leather. *Human Naugahyde*. She rotated the sample once more under the flat overhead light.

"That the bicyclist even found this is a bit of a miracle," Josh said, entering the room. "Has he been checked out?"

"He's clean. Just sharp-eyed," Kendall said.

"Our dogs turned up nothing more? Just this?"

"That's right," she answered. "Nothing else."

She put the sample into a clear plastic envelope and fixed a bar-coded sticker with a name and case number to the bottom edge of the packet.

"Off to Olympia," she said. The state lab was already running a DNA test against samples recovered from Celesta Delgado's hairbrush and toothbrush.

"Must have been a knock-down, drag-out there in the woods. You know, a place so remote no one could hear her scream," Josh said as he followed Kendall into the hallway.

"At least two people must have heard her scream," she said. "Celesta and her abductor."

She was right, of course.

Where was Celesta Delgado?

"Call for you, Serenity. On two."

Serenity Hutchins nodded at Miranda Jacobs, who commanded the phones outside the editor's and sales director's offices for all it was worth. Miranda, who never knew a day when a low-cut top and short skirt weren't appropriate for the office, was the gatekeeper, the story fielder, the person with the heads-up on anything worth buying out of the *Lighthouse*'s classified section before it even found its way into the paper.

Serenity set down her coffee and answered the blinking light on her office desk phone. She pressed the earpiece to her ear by lifting her shoulder.

"Article's a little thin on the facts," came a husky voice over the line.

"Most are," she said. "Which one are you talking about?"

There was a short silence. The caller moved something over the mouthpiece, sending a static crackle sound into Serenity's ear.

"The one about the brush picker." Another silence. Another muffled noise.

Serenity let out a sigh. She'd been a reporter long enough to know that readers always expected more than deadlines sometimes allowed. It wasn't as if there was any real information in the article, at least not anything that she could have really screwed up.

"Can I help you?" she finally asked.

"No, you can help yourself." The tone was unpleasantly cold.

"How's that?" she asked. "Did I make an error in the story?"

"Not an error of the kind you're probably imagining. An error of omission, that's all."

Serenity could feel her blood pump a little. "Just who is this, please?"

A slight hiss, then: "I'm the one who could tell you everything that happened to her."

His words came at her with the unmistakable air of authority, and they jolted her a little. *Everything. That. Happened. To. Her.*

Serenity looked around the room, trying to catch eye contact with someone—anyone. Miranda Jacobs had her face glued to her computer screen. No one else was in the newsroom.

"You're an asshole to make a crank call like this. And I don't care if you're a subscriber."

The voice on the phone laughed. "Oh, I'm not, Serenity. I'm a fan of your work. I just think you could use a little more depth in your reporting. Maybe I could tell you what happened. Like I did the other night."

Serenity banged her stapler on her desk and finally caught Miranda's eyes. She got up from her computer and started toward the young reporter.

"Who are you?"

"One who could tell you everything," he said.

Her face was flushed by then. "Then start talking. Tell me what you think I should know."

But the line went dead.

"Hello? You still there, creep?"

Miranda was standing in front of Serenity's desk by then. "What was that all about? Are you okay? Did that guy say something awful to you?"

Serenity shook her head. "It was that crank caller. Said he knew more about the missing brush picker out in Sunnyslope."

Miranda searched Serenity's eyes. "You sure he was *that* crank?" she asked. "You look scared."

Serenity relaxed a little and set down her phone. "Just a little unnerved. Did he call in on the eight hundred line?"

Miranda nodded. "Afraid so. Creepy *and* cheap."

Calls coming through on the toll-free line were untraceable on the phone console's ID.

"I wish those guys who get their rocks off calling in to the paper with bullshit theories about things would just get a life."

"Did he have a theory on the girl?"

Serenity shrugged. "I think so. He said he could tell me everything."

"Everything that was in the paper, I'll bet. And, sorry, but you know there wasn't much in there. No offense."

Serenity hated Miranda a little more just then. The *Lighthouse* wasn't the *Washington Post*, but she didn't have to rub it in. She worked there too, for goodness sakes.

"Maybe you should tell the Sheriff's Office?" Miranda suggested.

Serenity thought about it for a moment. "I suppose I could, but I really don't have anything to tell them. We all get crazy calls."

"That's the truth."

Miranda went back to answering the phone.

Outside of Gleeson's Grocery, one of those locals-only minimarts that was Key Center's primary gathering place, was a bulletin board. Before the Internet and even before the local paper started a Key section, the bulletin board had been the primary vehicle for yard boys filling in the long days of summer, loggers looking for extra work as homeowners sought to improve their views of slate-gray Puget Sound, and housecleaners in search of "mobile home or mansion" clients.

The boy and his father went past the bulletin board without so much as a sideways glance.

Inside, Gleeson's was packed with DVDs on one wall, a

"hot case" of fried foods on the other, and a small bin of produce, mostly of the kind that kept well: onions, potatoes, and
head lettuce. The rest of the store was laid out like a bowling
alley, with long, narrow lanes and shelves of canned goods
on either side.

Dan Gleeson smiled at the man and the boy, a warm look
of recognition on his face.

"Haven't seen you in a blue moon."

Sam Castile smiled. "Been a while. Nice to have some
time off. Me and the boy are going out on the boat."

"Weather's been rough lately."

"Yeah, it has."

Dan looked at Max, who stood silently beside his father.
"What can I get you? Turkey jerky? Healthy stuff, you know."

Sam answered for Max. "Nope, we want the nastiest, greasi-
est corn dogs you've got rolling around that hot case of yours."
He looked at his boy; the kid was smiling ear to ear.

A girl behind the cash register rang up the sale as the
store owner handed over a couple of corn dogs and packets
of yellow mustard.

The man's eyes landed on the counter. Light-blue flyers
were stacked next to a pink one that advertised a food drive
at the fire station later that week.

"The girl's dad brought those in. Said I'd hand them out.
Posted one on the bulletin board too."

Sam's heartbeat quickened, but he didn't show a trace of
concern. "Never a dull moment around here."

"You got that right."

He took a flyer and promised to post it. The headline was
in big handwritten letters:

Have You Seen Her?

"Look familiar?" Dan Gleeson asked.

Sam shrugged and started for the door, his son trotting

after him with a mouthful of nearly incandescent yellow mustard and batter-dipped hotdog. "The young pretty ones all look alike to me."

"That they do."

As he got in his vehicle, he noticed the blue flyer on the bulletin board flapping in the chilly breeze off the water.

Have You Seen Her?

He had.

No matter what she told Josh Anderson or Charlie Keller, Serenity decided that it was in her best personal *and* professional interest to hold back one little tidbit of information from both detective and editor. She didn't feel particularly great about the lack of disclosure, but the tradeoff seemed worth it somehow. The anonymous caller had confided a detail that was tantalizing for a young reporter hoping to make a name for herself—and looking to find a way out from this dead-end job. What he had revealed was etched in her memory.

"I popped my cherry on another girl," he'd said.

Serenity, at home at her kitchen table with the TV playing in the background, set down her pen. Was it truth or lie? Exaggeration or fact? The caller was hard to read with complete certainty. His voice was husky, foggy.

"What do you mean 'popped a cherry'?" she asked, although she was familiar with the expression meaning to lose one's virginity. But this man hadn't really been talking about sex: although he'd described what he'd done to the dead girl, it had been about violating her.

His pleasure, it was clear, was her pain. Her death was his orgasm.

"Done it before," he'd said. "Will most likely keep doing it. Until I get it right, Ms. Hutchins."

His words blasted a chill down her spine. He said her

name, and it startled her. Of course, he'd sought her out, dialed her number. *Wanted to tell her*. Even so, that he had used her name to conclude the conversation seemed so personal.

Ms. Hutchins.

The pervert was slightly polite, which unnerved her even more.

Chapter Sixteen

April 19, 1:15 a.m.
South Colby

She was naked, running through the deep green of the forest.
Overhead, she could see the contrails of a jet scratching the
powder-blue sky. Could the people in the plane see her? She
ran faster, her arms working like pistons as she propelled herself up an incline between a hemlock and a fir. Where to hide?
Who could help her? Sweat oozed from her pores, and she ran
faster and faster. Would she have a heart attack? Would she
fall to the ground into the black mud, be sucked into the mire,
lost forever? The woman was screaming as loud as she could,
but it was for naught. There was no one to hear her screams.
At one point she dared to look behind her, and she could see
the form of a man rushing toward her.

"Help me! Help!"

"Babe, what is it?"

Kendall shot up in their bed; her husband had turned on
the light and was putting his hand on her drenched shoulder.

"Oh," she said, realizing where she was. *Who she was.* "Oh, Steven, it was so real."

"A bad dream?"

She sat on the edge of the bed, looking out across the black waters of Yukon Harbor through the window, its antique glass rippling the view.

"Yes. I was running from someone."

"You're safe now."

She blotted her face with the sleeve of her robe. "I know, but it was so real."

"Just a dream," he repeated.

Kendall knew he was correct, of course, but she didn't tell him the part of the dream that seemed so troubling, so very disconcerting. It wasn't that *she* was running from someone. She wasn't herself in the dream at all. Kendall was sure that the woman in her dream was Celesta Delgado.

"I'm going to get some water," she said, heading toward the door.

As the tap ran, Kendall thought of the woman she would never meet. Coworkers at Azteca adored her. The owner of the brush shed had not one single harsh word for the young woman. And, of course, Tulio Pena had insisted from the very beginning that something very dark had occurred that afternoon in the woods. The clump of hair all but confirmed it.

She drained her glass, set it next to the sink, and went back to the bedroom, stopping only for a moment to check on Cody. She wondered if her son's mind ever conjured up such frightening images as she just had. Were his dreams empty, blank? Was autism a cocoon that kept a person buffered from the pain of the world around them?

Is it better to know fear, she asked herself as she pulled up the covers next to Steven, who was fast asleep, *so that you can appreciate love and the safety of those around you?*

In her job as a detective, Kendall had seen terror and its

opposite over and over. She wasn't sure if she had the answer to her own question.

The row of flowering cherry trees had dropped a blushing blanket of snowing petals on the ground outside the Kitsap County Sheriff's Office. Several cars circled the front of the building trying to find a place to park in response to TV reports that a Navy aircraft carrier was coming into Bremerton that morning. A small group of people, Kendall Stark among them, gathered to observe the ship as it came into view. She stood with coffee cup in hand, feeling rushed and tired at the same time. She wore tan slacks, a crisp white shirt, and an ice-blue sweater, her hair a little more spiked than she liked, given a night of slumber interrupted by the dream of the frightened young woman.

Later, Kendall would recall the dream, wondering if it had been something more than the workings of a mind trying to solve a problem.

Serenity Hutchins, clunky old newspaper-issue Nikon camera in hand, nodded at Kendall as their paths crossed in front of the Kitsap County Administration Building.

"Here to take some shots of the carrier?"

Serenity smiled. "That and whatever else they tell me to do. Jesus, I know Keller won't run this story anyway—not if there's some major breaking news about a missing llama in Olalla or something."

Kendall retuned the smile. "Nice job on the Delgado story."

"Thanks. Any update?"

Kendall shook her head. "I'll let you know. But between you and me, nothing."

"I got another call from the weirdo the other day, saying he knew something. I called Josh—Detective Anderson—about it."

"I heard," Kendall said. "I'm sorry that you've been getting those. It can be very upsetting. I know."

Serenity slung the camera strap over her shoulder. "Our jobs are sort of alike in that regard, Detective."

Kendall sipped her coffee as they walked toward the front door of the Sheriff's Office building, pink petals swirling underfoot.

"You're right. We both want the answers to the really hard questions, don't we, Serenity?"

The reporter raised her camera to take a shot of the fading cherry blossoms.

"Yes. But in my case, I have to take on whatever my boss says is important." She looked at her watch. "Like the new dry cleaner opening up on Bay Street. I can't afford to dry-clean anything on my salary, but off I go."

Serenity Hutchins was like any other person in Port Orchard, Kendall reflected: she was doing what she needed to until that big break came.

As Celesta Delgado had.

A few minutes after returning to her desk, Kendall's phone rang.

The caller identified himself as Bernardo Reardon, a detective with the Mason County Sheriff's office. He prattled on for a few moments in the congenial way cops do before cutting to the chase.

"You might want to take a drive over here," he said. "I think we might have found your missing brush picker. Or rather, what's left of her."

The last words pierced her heart

What's left of her.

"What makes you think it's our missing woman?"

"Height, weight, age—it's all good. Of course, it could be someone else, but if so, no one's reported this lady missing."

"I see. Decomp?"

"I've seen a lot worse. But like I said, come on over and

take a peek. We're about done with processing what we can."

Kendall's eyes landed on the poster that the Kitsap Crime Stoppers had made, with its lovely photo of a beaming Celesta Delgado. It offered a one-thousand-dollar reward.

A life was worth more than a thousand dollars, she thought.

"All right," she said. "I'll see you in an hour."

"Can't wait," the caller said.

She found Josh Anderson chatting with a young woman who worked logging evidence in the property room. She was laughing a little too loudly to be discussing business, so Kendall felt no compunction about interrupting.

"Ride out to Mason County with me?" she asked.

Josh turned away from the woman, and it was obvious that she was only too glad for the break in whatever story he was telling. She returned to the work she had been doing before Detective Anderson showed up.

"Sure. What's up, Kendall?"

"Delgado."

He studied her face. "Not so good, huh?"

Kendall shook her head. "I'm afraid not."

Chapter Seventeen

April 20, 10:30 a.m.
Shelton, Washington

The Shelton, Washington, Chamber of Commerce likes to brag that the city of more than eight thousand is the "Christmas Tree Capital of the World." In fact, the town has always been about trees, Christmas or otherwise; for a century, it exported logs and lumber, long before firs festooned with tinsel were thought of as a commodity.

The city is quintessential small-town Pacific Northwest, with past glories based on once-abundant natural resources now supporting attempts to coax tourist dollars. Every spring, the past is celebrated with the annual Forest Festival, with food booths, logrolling, and chain-saw competitions.

It was the festival that reminded the people that Shelton, Mason County, had been established on the southernmost edge of Puget Sound for a purpose. Smoke still curls from the Simpson Lumber Company's mill. Old-timers and current employees take a deep breath whenever possible. They know the plume smells like house payments, new cars, and kids' college educations.

The last time Kendall Stark had been to Shelton was the previous January, when she attended a candlelight vigil for a little girl who'd been raped and murdered by her neighbor, a registered sex offender still at large. Kendall had gone with her sister and some friends, not because they knew the little girl, but because her story had been so heart wrenching that they simply couldn't stay away. She came in her street clothes, of course. She didn't want to attract attention; she just wanted to hold one of those cheap, drippy candles to tell the world that Rikki Jasper would not be forgotten. Kendall remembered how she'd looked at the crowd and wondered if the perpetrator was among them.

Thoughts, she was sure, that also consumed the law enforcement officers who oversaw the case.

Kendall parked the SUV in a visitor's spot in front of Mason General Hospital on Mountain View Drive, the city's hospital and morgue. Moments later, after a receptionist buzzed him, Detective Bernardo Reardon came for the Kitsap County homicide investigators. He was a tall, thin man, with a Fu Manchu mustache and dark plum-pit eyes. He smiled broadly as he walked toward the sitting area, where Kendall and Josh had been waiting on some upholstered chairs next to a dying philodendron and a surly receptionist who was busy chewing out her boyfriend.

"Look," the receptionist was saying, oblivious to her visitors, "there are plenty of other fish to fry around here . . ."

Bernardo rolled his eyes. "Welcome to Mason General Hospital and our morgue. Come on back," he said, and they followed him to a private room where friends and family waited to identify the deceased. It was stark and empty, and smelled of alcohol-based cleaner.

He motioned for the pair to sit, and tapped his fingertips on his file folder.

"The vic was found by some birdwatchers at the Theler Wetlands," he began.

The Mary E. Theler wetlands were at the head of Hood Canal, an elbow of salt water that protruded into the rugged interior of Kitsap, Mason, and Jefferson counties. A favorite of day-trippers and bird-watchers, the saltwater marsh just outside Belfair was traversed with a web of elevated board-walks. Kendall, Steven, and Cody had been there several times, with Cody tucked snugly into his father's backpack, back when nature walks seemed to hold his interest. Sun on his face. Birds in the water. The movement of the reeds along the shore.

It was a lovely place to visit, and, apparently, to dump a body. At least, a killer thought so.

"We've got a touch of decomp going, so be ready for that," he said, looking mostly at Kendall. "I can still smell her from here. Anyhow, she matches the description of your missing brush picker. Pathologist has already swabbed and examined for trace, but like I said, she's a mess."

Josh jangled the change in his pocket, a habit that he had whenever he was bored or a little anxious. "Sounds good. Where do you guys break for lunch around here?" he asked, more concerned about his stomach than the dead girl they were about to see.

Kendall shot him a look, but he deflected it by mouthing, "Low blood sugar."

"Logger's Bar and Grill is always good," Bernardo said, opening the door to the morgue.

He handed the Kitsap detectives face masks but wasn't fast enough. The scent of the dead surged forward, and Kendall felt her stomach stir. She shot a cold stare in Josh's direction.

"How could anyone even think about lunch? Now or ever?"

Reardon responded first: "Detectives, one word of warning: our victim has no hands."

The dead woman had been laid out in a dark blue body

bag, which was split open like an oven-roasting bag to keep the putrid juices from spilling out onto the table, and to the floor. Long dark hair curled around her face and the nape of her neck. Even in that condition, it was clear that the victim had once been a pretty young woman. Her eyes were half-open, seemingly staring upward at the fluorescent lights overhead.

Kendall thought of her dream of the woman running through the darkened forest the night before. *What had the woman seen before she ended up on that table, so far from home?*

Bernardo peeled back the edge of the plastic body bag obscuring the victim's arms.

"The other one's the same," he said, indicating where her hand had been excised from her wrist.

"Looks pretty clean," Josh said, bending closer to get a better view. "That's what the pathologist said. No hesitation with the cut here. This wasn't some mad, frenzied stab job, but a clean cut."

Kendall didn't dare turn away, although it passed through her mind that no one should have to see whatever the monster had done to the woman she knew had to be Celesta. She didn't use her name. It seemed easier to call her "the victim" or "the body" when the trio went about their business.

"Can I see the victim's other arm too?" she asked, her voice slightly muffled through the mask.

"Suit yourself," Bernardo said, walking around to the other side of the table. "Just as ugly."

"Did your pathologist indicate if the victim was alive when this injury was incurred?"

The clinical talk was the best. Kendall plucked the words out of a textbook when she really wanted to say "Did she suffer?" or "Did the sick, twisted piece of garbage who did this to her do it after he killed her?"

"Postmortem. Almost a hundred percent sure."

The answer brought a little relief.

"Did you find the hands?" Josh asked, stepping closer to get a better view of the injuries to the body.

"Nope. And believe you me, we looked. Don't want some kid feeding a bag of day-old bread to some ducks to turn up a finger or something."

"When you say your pathologist indicated no hesitation, are you suggesting someone with unusual skill?" Kendall asked.

"Hunter, butcher, surgeon. You know, the kind of people who know how to move a blade."

Kendall looked over at Josh. "Logger or maybe brush cutter?"

Detective Reardon shrugged. "Could be. But one twisted perv, for sure."

Josh spoke next. "Any other injuries?"

"Pathologist says the girl was likely raped and tortured. Vaginal and anal tearing. Some ligatures on the ankles too. Hard to say about the wrists, for obvious reasons." He indicated a crescent of darkened skin on the body's right breast.

"Looks like some damage inflicted on the vic's breasts," he said, pointing. "Almost a perfect half circle, like a big hickey."

Kendall felt a wave of nausea work its way from her stomach, but she steadied herself.

"How long has she been dead?"

"A week, maybe less."

"Celesta Delgado," Kendall said, finally saying her name, "has been missing for more than a week."

Josh broke his gaze at the corpse and looked at Kendall.

"Maybe she was kept somewhere?"

Chapter Eighteen

Word traveled fast. Alarmingly so. Tulio Pena stood outside the Kitsap County Sheriff's Office smoking the stub of his last cigarette. The second he saw Kendall Stark, he dropped it and twisted the butt into the sidewalk.

"Detective Stark," he said, "was it Celesta? I heard they found someone, a woman's body." He was shaking and wrapped his arms around his torso, steadying himself.

Preparing for the worst.

Kendall shook her head. "No, Tulio. We don't know anything."

"The reporter called me. She says it was Celesta."

"We don't know who Mason County found. We'll have to run tests."

His black eyes were wet. "I want to see her. To make sure."

She moved closer and put her hand on Tulio's sagging

shoulder. "Look, I know you're hurting. But trust me, please, you don't want to do that."

"Trust you?" he repeated. "Trust *you*? I trusted that you'd find Celesta."

Kendall ignored the blame in his anguished voice. "Tulio, go home. I will call you when we know something."

"Detective, please. Please, if it is her, promise you will find out who did this. You will find him, right?"

Kendall wanted to give him the answer that he deserved, that all loved ones do. She wanted to tell Tulio that she would do whatever she could. She wasn't alone in her desire to figure out what had happened. The Mason County Sheriff's Office was working the case too. There was no way of knowing where exactly the crime had been committed, let alone by whom. Josh had insisted it was a turf war between rival brush pickers and that Celesta was a casualty. The missing hands bolstered his theory. Kendall, however, wasn't so sure. While it was possible that Celesta had been sexually violated as a part of some ritualistic torture, it seemed unlikely.

"Whoever tortured her and cut off her hands did it because he enjoyed it. Rape and that kind of behavior are incongruent with your idea that she was killed over a bunch of floral greens. Get real." she'd said to Josh.

Josh Anderson hadn't argued, because he had no convincing counterpoint. Instead, he'd just dismissed what had happened out in Sunnyslope on that warm afternoon.

"Whoever did it has moved on to harvest somewhere else. They don't have a green card. They don't leave a trail. They just fade into the woods. That's what happened with whoever killed Delgado."

It passed through her thoughts, but Kendall didn't want to say it aloud. At least not to Josh Anderson. By the time Celesta's body had been found in the Theler Wetlands, she already doubted busboy Scott Sawyer's story of trouble between Tulio and Celesta. And yet, there had been the purported threat.

If Celesta ever touched another man, Scott said, Tulio would make her pay. Kendall had talked with others at the restaurant, friends of both, and none thought Tulio would ever hurt Celesta. He was incapable of harming her in any way, let alone mutilating the body in such a grotesque manner.

As spring gave way to summer, a flotilla of boats gathered in Sinclair Inlet, and beach fires on the shores of Bainbridge Island sent a spray of orange light across the water. Summertime in Kitsap County was a mix of hot days tempered by rain on the occasions that most often count: Memorial Day, Fourth of July, and Labor Day.

There were no more calls to Serenity from the man who'd proclaimed the vilest of pastimes. Charlie Keller had told her to keep on the story, but there was nothing more to do unless there was some kind of break. Midnight Cassava's case went ignored, the assumption made by Port Orchard and Kitsap County law enforcement being that she'd run away. A third jurisdiction, the Bremerton Police, filed a report about a bloodied purse being found near the Parkade.

No one said much more about Celesta.

Except Tulio. He and the others who wanted to know what had happened out in the woods leveled charges of class and racial bias.

"If she were a white girl," Tulio said in one of his weekly visits to Kendall or Josh at the Kitsap County Sheriff's Office, "you'd know who did this to her."

Kendall was offended by the remark and told him so.

"Look, Tulio, don't ever say that to me. I want to know what happened to her as much as you do. I don't care if she's from El Salvador or Seattle."

Tulio balled up his fists as though he was going to pound the desk, but thought better of it. He relaxed his hand. "Then why haven't you caught who did this?"

Kendall didn't want to tell him that her partner still believed Tulio had killed his girlfriend.

"Sometimes these things take time. We'll find out."

"If you don't, then I will," he said.

Kendall didn't know exactly what Tulio meant, so she didn't push as hard as she might.

"We'll do our job. Leave it to us."

Chapter Nineteen

September 18, 8:45 a.m.
Port Orchard

Serenity Hutchins looked at the newroom's old clock and let out a sigh. It was almost 9 A.M. She glanced around to make sure no one noticed her overt boredom, especially since only a single hour of the workday had passed. She checked her notes, hoping that there was something stimulating there, something that didn't require a jolt of caffeine to get her going. There wasn't. She had a half hour to finish her story on the delay of the road improvements that the city of Port Orchard had promised to downtown merchants in time for the holiday shopping season.

She faced her computer screen head-on and tried to come up with a headline for her article. Then she typed:

County Shortfall Means Grinchy Holiday

It seemed a little over-the-top, but in her job as a reporter, writing humorous or subversive headlines was one of the few things with which she could amuse herself. Sometimes she slipped in a little inside joke. Now and then she purposely misspelled the name of an individual who'd rubbed her the wrong way.

"Sorry, sir," she'd recently said to an angry man she'd tussled with at a community meeting, "I have no idea how that happened."

The man's first name was Bob, not *Boob*, of course.

"I have an idea," he said, irritated and puffing into his phone on the other end of the line. "I don't like your attitude. I'd like to talk to your editor."

"It was an unfortunate typo," she said, loving every minute, her fingertip hovering over the button of her editor's extension. "Transferring you to the boss now."

She didn't wait for his response: she just clicked, and away he went. Mission accomplished.

Charlie Keller liked her, and she knew it. He'd chide her but back her up. He always did; he was that kind of editor. Once, after a heated confrontation with a churchgoer who objected to the paper's coverage of a South Kitsap High club for teen moms, he famously told his staff, "Newspapers would be a great business if we didn't have readers to consider."

Serenity didn't want to go to the county animal shelter to do an article on the dog or cat of the week. She didn't want to stop by St. Vincent de Paul on Bay Street to find a heartwarming story that showcased the "caring nature of our community." Growing up she'd read so many thousands of stories in the *Lighthouse* that she had scarcely given a thought to the fact that real people had to compile that information. Tedious facts. Boring. So mundane and appearing so regularly, Serenity wondered if they could just retype the same old papers and send them out the door.

From her desk, she watched Charlie set down the phone. The editor in chief was wearing his hopelessly out-of-date brown wide-wale cords and a cream-colored turtleneck that molded to his beefy chest. Unflattering as it was, it was his fall look.

He looked more excited than angry when he glanced over

the newsroom. Good. Bob, or Boob, hadn't made him mad. He fixed his eyes on the two other reporters. One was playing solitaire on her PC, and the other struggling with the school lunch menu: apparently, it changed just enough from week to week that it could not be cut and pasted. It had to be retyped, word for word.

"Get your butt over to Little Clam Bay out by Manchester," he said, approaching Serenity. "Some kids found a floater."

Her phone buzzed with a text message, and she looked distracted.

"A body, Hutchins," Charlie said, his eyes studying hers, seeing the glimmer of excitement that bad news always elicited in die-hard reporters. "A dead girl."

She glanced at her phone. "Going now," she said, taking her rust-colored cardigan draped over the back of her chair, her purse, a reporter's notebook from the office supply cabinet, and her camera. Her heart started to beat a little faster with each step. She'd heard the term *floater* before, of course, but the very idea that there could be a dead body bobbing in the waters of Little Clam Bay seemed—she hated herself a tiny bit for the thought—too good to be true.

Nothing ever happens here, she thought. *Except maybe today.*

Serenity took a cigarette from her grandmother's antique case and lit up as she dodged a few light raindrops in the parking lot. Her new boyfriend smoked, so she had taken up the habit in self-defense: to protect herself from the ashtray-kiss syndrome.

She noticed she'd left on the lights of her black 1999 Toyota Tercel, a temperamental car if ever there was one. She'd dubbed it "Hiroshima's Revenge."

You better start! We've got a floater today!

She turned the key, a slow grind, and then . . . *success*!

Her phone vibrated with the unanswered text message.

DEAD GIRL LITTLE CLAM BAY.

* * *

Seven miles out of town, the Little Clam Bay neighborhood was a Northwest crazy quilt of housing. Expensive custom homes were perched on the water's edge and backfilled with double-wide trailers skirted in plywood and kept dry with a patchwork of blue and silver plastic tarps. The bay was a narrow little inlet the shape of a shepherd's hook that reached in from Puget Sound and jutted through a cedar- and fir-trimmed landscape. At high tide it was a body of blue dotted with floating rafts, docks, and seagulls. On the flip side of the tidal schedule, the bay drained nearly dry. In summer, with the sun bearing down on the soggy bay bottom, the neighborhood smelled of rotting fish, seaweed, and the garbage that had been sucked in through the narrow channel and left scattered on the muddy floor. Sometimes careless boaters dumped garbage overboard in Puget Sound, and if their deposits hit the currents just so, Little Clam Bay, with its sluggish water flow, became a saltwater dump.

On the morning of September 18, Devon Taylor and Brady Waite decided that they'd skip school rather than force themselves through another state-required language assessment test conducted at Sedgwick Junior High. At fourteen, Brady and Devon were on the edge of trouble whenever the mood struck, which was often. It was nothing big—mostly skipping school and acting out in class when they bothered to slide behind back-row desks. They'd smoked some pot now and then and tried coke once, but ultimately the pair preferred video games and skateboarding to drugs.

Girls were also of great interest, but neither had plucked up the courage to ask one out.

They'd set up a kind of private clubhouse at Devon's, in a garden shed on the Taylors' lawn, which undulated down to the water's slimy edge. While they waited for Devon's mom to leave for her nursing administrator's job at the naval hospital in Bremerton, they smoked a couple of cigars they'd stolen from Brady's stepfather's secret stash.

"Even if I get in trouble for taking his stogies," Brady said between hacking coughs, "my mom won't be too mad. He's not supposed to smoke anyway."

"Your mom's a bitch," Devon said.

Brady's eyes puddled, and he let the smoke curl from his lips.

"Everyone's mom is a bitch. That's just the way it is, dude."

Devon didn't argue. "Speaking of moms. I wish mine would get her ass out the door. Cold out here this morning."

"Yeah, it is." Brady looked out the greenhouse window at the water. "Does this swamp ever freeze up?"

"It isn't a swamp, though it smells like one half the time. Only around the edges and not very much. Maybe froze twice since my dad moved us to Port Zero from Tacoma."

Brady seldom mentioned his father, and Devon took the opportunity to pounce on the subject.

"Ever hear from him?" he asked.

Brady took another puff before answering. "He calls Mom and she puts me on with him, but I can tell he's only talking to me because he has to. He doesn't give a shit about me."

"My dad's an asshole, but I guess having him around is better than nothing," Devon said.

Brady filled his mouth with more smoke and held it a second before attempting a smoke ring.

"Yeah, I guess you're right, dude," he said.

A beat later, the boys turned in the direction of the sound of a car's ignition turning over.

"Finally!" Brady said. "She's leaving. Let's go inside."

Devon flipped the latch on the door to the garden shed, sending a layer of smoky air outside. He looked over at Brady—alarm had suddenly filled his eyes.

"Jesus, someone is going to see the smoke."

Brady ignored his friend; his eyes stayed fixed on Little Clam Bay.

"You sick or something?" When he didn't answer right

away, Devon followed his best friend's sight line to the water. "What is it?"

Brady didn't say so, but he wished right then that he hadn't skipped school that day. He pointed at the water.

Devon's eyes widened. "Jesus, is that what I think it is?"

The boys walked closer, stepping on the frosty planks of the dock, their white and red Skechers slipping a little under their feet. Devon let his cigar fall into the water, making a sizzling sound as its hot cherry tip went black.

"We better call 911," Brady said.

Devon tugged at his buddy's hooded sweatshirt. "We're going to be in big trouble, you know."

"No shit."

"Maybe we should just pretend we didn't see it and just go inside and watch TV or something."

Brady shook his head. "But we did. And we have to tell."

His buddy was correct. In a morning of doing all the wrong things, they had to do what was right.

Chapter Twenty

Kendall Stark has just eased into her preferred parking slot—
close to the overhang that kept renegade smokers from the
Sheriff's Office and jail dry during the long drippy Northwest autumns and winters, when she saw Josh Anderson
grind out a cigarette and approach. He had his cell phone
stuck to his ear. The morning had been a difficult one, following one of Cody's restless nights. After a week in his new
school, there were doubts that he was adjusting, and she and
Steven argued over it. Cody, who usually did not betray emotion, was always aware when his parents were at odds. Words
or tears were not the barometer of trouble in the Stark family. A night without sleep was.

Cody, what do we do? How do we help you? she'd asked
over and over inside her head as she sat in his room, by his
bedside.

She rolled down her window.

"Some kids found a dead body in Little Clam Bay," Josh said. "Female, they think. Didn't want to get too close. Body's still out in the water. Coroner's en route."

"Nice way to start the day, Josh," she said, realizing that any hope for a better morning had been jettisoned.

"For the kids or us?"

"I was thinking of the woman," she said.

"Well, the kid who called CENCOM was crying. Worried not only about the body but about the fact that he'd skipped school today."

"Nice," she said. "That'll teach him a lesson."

"Take your car?" he asked. "Mine's in the shop again. BMWs are so damn touchy."

"Get in," she said. Josh never missed an opportunity to remind someone—anyone—that he drove an expensive car. Expensive, but always in the shop or the detail center. Josh Anderson practically needed a bus pass to get to work.

Kendall unlocked the passenger door and scooted aside some papers from Cody's school, and Josh slid inside. He immediately cracked the window to let the air come in and suck away the condensation. Kendall always seemed to keep the inside too warm for his liking.

"Hey," he said. "Did I say good morning?"

Kendall glanced at him as she backed out and turned onto Sidney Avenue. Rain pecked at the windshield, and she turned the wipers to the intermittent setting. "If we've got a dead woman, I'd say the morning's not so good," she said.

"You're right." His tone was utterly unconvincing.

Kendall Stark wasn't one of the detectives who got an adrenaline rush from the news of death. She'd tracked killers before. Catching them was the rush. Never the pursuit. And never the start of a case. The beginning of a case only seemed to remind her how fragile life was and how, in an instant of someone's choosing, it could all be taken away. She felt awash with sadness. Not Josh, though. He was nearly giddy. Kendall had seen that look on his face before. It was as if real life kicked in and stirred him only when it came with a measure of tragedy.

"Jesus, Josh, you don't have to be so happy about this."

He looked at her but avoided her eyes.

"Not happy. Just ready to get a little action going. We could use some around here. A homicide gets my juices flowing. Been boring around here all summer."

If she hadn't been driving, Kendall would have slapped him just then. "You don't even know if it's a homicide."

"It is."

"How can you be so sure without even seeing the body?"

"Because we've had no reports of anyone falling off a boat or off a dock. The only floaters we ever have in Puget Sound are drunk swimmers or kids who were left unattended. We know about those. This isn't the season for that. If the floater fell off a boat, someone would have called it in. She's a murder vic. Betcha a beer."

Kendall didn't bet.

"We'll see," she said.

In a very real way, the boys, the sheriff's detectives, and the dead body were bound forever. The five of them would always be connected by what had transpired that morning. *Forever.* In the summers when he would finally have a girlfriend, Devon would lie out on the dock and think of the dead body. Whenever Brady came over, they'd probably relive the morning they found it. Kendall would never drive by Little Clam Bay without recalling what had been discovered there.

Even Josh Anderson would point it out to those he sought to impress—a lover or even a young officer.

A van with a deputy from the Kitsap County Coroner's Office pulled in behind them and started to unload with the kind of speed that might have indicated a rescue rather than a recovery effort.

"You're the police, right?" Devon asked Kendall and Josh after they'd parked in the driveway. "The 911 operator said for us to stay put until you got here. Are we in trouble?"

Brady spoke before either detective could answer.

"We're supposed to be in school," he stammered, although it was unclear whether it was due to the chill in the air or the dire circumstances of their meeting.

"We leave that to your folks," Josh said as he watched a diver emerge from the black waters of the glassy bay. "You boys sit tight for a second, all right?"

"Where?" Devon said.

"Just stay here."

"Yes, sir. Will do," Brady said. The boys took a seat on a metal garden bench.

Kendall retrieved a pair of rubber boots from the back of her SUV and bent down to fasten them.

"Shoes are going to get ruined," she said, drawing her gaze down the wet lawn and glancing back at Anderson's black leather lace-ups.

He shrugged. "No kidding. I might have to expense them. They're almost new too."

Kendall doubted that. Josh was many things, but despite his oversized ego and reputation as God's gift to women, he was no trendsetter. He'd worn the same pair of shoes for the past two years. However, he never missed a chance to fatten his wallet at the county's expense.

A shiny red Volvo lurched into the driveway, and Belinda Taylor scurried from the car to the water's edge.

"What's happening here?" she called out. She was a tall woman clad in a Burberry raincoat and leather boots that sank into the damp lawn like a gardener's aerating tool.

Step. Squish. Pull. Step. Squish. Pull.

"Mom!"

"Don't 'Mom' me!" she said. "You are so grounded for skipping school!"

She turned to Kendall. "What's going on here? The boys are truant. They're not felons. What gives with the entire Sheriff's Office camped out on my front yard?"

"Mrs. Taylor," Kendall said, "I'm afraid the boys have made a frightening discovery."

She looked over to where Josh Anderson was crouched next to a body. Ms. Taylor instantly knew what she was seeing, even at fifty yards away. She worked in a hospital. She'd seen her share of stiffs, though not in her own backyard.

"They found a body floating in the bay," Kendall said.

Belinda Taylor's face went a shade paler. She reached for her son and pulled him close. Ordinarily, with his best friend present, Devon would have resisted. Right then, despite his age, a little motherly reassurance felt pretty good.

"Mom, I'm sorry we skipped school."

"Ms. Taylor, it was my idea," Brady said.

She shook her head. "That's not important. What's important is that you need to tell the detective what you boys saw. We'll deal with the other issue later."

A black Tercel in need of a new muffler pulled in behind the coroner's van. The detectives looked up and offered a slight nod to Serenity Hutchins as she stepped out of her car.

"The reporter is here," Josh said, letting out an exasperated sigh. "I'll handle her."

Kendall made a face. "Be nice."

Serenity started toward them, but Josh intercepted her before she got close enough to see what was going on.

The teens told Kendall that they had no idea who the victim was. In fact, they were a little embarrassed to admit they really hadn't gotten close enough to see her features clearly.

"It kind of creeped us out," Devon said.

"Big-time," Brady said.

Even if they had found the courage to get a closer view, it was apparent to everyone within ten feet of the body that there was one major obstacle.

The victim had no face.

Kendall made a few notes and looked back at Josh and Serenity, who were still talking.

Jeesh, she thought, *we've got a dead woman down here. Can't you give a quick quote and tell the reporter to back off?*

She left the boys and Ms. Taylor and joined a pair of coroner's assistants as they hoisted the corpse into a body bag.

The woman was about twenty. She was white, with small hands and thin ankles. She wore no shoes. Her blue jeans were tiger-striped on the crotch, markedly visible even with the fabric sodden with seawater. Too perfect to be the casual striping of an expensive pair of jeans that had been crafted to look old. She wore a pale green top that had been carelessly buttoned: the top button had been fastened to the hole in the second position. The blouse was cotton and had absorbed blood in two patches aligned with the dead woman's breasts. A cursory examination of the body indicated nothing out of the ordinary that might help ID her quickly. No special jewelry. No tattoos were visible. No purse and no wallet.

No nothing.

Whoever the young woman was, whatever she'd been in life, it would be up to an autopsy to tell her story.

"Tell Dr. Waterman I'll be around for the autopsy in the morning," Kendall said to one of the assistants. Dr. Waterman's place was the county morgue.

"Jesus," Josh said, "and I was beginning to think our dry spell would last into the holidays."

The summer had only brought one other murder: a Port Orchard teenager had been stabbed by his brother over a twenty-dollar bill. Before that was the springtime murder of

Celesta Delgado, the Salvadoran brush picker who had apparently been killed by a rival over salal and huckleberry.

"Yeah," Kendall said, "you were wishing yesterday for something other than a gun or drug case. Looks like your prayers have been answered."

Chapter Twenty-one

September 18, noon
South of Port Orchard

The drive from Little Clam Bay took longer than the trip there. The county evidently had some money in its coffers, because a couple of flaggers in orange vests were planted on Little Clam Bay Road as a yellow backhoe prepared to cut into the ditch. A row of twenty-four-inch drainpipes sat on a flatbed truck parked off to the side; at least, it was supposed to be off to the side. It jutted out into the roadway just enough to turn a two-lane into a one-lane.

Kendall rolled down her window and addressed the flagger, a woman of about twenty.

"Can't we just scoot by? I think I can make it."

"Sorry, but no. Yesterday's rain did a number on the shoulder. Be about five minutes, max."

Kendall pushed the button to raise her window. Rain had sprayed over her left side. As the car idled, she looked over at Josh, who was lamenting his ruined shoes and how he was sure to catch a cold. He'd unlaced his shoes in an effort to speed up the drying process.

"Turn the heat up, will you?"

Kendall obliged.

"She looked young," she said. "Maybe a teenager."

"The flagger?"

"The victim," she said, knowing that he was just playing with her.

"Yeah. She was."

"What do you make of the boys, Josh?"

"Young and dumb and full of . . . you know the rest," he said. "Just unlucky enough to skip school and more scared that their parents would find out they'd been smoking cigars than they were about getting in trouble for cutting class."

"Devon made a big point of saying that we'd find his DNA on the cigar he dropped in the bay." The flagger waved them on, and Kendall put the car in gear. "Maybe she was a student at their school," she said.

"Doubtful. They go to junior high. That girl looked older. But we can check it out. Let's get back and run the missing-persons database and see what pops up."

"I'll be surprised if she's from around here," Kendall said.

"Why's that?"

"Because she looked like a girl who'd be missed, that's why. The people around here call us if their kids are an hour late from the movies."

A sly grin broke out over his face. "That they do."

Kendall nodded without remarking.

"Let's run by Sedgwick," Josh said. "We ought to check out the boys' story, and it's on the way."

John Sedgwick Junior High was one of those immense edifices that looked authoritative and utilitarian at the same time. Its chief bits of architectural interest were the four pillars that flanked the front of the building: they were massive tubes of painted concrete. That was it. Form, no style. When Kendall Stark and Josh Anderson made their way toward the front door, a kid called out.

"You here about the dead body?"

Kendall turned toward the voice. It came from a skateboarder in low-slung black jeans, a blue hoodie, and a chain that went from, presumably, his wallet to his belt loop. He had dark blue eyes and the faint tracings of a mustache that he'd obviously been nurturing to look older, and maybe a little tougher. She recognized Matt Gordon despite his attempt at facial hair.

Josh looked at Kendall. "You know that kid?"

"Shoplifter, but not a good one."

"Officer Stark," the teen said, "we all know."

She didn't correct him by pointing out that she now carried a detective's shield.

"How's that?"

Without saying a word, Matt Gordon poked at the keys on his phone and held it out.

On his iPhone screen was an image of the tragic scene they'd just left at Little Clam Bay. Kendall noted the time stamp: twenty minutes *before* the Sheriff's Office had been notified.

"Devon and Brady need a lesson on priorities," she said to Josh.

"Huh? Brady blasted it out this morning," Matt said. "Let me show you another." The kid was grinning nervously now. Kendall had cut him some slack on the shoplifting case, and he was trying to be a good citizen. "Here."

This time it was a photo of Kendall and Josh leaning over the body.

"That's how I knew it was you and why you were coming, Officer Stark."

"Any more out there?" she asked, her tone flat to mask her anger.

"He texted everyone that he was putting up an animated

slide show on his MySpace later. Kind of cool that someone died around here, and we can watch how you solve the case. Like *CSI*. My mom loves that show."

Jesus, what's with these kids around here? Is everything a joke? she thought.

"Thanks, Matt. And by the way, it isn't *cool* that someone died around here. This is very serious and sad business. I'd appreciate it if you'd remind people of that. Okay?"

"Yes, Deputy. Will do."

Josh spoke up. "It's *Detective* Stark. She's a *detective* now. Not a deputy."

Kendall suppressed a smile. It was the first time that Josh had done that. For a man who was a relentless self-promoter, he simply didn't believe in building up someone else, because if someone was his equal, it diminished him.

She turned to the boy. "By the way, I'll need your phone."

The Kitsap County detectives went past the hideous cement pillars and into the administrative offices, where they had a brief conversation with the school's assistant principal, a nervous man with caterpillar eyebrows who was about to consume a limp chef's salad. It was doubtful that anything but an inquiry from the Sheriff's Office could have interrupted the meal.

Gil Fontana set down his plastic fork and verified that Devon and Brady were decent students, not overly prone to mischief.

"Those two are harmless," Gil said, "given what we deal with around here." He looked down at the contents of an open file folder to refresh a memory that couldn't possibly have held any real awareness of those boys: there were hundreds like them at the school. "Let's see, they've skipped school only twice before and never have been the subject of any major disciplinary action."

"Any female students reported missing in the past few days?" Kendall asked, looking past Gil as he fidgeted in his leather office chair. A poster on the wall indicated that John Sedgwick Junior High "celebrated" tolerance, diversity, and sensitivity.

"No female students missing. A few out sick, but junior high girls take advantage of their cramps to miss school."

Kendall thought of saying something like "cramps" were no laughing matter for a young girl and that he needed to re-think a few things.

The poster caught her eye again.

"I see that you celebrate sensitivity here," she said.

Gil plastered on a smile. "That's right. The state requires it."

Kendall stood. "Good. Too bad it has to be required. By the way, you've got a problem here, Mr. Fontana. A young woman's death is not something to be *celebrated* on My-Space or Facebook or Twitter, for goodness sake. Those boys—who you seem to feel are no problem—have some serious issues."

The assistant principal's face turned scarlet. "What are you getting at, Detective?"

"Aren't you concerned that they broadcasted a photo of a dead body to everybody in this school?"

Josh followed Kendall to the door. He didn't say a word, but he clearly was loving the exchange.

"These are the times we live in," he said, a discernible smirk on his face.

Kendall masked her anger with a smile. "At least I doubt you'd want the school to be known for that kind of thing. Am I right?"

"What was that all about?" Josh asked as they got back in Kendall's car.

"Seriously? You don't think the whole world is going to hell in a handbasket? It's like a school full of sociopaths."

"I guess so," he said. "I never thought of it that way."

"Well, you should. How would you like it if someone took a photo of your son like that and sent it around for a bunch of gawkers?"

"I wouldn't. You're right, Kendall. I wouldn't at all."

Serenity Hutchins slid back behind her computer. Charlie Keller was stomping around the office like a beat reporter in one of those 1940s movies that glorified the "scoop." She wondered for a minute if her boss could possibly be *that* old. Her archrival, Joy—whom she called "Joyless" behind her back—was fuming in the corner that she was stuck doing that season's "Fall into Halloween" Web blitz, an assignment that reeked of getting under the covers with advertisers. The paper's copyrighted Spooky McGee character, a pumpkin-headed seagull, implored shoppers to head for the sad little mall at the base of Mile Hill Road. Joy was stuck with coming up with content to support the program.

She had already used Buoys and Gullfriends, Head Over to the Mall as a headline, and she wanted to die.

Joy looked up, her face contorted in an unattractive grimace. "Serenity, you need any help?"

"No, thanks, I've got it handled. Besides, you're up to your neck in work yourself."

Joy sighed. "Not what I thought I'd be doing when I graduated from journalism school," she said.

Charlie's deep voice boomed from across the newsroom. "We all have to start somewhere."

But we don't have to end up here. Like you, Serenity thought, but didn't say it.

"How's the dead girl story?" he asked, now at her desk. "This is front-page, Hutchins. And as you know, we don't get a lot of front-page stories around here."

Serenity didn't say so, but it troubled her that her mood

had shifted from boredom to the rush of excitement that came with the discovery of the dead woman in Little Clam Bay.

"I'm on it. Nothing much yet."

She'd tried to get the detectives to tell her something about the case. Was it even a homicide or just a boating accident? No one would say. She talked to the boys and their mothers for about ten minutes, but there really wasn't much she could write about that. She stared at the empty window of her computer screen.

"We want to lead with the dead body," Charlie said, now hovering. She could feel his hot coffee breath on the back of her neck.

"Figured that," she said. She half expected him to give her some kind of lecture about how things were done "back in the day." She liked Charlie all right. He was smart, was an excellent writer, and seemed compassionate enough. But he didn't seem to get the irony that he'd landed a final gig at a paper that was one step above a shopper.

"It'll be short. I took some photos of the kids who found her, but I didn't get much out of them. The detectives—Stark and Anderson—gave me the brush-off, pending the coroner's report. We might not have much in the way of any real info. No who, what, why, anyway."

"Okay. Do your best. I need it in an hour."

Serenity dialed Detective Anderson's number, but it went to voice mail.

"Detective, it's me, Serenity. I need whatever you've got. Keller's riding me hard right now. Let me know something, okay? Call me on my cell. You've got the number."

Serenity looked at her computer screen. The story for tomorrow's front page was thin, but what more could she really say? She had agreed not to identify the boys. The detectives had given her next to nothing. A body was found. *That was it*. The subject was so tragic, there was no room for clever wordplay in the text. She had to stick with the facts.

Body Found Floating in
Little Clam Bay

Two local boys found the body of an un-
identified young woman floating on Little
Clam Bay yesterday morning. The boys, both
14, were skipping school when they made the
grisly discovery in the water fronting 1527
Shoreline Road.

"We weren't sure if what we were seeing
was really a dead person," one of the boys said.
"She was out there floating. It was pretty random that we discovered her. We, you know,
shouldn't have been there."

Neither the Kitsap County Sheriff's Office
nor the coroner's office had any immediate
comment.

After dropping the file into a folder on the server, Serenity swiveled in her chair and got up to leave. She decided she'd head across town to the Sheriff's Office to find out what she could. More than anything, she hated being ignored.

What did it take to get a decent story around Port Orchard, anyway? She asked herself.

Later, the admonition "be careful for what you wish for" would come to mind and haunt her dreams.

Chapter Twenty-two

The house at 704 Sidney Avenue had a history both mundane and macabre. It was a place that passersby and drivers skirted past, disinterested. Certainly, in its eight decades of existence it played out a thousand family dramas and joys. Most places that old have. Babies were born. Kids went to school. Teens went to the proms. Memories were made.

All of the things that make a house a living thing had transpired there.

Yet, this place was a little different. There was a touch of strangeness and darkness about the house as well.

One time in the 1990s, a woman who stopped by the house and spoke to the present occupants told a tale of her mother's suffering with cancer.

"Dad couldn't stand her constant crying all night," said the visitor, who had once lived there. "So we set her up in a tent in the front yard. Dad put her out there so he could get some sleep. Seems a little cruel now when I think of it. But back then, it was a good solution."

Not surprisingly, others who lived there reported that the house with an obscuring tree that had been lovingly planted by the first owners had a weird, sad vibe. Most who felt it did so only after learning that the place was the final stopping point for the dead of Kitsap County.

The house adjacent to the Sheriff's Office back parking lot was the Kitsap County Morgue. It is doubtful that any other morgue in America was quite as homey.

The coroner's offices were upstairs in what had been a dining room, living room, two bedrooms, a bathroom, and a kitchen with a battered blue linoleum floor. Throughout the house, with its coved ceilings, pale gray paint, and thick-cut moldings, were the remnants of the dead. The staff stored formaldehyde-soaked tidbits of people in plastic bags set in large plastic tubs like the ones families use to store Christmas decorations. A built-in nook held teeth and a floating finger in small jars. Each body part was a clue to the unthinkable things that people did to each other. Despite the accoutrements of death, the upstairs was a staid, quiet office. Phones were answered, mail sorted, budgets balanced. If things were a little disordered, it was because the space was so small.

And body parts took up a lot of space.

Downstairs, however, was where the work that leaves a Rorschach pattern in crimson on a pristine white lab coat was done every time a stiff rolled in on a gurney. Early in the morning after the Little Clam Bay body was found, forensic pathologist Birdy Waterman put on her scrubs in the small dressing area in the converted garage that was a most unlikely autopsy suite. She checked the body logbook on a table next to a chiller that held six bodies at the time. It had only been full once or twice in the county's history. While a couple of hundred bodies were autopsied every year, they were dispatched to funeral homes—mostly for cremation—within twenty-four hours of their arrival on Sidney Avenue.

"Move 'em in and move 'em out" was a phrase favored by the county coroner, an affable fellow named Kent Stewart who'd been elected to the position for a dozen years. He was more than an elected glad-hander. He was also a skilled manager of an ever-shrinking budget. The day before the dead body from Little Clam Bay had come in, Kent purchased four new office chairs from Boeing's surplus store south of Seattle. The total cost was $28.

If Kent Stewart was the "face" of the coroner's office, Birdy Waterman, a forensic pathologist, was the chief cook and bottle washer. Her hands were on everything. That was fine too. Kent only occasionally came downstairs to see what was happening in the morgue—mostly in the summer, when a decomposing body sent a stench up through the floorboards.

"Downstairs is your domain," he said time after time. "Call me if you need me."

With the exception of days that started with an autopsy, Kendall Stark never wore jeans to work. That morning as Steven organized Cody's things for school, she packed an overnight bag. She moved around their bedroom, silently, gathering up a pair of slacks and sweater that she could wear while Dr. Waterman completed her examination.

Steven emerged from the bathroom and looked at the bag she'd filled.

"I was going to tell you to have a nice day," he said, thinking better of it.

She pressed her lips into a slight smile. It was meant to acknowledge his support.

"I could barely sleep last night," she said. "All I could think about was that dead young woman."

"I know," he said. He stepped closer and looked into her eyes as he held her hands.

"That's what makes you good at your job, Kendall. You give a shit. Not everyone does. Some people sleepwalk through their lives, never really noticing why they're here."

She knew he was right, but she also wondered if he was talking about his own work. He'd been down about it, telling her not long ago that he "hadn't dreamed of this life, this job" when he was a little boy. She'd tried to support him by reminding him that he was so good at selling ads.

"A trained chimp with half a personality could do what I do," he'd shot back. His demeanor was slightly sardonic, but not so much that Kendall could be sure just how he really felt. She was left to wonder. When Steven talked about his disappointments in life, was he talking about her? About Cody?

She picked up her overnight bag.

"When I think of why I'm here," she said, "I know it's to help people, to bring the lost back home."

Steven kissed her and playfully touched her hair. "You'll find out what happened to the girl," he said.

She didn't say how she felt about Celesta Delgado and how she'd failed to find her killer. Mason and Kitsap counties postured over who owned the case: the jurisdiction in which she had gone missing or the one where her body was found. She didn't tell Steven that she'd had an encounter with Tulio Pena at the Albertsons supermarket on Mile Hill and how he'd accused her of not caring, of giving up.

"I'll do my best," she said. "See you tonight."

Chapter Twenty-three

Birdy Waterman looked up as the frosted-glass door swung open.

"Morning, Detective," she said, as Kendall let herself inside.

"Sorry I'm late," Kendall said taking off her jacket and hanging it on a hook near the logbook.

"You're not late. Just in time, in fact." Birdy rolled on a pair of gloves. She looked at the overnight bag. "Oh, goody. Why didn't you tell me we were having another sleepover?"

Kendall smiled back. "A surprise," she said.

"Where's Anderson?"

"Good question, Doctor. He said he might be late, so I waited for him at the office. Never showed up."

Kendall went into the small dressing room and put on a set of scrubs, emerging a few moments later to ask the question that had haunted her after seeing the body.

"What happened to her face?"

She stopped a few paces behind the pathologist as Birdy unlatched the enormous refrigerator and rolled out a sheet-covered corpse to a space on the far side of the room.

"The catchall is 'animal activity,' and I suspect I'll be able to pin it to a seal. There are some teeth marks where the nose was excised."

She watched as Birdy gently peeled back the pale green sheet.

"See here?" Birdy said, pointing with her gloved index finger. "Those small tears form a pattern. Each is spaced two inches apart."

Kendall leaned a little closer to get a better view. She took in the acrid scent of the corpse, which made her stomach roil only a little. Then it passed. She found it strange that the sight of the body had such a fleeting impact. Certainly, she'd already seen the woman at Little Clam Bay, but in the outside world the smell of the dead can be somewhat ignored on a cool damp day. Not possible, she knew, in the confines of the morgue, where bright light, sterile surfaces and the faint odor of cleaning supplies can't completely foil the assault on a person's olfactory senses.

"I'm thinking a sea lion pup," Birdy said, barely glancing back at Kendall. "Humans aren't really good eating, of course, and even an orca will pass one up. Sharks too. I think a pup did a little nibbling here and there and then gave up. Animal DNA could confirm, of course. Did I tell you about the body found in the woods by the golf course at Gold Mountain? Had to take bite impressions to the University of Washington. Turned out it was a bobcat, not a cougar."

"I guess that would make a difference," Kendall said, somewhat tentatively.

Birdy looked at the detective. "Actually, you're right. It did. Bobcats are aggressive only to a degree and can be fended off with a well-placed poke of a nine iron. An angry cougar, however, is another matter."

Birdy lowered an overhead lamp and took a pair of chrome Fiskars, sliced off the woman's clothing, and deposited it into clear plastic evidence bags. While trace evidence was always possible, it was highly unlikely on the outside of the clothing. The body had been in the water for a while, at least a couple of days. Sometimes hairs and fibers were protected in the interior of a garment. That, both women knew, was a long shot. The choppy waters of Puget Sound were like a Kenmore washer on a heavy-load cycle.

The pathologist took a succession of digital photos, some with flash, and others without.

Kendall used a Sharpie to mark the bag for the sliced jeans, then another for the now-shredded green blouse. She'd take them back over to the crime lab for drying before any additional examination. Drying would preserve evidence and make the stink of the clothing somewhat bearable.

Feeling strands of her long black hair fall from the band of her disposable head covering, Dr. Waterman stepped back from the autopsy table. She took off a glove and tucked in the stray locks.

"There will be no contamination on my table," she said, putting on a clean glove.

Kendall nodded, although the remark seemed more for the pathologist than her audience.

As she worked in her basement autopsy suite, Birdy Waterman spoke in measured tones, her voice betraying no emotion. It didn't matter. She'd conducted hundreds of autopsies and knew that each one was a professional obligation and a personal burden: each one broke the doctor's heart.

". . . the victim, a well-nourished female age seventeen to twenty-five, five feet, two inches in height, 110 pounds, dark blond hair, blue eyes . . ."

She hesitated as she thought of a way to clinically describe the horror of what she was seeing. "There are no facial features, likely due to animal activity, postmortem . . ."

She noted that there were no distinguishing marks on the woman's body.

She didn't get the tattoo urge that so many of her age had, she thought.

The condition of the victim's teeth indicated reasonable if not excellent dental care. The dead woman or girl was not a meth-head. She was clean, well cared for. Dr. Waterman swabbed the dead woman's mouth and clipped her soft, unpainted fingernails, and Kendall collected each snip into poly bags.

"I don't see anything under the nails, but you never know what your guys can find in the lab," she said.

Kendall nodded. "I'm always amazed at—and appreciative of—how the smallest things can point to a killer."

Next, Dr. Waterman focused the beam on the victim's ears, then cheeks, a part of the face that still remained relatively intact. She swabbed again. Fibers and hair had adhered in a couple of places on the cheeks. She swabbed more.

Adhesive, she thought, before catching Kendall's eyes. "Our victim might have been restrained or gagged by some kind of tape."

"Photo?"

The pathologist stepped back to allow Kendall to get closer for more photos, macro views of faint gummy striations.

"Okay, now for the reason she's here on my table," she said as she flexed the woman's wrists and noted the dark bands of contusions that encircled them.

"Victim shows evidence of ligature on both right and left wrists."

For the first time Kendall noticed parallel lines of dirt and bruising. Faint, yet there nonetheless. Her camera's shutter sounded six times in rapid succession.

"She was tortured. Held captive. This is too brutal for some sex game gone bad."

She was referring the case of Sheila Wax, who had died

the year before when a so-called breathing game went too far. Kendall had worked that case.

Birdy ran a stream of water over the nude torso. Dark, congealed blood ran along the drainage gutter of the table.

"This is far more than torture," she said, locking her eyes on Kendall. "Victim's areolae on both breasts have been excised," she said.

Kendall felt the familiar shudder of sickness that sometimes came in the basement autopsy suite, no matter how seasoned she believed herself to be or how prepared for the aftermath of murder. She steadied herself while Dr. Waterman pointed to the edges of the wounds.

"See this?" she asked, taking the tip of a scalpel and lifting the pale skin. "A cut, not a tear. Definitely not animal activity, like the face."

Kendall studied the wounds. "Postmortem, like the animal activity?"

"Hard to know for sure, but when I see things like this, I pray to God that the victim was dead before whoever it was took it upon himself to cut her. We had a case a few years back in which a man hacked off his wife's hand and then drove her to the hospital."

"How thoughtful." Kendall took some more photos.

Birdy turned her attention back to the corpse. "This is the work of a sexual sadist. He bound, gagged, defiled, tortured, and cut her, and kept part of her body for a souvenir."

Kendall knew what the pathologist was getting at. "Someone who commits this kind of crime doesn't just stop."

"That's right, Kendall. Someone who does this has to *be* stopped."

Finally, the beam of the pathologist's handheld light found the woman's vagina. It was just another invasion of the dead woman's privacy that had begun when the two boys skipping school had found her and sent out photos to their friends at school. For Dr. Waterman, probing in a woman's most private area was the necessary evil of finding out what had happened, and it always felt like a violation, no matter how many bodies she'd autopsied.

More photos. *Flash!*

Next she bent her knees slightly, bore down, and rolled the body onto its side, then onto its stomach. She walked to the end of the autopsy table and gently spread the woman's legs apart.

"Indications of trauma in both anal and vaginal cavities . . ."

Dr. Waterman winced a little and amended words: "*Severe* anal trauma . . ."

The exterior exam complete, Dr. Waterman went for the garden loppers that she'd purchased on her expense account at the local Ace Hardware off Mile Hill Road. The bright-green-handled loppers were the ideal tool for cutting through the ribs. While Kendall looked on, the doctor made her Y-incision from shoulder to shoulder and down between the mutilated breasts. Then she reached for the loppers.

Kendall watched, listened, and wondered.

Who did this to you? Who are you?

Kendall always thought of the dryer in the Kitsap County property processing room as a "clothesline of death." She carefully logged in the victim's clothes and hung them in the dryer. It was a bulky piece of equipment that functioned more like a warming oven than a spin dryer. Clothing hung limply until it dried to crispness. Body fluids and, in the case of the Little Clam Bay victim, seawater would provide a stiffness like starch.

Heavy starch.

"How's our girl in the morgue?"

It was Josh.

"She's still dead," Kendall said, a little irritated that he'd missed the autopsy. While it wasn't required to have two investigators there, murders were so infrequent in Kitsap County that an extra pair of eyes and hands would have been useful.

"Anything out of the ordinary?"

Kendall closed the glass-fronted door. "You mean like the fact that some freak cut off her nipples, raped her, and tortured her? That kind of out of the ordinary?"

"You seem pissed off at me."

Kendall peeled off her latex gloves and threw them in a receptacle.

"I could have used you there, Josh."

Josh murmured something about being sorry before he made his excuse.

"I had an interview with the paper that I couldn't get out of. They've been hounding me. I'm getting a feature story. Probably front page."

"I doubt that," she said, heading toward the door.

"Huh?"

"A dead woman trumps a self-centered cop any day."

Chapter Twenty-four

September 21, 1:30 p.m.
Port Orchard

Later that afternoon, Kendall Stark fixed her eyes on the autopsy report as Birdy Waterman went about her business going through the department's supply manifest for new orders. She was low on blades and the heavy needles used for the sometimes hasty and careless suturing of a victim, post-autopsy. Birdy wasn't like many of her contemporaries who had graduated from medical and law school with the full acceptance that the dead they'd see in the course of their careers should only be viewed as evidence, nothing more. She had gone to medical school at the University of Washington on a scholarship for Native Americans. She never said so, but she was more concerned about helping the spirits of the dead find their way home. A clean autopsy, given with love and respect, was preferred over the crime-fighting approach of so many. She was a scientist, to be sure, but a compassionate one who knew that life was a continuum and death was not the end. For that reason Birdy always ordered the finest-size needles she could, even when the medical supplier didn't see the need for the tiny stitch.

Kendall looked up from the sheaf of papers. "You're certain that missing tissue from the victim's face was postmortem?"

Birdy stopped making hash marks on the supply list. "There are some indicators that she'd been battered on her face, but it's hard to say with complete certainty."

Kendall locked her eyes on the pathologist. "Cause of death?"

"Manner of death: homicide, for sure," she said. "But she's been in the water for some time, and it's hard to say if she was suffocated or strangled. I'm concluding asphyxiation. Found adhesive around her cheek area, indicating she was gagged with tape, most likely good old duct tape."

"Tortured?" Kendall asked, although she knew the answer.

"Raped vaginally and anally. No semen. My guess is the perp wore a condom."

"Considerate of the bastard."

"More likely careful. At any convention of my ilk you'll find a symposium on the *CSI* effect. Perps are boning up by watching forensic TV shows to find out how to avoid detection."

"So I've heard," Kendall said. "We can thank Hollywood for that."

Birdy nodded, and Kendall followed her into the chiller, indicating she had something she wanted to show her. She held up the dead body's right arm. "See the discoloration there?"

Kendall noted the faint purple and black striations that ringed the thin, delicate wrists.

They'd discussed them at the autopsy.

"Wire, not rope. You can see how the binding dug into the skin, nearly slicing it?" She flexed the wrist and nodded for Kendall to come closer. "You don't even need a scope to see that despite the fact that the water plumped her skin up a bit and softened the grooves, there are several rows of indents."

"I see. Bound with wire. Postmortem too?"

Birdy let the wrist rest on the stainless table. She set it down gently, as though the body could still feel the chill of the metal.

"Not at all. My guess is that she was bound with wire for a time, and then the wire was removed. There was some tissue healing. Then, of course, she was put out of her misery by the perp."

Kendall felt a chill and pulled her sweater tighter around her torso. She let her hands retract tortoiselike into her garment's long sleeves.

"Are you saying she was held captive?"

"Stomach is empty. In fact, I have no indication that our victim has eaten anything for at least five days. Nothing."

"Anything that will help ID her?"

Birdy shook her head. "Not really. No tattoos, decent dental work, no nothing that would give us a leg up to run any kind of check in the system. Anyone matching her in your missing-person's database?"

Kendall shook her head. "Not so far."

"There's also this," Birdy said, pointing to some tiny specks lifted from the victim's vaginal walls. It was hard to say exactly what they were. Dr. Waterman narrowed her focus as she twisted a swab into the light next to her autopsy table. There were six small flecks. They appeared opaque, not transparent or translucent. It was hard to say what color they were. One side seemed off-white; the other a reddish hue. She deposited the swab into a plastic bag and secured it.

"This one's for the lab team in Olympia," she said. "Who knows where this will lead, but in the meantime you might need some extra help to ID this one. Help of the artistic kind. Who is this girl?"

In the basement of the tidy white house on Sidney Avenue, Birdy Waterman covered up the morgue's sole dead body while

Kendall Stark looked on. The two of them silently pushed her into the chiller.

Neither woman spoke, although both were thinking the same thing.

You were someone's daughter, sister, maybe even a wife. You are being missed by someone. Someone out there—besides the killer—is wondering where you are right now.

If no one claimed the body in a week, they'd bury her in a Port Orchard cemetery, in the no-man's-land that local law enforcement from Seattle to New York called Potter's Field.

PART THREE
Skye

The only games that matter are the ones that I want to play. Shut up and enjoy the ride.

—SOME OF THE LAST WORDS SHE EVER HEARD

Chapter Twenty-five

Cullen Hornbeck picked up his phone and looked at the number to call his ex-wife, Sydney, at her home in Sedona, Arizona. He hated making the call, but he had no choice. Cullen had hoped that his own phone would ring with a call from Skye telling him that she'd hitched to Arizona. She'd grown tired of Vancouver's rain, the overabundance of blue and green as mountains and trees conspired to hem in British Columbia's largest city. Skye was twenty-four, a young woman who was the curious mix of her mother, a silversmith and jewelry designer, and her father, the chief financial officer of an import/export business that procured Asian antiquities. Cullen was drawn to the arts, but his emphasis had been on the business side of things. Sydney was the proverbial free spirit, the kind of woman who seemed both buoyant with her flair for fashion and design yet weighed down by the realities of an artist's life. She had left Cullen and Skye, a fourth-grader then, with no plans other than to "find her center" and the life that the creator had devised only for her.

Although he followed strict process flow for his import business and knew his way from Point A to Point B on most matters, Cullen was left to raise his daughter without a road map. A girl, he quickly learned, required a completely different set of skills. A young girl was not a commodity. When Skye had her first period three years later, Cullen drove to a drugstore at breakneck speed and visited the male's most unfamiliar aisle, only to return home to his amused daughter with a box of Kotex supers.

"I think I need to get some pads, Dad," she'd said, allowing a smile to cross her face. "I don't think what you've picked up will work for me. But I'm new to this, so what do I really know?"

Cullen felt his face go hot. The errand had been embarrassing, of course. This was his daughter, a young woman, at least biologically. He'd miscalculated. He'd failed where Sydney would have succeeded.

He wondered if this was one of those times too. Skye had been restless in the past few months. She'd graduated with a degree in art restoration from the University of British Columbia. She'd thought she could straddle her parents' worlds, perhaps. Maybe bring them together in some way. Yet, over and over, she let it slip that she wanted adventure.

"I want to do something off-the-wall, Dad," she said, looking at him intently. "Something fun—dangerous, even."

"You've backpacked across Europe and the U.S. Isn't that dangerous enough?"

Skye laughed. "No. I'm looking for a life experience, Dad. I don't want to . . ." She hesitated. "You know . . . end up like Mom at thirty-five or you, sorry, at fifty."

He furrowed his brow, feeling a little stung. "Exactly, Skye, what do you mean?"

She knew she'd hurt him. Her eyes pleaded for understanding. Her choices were her own. She was trying to be the woman she wanted to be.

"I'm sorry," she said. "That came out a little harshly."

"You can say that again."

She didn't take the bait. "What I can tell you, Dad, is that I want an adventure. I want to do something that I can remember always. You know, something that doesn't fit within the prescribed boxes that you've followed in your life."

Cullen put his arms around his daughter. "You and your mom were always the boxes that I could never checkmark cleanly."

So there he sat, replaying that conversation, staring at his phone. He'd gone to work the previous Friday, and she was gone when he returned.

There was a note, of course.

Dad, I've left on my adventure. I'm not sure when I'll return, but I'll call you soon. Don't tell Mom.

Skye never called. Cullen was unsure when he should start to panic. Was it after three days? Or four? By the sixth, he'd made inquiries with the Vancouver police. He notified the hospitals.

"Were you and your daughter getting along all right?" the cop in the Missing-Persons Unit had asked, in a tone suggesting boredom more than concern.

"Yes, we were," Cullen shot back, a tad defensively. "We've had our moments, but this wasn't a running-away-from-home situation. She's twenty-four."

"That's right," the cop said. "She's an adult. If she wants to disappear for a little while, she's entitled. Lord knows, I'd like to vanish sometimes myself."

Cullen wanted to snap at the man: *This isn't about you. This is about my daughter and the fact that I'm a complete failure as a father. This is about the fact that she might be at her mother's, and I hate calling up the bitch to concede said failure.*

Cullen said none of that. He thanked the man and dialed his ex-wife. Before he could even get to the point of his call, Sydney cut to the chase.

As she always did.

"Is Skye all right?"

He wondered for a split second how she'd known the reason for his call. Then he remembered: Skye was all they had in common anymore.

"I was hoping you would be able to tell me," he said.

"Me? How am I supposed to know how she's doing? I haven't heard from her for a couple of weeks."

Cullen could feel the air drain from the room. "I thought you two were talking again."

"That's beside the point." Her tone was sharp. "Are you calling me because you don't know where our daughter is?"

He hated how Sydney occasionally deigned to use the modifier *our* when referring to the little girl she'd left behind. On a whim. A selfish whim!

She's my *daughter. And I don't know where she is!*

Instead, he swallowed hard and let the bile drop back down his throat. "Look, Sydney, I'm calling to let you know that I'm a little concerned about Skye. She's been gone for about a week. I was half hoping she was headed down your way."

"Gone? Like missing?"

Cullen gulped. He hated the woman on the other end of the line. He imagined her in a house swimming in crystals, diaphanous fabrics, and beaded curtains that she tied back with a string of bells from an import store.

"Like missing, yes."

The sound of wind chimes clattered in the background. "Of course, you thought I had something to do with her finally getting out of that rain gutter, Vancouver, right?"

"No, it wasn't that at all. I just thought . . ." He let his words trail off to silence.

"Cullen?" Again her tone was ice, as it had been since the day she left him.

"Yes, Sydney, I had hoped she'd gone to see you. She was seeking an adventure somewhere, and you wrote the book on that one, didn't you?"

His words were meant to punish. It was as if Skye's words about the reason Sydney left them were a double-edged blade. She'd pierced him with it, and he'd shoved it right back at his former wife.

Syndey was silent for a moment.

Was she remembering? Was she sorry? Was she only angry that every call—every call spaced out over a fourteen-year period—had ended just the same?

"Good-bye, Cullen. I'll let you know if I hear from her. You do the same."

Click. The call was over. Cullen Hornbeck felt sick to his stomach. If his grown daughter had any friends, he didn't know them. If she had any real connection to another human being besides himself and her mother, he didn't know who it would be. The police had said she was an adult and could damn well do what she wanted. He felt like screaming into the phone at the officer, who didn't seem to care.

"She is all I have! She might be an adult, but she's fragile. She's dear. She's headstrong. She would tell me where she would go. Not disappear for a week! She loved me."

Still carrying his phone, remembering the seven minutes he'd spent on the phone with Sydney, he flipped on the light in his daughter's bedroom. At her urging, he'd redecorated the room after she went to college. Yet, there were remnants from her childhood. In the corner by a window there was a hammock that was brimming with Beanie Babies she had collected in grade school. He remembered how thrilled she'd been when she found the purple Princess Diana teddy bear at a Surrey five-and-dime. He picked up the bear and looked at it for a moment before setting it back among its cadre of animal friends. There was also a poster of Justin Timberlake on the back side of the door.

He'd kidded her about all of those things when she left for college. He'd threatened to redo the room into an exercise room.

"Like you'll ever exercise," she'd said.

He recalled how he patted his slightly doughy abdomen and shrugged. "Oh, I don't know. Next time you come home, I might have a hard body."

"Ugh. That's the last thing a daughter wants to hear about her dad," she said.

They had both laughed. And he'd vowed right then not to change a thing.

She didn't seem to see a need for it, either. It was a shrine to a time that had come and gone.

Cullen snapped his phone shut and sat at her desk. Her laptop was gone. There was nothing to rifle through. No papers in the trash. Skye had vanished.

Sydney Hornbeck Glyndon put down the phone and looked at the photo of her daughter staring from the art niche that she'd had specially created when she and her new husband, Brannon, built their Arizona dream house. Originally she had it in her mind as a place to spotlight one of her bronze sculptures of children. She'd always loved children, although she'd never quite been able to put aside her own needs for the one child who really mattered. She felt a chill in the air despite the heat that oppressed the valley that time of day. She knew that Cullen was more than concerned. He was scared. She could remember the last time she'd heard that in his voice.

"You're leaving us forever," he'd said when he saw her bags packed and lined up like a row of mismatched sentinels at the front door of their Vancouver home.

"I don't know," she'd answered, not looking at him.

"What am I supposed to tell Skye?"

Still refusing to meet his gaze, she replied, "Tell her what she should already know. I love her."

"You have a great way of showing it."

"She'll understand someday. Sometimes a woman needs freedom. You're a kind man, Cullen, but I need to be me. Not someone's wife."

"And not someone's mother," he'd said as the door shut.

Chapter Twenty-six

September 26, 10:44 p.m.
Key Peninsula

There was something comforting about speaking to a machine, if comfort had ever really been a concern. Which, of course, it hadn't. Sam Castile had never done a thing in his life other than find ways to feel good. Sometimes he wondered if his desires worked on some other plane, in a world far from those of other men. Other men seemed to strive. They seemed to seek to protect. It seemed that other men just wanted to ensure that they were always at the top of the heap, the winners of the competition. *Control.* What gave him a charge—both sexual and intellectual—were the hunt, the capture, the destruction of someone weaker than he was. It was primal. When he watched those other men with their pretty salon-cut hair and Macy's clothes lament the challenges of their jobs, he wanted to laugh. They were playing a game that they could never really win. They'd been told by women how it was to be a man.

How they should be. Feel. Do.

By doing so they'd lost any real semblance of manhood. Sam saw the ruse for what it was and almost pitied those who didn't understand that, in the case of domination and submission, there could only be one victor.

Sam loved the fight, the moment in which his prey acquiesced, fell limp, gave up. He loved the screams for mercy, the promises to do whatever he wanted, when he wanted.

Before he could tell her how dark his thoughts were, he talked into the machine. No judgments. No assessments about what he was doing. Just the cool sound of his voice as he recounted how things operated in his universe.

Where he was king.

"Me again," he began, "I've been thinking about Number Three the past few days. How her skin felt, all wet, warm, soft. She was the prettiest one. She was the one teenage boys would dream about boning. Not all of them have been as hot, as weak. She was compliant. She did what I commanded. She was mine, like a pet. Like a toy."

He could feel the bulge in his leather underwear grow with the recollection of what she'd been like. He slipped his right hand into his waistband, feeling the warmth of his own body. Liking what he felt. Rubbing his penis. The shaft, the head, his testicles.

All of it was feeling so good.

"She could have been my pet longer. She could have done what I wanted her to do. But no, she had to get some ideas of her own. Stupid bitch. She hurt me. She found a goddamn screwdriver and actually tried to kill me. Kill *me*! That stupid bitch!"

Sam opened his desk drawer and retrieved two black metal binder clips. He clamped one on his right nipple, the other on his left. He winced and gulped. The hurt was good, what he imagined it felt like for his victims when he brought them to the edge of passing out with pain.

He was nearing climax as the images of her surrender came faster and faster. He worked his right hand faster and faster, leaning back in his brown leather office chair. Thinking of how he had snuffed out her life, and the relief that came with it.

"Oh, you stupid bitch. You shouldn't make me mad. I'll goddamn slice you up like a deli sandwich."

His mind conjured up the brutal images of his own hands, his hairy knuckles, white with tension as his fingers squeezed her slender neck. The struggle. The quiet, coughing scream that ended with her falling limp. He'd started to roll her over, determined to put himself inside her in a way that he was sure she'd like. If she were alive. To his disappointment, she'd soiled herself.

"Jesus," he'd said, "you piss me off. You could have been such a good bitch. A clean bitch. I don't like a dirty whore. You shouldn't have tried to hurt me. I'm the boss. You belonged to me."

As he remembered her, how she had been, he thought how much he might enjoy it if he could tell a living person what he'd done.

He spoke into his recorder.

"No one really knows what it takes to be me."

Once he'd finished all he needed to do, he clicked on the Web site for the *Lighthouse* newspaper. How he loved seeing his work, reliving the glory of the last moments of another's life. It excited him once more.

Here I go again, he thought, feeling another erection swell.

Kendall Stark tucked Cody into bed as Steven looked on. The nighttime ritual was as it had always been, quiet and peaceful. She kissed him on his forehead, still warm from his bath after dinner. Cody's eyes fluttered, his lids heavy with sleep.

"Good night, my baby," she said.

She imagined a smile, yet there really wasn't one.

"He had a good day," Steven said. "He seems happy in the new school."

"He's adjusting," she said. "We all are."

Steven put his arms around her waist as they left their son's bedroom for their own.

Kendall looked at her husband and nodded, although she was unsure what he had said. She hated more than anything that she wasn't living in the moment. She was far away on the shores of Little Clam Bay with a dead girl, a girl without a face.

Chapter Twenty-seven

Not surprisingly, a number of forensic artists find their way to the profession because of an interest in criminology. These were the kind who stayed up late watching crime and cop shows, feasting on criminology. They had artistic skills, of course, but artistry wasn't the driving force for their careers.

Margo Titus, a good-looking brunette who always wore her hair up in a messy bun, with frameless glasses on a gold chain around her slender neck, was from the other camp. She'd been an artist first. She drew Sparky in the margin of a magazine reader response card when she was eleven years old, waiting for her mother in an Idaho doctor's office. She wore all sixty-four of her prized Crayolas to nubs, even the ugly flesh-toned one. She won two school competitions for her artwork by the time she was in junior high. One was a sculpture of a woman walking a dog that landed her in a coffee-table book, *KID ART!*

There was no mistaking it. Margo Titus was going to be a fine artist, a sculptor. She was going to sell her pieces in galleries in New York. She was so talented that if she stuck with it, she was told by all her teachers, she could be the artist that generations would remember.

"You are the kind of student that teachers dream of having but once in a lifetime," said her high school mentor, a woman who wore knee-length skirts and copper bangle bracelets. "You are going to do all the things I dreamed about when I was your age."

Dreams, Margo learned, do die. Her pieces never caught fire like she and others had hoped. They were dismissed as too provincial. Sweet but forgettable. She ended up moving back to Boise and waitressing at a downtown martini bar for a couple of years before going to Boise State for classes in forensic science, inspired by a TV show spotlighting how artists could put their skills to use in helping others.

"The most important thing in the world isn't how a piece of art goes with your couch and love-seat set," she told an artist friend when she made up her mind.

Three years later she was doing facial reconstruction out of a studio she called The Face Lab Inc., in Portland.

Kendall Stark contacted Margo to work the Little Clam Bay case. They'd met at a Seattle conference several years earlier. When Margo answered the call and the two women exchanged some personal updates, Kendall was very direct on two key points.

"We have a limited budget up here, but we also have a case that needs solving."

"I'm sure I can work within your parameters, Kendall. What's the case?"

"A young woman, early twenties, found floating in one of our local estuaries. We've put the word out, but, you know, sometimes a description isn't enough."

"Decomp?"

"No. Not too bad."

Margo knew that sometimes a morgue photo required a little help too. Facial expressions, the way a person's mouth and eyes work together to form a true representation of what he or she looked like in life, were sometimes crucial to finding out just who they were.

"There is some tissue damage. The coroner thinks it was animal activity."

"How bad?"

"Parts of the mouth and nose."

"Eyes in place? Brows?"

"Yes. Barely."

"That's fine. I've worked with a lot less."

"I know that they closed the case on Ridgway's 'last victim' because of you," Kendall said, indicating the case profiled in a police journal that featured Margo's work. The article had recounted the discovery of a small skull near Star Lake in south King County, Washington. Over time, seven more bodies had been found in the vicinity, most together in a single cluster of grisly mayhem that shocked the Pacific Northwest nearly as much as the Ted Bundy murders had over the previous decade.

The article had concerned the skull of a young African American woman—or maybe even only a girl. No other personal effects. No bones. No nothing. Just the dark gray skull found by hikers among the sword and bracken ferns that fill in the lush undergrowth. The "last victim" went unnamed until six months after the trial, when Margo took up the challenge because, according to the article, "every mother deserves to know what happened to her daughter, no matter what. I don't care if this girl was a prostitute or a gangbanger. At one time she was someone's precious baby girl."

It turned out that the Star Lake location was Green River Killer Gary Ridgway's body dump site. Margo's work gave the victim back her name: Tammy Whitman.

Kendall admired the humanity and respect for the victim that was an essential part of Margo's work. Being murdered was heartbreaking enough. To be a victim with a Jane or John Doe bracelet in some Podunk morgue was an insult to whatever life that person had led.

Or to those loved ones or friends who were out there, wondering just where he or she had gone.

"I'm assuming that a 2-D image is acceptable," Margo said. "How soon can you send me facial measurements? Photos?"

"How does this afternoon suit you?"

Margo laughed. "This is one of those you-need-it-yesterday requests, isn't it, Kendall?"

"Not really. Sooner is better than later."

"All right. Get me the material, the coroner's contact info, and I'll see what I can have for you in, let's see . . . a day or two?"

"Next time you're in town, martinis on me," Kendall said.

After she hung up, Kendall went looking for Josh Anderson. Help was on the way. Without knowing who the victim was, there was no way they'd catch the killer.

Everything always started with the ID.

Most of her contemporaries worked solely on the computer, but Margo Titus still loved the way colored pencils and Conté crayons felt against the smooth surface of high-quality rag paper. She found greater success in bringing the material to life by using the old-school methods that she'd first picked up to make her reputation, her legacy, as a fine artist. After working to specific measurements on a transparency atop the photographs, she'd draw, color, and then scan the image for manipulation in Photoshop.

On a row of shelves above her worktable were three sculpted heads that she called the "Janes." Although they'd been found in three different states, they shared the unique bond of being Jane Does. All three were crafted with such realism even Margo thought their eyes followed her about the room. Sometimes she wondered if their vigilant gazes were meant to remind her that she'd failed to determine who they were.

Who is missing you three?

Next to the Janes was a framed portrait of Margo's husband, Dan, and their sons, Jacob and Eli. Below the shelves was a corkboard decorated with the whimsically macabre drawings of her boys, depicting their mother at work in her studio. Heads on the table. Morgue photos scattered like confetti. A paintbrush in hand.

I'd love to be a fly on the wall when the boys are talking about my work at school, she'd thought more than once.

She looked down at the photos and the autopsy report, all of which she'd printed out.

"You won't be one of the Janes," she said. "Not if I can help it."

Margo stirred some sugar into her licorice tea and turned on her CD player. The liquid notes of a Stan Getz samba filled the air. She'd have played it louder, but she didn't want to miss a call if her boys or husband tried to reach her. There was something soothing about the samba, with its sliding percussion overrun by a soaring saxophone. It gave her a calm energy.

"Let's see who you are, little one," she said as she undertook her distinct blend of science and art.

She had no one to consult with as she began to work. In cases she'd worked for the Portland and Boise police departments, she'd had the opportunity to interview witnesses who'd seen a perpetrator. She would inquire carefully, probing into the memory of the viewer. It was a collaborative process as the witness offered up the cues of recognition fixed in his or her memory. The slant of a brow. The flare of the nostrils. Lines on a forehead. So much information was held in a person's recollections that the true skill came in digging it out as much as the application of any artistic skills.

But this one had no one to speak for her or who her killer might have been.

Chapter Twenty-eight

They had made love all night long, and as she positioned herself on the toilet in the darkness of his bathroom, Serenity Hutchins knew that she'd gone too far for the story. It wasn't that she wasn't attracted to him. He worked out, and, despite being old enough to be her father, he had a nice physique. The last guy she'd dated was much younger, but his body was a doughy mess. She finished going and debated for a moment whether or not she should flush. She didn't want to wake him.

If I wake him, she thought, *he'll want to do it again.*

She risked it. Whoosh! She squinted in the faint light coming through the mini-blinds as she washed her hands.

"Baby, come back to bed."

"Coming. But Baby's tired," she said.

"We don't have to go to work tomorrow," he said as she moved toward him in the darkness.

"I do," she said. "I have to get some sleep. I have an event to cover in Manchester. A salmon feed or something."

He put his mouth on hers.

"Oh, Josh, don't you have a crime to investigate?"

He nuzzled her. "Kendall is working the hard stuff. I'll just lay here and enjoy you."

The face staring up at her was young and pretty. She had a slender nose and a mouth fuller on the lower lip that gave her a slight pout. It was very late, and the chill of an early autumn seeped through the windows as Margo Titus stepped back from her worktable. The face she'd painstakingly restored seemed more melancholy than most that she'd created. Margo never created a face that would cause someone to smirk: a cartoonish visage that somehow made a joke out of the victim. Some forensic artists offered up images that, while possibly very accurate, cast a distinctly creepy vibe.

Margo wanted the kind of countenance that spoke to the viewer. She sought an expression that triggered a genuine emotion of concern. This face looking up at her was a sad one. A heartbreaker. It was the face of a pretty young woman, one who had to be missed by someone.

Somewhere. But where? And by whom?

She looked at her wall clock. It was 4 P.M. She had time to finish up, get to Whole Foods, and have dinner going before her family assembled around the table. After working on the rendering with such deliberation, such intensity, she could still set it aside when it came to being a wife and mother. It wasn't that the morgue photos were expunged from her memory, but they were stored in a place separate from the world that saw her as something other than a woman who draws dead people.

Margo scanned her artwork and prepared to send it via e-mail it to the Kitsap County Sheriff's Office. It would be quicker than a phone call, and she had to get going.

Kendall, I hope this helps in your investigation. There's a little guesswork because of the tissue damage, but I think

> this should be close enough to get the attention of anyone
> who knew her—provided they see the rendering. Good
> luck. Let me know when you identify her. She deserves
> that, along with justice for her killer.

Before she pushed SEND her eyes lingered on the damage
to the right breast. The cut looked so clean, so precise. It was
as if a diamond of flesh had been removed from the dead
woman's breast.

Sweet Jesus, she thought. *What kind of maniac would do
that?*

As he tore at her, ripping her underclothing, commanding
her to do this and that, she flashed on how it had started. The
first few times Sam Castile made a shopping list for Melody,
she saw nothing interesting in it. He wanted a motion detector, a fourteen-foot steel chain, and four brown tarps. The
items were mundane, utilitarian. Melody looked at her husband's list, added a few things she needed for herself, and
pointed her silver-colored Jeep in the direction of Home Depot
and Costco. Sam Castile had made it clear that the tarps he
required were not blue, which were the ones most commonly
sold by local stores. The brown were certainly less conspicu-
ous when placed over a leaky roof, a cord of wood, a chicken
yard. He wanted the chains to be polished steel, not galvanized. He said galvanized links were weaker. The motion detector had to be top of the line.

"If someone's out there, you know, lying in wait," he'd
said, "I want fair warning."

He was concerned about her safety, or so she had first believed.

The motion detector morphed into a trio of the devices.
One was affixed to the side of the house, casting a beam whenever an errant deer wandered by. The other pair stood guard
along the winding driveway that meandered through the heavy

fringe of salmonberries, sword ferns, and a tangle of ocean spray leading to the house.

"If you want to run a day care out here, babe," he'd said, "you'll need to make sure the kids are safe."

In the beginning she'd believed her husband. She thought that Sam's words of concern, his need for protecting her and the children, were genuine.

That, of course, was only in the beginning. But there was no day care. There was only isolation.

Sam installed motion detectors fifteen feet past the farm gate, which they kept chained tightly. Visitors hated the gate more than anything: there was no way of tripping it so that it would open without them getting out of the car, unlatching the chain that held it in place, swinging the gate open, driving through, and then getting out of the car to shut the gate. It was a colossal hassle by any measure. In the early days, at least, if Melody had any designs on sharing a cup of chamomile tea with a girlfriend from next door, the gate obliterated them.

No one came over unless they absolutely had to.

Her tuxedo mocha on her desk, Kendall Stark looked intently at the image of the Little Clam Bay victim as Josh Anderson strolled into her office.

"Hey, you," he said, sitting down, "what do you have there?" He seemed more upbeat than usual, and certainly more upbeat than the moment called for.

"Margo's rendering of our victim."

"Let me have a look," he said, reaching for the photo printout. "Good-looking girl. Sure doesn't look like what we saw on the scene."

"That's the point," Kendall said. "We're looking at trying to find out *who* she is, not scare people away."

"I know. I was talking to the sheriff yesterday. He thinks we should use this case to spark some better relations with the local media."

Kendall took her eyes off the photo and studied Josh.

"I wasn't aware there was a problem with local media. Are we talking about KIRO TV and what they said about our jail?"

"No. More local. Local like the *Lighthouse*."

"I thought we were good with them," she said.

"There have been some complaints. You know, from the publisher to the sheriff. Says we don't give them a heads-up on anything. You know, blah blah blah, you only talk to us when we cover your stupid office pancake feed for Kitsap Crime Watch."

"No one mentioned it to me," Kendall said, taking a sip from her coffee.

"No biggie. Sheriff thought we should toss them a bone now and then. Maybe I could take this over to the paper myself."

Kendall thought for a moment. Josh's ulterior motive was so transparent, she wanted to laugh.

"I'll give it to Serenity what's-her-name," he said.

"That's all right," she said, pulling the photo back from Josh's grasp. "I'll take it."

Josh looked a little disappointed.

"She's too young for you."

"Who is?"

She scolded him with a cool look before answering. "Serenity Hutchins."

"I don't know what you're talking about, Kendall."

Kendall nodded. "Never mind. I was only joking."

But she wasn't, of course. She almost never joked.

Serenity Hutchins was hunkered in front of her computer screen when Kendall made her way across the small newsroom.

"I want to talk to you. I have something I need to discuss with you."

Serenity looked up. "You do?"

"Yes, I do." She dropped a photo on Serenity's chaotic desk.

Serenity looked at it for a long time, her eyes finally returning to the detective's.

"She was pretty. Who made this?"

"A forensic artist from Portland. Her name and number's on the back, in case you want to interview her. I'm giving this to you first. It goes out to the Seattle, Tacoma, and Bremerton media tomorrow."

Serenity nodded. "I'm all over it, Detective."

"I'm sure you are."

Kendall turned toward the door. She didn't hear the reporter thank her, although she did. She was focused now on the part of police work that depended on the public and whether or not someone would help her find out the name of the dead woman. She brushed past a girl talking to the receptionist at the front desk. She didn't know right then that she had walked past a young woman who had also caught the killer's eye.

She didn't know there were others too.

Melody Castile had one thought that reverberated in her mind. It was a kind of mocking refrain that she knew no longer carried the kind of weight she might have hoped. *Better her than me.*

The figure on the filthy mattress was streaked with blood and her own feces. Fear had caused her to let go of all bodily functions. She was weak, barely breathing. Her mouth had been covered by the now-familiar silver-gray duct tape.

"Clean her," Sam said, unbuttoning the snaps on his blue and red flannel shirt. *Pop. Pop. Pop.* His undershirt was torn, and he pulled that over his head, flexing his biceps and his triceps for his adoring audience. "Then Baby and Daddy are gonna play."

He stepped out of his jeans, kicked them aside, and stood there nude, his penis already hard.

"Is she okay?" she asked.

"She's alive," he said, "so I guess not." He let out a laugh and bent down. The woman on the plastic-covered mattress couldn't speak, but her eyes were flooded with terror. He slapped her, and the woman shook. "See, she's alive."

"Good. That's good."

"Now, get naked," he said, looking over at Melody, who was already unfastening her bra, "and let's have some fun— you know, until one of us can't anymore."

Melody reached for the baling wire and grinned at him.

"Want me to spin my web?" she asked, already knowing the answer.

Chapter Twenty-nine

October 5, 3:30 p.m.
Key Center, Washington

The drive out to her sister Melody's place took almost an hour. Serenity Hutchins kept her radio on an eighties music station playing hits that were popular before she was born. She listened to the Waitresses' song, "I Know What Boys Like" and wondered how come music wasn't fun like that anymore. Her sister, Melody, and her husband, Sam, lived on almost five acres in a log home just outside of Key Center on the Key Peninsula. The Castiles had a son named Max who had just turned eight. In fact, the gathering that afternoon was to celebrate the boy's birthday and the last sure sunny day before the Northwest rains kicked in and stole the last of the summer. The music was loud in her little black car, but more out of habit than a desire to blast her eardrums. Serenity had gone so long with a loud muffler that after she finally fixed it, she'd gotten used to a decibel level that threatened hearing damage.

Relationships between sisters are always complicated. Any sibling can vouch for that. But with a ten-year age gap, Serenity and Melody shared little more than the commune-style names their mother had given them.

Melody had resented her sister from the time her parents brought her home. She'd suddenly been demoted to helper and sister instead of the center of the universe. Whenever her mother and father left Serenity in the care of her sister, she'd feign attentiveness until the door shut behind them.

She never changed Serenity's diaper. She never gave her a bottle. She just let her cry it out until she saw the headlights of her parents' car in the driveway.

Later, there were hair-pulling, screaming, and setups to get her in trouble. Serenity was far from perfect. She'd learn to give as well as she got. One time she found a condom wrapper in a park and planted it in her sister's room. Melody got a beating from her dad and a smile from her sister. Both sisters held memories distorted by their own wants and wishes. Theirs was a relationship in a constant mend.

At least they played at it as though they cared. Attending Max's birthday barbecue was part of the game.

Serenity parked her car and knocked on the door.

Sam, dressed in blue jeans and a faded red shirt, answered. He was forty-four, broad-shouldered, and a little more than six feet tall. On this particular afternoon his black hair was wavy and a little long, swept back from his forehead. Sam Castile was a man of a thousand looks—facial hair that changed from a full beard to a goatee and then back to a Fu Manchu. He was handsome in a Marlboro Man way, weather-beaten and a little too tan.

"Your sister was thinking you forgot," he said, letting her inside.

"She always thinks the best of me."

Sam shook his head. "Now, now."

"She started it. Or you did."

There was some truth in what she said, and it only made

Sam Castile suppress a smile. He loved lighting the fuse between his wife and her little sister.

Max ran up to his aunt, eyeballing the small package wrapped in blue tissue paper she held at her side as he hugged her.

"For me?"

Serenity kissed the top of his head. "It sure is, Max."

The boy reached for it, all smiles.

"Video game?" he asked, taking the present.

"You'll see."

She followed her brother-in-law into the kitchen, where her sister was slicing onions and lemons.

"Need some help?" she asked, finally.

"I thought that was you driving in. Do you really have to blast the neighborhood with your music?"

Serenity wanted to say, "What neighborhood? You live out in the middle of nowhere." But she kept quiet.

"Really, what can I do?" she asked.

Melody went about her chopping. She was a pretty brunette who wore her hair pinned back even when she wasn't in the kitchen. A silver pendant hung around her neck like a swinging pendulum as she attacked an onion with her knife. Melody had light blue eyes, so pale, that sometimes, when the light hit them just so, they looked like shiny black beads floating in pools of white. Her skin had always been flawless, although Serenity thought she could finally see the tiny creases around her mouth from smoking and too much sun.

You're getting old, sis, she thought.

Sam took a beer from the refrigerator and held it out to Serenity.

"No, thanks," Serenity said.

He removed the top and started to drink.

Melody just kept slicing, filling the air with the scent of onions and lemons, the garnish she'd planned to adorn the salmon that her husband had caught on one of his overnight fishing trips.

"How's work?" he asked.

Serenity shrugged. "Oh, you know, boring most days."

Melody ran a fillet knife along the fish's spinal column, expertly separating the bone from the rosy flesh.

"I'm glad you're getting so much out of your college degree." Melody never missed an opportunity to say something about how her parents had put Serenity through school when she herself had had to drop out.

"Seems like you've had some interesting things to write about lately," Sam said.

"You mean the election of the Fathoms o' Fun Queen?" Serenity said, her tone deadpan.

"I missed that one," he said. "I'm talking about the dead girl in Little Clam Bay."

Serenity nodded and started to talk about the forensic artist in Portland and how she'd been the first to publish the photograph, but her sister cut her off.

"Grill hot enough, Sam?" Melody asked, interrupting the conversation.

Sam winked. "Always. Come on, Serenity, you can help." He set down the last of his beer and headed for the French doors with the salmon.

While Serenity held the platter and he scraped tiny bits of burned-on black off the grill and into the fire, they talked about the murder case, the weather, the fact that her sister could be such a bitch.

Serenity looked across the backyard while he worked the grill. Sam was using charcoal briquettes instead of gas, and she liked the old-school touch. Sam was a traditional guy, and, coming from a family with a father who wasn't, Serenity could see why her sister was attracted to him. Sam's hair was still licorice black, as thick as it had been in high school. The lines on his face only accentuated his handsomeness, as if dimples and prominent cheekbones needed to be underscored. His eyes sparked intelligence and fire, more golden than brown. He was a man's man, the kind who put in a full day as an inspector at the shipyard, a soda with his buds at Toy's Topless in Gorst, then went on home to his wife and son. All in all, Serenity figured, her sister had been reasonably lucky in love. As lucky as she deserved. On the other hand, Sam could have done a little better.

"Been out on the *Saltshaker*?" Serenity asked. "Or is it too cold now?"

The *Saltshaker* was Sam's pride and joy, a thirty-five-foot Sea Ray cabin cruiser that was more than twenty years old. Sam had babied it in every possible way. He hosed it off. Waxed it. Redid the galley and the head, and put in new vinyl on the seat cushions that served as a banquette at the dining table.

"Every now and then. Half the time alone. You know your sister."

She poured herself some iced tea. "Yeah, she always hated the water."

"Maybe I can get you to come aboard sometime?"

"I'm a little like Mel that way. Probably the only way."

Sam laughed. "I get what you're saying."

"What's up with that?" she asked, changing the subject.

"What?" He tried to follow her line of vision, but didn't catch what she was talking about.

She pointed to a mobile home tucked behind the trees.

"Oh, that. Been here forever. Just didn't have the sense to have the previous owners tow it away. Wish we did. A damn eyesore."

Serenity grinned. "Fits in with the sketchy neighborhood. No offense."

The barbecue splashed some fire, and Sam jumped backward a couple of steps.

"None taken," he said. "We like the seclusion of the place. Some people pay a premium for it. For others it's all they can afford."

Serenity knew what he was talking about. It was the perfect last sunny day of the season.

At least, she thought so.

* * *

Sam Castile had seen that look on his wife's face before. Cold. Bitter. Pissed off.

"She got him a goddamn video game," Melody said.

Sam turned down the blanket on his side of the bed. "Your point?"

"Jesus, Sam. She's supposed to be educated. Doesn't she know that Max will end up a big, fat, stupid couch potato if he hangs out in front of the TV screen playing when he should be doing something better?"

He peeled off his underwear and T-shirt. "She was trying to be nice."

Melody knew what was coming. She went for the bottom drawer of her dresser and, from a stack of twenty identical undergarments, pulled out a filmy, frilly bra and panties. "She knows how I feel about this stuff. She doesn't care. Never has. She just does what she wants."

"Lighten up," he said, now running his hand over her small breasts. "We do what we want, too."

Melody was about to make another cutting remark about Serenity but didn't. Her tirade just then had been a lapse in the kind of control that she needed. She could hate her sister, be jealous of her. She could think anything she wanted. But she wasn't in control. She never had been.

"I want to play now, babe," he said. "Been a long day."

She knew what he wanted, and she rolled over onto her stomach. There was no love in their lovemaking. It was more of a punishment, an endless poking and prodding. A game in which she was always the defeated and he the victor.

Everyone gets what they want, she thought. *Everyone but me.*

Only once since her life became dark and completely undone had Melody Castile reached out to anyone for help. She had phoned Serenity and asked if she'd meet her for lunch at the Shari's just off Highway 16, near the first Port Orchard exit.

"What's the occasion?" Serenity asked after the hostess had seated them in a window booth looking out at the highway. "My birthday isn't for six months."

Melody wore nineties-style pale blue jeans and an olive sweater. She never had anything new. She looked old, tired. Even her hair, which had been the true marker of her beauty, was dull, pulled back in a loose ponytail held together with a scrunchy.

Who still wears scrunchies? Only my sister, that's who, Serenity thought.

Melody ordered coffee and a slice of strawberry pie. Serenity ordered apple. She thought no pie without a top crust was a real pie.

"You look like shit, by the way," Serenity said.

"Thanks, I needed the compliment. You always know what to say."

Serenity could see that her sister was troubled. Her eyes stayed fixed on the traffic blur outside. She wanted to tease her more, kick her a little when she was down. There hadn't been too many times in childhood when the balance of power had been in her favor. They were sisters in name only. Serenity had longed for something closer, something that approximated a genuine bond. She'd given up on that.

If Melody was waving a white flag just then, Serenity didn't see it.

"So what's up? Is it Mom?"

Melody set her fork down and looked at her sister. "No. It isn't. It isn't Max. It isn't you. It isn't Sam. No, really. This is about me."

"And how you're stuck out in the country, wasting your precious years?"

Serenity knew the words were harsh, but she'd already let them out of her mouth.

Melody reached for her purse. She pulled out a twenty and put it on the table.

"Never mind," she said, edging toward the end of the booth.

"Mel, I'm sorry. What did you want to talk about?"

"Nothing. It's all right. Never mind."

Melody Castile knew that she was alone. It had happened so slowly that there was never a point at which she could have stopped it. *Alone*. And if she was sleeping with the devil, then she knew just what that made her.

With satellite dishes affixed like mushrooms on rooftops around the residential neighborhoods of Vancouver, getting a feed from U.S. TV networks was no longer the challenge it once was. In the years of rabbit ears and roof- or tree-mounted antennae, it was a lucky family who could pick up Seattle TV stations. Despite the fact that satellite TV brought in the possibility of picking up L.A. or New York TV, old habits died hard. Certainly, Cullen Hornbeck could watch anything he wanted, but he still stayed fixed on Seattle's venerable KING-TV for its evening news broadcast. Since he traveled to Seattle a couple of times a month on business, it made perfect sense to stay current on the goings-on down there.

It had now been two weeks since his daughter went missing. He'd seen her face in the crowds at the local market. He'd heard her voice over the loudspeaker at the airport. He'd tricked himself at least twice a day into believing that she was all right and it was her finger that was tapping him on the shoulder when no one was there at all.

He splashed some Crown Royal over a couple of cubes of ice. *More*, he thought.

Another splash.

He rolled the smooth, sweet alcohol in his mouth and down his throat. He could feel the slight burn of the whiskey as it sent a shock wave of warmth through his body. The ice crashed against his lips as he swallowed more.

The anchorwoman, a striking blonde who'd been on the air since he was a teenager, announced the next story.

"They are calling her Jane around the morgue in Kitsap

County, but they know that's not her real name. The county coroner is hoping that someone watching this broadcast can help identify her . . ."

The TV showed a body of water, and a reporter, a black male in a puffy orange vest that made him look more road improvement worker than journalist, started to speak.

"Two Port Orchard boys skipping school two weeks ago found her floating right here in Little Clam Bay."

Cullen poured another shot, keeping his eyes fixed on the screen. When Skye's Siamese cat, Miss Anna, rubbed against him, he ignored the impulse to pick her up.

"She was young, in her twenties. She was wearing—"

Cullen set down the glass, missing the tabletop. The tumbler shattered, and Miss Anna ran for a place under the table.

The clothes look as though they could be Skye's. The age is right too.

His heart raced. He disregarded the broken glass and stared at the TV.

". . . the young woman's injuries were so severe that a forensic artist was brought in to re-create what she might have looked like in life."

A woman identified as the coroner came on the screen. Birdy Waterman held up a drawing. Cullen felt relief wash over him. The image was all wrong. The girl in the rendering had a kind of vacant stare. She wasn't vibrant and full of life.

Of course, he told himself right away, *she was dead.*

"This is an artist's representation of what our victim might have looked like. It isn't a photograph of her," Dr. Waterman said. "If you are missing someone who approximates this image, please contact the Kitsap County Sheriff's Office."

The blond woman came back on and read a phone number. Without even thinking, Cullen Hornbeck wrote it down.

It can't be her. She isn't dead. She just can't be.

It passed through his mind that he might not have the courage to dial the number. Not *knowing* still meant hope.

Chapter Thirty

Kendall Stark and Josh Anderson fielded the calls after the story featuring the Little Clam Bay victim rendering ran in the *Lighthouse* and on TV. Calls came in fits and starts throughout the morning and into the afternoon. Sometimes it was clear that the person on the other end of the line was heartbroken or an attention seeker. Sometimes a little of both.

"Looks like a girl I worked with at the Dinners Done Right on Bethel Avenue."

"My sister has been missing for two years. Might be her."

"My aunt."

"Best friend from high school. I think."

"My daughter."

There were dozens of such calls. But only one had some information that promised some real potential.

It was from a man in Vancouver, British Columbia.

"Was the blouse a Trafalgar?" he asked. "My daughter's

missing. I saw that the girl you found was wearing a green blouse."

Kendall looked at the list of clothing found on the victim.

"Sir," she said, "how long has your daughter been missing?"

"Three weeks yesterday," he said. "Is it my daughter that you've found?"

Kendall could hear the man's heart shattering.

"I don't know. But the blouse is a Trafalgar. Can you come to Port Orchard?"

Kendall had seen the all-consuming look of loss on the faces of others who'd sat in the waiting room, next to the array of magazines on a glass-topped side table. The magazines were well worn but barely read. They were brought in by thoughtful staff members, the address labels neatly removed with scissors. Cullen Hornbeck sat slightly stoop shouldered, as if the air had been let out of his body and he'd refused to take in any more oxygen. His eyes were black buttons, unblinking and sad.

"Mr. Hornbeck?" she asked as she stepped into the room. "I'm Detective Stark."

He stood and extended his hand.

"Yes, I'm Cullen." He looked around, catching the eye of the only other person waiting to see law enforcement, a gray-haired woman with a peeled orange and a *People* magazine. The woman went back to her reading.

"Thank you for seeing me," he said.

"Of course, Mr. Hornbeck. We've already sent for your daughter's dental records. We should have them this afternoon." She looked at her watch. "Or they could be here even now, waiting in the coroner's lab for log-in."

She motioned for him to follow, and the pair meandered through the lobby, behind the receptionist's desk, past several unoccupied cubicles. She opened a door and led him inside a grim little room with two chairs and a black metal table.

"Coffee?" she asked.

"No, thank you, Detective."

"All right, then."

"It has to be Skye," he said. "The girl you found." His tone was slightly demanding, and Kendall found it a little off-putting. It was almost as if he was *insisting* that his daughter be identified as the Little Clam Bay victim.

"Sir, as I told you on the phone, we won't know until we compare her dental records or barring that, DNA from your daughter. You brought her toothbrush?"

"Yes," he said, his eyes welling with tears. "Right here." He pulled a bright red toothbrush clad in plastic wrap from his breast pocket and slid it across the table. "I also brought her hairbrush. I know that sometimes that can be helpful."

"All right. Thank you."

"Detective, you've never asked me why I know that the dead girl is Skye."

"You saw it on the news."

Cullen shook his head. "No, that's not all of it. That's not how I found you to call. It's deeper than that."

He looked at Kendall, wondering how many times she'd been faced with a man in his shoes.

"How is it?"

He took a breath. "I saw her picture on the missing girls' Web site."

Kendall was unsure what Internet site he was referring to.

"Sorry? Someone put up a photo of your daughter to help get the word out that she's missing?"

"No," he said. "Someone put up a photo of the body you found in Little Clam Bay."

Kendall had known several cases in which armchair detectives—or cybersleuths, as they liked to call themselves—had put up victims' photos, sometimes gruesome and offensive images, with the hopes that they'd strike lightning and glean a nugget of truth from the gawkers that flock to such sites. She knew that despite the confiscation of their phones, the images that Devon and Brady took of the dead woman had been floating around the Internet like a heartbreaking calling card.

"I have this feeling in my gut. It is like the blade of a knife stuck in so deep that it presses against my spine. I know that my daughter is dead. I know that she's never coming back."

He pulled out a photograph and handed it to her.

It was a pretty young woman wearing the green blouse.

"She's pretty. Very pretty."

"Smart too."

"Where's Skye's mother? Has she heard from your daughter?"

Cullen shook his head. He had a hangdog expression that made Kendall want to proceed with gentleness.

"Maybe she knows something."

"I doubt it. The woman only knows one thing—and that's how to live her own life, unencumbered. She never loved Skye."

"I'm sure you're wrong, Mr. Hornbeck. All mothers love their children."

"Look, all mothers are supposed to love their children. It is supposed to be automatic, natural. But it isn't so."

Kendall looked down, feeling the man's pain swell to the point where it was palpable. She wanted to argue with him about what Skye's mother felt. She was sorry for her too. Her daughter was dead, and whatever had transpired between them would never get resolved.

"I'm sorry," she said. "I had no business presuming how anyone felt. That's between them."

Cullen looked hard at her.

"That it is," he said.

"A bay view will be fine," Cullen Hornbeck said as the Holiday Inn Express clerk slid a plastic key card across the front desk. She was a chubby girl, a brunette with lively brown eyes that she accentuated with a heavy application of mascara. She was younger than Skye and by no means a ringer for Cullen's daughter, but the front-desk girl's very aliveness taunted him. Picked at him. She tilted her head as she watched the hotel's newest guest complete the requisite paperwork. She smiled a friendly smile.

"Canada, huh?"

"I'm afraid so."

He noticed that the girl wore braces and had three holes pierced into each ear.

Skye had had braces when she was fourteen.

Skye had two . . . or was it three holes in each ear? How was it that he couldn't be sure?

"My mom goes up there every six months to get the aspirin with codeine. Can't get it here."

Cullen didn't say a word.

"We have free continental breakfast tomorrow at six. If you're looking for dinner tonight, the Chinese place across the street is pretty good. Try their rainbow pot stickers and sesame balls."

"That sounds good," he said, knowing that the idea of any food whatsoever was the furthest thing from his mind.

His hotel room door secure, Cullen threw his suitcase on the bed and turned on the shower. He turned on the TV, louder than he would need to hear it, but not so loud as to be a nuisance to the other guests. He drew back the bedspread and dropped onto the pillow. He thought of how his daughter had always felt hotel bedspreads and pillows were full of "cooties" and that no one in their right mind would touch his or her bare skin to either. Deep within the folds of the poly foam, he began to scream. At first there were no words but the guttural cries of a man who had lost everything.

Finally, the pillow consumed his grief, keeping his words tucked inside.

"Skye, no! Please come back to us! Come back to me!"

* * *

Sam Castile knew the value in "mixing it up," as he liked to call it when it came to dealing with the women he stalked, used, and discarded. The only method that was off limits was gunfire. Even the most inept police department had access to labs that examined the lans and grooves of a spent bullet. Ballistics ensured that a killer could be traced. That is, of course, if the gun could be found and matched to the killer. Certainly, he could have stolen a gun. But even that upped the ante for the risk of detection. So many killers in the *Encyclopedia of Crime* that he kept on the shelf with other, less useful books had been caught because they'd committed another crime.

Ted Bundy had been pulled over on a traffic violation in Salt Lake City. He'd attempted to elude police by driving through stop signs. *With his headlights off!* When he finally gave up, cops found an ice pick, handcuffs, and a pantyhose mask in the vehicle.

The serial killer's traveling kit.

The Night Stalker, Richard Ramirez, screwed up his string of fourteen murders in the L.A. area when he was traced to a Toyota stolen from some restaurant goers in the city's Chinatown. It was, Sam thought, a stupid move. If Ramirez had kept his focus, he'd have been able to keep his string of murders alive.

No killer likes to be told when they are finished doing what they do best.

Aileen Wuornos, who took it upon herself to rid Florida of purported philandering husbands and male abusers by killing the men she picked up for sex, was another one who could have prevailed if she hadn't been so careless with her associated crimes. She was traced to a stolen car belonging to a dead man. Pawnshop receipts for victims' belongings were mottled with her fingerprints.

Kill for sport or to make a point, not for money, stupid bitch!

So there he sat, thinking of what he might like to select from his smorgasbord of murder. What would be the most memorable way to steal the life from someone? What would fuel his desires? How would it play back when he remembered? Would it make him hard? Or would it merely frustrate him because there were not enough aspects to conjure a decent erotic fantasy?

Who would it be?

Chapter Thirty-one

October 8, 9 a.m.
Port Orchard

Lighthouse publisher Tad Stevens scurried out of his occasional office and stood under the YOU AUTO BUY and LET'S GROW REVENUE banners that had been plastered on a nearby wall to motivate the long-suffering advertising staff.

"People, I need your attention. People, I need your attention now."

Mr. Stevens, as he insisted on being called, was the owner of the half dozen small papers that made up the struggling chain that caught the ad revenue and news crumbs that the Seattle papers apparently deemed too insignificant. Mr. Stevens was a remarkably neat man with a small frame, soul patch on his chin, and rimless glasses that held the DG logo of Dolce & Gabbana at the right temple hinge. He lived alone with his two Pomeranians, Hannity and Colmes. Editor Charlie Keller, for one, insisted that everyone in the newsroom show the publisher respect.

"Whenever he's in the office, be nice," Charlie had instructed them. "When he's gone, you can call him *dipshit* if you like."

No one had a problem following Charlie's lead.

"People, no one likes the idea of capitalizing on tragedy. But that's what papers do better than any entity other than maybe police departments and the medical profession," Mr. Stevens said.

Let's not forget the lawyers, Serenity thought.

"We have a golden opportunity to kick some ad revenue and readership butt, team."

Golden opportunity? I'd like to kick someone's butt, she thought some more. *But it isn't a reader's or an advertiser's.*

The publisher went on, his enthusiasm swelling: "It appears a serial killer might be at work right here in our own backyard. We've got the dead woman in Little Clam Bay and what's her name . . . the brush picker."

Jesus, do you have to be gleeful? Two women are dead. This isn't the biggest thing to hit Port Orchard since the Wal-Mart went in.

Serenity wanted to say something but stayed quiet. Not something she was particularly good at, either.

"We need to be tough," he said. "We need to *own* this story. We need to sell our expertise as the local paper with its hand on the pulse of a major case. If this serial killer case gets the kind of traction I'm thinking, we'll be able to sell photo rights to media outlets across the country."

He looked over at Serenity but didn't say her name.

"There will be opportunities for all of us. TV interviews. Maybe even a book. But our focus now is claiming this as a *Lighthouse* exclusive."

Next he lowered his impeccable DGs and looked over at Travis Janus, the backup sports reporter who also did the paper's Web site.

"TJ, let's think out of the box on this. We need to enrich the content that we have up now. I'd like to see photos and docs pertaining to the case. If you need content to connect the dots, Serenity will help out."

Serenity nodded, but knew that TJ wouldn't ask her for anything. The Web was his bailiwick. He didn't take advice from anyone. Supposed computer experts never do.

"You see this?"

Steven Stark, sweaty from his early-morning run from their place to Manchester's boat launch and back, handed Kendall the morning's edition of the *Lighthouse*. Cody was at the table waiting for a pancake and Kendall set down the spatula.

SERIAL KILLER STALKING KITSAP?

The story with Serenity Hutchins' byline ran at the top of the front page and featured two photographs. The first appeared to be Skye Hornbeck's high school photograph; the other was one of the images that Tulio Pena had provided for the feature story that ran after his girlfriend, Celesta, was reported missing.

"She makes a reasonable case that the two are connected," Steven said.

"Oh, she does, does she?"

"I'm just saying," Steven said, taking a seat at the table.

Kendall started to read while the pancake on the griddle began to burn. Serenity noted how the women were of approximately the same age, on the petite side, and both wore their hair long.

"She's describing half the county," Kendall said, looking up at Steven. "I thought that was a stretch. But that's not where she won me over."

Kendall read on as the *Lighthouse* reporter indicated that the fact that both dead women had been butchered in too similar a fashion to ignore. She'd interviewed a profiler who lived on the Internet and offered no real credentials but was always handy with a quote. The article concluded with an over-the-top line that made Kendall wince and her husband laugh.

"Boston had its Strangler. New York had Son of Sam. Are we being plagued by the Kitsap Cutter?"

Steven got up from his chair and flipped the burning pancake.

"She's trying to sell some papers," he said. "Nothing more, I'd wager."

Kendall put the *Lighthouse* on the counter and squeezed some syrup on Cody's short stack.

"Only one problem, honey," she said, hesitating a little. "We've never released the extent of Skye's injuries."

"Wasn't she there when the body was pulled from the water?"

She put the plate in front of her son and watched for a second.

"Want Mommy to feed you?" she asked. Sometimes Cody didn't want any help. This, it turned out, was one of those mornings. He took the fork and started to eat. Kendall looked back at Steven, who was flipping another pancake.

"What was the problem, Kendall?" Steven asked, obviously curious.

"Serenity was there at the crime scene, but she couldn't have seen what Dr. Waterman and I observed during the autopsy. We've never released the information about the cuts to her breasts."

"Then how did she know that?" he asked.

Kendall set down her coffee. "That's what I'd like to find out."

Kendall Stark shut her car door with so much force, she actually slammed it. Josh Anderson, snuffing out a cigarette in the parking lot of the Sheriff's Office, winced from twenty yards away. His startled look was the only good thing that had happened since her husband pointed out the lead article in the newspaper.

"Did you tell her about Skye Hornbeck's wounds?"

Josh looked as blank as he could. "Tell who?" he asked.

Kendall crossed her arms and stared at him. She kept her voice calm, but there was no mistaking how she felt. "Don't bullshit me, Josh. Did you tell Serenity Hutchins about the condition of Skye's body?"

He shook his head. "No. Why would I?"

"Because you think she's hot for you. Or something like that. The older you get, the more stupid you get."

Josh took a step back. He'd never seen Kendall so heated.

"Look, I never told anyone about that," he said.

She jabbed a finger at him. "Like I'm going to believe you? Look, I know you've been seeing her. What is she, twenty-one?"

"No. I don't know. I haven't told her anything."

Kendall knew that her face was red, but she didn't care.

"We look really stupid, you know."

"Is that what this is about? Looking stupid, Kendall?"

Kendall turned to go inside. He was partially right, of course.

"Don't even go there," she said. "If we have a serial killer, then we have bigger worries than anyone's ego. That includes yours and mine."

Josh followed her inside, but Kendall was too angry to say anything more to him. When they found their offices, she shut the door. A blinking red light on her phone indicated a message. She dialed the code for her voice mail.

The voice was familiar.

"Detective Stark, is it true? Did this Kitsap Cutter kill Celesta?"

It was Tulio Pena. His voice was in shards.

Kendall felt a kind of sickness wash over her. It was the

feeling that came from letting down someone who had depended on her. She could blame Josh for leaking information to Serenity. She could even blame him for insisting that Celesta's murder had been the result of a turf battle over floral greens. She could even tell herself just then that she had done the best she could.

But that was a lie.

"I want you to call me," he said. "I want you to tell me that you are still trying to find who killed Celesta."

Kendall hung up and drew a deep breath. She dialed Tulio's number. Her heart was heavier than the anchor her father had used to lock their boat into a fishing spot on the east side of Blake Island when she was a girl.

"I'm so sorry," she began, "that you had to read that in the paper . . ."

As she spoke to Tulio, she had no idea that things were about to get worse.

Margo Titus had done her job and the outcome was what she'd prayed for: an identity revealed. She put away the files that she'd accumulated on the case. It was always a great relief to store the bits and pieces she'd used to help find out who was who. While the vacant-eyed Janes looked on, Margo's eyes landed on the autopsy photo. For the first time she noticed a series of very faint red impressions on the victim's neck.

Skye Hornbeck's neck, she corrected her thoughts.

She dialed Kendall's cell number.

"I was just thinking of you, Margo," Kendall said. "I meant to call. I'm guessing you heard the news."

"It isn't about that. They don't always end this way. I'm glad that this one worked out."

"Me too."

They talked about the case, the cause of death, the fact that Kendall had been in touch with Skye's father.

"I don't know if it is anything," Margo finally said. "I was looking at the photos, and I noticed marks on her neck. I don't know if you have a serial up there or a onetime psychopath, but he might have taken a trophy."

Kendall, pulled the photos and began flipping through them. "A necklace?"

"That's what I was thinking."

"Her father mentioned one."

"If the killer took it, he took it without unclasping it."

Kendall saw the series of faint red marks in one of the autopsy photos.

"I see it."

"Of course, I could be wrong. But I worked a case in Red Bluff where the perp kept all his vics' brassieres in a laundry bag under his bed. One in Oklahoma City kept his vics' earrings."

Kendall Stark stood in line behind the other county workers looking for their caffeine buzz. She'd had a restless night with Cody and the case. The press accounts fueled by Serenity Hutchins hadn't helped, either. She wasn't sure right then what was weighing most heavily on her mind. Her son didn't— or couldn't—use words to indicate that the Inverness School had been a stunning disappointment for him too. It was hard to gauge a shift in his awareness. At times, he showed no emotion whatsoever.

Kendall, who didn't favor a foundation for her makeup, applied some concealer under her eyes. Her hair was in need of a cut or a double-dose of hair product. She didn't look good, and she didn't need anyone to tell her so. What she needed was that mocha.

She felt an abrupt peck on her shoulder, and she turned around. It was Serenity Hutchins.

"I know you don't think much of me," Serenity said.

Kendall let out a sigh and knew she'd lost her place in

line. There was no way they were going to have that conversation right there. She indicated for Serenity to follow her to a table by a large window filled with the view of the inlet. They sat facing each other.

"It isn't about you. It isn't personal," Kendall said.

Serenity was upset, but it was unclear right then if she was angry or embarrassed. She'd gone after Kendall, but she seemed to pull back a little.

"I'm doing the best that I can," she said. "I'm trying to get at the truth."

Kendall knew better than to say what she was thinking, but she couldn't stop herself.

"Look, I just don't like your methods, Serenity."

"My methods?"

Kendall allowed a slight glare of condemnation to zero in on Serenity's unblinking eyes.

"Yes, your methods. I really don't want to get into it. Can we leave it alone?"

"No. We can't. I have a job to do too."

Kendall looked out the window. "Fine. We all do."

Chapter Thirty-two

October 15, 9 a.m.
South Kitsap County, Washington

A long gravel and mud road led to the parking lot and then a
wide path followed a steep embankment to the pristine sandy
beach at Anderson Point. The location was not for the infirm
or the underexercised. It was so difficult to get to, and, despite its status as a county park, it had very few visitors. It
was almost always deserted. Lovers came to have sex behind
a burned-out cabin, hidden from view by a three-foot barrier
of silver-gray beach grass, all blades bent away from the
surfside. On the hottest summer days, mothers took their little ones there to dig in the sand and collect bleached-out
clamshells while they listened to music on iPods or read the
windswept pages of a paperback novel.

Mostly the park was empty, beautiful, and quiet as God
had intended it to be. Mid-October brought a blast of cold air
off the Colvos Passage, but that didn't stop the diehards who
jogged from the parking lot to the beach. On October 15, an

early-morning jogger made his way down to the water, running the switchbacks at a better clip than he would be able to do later when returning to his car. Everyone, especially joggers, knew that the trip down to the beach was much easier than the steep climb back to the parking lot. He crossed over the grass-tufted dunes and faced out over the narrow passage that separated Kitsap County from Vashon Island. He heard a seal bark and watched some seagulls battle over something good to eat fifty yards down a beach strewn beautifully with grass, wood, pebbles, and, finally at the water's edge, sand the consistency of cake sugar. The gulls were making such a ruckus that the jogger altered his course and worked his way down the beach, heading south. The tide was out a little, and his running shoes stamped the sand. He breathed in the air and was about to turn back when he noticed seagulls screaming at each other as one tried to fly away with its prize. Whatever it was, the bird dropped it and it fell to the beach.

Jesus, what's that? he thought.

The jogger walked closer and bent over to get a better view. *Was it the leg of a hapless sea star?* He pushed at the object with the tip of his dirty blue running shoe. It was slender and wrinkled, with a tapered end and a tattered one. He nearly jumped out of his skin.

A human finger.

As he spun around with his back to the sound and dialed 911 on his cell phone, he noticed a cacophony of gulls twenty yards away, near a neat pile of driftwood. He made his way toward the squawking birds, as a tugboat passed a half mile down Colvos Passage.

This isn't happening, he thought.

Cradled between two parallel logs was a human body.

A woman.

Nude.

Although he strained to see exactly what he was looking at, the jogger took a step backward, his heels sinking in the sand.

The 911 operator answered and he coughed out the words, "I found a human body, I think. Out here at Anderson Point."

"You *think* so?"

"I *know* so, it's just that . . . well, I found *most* of a human body."

The corpse was missing more than a finger.

"This lady has no head."

Over on the Key Peninsula, Melody Castile was lost in her thoughts again. She turned over her purse and let its contents fall onto the bleached maple kitchen table. A few coins rolled to the floor, but she paid them no mind. Nor did she take a moment to view the mini photo album that she carried wherever she went. Inside were the incongruent, nearly Betty Crocker–inspired photos of her with her husband and little boy. She fished through the brushes, the tissue, the car keys—everything that she carried with her—in search of the waterproof mascara that she was just sure was there.

And then she found it. She pulled the cap from the top to expose the slender wand and applicator. The makeup had been in her purse for some time—since the previous summer when she swam at the Gig Harbor YMCA.

Good, she thought, seeing that there was plenty of the dark pigment left. *This should be perfect.* She considered a coppery-red lipstick too, but dismissed it out of hand because she knew that her husband didn't like the messy way lipstick sometimes transferred.

The oversize chest freezer in the Fun House was in the very back of the old mobile home, behind the false wall that allowed a modicum of discretion and security. Even if some kids wandered in to find out if it was a good place to get in trouble, they'd never find the mattress or the freezer.

Just boxes of things that weren't worth bothering with.

* * *

It was a gruesome gathering. Kendall Stark, Josh Anderson, and Birdy Waterman stood over the headless corpse in the basement of the Kitsap County coroner's office. Even Josh, who'd never missed an opportunity to make an off-color remark, was silent. The acrid scent of the deteriorating tissue and seawater was only too familiar.

Celesta Delgado.

Skye Hornbeck.

"If we ever doubted before, we have a serial," Kendall said. "Don't we?"

Dr. Waterman nodded as she worked her light over the dead woman's torso.

"The question," she said softly, "at least for now, is just who this is?"

Kendall nodded. "If she's local and reported missing, we might be able to pinpoint who she is."

Even without a head.

"Midnight Cassava," Josh said. "She's been missing since the second week in April. Or thereabouts. Hard to tell with her comings and goings. Hooker, you know."

"Marissa," Kendall corrected, ignoring the hooker remark.

The pathologist looked over her glasses at Josh and Kendall. "Did she have any children?" she asked

Kendall nodded. Suddenly she no longer smelled the decomposition of the body. "Yes, a little girl. She's living with her grandmother now."

"This woman has had at least one baby. See the stretch marks? Internal exam of the uterus will verify it. Her name wouldn't happen to be Tasha, would it?" Birdy asked.

The beam of the light illuminated a wrist tattoo of letters spelling out T-a-s-h-a, each character separated by a tiny daisy.

Kendall thought of the little girl. Her mother was a prostitute and had died the kind of unspeakable death that no one, no matter how she lived her life, deserved.

Striations around the wrist were visible. Like the others, likely made by wire bindings.

"Was she restrained? Like Skye?"

"I can't be sure," Dr. Waterman said. "There's some obvious freezer burn here. See that dark patch of skin along the arms?"

The pallid limbs of the victim had broad markings that ran from the shoulders to the hands. The right hand was missing the index finger.

"Why cut off just one finger?" Josh said. "I mean, if you're going to lop off someone's head for fun, why bother with a single digit?"

The pathologist shrugged. "My guess is that he didn't mess with cutting off her finger. Those damn gulls did. Look at this cut. More of a tear, really. Not like the head."

Indeed, the neck was the most obvious and shocking injury Kendall had seen. It was a blood-clotted stump. Tissue and vertebrae pushed upward like a mushroom from the remarkably clean cut that had severed the head from the body.

"Look at how precise this is," Dr. Waterman said. "This was no hacking but a careful—and I'd say *skilled*—decapitation."

Josh popped an Altoid mint into his mouth, as if the fresh taste of the candy would mitigate the stench of the room. "Who has that kind of—as you put it—skill? A taxidermist? A French Revolution reenactor?"

Birdy let a slight smile break across her usually serious face.

"That'll be your job to figure out," she said. "I'm just calling it like I see it, Josh."

Next, scalpel gleaming, she made her Y-incision, slicing the skin shoulder to shoulder, then down the sternum.

"I suspected this," she said.

Kendall bent closer. "What's that?"

"See the crystals here?" She pointed to the edge of her

scalpel next to the heart. Thin wafers of ice glistened like tiny diamonds on deep-red velvet.

Kendall indicated she did.

"This lady's been kept in a freezer."

Josh Anderson's cell phone sounded, but he let it go to voice mail.

A beat later, Kendall's buzzed. Thinking it might be something about Cody at school, she snapped off her glove and reached for her phone. It wasn't the school. It was the number for Serenity Hutchins. She ignored it.

"Your reporter girlfriend is certainly quick on the story," she said to Josh, who seemed to shrug it off. Birdy regarded the two detectives and spoke up.

"Now that you mention Ms. Hutchins," Birdy said, "I was wondering how she was able to write such an incisive story on victim two."

Josh looked a little embarrassed, his face darkening. He stepped away from the autopsy table and put his hands out as if to push back.

"I didn't tell her about the cuts," he said.

"Of course you didn't," Kendall said. "You'd never kiss and tell."

"But I didn't," he said. He looked intently at both women. "Not this time."

Chapter Thirty-three

October 15, noon
Bremerton

The hospital chapel had seen ten thousand tears. Maybe a million. It was a dour little room with four pewlike benches upholstered in dusty olive and facing a simple brass and wood cross. Very modern, or at least it was modern in the 1970s, when having a hospital chapel was part and parcel of dealing with dead patients.

Donna Solomon said nothing at first. She simply buckled over, hugging herself, as Kendall Stark told her the news.

"I'm sorry," Kendall said. "This is such sad, sad information to take in."

Donna found the strength to draw in a deep breath. Her eyes were flooded by then, and tears started to pour down her cheeks, collecting in the corner of her mouth.

"It is, it is . . ." she finally said.

"No one should ever have to go through this. Few people have."

"Thank you for telling me before the papers put something out there."

Kendall put her arms around Mrs. Solomon. Her daughter had been missing since mid-April. She'd thought, hoped, that Marissa had gone somewhere to be with a boyfriend.

"I always thought she'd come back. She did love her baby, just as I loved her."

"I know."

"Can I see her?"

Kendall shook her head. "That wouldn't be a good idea. Her body isn't completely intact. I'm sorry."

Donna Solomon dabbed at her eyes with a tissue from a dispenser on a table.

"What do you mean, intact?"

"The body was in bad shape, I'm afraid."

Kendall didn't want to tell her the details just then. She studied Donna's reaction, and she seemed to be satisfied.

Devastated. Resigned. Satisfied.

Kendall Stark could have cried when she saw the headline in the *Lighthouse* the next morning. It was beyond anything she could have imagined.

HEADLESS IN SOUTH KITSAP: THE CUTTER STRIKES AGAIN!

Despite the fact that Kendall was suspicious that Josh had tipped off the young woman, there was the distinct possibility that Serenity had gotten the information from the jogger or others at the scene. Even so, she poked her head into Josh's office to give him a piece of her mind. He was gone. Next on her list was Charlie Keller.

She wouldn't even bother with Serenity.

She dialed his number, and the editor got on the line.

"Big happenings in Port Orchard, Detective."

"Look, Charlie, I like you. I like the paper. I don't even mind it when you get things wrong. But don't you have any kind of decency over there?"

"I don't know what you're getting at."

"How did you get that information? Couldn't it have waited a day before you blasted it to everyone that the victim had been decapitated?"

"The news doesn't wait."

Kendall sighed. Of course he was right.

"No offense, Charlie, but the *Lighthouse* is hardly CNN. It could have waited."

"Ouch," he said.

"Don't you care about the victim's family? They'd barely been notified."

"That's your job."

There was no point in the call, and Kendall Stark knew it. She'd dialed the *Lighthouse* editor to give him a piece of her mind about ethics, dignity, and concern.

All of that was lost on that bunch.

Serenity watched her boss turn off his office speakerphone. Despite Charlie Keller's bravado during the call with Kitsap County detective Kendall Stark, he didn't look happy. In front of him was a stack of messages from national media outlets ranging from Fox News to CNN. Kitsap was making the news in the way that forgotten little burgs gain overnight notoriety when evil presents itself.

"She was pretty hot, wasn't she?" she asked.

Charlie Keller fanned the messages on the desk in front of him.

"Yeah, she was. Too bad. I like her. She does good work, and we don't advance a story very often without the help of the police. No offense to you."

"I don't know what you're getting at, Boss."

He shook his head, not looking up at her. His eyes still

riveted on the messages. "You know. And I'm not saying that you're not doing a great job. But really, it won't look good for the paper if some blogger points out that our reporter is getting her info from her cop boyfriend."

Serenity looked surprised. She hadn't said a word about seeing Josh Anderson.

"Well, for your information, Josh didn't tell me this info. Not this time. I have more than one."

"I'm sure you do," he said. "But let's watch this, okay? These things have a way of biting people in the ass. And you don't want your ass chewed, believe me."

Serenity nodded. "You're right. I don't."

Jamie Lyndon was petite, but she had nerves of pure carbide. If she hadn't been too slight in her build to take on all the physical requirements of the qualification exam, she would have been happy to be a corrections officer at the Kitsap County jail. At a breath under five feet and not quite a hundred pounds soaked to the skin, she eventually found her niche with a headset firmly in place as a 911 operator working at Kitsap County's central communication center, CEN-COM. Less risky. Less fun, to be sure. But her cool demeanor always served her well in a job that demanded calmness on the rocks with a splash of humor.

"Must be a full moon," she said to her coworker, Sal, as they fielded call after call. "Werewolves and teenagers, if you can tell either apart on a night like this."

"Yup, the board's on fire tonight, for sure," returned Sal, a part-time communications officer, part-time student, and full-time single dad. "That's what we live for around here. Love it when we're busy."

"Me too—" Jamie began to answer before swiveling around to face her console and another call.

"9-1-1. What are you reporting?"

"Hello?"

The voice on the other end of the line was female, soft-spoken. So much so that Jamie couldn't quite make out what she was saying.

"Can you please speak up?"

"Okay. I just don't want anyone to hear me."

"Is this an emergency?"

"Yes. It is. I think it qualifies. It's about a murder."

"All right. Can you be more specific?"

"The dead lady at Anderson Point. I know the guy who did it."

"Who is this? Where are you calling from?"

"I'm not saying. And don't try to catch me. This phone's about out of minutes, and I'll just get another from the gas station."

"All right. Who are you talking about?"

"The dead lady."

"Yes, I know that. I mean, who is the guy you've alluded to?"

"I'm not saying." The woman paused, as if she hadn't contemplated that she'd be asked such a simple question. "I can't. But I want you to know that he's not a monster."

Jamie knew enough from the newspaper and the Sheriff's Office scuttlebutt that the caller was wrong. The man who had murdered and dumped Jane Doe in the frigid waters of Puget Sound was nothing less than a monster.

"You need to talk to someone, provided you really do know something."

"I do. I do."

"Now we're getting somewhere. You called for a reason."

"I was feeling sorry for the dead woman. She didn't deserve to die. Not in the way she did."

Jamie pressed the caller. She had a way of pulling up just a touch of sarcasm to make someone spit out what they had to say.

What she needed them to say.

"Is that so? Tell me something we don't know."

There was a silence for a second, and Jamie wondered if she'd pushed the caller too hard. "The dead girl has a small crescent-shaped scar above her right knee."

In case the information was accurate, Jamie pushed a little harder. "Where is he?"

"I've already said too much."

"You've just got started. You don't make a call like this and then just drop it. Who is he? This man who did this?"

"I'm not saying."

"Who is he to you?"

"This call isn't about me."

Jamie took a breath. She wanted this woman to do the right thing. It was, after all, the reason she called in. *Or was it?* They had their share of crazies phoning 911. One man called at least once a week with the tale that he was sure a young girl was being tortured in the apartment above his. The police were routinely dispatched for the sole reason of making sure they were not at risk in any potential lawsuit— in case there really was a girl being tortured on the third floor of the Marina Apartments.

"How do we find him?" Jamie asked.

A slight hesitation, some kind of a tapping sound. "You won't."

"How do you know? Do you know him?"

"I love him, and I serve him."

Jamie felt the air suck out of the room.

"Please hold the line, will you? I think you'll want to talk to one of the sheriff's detectives. Hang on. Okay?"

There was no answer. She heard a door slam and some muffled sounds.

"Are you there?"

Still nothing.

A man's voice cut on to the line. "My bitch is done talking to you." The voice was deep, cold, unforgettable.

Sal looked up from a computer screen, where he had just logged in the basics of his latest call. "What was that?"

"Some woman, first. Some *man* at the end. Says she knows who killed the woman out on Anderson Point. It sounded like she knew something. The man shut her up."

"Get the number? Location?"

"Disposable cell phone, she says."

"God, we hate those."

Jamie sighed. "Yeah, we do."

"Think she was for real?"

"I'll forward it to the Sheriff's Office. That's their job. Ours is to answer the calls." She turned her attention to the call light flashing from her console. "God, here comes another."

Jamie pushed the button on her handset.

"9-1-1. How can I help you?"

The caller was inquiring about the neighborhood block watch program. Jamie politely reminded him that those types of inquiries were not an emergency.

"Try back tomorrow. Use the help line. This is for emergencies only," she said.

She rolled her eyes in Sal's direction, and he, too, was handling a call.

Jamie wrote up a brief note on what the caller had said about the corpse on the shore at Anderson Point and forwarded it to her floor supervisor. She'd noted the call log accession number, which would allow investigators the ability to pull the recording of the call so they could listen to what was said—and how it was said.

Jamie Lyndon had a pretty good feeling that this particular call would lure some ears sooner than later. And she was right.

The next morning, Kendall Stark looked at the CENCOM report about the nighttime caller and the chilling message that she'd relayed to the operator. It was only two paragraphs long, but it provided a crucial piece of information.

She looked up at Josh as he strode into his office, coffee

in hand and a smile on his face as if he was going to tell a joke.

"What's with you?" he said. "It's too early for this to be a crappy day already."

She indicated the report with a tap of her finger. She had also downloaded an audio file of the call.

"One of our operators took a call last night. If it's genuine, and I have no reason to believe it is . . ." She let her words trail off.

"Yeah?" he said, sliding into a chair.

"This is a theory," she said, "and I'd like to tell you, but . . ."

"But *what*?" He looked impatiently at her and took a swig from his dirty mug.

"I don't want to read about this in the paper. Okay?"

"I thought we were beyond that, Kendall."

"I hope so," she said. "And because I need you on this case, I'm willing to give you my trust just one more time."

Josh didn't offer up a quick retort; instead, he just nodded.

"The so-called Kitsap Cutter isn't acting alone," she said.

"You mean like Bianchi and Buono?"

He was referring to the Hillside Stranglers, who'd raped and murdered ten women in California in the 1970s. The crimes were notorious for many reasons, one of which dealt with how the two acted in tandem. They shared a psychopathology that entwined them in such a way that enabled them to act out on their fantasies together, each stoking the sick desires of the other.

"Not exactly."

She played the recording.

"I love him, and I serve him."

Josh stared at Kendall as the audio concluded.

"More like Bianchi and Betty," she said.

"The Cutter's accomplice is a female?"

Kendall nodded. "It fits the evidence. The cleaned-up victims, the hesitation in some of the cuts, the way he's been able to lure victims without tipping them off."

"They weren't afraid," Josh said.

"That's right. Because *she*," Kendall indicated the report once more, "*the caller,* was there too."

Chapter Thirty-four

October16, 9 a.m.
Port Orchard

Kitsap County Sheriff Jim McCray, a stern presence who rose up through the ranks when he won a neck-and-neck election two years prior, called Kendall and Josh into his office. It was just after 9 A.M., and the day felt like trouble already. Jim McCray was a hulking figure at six-foot-five and two hundred and fifty pounds. He had deep-set brown eyes, which seemed to penetrate more than stare.

"Look," he said, as the pair took chairs opposite a desk loaded with paperwork that needed tending, "you two are great detectives."

Josh glanced at Kendall. "I have a feeling we're getting an award," he said, his tone sardonic and a little resentful.

"Or about to be fired," she said.

Jim McCray allowed a rare smile.

"Neither. But the fact is we need some help here. The FBI is going to assign some resources out of the Seattle field office. Mason County and Pierce County are going to put a guy—or gal—on the team, too."

The gal reference was a nod at Kendall, and it wasn't meant to be sexist, just a correction from a man who was still working on his human resources skills.

Josh didn't like what he was hearing one iota. "Sounds like you really don't think we can do the job," he said.

Jim shifted his frame in his chair. "Not that at all. We're getting pressure. And I'm not just talking about the *Light-house*."

Kendall knew that he was referring to Serenity's latest story and the accompanying editorial that called for the obvious: JUSTICE NEEDED FOR CUTTER'S VICTIMS NOW.

"Who's leading the task force?" she asked.

"The FBI has enough to do with their terrorism investigation in Blaine," he said, referring to an Iraqi national who had been caught at the Canadian border crossing with a trunk load of plastic explosives and a schematic of Seattle's Space Needle, "but to answer your question, they're leading."

"Jesus," Josh said, "we've just started here, and you're letting us get stepped on."

The sheriff tightened his mouth and munched on his response. "We blew it with Delgado, and everyone knows it. We have to pay the price for our blunder by eating a little dirt."

Kendall looked at Josh. He was fuming.

"It was a mistake," she said. "And I'm sorry about it."

Josh looked out the window. He'd been written up for outbursts in the past. He'd been to anger management training. He counted to five. There was no need to count to ten.

"Fine," he said.

A discernable pattern marks the surge of Puget Sound. Most currents follow the ebb and flow from the Strait of Juan de

Fuca, that choppy channel of Pacific blue that isolates Washington from Vancouver Island. The currents are swiftest there, petering out considerably as islands and peninsulas impede the natural movement of tidal waters.

Kendall maneuvered her SUV into a tight space in the visitors' parking lot adjacent to the Veterans' Home in Retsil, only a few minutes east of Port Orchard. From the water, ferry passengers on the Bremerton–Seattle run caught a glimpse of the building, looking stately and grand on a bluff that soared above the lazy tide lines of the beach that scurried over to Rich Passage.

Kendall reviewed the locations of where Celesta, Marissa, and Skye's bodies had been discovered. While nothing was absolute in the investigation, she and Josh shared the general feeling that the killer lived in the northern part of Kitsap County.

"Shoving a dead woman into the water is a nighttime activity," Josh had said after a short meeting with the sheriff and a speakerphone connected to members of the task force. "The killer cruised to the Theler Wetlands and plunked Celesta where he thought no one would find her—in the shallows near Belfair. Reedy there. Weedy there."

"He didn't really hide her," Kendall said. "He wanted us to see what he'd done."

Josh shrugged. "Maybe. But my gut's been at this longer than you, and I don't agree."

Kendall found her way across the lot to the front entryway of the Veterans' Home. She had a date with an old family friend.

Peter Monroe was eighty-seven—a still-with-it eighty-seven—and lived on the second floor in the remodeled section of the nearly century old institution. He was reading Clive Cussler's latest tale by the window when she appeared in the doorway. He looked up and moved his book to his lap. His hands were twisted into gnarly kindling; his eyes were now faded denim. He slowly got up and gave Kendall a hug.

"Hi, Mr. Monroe," she said as warmth came to his white-whisker-stubbled face. Though he told her after high school graduation that she could call him Pete, she never could do it.

"How's my favorite marine biology student?" he asked, a reference to the classes he had taught at the university before retiring at seventy-nine.

"I'm fine," she said. She'd taken a couple of courses from him out of personal interest, but also because she'd known him growing up in Harper. The Monroes had lived down the street from her family's home on Overlook Road. "Still looking at the water from my front window and appreciating all that goes on under its surface."

"You said you wanted to talk about currents." He lowered his rimless glasses and looked at her. "What's this all about?"

As Kendall pulled a folded paper from her black leather shoulder bag, she noticed a framed photo of Mrs. Monroe on the bed stand. She'd been gone for at least ten years. She felt a flush of sadness. He'd been alone a good long time. He had children, of course, but she wondered if they visited often. It was too personal to inquire, so she didn't ask about them.

He took the paper and moved it into the sunlight, and Kendall sidled up next to him, so she could view her chart as he did. "The red dots are the locations where the bodies were recovered," she said. "I'm wondering how the killer can get around so easily, dumping victims without any detection. They're not really a cluster of dump sites." She stopped herself.

Kendall hated that she'd even used the word "dump," as if the women were nothing but trash.

"Hood Canal is interesting," Pete said, sliding his glasses back up the bridge of his nose to get a better look at the swirling rings laid out by an oceanographer and a cartographer. The rings were spaced at varying widths, like the lines on a piece of driftwood. "I used to go shrimping there with Ida and the boys."

"Those were happy times," Kendall said, catching the look of a specific memory in his blue eyes.

Pete peered at Kendall over the brims of his glasses. "Yes, but that's not why you're here. You're wondering if the *perp*— that's the word you detectives like to use—went all the way to Belfair to drop off Ms. Delgado's remains?"

Kendall hadn't used Celesta's name, nor was it on the map. Just Victim One, Victim Two, Victim Three. Mr. Monroe still read the paper. *Good.*

He went on. "Rough weather notwithstanding, the currents and tidal oscillations are a little sluggish here by the bridge," he said, indicating the floating bridge used to traverse the narrowest part of the channel from Kitsap to Jefferson County. "Not knowing where he put her in the water, of course, my guess is that she couldn't have been dumped off the bridge and floated all the way to Belfair. Not likely. If he put her around here," he said, pointing to a location about a quarter mile from the bridge, "she'd ride the tide to the location in the wetlands."

"How long would it take her body to travel that far?"

His answer was immediate, though not precise. "A few hours. Half a day at most."

Kendall pointed to Little Clam Bay and Anderson Point, on Colvos Passage across from Vashon Island.

"Currents flow northerly on the Seattle side of Vashon," Pete said, "and southerly on the side where you've indicated here and here." He tapped a twiggy fingertip on the two red dots.

"So if we found some evidence related to one victim here near Anderson Point," Kendall said, taking it in, "you're telling me that the *perp* likely dropped the evidence north of Olalla."

Pete nodded. "Yes. The passage is busy there, but not as busy as the east side of the island. I'd say if someone wanted to get rid of something overboard he would do it around Fragaria, maybe a little further north around Southworth. Not as far as Harper, where you live. The current's too weak there."

"Right," she said, looking at the boat launch at Southworth. "That's the only place along the whole passage where he could launch a boat other than here. No other ramps until way south until you get to Olalla."

Little Clam Bay, where Skye Hornbeck's remains were found, was less problematic.

"No doubt that the body caught a current right about here," he indicated a location off Blake Island to the east of Manchester. "Current flows this way," he said, drawing a line near the Naval Supply Center. "The body likely got sucked into the bay, here. Not easy to do. But doable. Terrible clamming there, by the way."

Pete folded the paper and returned it to Kendall. "Sure, it's possible that your perp is flitting around in a speedboat; my guess is that the boat's a larger one. It would need to be a boat of some size to chug through the waters from Hood Canal to Southworth."

"A commercial boat? Tug?"

"Possibly, but also a large pleasure craft. My point being, I'm doubtful he's launching his boat off some trailer at Harper or Southworth. Must be moored somewhere around here."

Kendall bent down and kissed his forehead.

Pete Monroe actually blushed.

"What did I do to get that?" he asked.

"Just because you're a great man and I want you to know it."

He smiled broadly as she gathered her things to leave.

"Come back and see me soon, okay?"

"There's no doubt about that," she said.

Max Castile knew that his parents had their secrets and there was no asking about them. The mobile home was off limits, of course, but so was the old Navy trunk kept at the foot of their four-poster. It had his dad's name stenciled in block letters, CASTILE, and the black-and-white dial of a combination lock of the type that he'd seen used by kids to secure bikes to the metal railing behind the school.

For as long as the boy could remember, his father kept the trunk locked. The one occasion that it wasn't was the time he looked inside. His dad was at work and his mom was doing something in the back of the house when Max's curiosity got the best of him. The lid was heavy, and he had to pull hard to swing it open.

On top was a covering of thin, dark fabric. Max turned the edge and immediately caught a glimpse of silver. *Chains.* He pulled back more of the fabric to reveal a leather whip coiled and twisted into a figure eight, just like all the electric extension cords hanging on pegs in his father's garage. He wanted to play with the whip, but he didn't dare reach for it.

Something else caught his eye. He blinked. Next to the whip were various flesh-colored tubes: replicas of enormous penises. They reminded him of a horse's he'd seen once when he was over at a friend's house when he was five. The kid had told Max what it was, and he hadn't been able to take his eyes off the stallion. He looked deeper into the trunk and saw a pile of magazines with covers showing men wearing masks and woman bound with cords.

Pleading. Begging. Screaming.

The images scared the boy, and he let the lid slam shut. *Thud!* He heard his mother's footsteps and ran out of the room.

"What's wrong?" she asked, catching him near the kitchen doorway.

"Nothing," he lied, not looking her in the eye.

Melody studied her son, taking in his fear and wondering what he'd been up to.

Twenty minutes later he returned to his parents' bedroom, drawn to whatever he'd seen. This time the box was locked.

Chapter Thirty-five

Melody Castile turned to her husband and flashed an uneasy smile. It was subtle, and she turned her head as quickly as she could and faced the window. Rain splattered against windowpanes with broken seals, making the trailer fifty yards away hard to see. She knew what was coming.

"You coming to the Fun House or not?" Sam asked.

"The boy's restless, Baby." Melody looked in the direction of the TV room. Max was watching some kind of Japanese anime cartoon that held his imagination captive. He wasn't restless in the least.

"Daddy wants you there," Sam said. He was demanding, his meaning implicit: *either you come now, or you'll pray you did later.* "Don't make me get angry."

She looked directly at him. "Baby wants to be there, but you know the boy needs me too."

He shifted his weight on heavy work boots that had tracked in fir needles and the leaves shed by the willow she'd planted when they first moved onto the property. Corkscrew willow. She'd imagined that she'd be harvesting the curling stems for floral projects and craft shows. She had no idea that she'd have to abandon all that she'd dreamed of in order to fulfill his needs in the Fun House. The best she could say of herself was that she was a reluctant participant. But not all that reluctant. She'd done everything he'd wanted, when he told her to do it. She knew that if the unthinkable had ever occurred and they were found out by the police or someone else, she was going down too. She'd been there. She'd helped him.

And sometimes she had even enjoyed it.

"Fun House," he said. *"Now!"*

Melody took a bottle of olive oil from the kitchen cabinet and followed him outside, across the wet grass, past the drippy willow stems, and between two firs that acted like shutters to the doorway of the mobile home. She filled her lungs with air and followed him. It was a single-wide, in decent shape, but outdated in a world in which only a lowlife Kitsap methhead would call such place home. He'd ripped out the kitchen and knocked out the wall between the two bedrooms. He'd burned most of the garbage, filling the air with black smoke.

She was sure a neighbor would call in the illegal fire, and when she told him so, he'd looked at her with those cold eyes.

Eyes that she found full of cruelty, but in a way that made her lust for his touch. She'd never recoil from him.

But that was before the Fun House became what it was to be.

One afternoon he showed up with two old queen-size mattresses he'd purchased from Craigslist. She looked at them and made a face. She indicated a big stain that looked like dried blood.

"Those are nasty," she said. "Someone had her period all over that one."

"Baby, don't worry. I'll make it nice for us."

She helped Sam carry the mattresses one at a time across

the yard into the single-wide. She heard the laughter of children on the acreage next door as they played with the family dog, a German shepherd that they insisted would protect them from prowlers. With the truck bed empty, she noticed a box of chains and a spool of wire.

"What's that for?"

He offered a smile, his lips barely parted. "That's for me to know and you to find out, Baby."

In time, yes, she'd find out.

From the beginning, Sam reminded Melody what was at stake and that any failure of their secret would be her fault alone.

"Look, I'll kill you and go have a pizza before I do any time."

She simply nodded. Her heart fluttered, but she only agreed.

"No one knows what goes on here besides you, me, and the girls we pick up here and there. They won't say anything, that's for sure. They'll never get the chance to."

"I love you," she said. "I just want you to be happy."

"I might have been happy if I'd have married someone other than you. But you'll do what I want nine times out of ten, and that'll be enough to keep you breathing."

It was a threat, and it excited her.

"I promise to be good."

"Good isn't what I want or need. I like my women a little on the rough side, bitch. You know, sweet like a soft cookie, but with the crunch of nuts inside." He let out a laugh.

She laughed, too, as if what he'd said was the funniest thing she'd ever heard.

It was too much of a reaction, and his eyes shot her a *shut up* glance. She shut up right away.

Kendall answered Dr. Waterman's message with an in-person visit. She needed some space to think, and the walk across the parking lot from the Sheriff's Office to the morgue was about as good as it was going to get. She found the county's forensic pathologist eating some slightly congealing ramen at her desk in what had been the dining room of the sad little house that served as the county morgue. Birdy set her mug of noodles down and greeted her with a smile.

"Such service," she said.

"We aim to please, Doctor."

Birdy motioned for her to sit, and Kendall obliged. "I know. I'm glad you came over. I have something for you. Lord knows you could use it."

The last sentence wasn't meant as a dig, and Birdy regretted how it came out. "You know what I mean. We all could use a break."

Kendall nodded. "You can say that again. Have you got something for us?"

Birdy folded back the metal clasp of a manila envelope and pulled out a four-page report, most of which was boilerplate and protocol.

"About those paint specks."

Kendall scooted forward on the chair. "You've got something, haven't you?"

"Nothing as definitive as you'd like, I'm sure, but something yes. Lab results came back this morning. Not only did the ladies in Olympia—with an assist from the feds' lab—confirm the chemical makeup and date of the paint—1940, prewar—they determined that the outer surface of the paint indicated some wear."

"'Some wear?'"

"That's right," Birdy said, drumming her fingernail on the report. "It appears that the object inserted into our victim was likely a household item: eggbeater, rolling pin, potato masher."

Kendall didn't say anything, and Birdy filled the silence with more information.

"The postmortem damage to her vagina fits the kind of shallow penetration of a painted dowel pin—you know, four inches or so. Whoever raped her after death used some kind of old kitchenware. I'm about sure of it."

"Why would someone do that?"

"That's your question to answer, but the truth is, Kendall, we never really know what triggers the darkest and the unthinkable. The killer could have picked up a rolling pin because it was handy or because using one in such a vile way held some meaning for him."

"Like he hated his mother," Kendall said.

Birdy put the report back in the envelope. "That's one possibility, I suppose."

"Obvious as it is."

"Right. Remember the murders in Spokane ten years ago? I know this is a bit before your time. They called him the Grandma Killer?"

Kendall searched her memory. "Yes," she said. "I think he killed four women, all elderly."

"Yes," she said. "The media—and my colleagues in law enforcement—were all but certain he was targeting older ladies because of some anger against them or some sexual compulsion. A classic rage killer."

Kendall was unsure where the conversation was going, and the look on her face signaled the pathologist to wrap it up.

Which she did.

"Point being, the killer wasn't targeting older women because he was *attracted* to them. They were simply random picks based on opportunity. They'd spent months profiling a killer they thought had a granny complex for nothing."

"He was just lazy, right?"

Birdy nodded. "That's right. So what I'm getting at is, I don't think that our Kitsap Cutter has anything against his mother per se. I think we've got a man who is an opportunist and is looking for women he can control, defile, and do with as he pleases. And there's one more thing. I'm all but certain that our killer has an accomplice."

"What makes you say that?"

"Some alleles were picked off the paint chips. They don't match each other. They come from more than one person."

"Is the Cutter a killing team?"

"That's my guess. Of course, it might merely mean there was trace from the grandma who owned the old rolling pin. DNA, like fingerprints, is not time/date stamped."

Kendall Stark parked her child-fingerprinted SUV in the lot behind Bay Street in an oil-stained lot that looked out over Sinclair inlet at the Navy ships across the water in Bremerton. The Olympic Mountains, rugged and bare of snow, were an awe-inspiring backdrop. She glanced at the moored ships, gray and enormous, like whales lazing, and then proceeded to one of the antique stores that lined much of Port Orchard's downtown thoroughfare. She was on the hunt for classic kitchenware, items that had once lovingly helped to prepare meals, but now had been used for the unthinkable.

Most stores had "a little of this, a little of that," but one seemed the most likely place to learn more. It was Kitchen Klassics, a hole-in-the-wall shop, just steps away from the library, a popular tavern, and a bail bondsman's office that were the three busiest places on the main drag of town.

Adam Canfield, a man who wore a cardigan and a bow tie every day of the year, nodded at Kendall as she came inside, ringing the bell. He set down his supersized mug of black tea and lit up with recognition.

"Hi, detective," he said, brushing back a lock of prematurely salt and pepper hair that hung foppishly fringed on his suntanned brow.

Kendall had known him since high school when they worked on a production of *Brigadoon*. She'd been Fiona; he was a set decorator.

"Adam, I'm on a mission, and I think you're the one to help."

"A *case*." He raised an eyebrow. "*The* case?" he asked, without saying the obvious.

She smiled at Adam. He was complete gossip, but an effective one when it came to feigning confidence. He should have been an actor.

"I can't talk about the specifics," she said. "But I'm hoping you can help."

He moved his tea aside and leaned on the glass case that served as a counter, his elbows sliding a little.

"I'm here for you," he said.

Kendall described the color, size, and age of a particular kitchen item.

"I'm thinking a handle on a cook's tool."

Adam resisted the urge to offer up some kind of innuendo. "Red or red with a white underglaze?" he asked.

She pondered the lab's report. "Yes, there was a white underglaze."

"Good, that makes it more interesting," he said. "And more valuable. Follow me."

Adam led Kendall between rows of old appliances and dining sets to a large locked case. Inside were crocks loaded with rolling pins, potato peelers, and tools with purposes unknown to the Kitsap County investigator. Adam unlocked the case and reached for a rolling pin with cherry red handles.

"Made only one year, 1938, in Germany," he said, giving dough roller a spin as he handed it over.

Kendall stopped the whirling pin. "What happened?"

"Company went TU," he said. "The war, Jewish company, Germany."

Kendall rotated the pin. The dowel was not stationary like some rolling pins, but inside ball bearings turned the cylinder. It glided over pastry like a vintage Ferrari, smooth and with style.

"I see," she said.

"Retails for about $400. You can have it for $375."

Kendall handed it back. "Thanks, Adam. But I'm more interested in who else might have wanted one of these."

He locked the case. "I've sold a couple since I've been in this location. Highly collectible, this stuff. Few people appreciate something so simple, so rare. "

"How are your records?"

Adam grinned. "They suck, but I could do some digging."

A while later, Adam Canfield was on the phone. Kendall was sitting in her office with Josh Anderson going over the minutes of the last task force meeting, taking their lumps and wishing they'd been able to put an end to the Kitsap Cutter case before things had spun out of control.

Even more so.

"Hi, Kendall, *er* Detective," he said, correcting himself.

"Hi, Adam," she said, "have you got some good news for me?"

"I don't know if it's good news. But it is news. I dug through the files. God, I wish I made enough dough to hire a full-time bookkeeper. It isn't easy being in retail, you know."

"I'm sure, Adam. What did you find out?"

"Three names: Katrina Dodson, Melody Castile, and Veronica—she likes to be called Ronni—Milton. All of them have purchased something in that old line I showed you."

She wrote down the names. *Something* seemed so vague, and she asked him about it.

"My records are lousy. *Lou-zee.* I don't know what they bought. You'll have to ask 'em. Kat and Ronni live in Port Orchard. Melody's out on the peninsula."

Josh Anderson's eyes flashed recognition at one name on the list, and when Kendall hung up, he wasted no time telling her what he knew.

"Melody Castile is Serenity's sister. She's one of those collectors, big-time. About all she does. I'll run this one down."

Kendall didn't have a great feeling about Josh "running

down" anything when it came to Serenity Hutchins, but she agreed. She'd follow up on the other two vintage kitchen collectors. She always did two-thirds of the work when she and Josh worked a case together, anyway. Why should the Cutter be any different?

Josh Anderson pulled the cork from the slender neck of a wine bottle, sending a nice pop into the air.

"You'll get a kick out of this," he said to Serenity as he poured some wine into the last two goblets that his wife had left when she packed up (his *first* wife, not his *last* wife). The pair were holed up in his condo in Bremerton, taking in the view of the moonlight water and a passing pleasure boat.

Serenity tasted the wine and nodded in approval. It was a crisp chardonnay that she favored, and Josh knew it.

"What's that?" she asked.

"You mentioned your sister being a kitchen junk collector."

She rolled her eyes. "Among other things."

He nodded. "Yeah, among other things."

Condensation clung to her glass, and she wiped it away with a paper napkin.

"Her name came up today on a list of buyers of stuff that may be related to the case."

Serenity wasn't sure what he was talking about, but she didn't press for details right then.

"My sister's a little loopy and her husband is a creep, but since my folks died they're pretty much all I have," she said.

He drank some wine. "You don't mention them much."

"We're not close. Sometimes I wish we were," she said.

"I know how that goes."

Chapter Thirty-six

Max Castile had begged for months to be Indiana Jones for Halloween. At first Melody had been surprised by the choice. It seemed to be a character out of her own childhood and an unlikely candidate to inspire the imagination of a child of today. She had her sister to thank. It was an Indiana Jones video game that Serenity had given Max for his birthday.

She took out her mother's old Singer sewing machine and worked day and night at the kitchen table, taking one of Sam's work shirts and reducing it in size for her little boy to wear. She'd found an appropriately beat-up fedora at the Gig Harbor Goodwill that smelled of someone's grandpa.

Max had found the whip.

"Mom, I love you," he said, holding up the small black riding crop with a silver skull at its knob end. "This is so cool."

The whip was not part of the costume she was making but

had been among the toys that she and Sam employed in the Fun House.

"Where did you get this?" she asked, her voice a controlled scream.

Max looked confused and then burst into tears.

"I'm sorry. I'm sorry. I thought you got it for me, Mom."

"This is not for you," she said, taking the whip back.

The little boy ran from the kitchen. His mother did not follow. She didn't know what to say or whether it was worth making any more issue of it.

She turned the machine on and started sewing.

Melody Castile had been the star of Sam's little productions nearly since the time they were first together. At first it made her feel uncomfortable, doing the things that he insisted turned him on. When it came to lipstick, he wanted her to wear bright red, not muted shades of brick and persimmon. Candy Apple was the color he desired on her lips. He wanted her to wear crotchless panties that he purchased off some Frederick's of Hollywood–type site on the Internet.

"For my all-access pass," he said when he gave her the sheer underwear with the slit on the front panel.

Sam's requests escalated over time. No longer did he seem to be content to make her over into his version of sexy. He had her *do* things. Oral sex in a bathroom at the Space Needle. Allow him to slip his fingers into her vagina while they waited in the drive-through line at the Port Orchard Starbucks. Each time she acquiesced, the line moved closer toward the sordid.

"Baby, I need you to put this on and be my dirty little bitch."

He handed her a short dress, pale blue: it looked like the kind of garment a flower girl might wear at a summer wedding.

"No panties, bitch," he said as she dressed.

What is this game? Why am I doing this?

"I want you to put this inside of you, bitch," he said, handing her a clear Lucite dildo. She'd never seen it before. It was enormous, shiny, like a phallic icicle. God only knew where he'd purchased it. At one of those seedy sex shops near the Navy base in Bremerton? Or in Tacoma at that suburban-style superstore, Castles? There, a credit card and a taste for the wild side could get a customer Jenna Jameson's vagina or Johnny Wadd's penis made of rubber or silicone with a star-burst on the package proclaiming that it was dishwasher safe.

"Get on the bed," he said, pushing her slightly, as his digital camera started to whir.

It wasn't just that his voice was demanding: It was more that she *wanted* to please him. Melody knew that men sometimes needed something more than the usual. She wanted to help him, to please him. So she obeyed.

He took off his pants and underwear but not his shirt or socks as he stood before her. He almost never took off his socks when they had sex. Yet, she had to be devoid of all clothing and jewelry, down to her wedding band. It was what he preferred.

"Legs up. Spread your legs, bitch," he said. "Higher."

He held out his camera.

"But you can't take sexy pictures of me, baby, if you can't see my face," she said.

She didn't tell him that she'd spent a half hour on her hair and makeup, thinking that the sexy pictures he had in mind were more *Playboy* than *Hustler*. She was a pretty woman who didn't need a heavy hand with the lipstick or blush, but he liked her to "paint it up" a little. She'd even put a little foundation on the thin white stretch marks she carried after childbirth.

He laughed. "Bitch, I don't care about your face."

She looked a little hurt, and he seemed to respond to her concern.

"I want to show these to my friends. If they see your face, they'll know it's you. Then they'll hit on you. I don't want that."

She relaxed a little.

"Good, bitch. Now, put it in!"

Later she would think back to this moment, wondering if she'd crossed over to a dark and dangerous side. Was this her turning point? If she'd said no to the photos, the dildos, the leather straps, the chains . . . would things be different?

"It hurts," she said.

"Oh, bitch, that's good. That's how I like it. That's how you like it too."

She lay back on the bed, feeling sore and ashamed. Whatever questions she had about what they were doing stayed unasked.

A few days later he came home from the shipyard, beaming. She was in the kitchen.

"I showed your pictures to some of the guys," he said, cornering her in the kitchen while she prepared dinner. He spoke in low, conspiratorial tones. It was as if they'd done it together as a team. She'd felt she was just an object under his direction. But he seemed to suggest more. *Your pictures.* It made her feel good. "I didn't tell them it was you, just some bitch I photographed."

There was pride and excitement in his voice, and it stirred something in her. It was dark, nasty, and wrong on every level, but she wanted more. She wanted to make him happy.

"I'm glad to be your hot bitch," she finally said, sliding her pink top up to reveal her breasts, still round and lovely even after having had a child. "Pinch me hard."

Sam complied, taking her nipples between his rough, callused fingertips and twisting as if he were turning a stuck cap on a ketchup bottle. He could feel her tense up in pain, and it aroused him. She reached down and grabbed his crotch, feeling the power of her own.

"Good girl," he said, twisting her harder.

"Yes, I am." Tears rolled down her face, and her knees buckled. "I'm a very good girl, Daddy."

He kissed her, his breath smoky and sweet from a beer he'd had with his friends.

"I want you to put it in me," she said, almost pleading.

"My bitch wants it bad?"

"Oh, yes," she said.

"Real bad?"

"Yes, Daddy, yes."

He took his hands off her breasts and smacked his palms against her shoulders, sending her backward into the counter. A dinner plate fell and shattered.

"Only *I* say when!"

She pulled herself up as their son, Max, entered the room.

"Mom, what happened?" he asked, looking first her, then at his father. "Dad?"

Sam turned away, and Melody gathered herself. "We're fine. Mommy just slipped. Dinner's ready in five minutes."

Max stood in the doorway for a beat and then went back to watching TV.

"Good, bitch," he said, his voice a whisper. "You know just what to do."

Melody Castile dreaded the encounter for more than a week. Her husband had rented a motel room in Tacoma a couple of exits south of the mall. She got a babysitter and had her hair done at the Gene Juarez Salon, a big splurge.

"I like your hair that way. Special occasion?" the sitter, a neighbor girl, asked as the couple was headed out the door.

"Any time with my husband is special," she said, feeling her heart beat a little faster under her blouse.

"When will you be home tomorrow?"

"Early afternoon. There's a frozen pizza you can fix for lunch."

The conversation was mundane, constructed on what had to be said. What was an acceptable bedtime? Which snacks were okay, and which were verboten. The conversation with the sitter was a part of the deception that had started to over-run their lives. Soon everything was a lie. What they did. Who they were doing it with.

Except for their love. That would always be grounded in truth. And fear.

She told herself over and over that it was like going out on a double date, except there would be three of them. He had promised that the guy was "clean" and "in good shape" and that "he thinks your pictures are hot."

His name was Paul. He was in his late thirties, divorced, no kids. He'd made the remark that swinging as a single would be a better use of his free time than trying to find another woman to settle down with. *Women are heartbreakers*, she sensed he was thinking, although she also sensed that he'd never ad-mitted to Sam or anyone that his heart *had* been broken.

Melody remembered little of the encounter, and what she did recall came to her in pieces like the colors of a kaleido-scope, moving, turning, never really fitting into any identifi-able shape. Her husband tied her up and took pictures as Paul penetrated her in every orifice. Repeatedly. After he could no longer maintain an erection, he used the neck of a champagne bottle that he'd brought along "to get us all in the mood." Sam put down the camera and let Paul take pho-tographs of her while he "tickled" her nipples with the tip of a hunting knife.

At one point Melody remembered looking down on her-self as one man straddled her, forcing his penis in her mouth, while the other entered her anally. She could not be sure which of the pair of sweaty men was her husband and which was their playmate. When the man ejaculated into her mouth, he rolled out of view. In a mirror over a cheap dresser, she could see her face, smeared makeup, puffy eyes, and a small river of tears.

"Take it, whore! Take it!"

When she woke up the next day, Paul was gone. Sam was next to her, spooning her naked body with his own.

"Fun last night," he said. His breath was hot on the nape of her neck, and she fought the urge to recoil.

Melody moved her head slightly, indicating her approval with a nod. But she swore to herself that she'd never do that again. How had it gone so far? How could this man who loved her so brutally violate her with another man? It was cruel. Scary. She would never get herself into that kind of a situation again. Not one in which *she* was the object of her husband's twisted fantasies.

If there were any more three-ways, there'd be a second woman.

And I don't care what happens to her, she thought. *So long as it isn't me and as long as it keeps my love happy.*

When he offered up an alternative scenario, she jumped at it.

"I was thinking," he said as she helped him shove a new chest freezer into a corner of the old mobile home. "Wouldn't it be hot if we, you know, caught someone?"

"'Caught?'"

"Yeah, you know, snagged some chick that we could play with together."

Melody's heart raced. "A woman?" she asked.

Her husband's eyes flashed that look that she knew better than anyone. It wasn't a question. It was a demand. "That's what I was thinking."

"I like it," she said. "Sounds like fun."

Melody Castile brought a bag of Nacho Doritos to pass the time by feeding the seagulls. She drove all over Kitsap County before finding herself on Olalla Valley Road in the very southern part of Kitsap County. Just after the Olalla Bay Bridge, she crossed the centerline and parked, her car facing traffic. If there was any. A young man sat in his pickup truck twenty yards ahead, his window cracked, smoke sliding out into the sea breeze. She opened the car door, found her footing on the rocks that edged the causeway, and ambled down to the water. She was alone. Her hands dipped into the Doritos bag, her fingertips turning orange. As if on cue, the birds came.

As they circled around her, pulling the DayGlo snack from her fingers, she winced at the pain.

The girl begging for her life.

The shadowy figure of a man as he penetrated a woman's severed head.

A baby crying for its mother.

The images that came to her mind were raw. They brought a visceral response that shocked and soothed her at the same time. The birds mistook her orange-colored fingertips and bit her. Blood rolled down her wrist.

The smell of sex and murder.

The taste of a man after he'd finished having sex with a dead girl.

The light that went out in a young woman's eyes as she tumbled into the depths of her terror.

Melody continued feeding the birds as a man with a clam bucket and shovel walked toward her.

"Hey, you okay?" he asked.

She didn't respond.

"Those birds are hurting you."

Snapped out of her thoughts, she turned toward the man.

"You all right?"

Melody's eyes were dilated and scarcely showed the recognition that another human being had asked her a question.

The man put down the bucket and shovel. "Seriously, you all right?"

The last of the Doritos were snatched by a particularly aggressive gray gull.

"Fine. Yes. Fine." She smiled at him. "Just lost in my thoughts, that's all."

Weeks passed and the temperatures dropped. Northwest rains came and turned maple leaves into a sodden mass. Detectives Kendall Stark and Josh Anderson felt the case of the so-called Kitsap Cutter grow cold. The FBI's famed Behavioral Science Unit was consulted, but offered up nothing more than what an avid viewer of *Forensic Files* could: the killer was a white male, in his late thirties to forties, and likely had someone who helped him either with the procurement or torture of his victims.

Kendall put it this way on an interdepartmental memorandum:

> There's no doubt he's a sexual sadist, but he's also scrupulously careful. We may be in the unfortunate position of waiting for someone to come forward or another victim to turn up.

Chapter Thirty-seven

December 10, 5:30 p.m.
Key Center

The voice on the phone spoke in husky, quiet notes. Serenity Hutchins had to strain to hear as she swiveled away from the TV playing in her apartment kitchen. She might have even hung up out of annoyance like she had with other callers to the paper.

She didn't this time.

"Too bad you don't have all the facts about my latest little project."

"You again? Just who are you?"

"Does it matter?"

"I think you should tell me who I'm talking to." With the phone pressed against her ear, she undid the latch to the dishwasher. The washing cycle stopped. But the damned TV was still playing in the background.

"Can you speak louder?" she asked.

"I could, but I don't want to wake the baby," he said, his voice still very low.

"Who are you?"

"I'm the one who knows the truth about the body in Little Clam Bay."

Serenity hadn't been on the job long, but she knew the ring of truth when she heard it. She popped the phone from her ear and looked at the Caller ID window. The code, like the other calls, indicated a calling card, not a phone number and a name.

"How is it that you know?" she asked.

"Do you need me to spell it out? Are you really as stupid of a bitch as you come across in the paper?"

She ignored the personal insult, and as far as insults go, it wasn't the worst aimed at her by a reader of the pages of the *Lighthouse*.

"I guess I am," she said. "I do need you to spell it out."

"I put her there."

Serenity felt the downy hairs on the back of her neck rise up. The man's voice was utterly emotionless. There was no reason to believe him, but neither was there any reason to dismiss what he was saying.

"Who are you?"

A short pause.

"Seriously, you think I'm going to tell you that?"

"What are you going to tell me?"

"I'm going to tell you how much the girl begged for mercy. I'm going to feed your nightmares for the rest of your life. Or I'm going to hang up and tell someone else. You choose."

Serenity reached for some paper in the drawer under the phone. She moved the ballpoint pen in cyclone curlicues over its surface, but it only scratched the paper. She reached for another, a red pen, and found success.

"Tell me."

Another short delay. She thought she heard someone talking in the background, but she was unsure if that was the caller's radio or TV.

"You'll ask no questions," he said.

"But that's my job."

"Or I'll tell someone else."

Serenity felt the flutter of fear, the kind that comes when making a deal with the devil. She didn't know it, but in a way that was exactly what she was doing.

Steven Stark strung the lights on eaves of their home. He'd used a combination of blue-and-white LED lights that seemed too dim to really do the job.

"Interesting, in a subtle kind of way," Kendall said. She had joined Steven and Cody on the driveway to get a better view.

"I know what you mean," Steven said. "I actually like the gigantic bulbs that my folks used to put up. Energy hogs, but they at least told the world that you'd bothered to decorate."

Cody's eyes traced the string of lights that his father had hung with the taut precision of a perfectionist.

"Pretty," he said, a broad smile over his face.

"I think so, too, baby," Kendall said.

The three went back inside the house with the promise of hot chocolate. The moment outside had been a welcome escape from the Christmas card that she'd received that day at the office. She hadn't opened it. She hadn't wanted to.

Now it was time.

The address was from Vancouver, British Columbia. Hornbeck was the last name.

While Steven poured milk into a saucepan, Kendall pulled the envelope from her purse and opened it.

The front was a picture of a Madonna and child. Inside was a message signed by Cullen Hornbeck. Two photographs were also enclosed. She read the message first:

I want to believe that you are doing your best to find out who killed Skye. It has been months since she was

found. I think of her every day. I want you to think of
her too.

The first photo was a picture of Skye with her father at
some kind of sporting event. They appeared to be laughing.
Her hand rested on his shoulder. On the back of the photo,
Cullen had written:

These are the memories that I wish were at the
forefront of my thoughts of my daughter.

The second photo was one of the images taken by the
teenage boys who'd found Skye's body while skipping school
that September. He wrote:

This is what I see every night in my dreams. Please
don't forget about her.

Kendall set down the card and photos, her eyes damp
with emotion.

"What is it, babe?" Steven asked.

She turned to Cody. "How about you get your jammies
on?"

Cody spun around and went down the hall to his bedroom.

"Skye's father," Kendall said, indicating the card. "But it
is more than Cullen. Tulio Pena. Donna Solomon. All of them.
All of them are facing the holiday without their loved ones
and no answers to let them rest in peace. This isn't right. We
have let them down."

"You haven't." He put his arms around her.

"I don't know what more we can do. The FBI has taken
its sweet time to tell us what we already know. We have a serial killer somewhere around here. He's a sexual sadist. We
know he lives somewhere in a fifty-mile radius, which means
Kitsap, King, Mason, and Pierce counties."

"And he's stopped killing," he said.

She shrugged slightly. "The last profiler we talked with said it was likely that he has moved from the area or . . . get this . . . is *taking a break*. Or it is possible that he's killed and we just haven't found the next body."

Cody came into the kitchen. He'd changed into his pajamas. Green tree frogs ran up and down his flannel legs.

"Hot chocolate is about ready," she said, looking at first at Steven, then at her son. "Let's find a book, and I'll read to you."

She tucked the photos back into the card and slid it under her purse.

What next? she asked herself.

Despite her best efforts, Kendall had come to grips with what most seasoned investigators of serial killers learn, piece by bloody piece. The perpetrator is only caught when he makes a stupid mistake.

It was only a matter of time. And yet, at the same time, that meant that someone else would have to die. Someone else would be made to suffer.

The voice on the end of the line was hauntingly familiar. It was husky, slightly modulated in a way that sounded as if he had been out for a run and was trying to rest up as he spoke.

"You fixing dinner for someone special tonight, Ms. Hutchins?"

She looked at her caller ID. The screen indicated: OUT OF AREA, PRIVATE.

"Who is this?" she asked. She was in her car about to unload her groceries when she picked up the phone. She turned off the engine and looked around.

"You know who it is," he said.

It was him.

"I'm going to call the sheriff."

"You mean that cop you've been screwing? Good for you. Call him, and you'll miss what I have to say to you."

Serenity rolled down her window and looked around the apartment complex parking lot. A little boy and his brother rolled past her on skateboards toward the play area. A girl walked her dog. There was no one else around. She looked in the backseat of her car, even though it was packed with groceries.

"What do you want?"

"Like all good boys, I want to play."

"You're sick."

He laughed. "That's what I'm told."

"I'm hanging up," Serenity said, although she didn't. She couldn't.

Silence on the other end.

"You still there?" she asked.

He laughed again. "I knew you'd want to hear more."

"What do you want to tell me?"

"I just wanted to give you a heads-up, that's all."

The phone went dead.

Chapter Thirty-eight

January 15, 1:25 p.m.
Olalla, Washington

It was a running joke in rural Kitsap County that if you ever wanted to get rid of something, just stick it off to the side of the road with a FREE sign: No matter what it was—hideous couch, broken lawn mower, TV console turned into an approximation of a minibar—it would be gone in the blink of an eye. It seemed that the southern end of the county was blessed with a good portion of the population who just couldn't pass up a bargain without tapping the brakes. Indeed, it was a kind of protocol to the disbursement of the unwanted. No one ever dumped anything at the makeshift free-for-all. People only took.

On the morning of January 15, Ken Saterlee set out two boxes of half-used interior paint and a few other odds and ends from a construction site that he'd worked the previous month as a "punch man." His wife hated the Sunshine Yellow color that he'd thought was a major score. By 10 A.M., after he returned from coffee, he noticed that there were *three* boxes next to his driveway off Willock Road, just south of Port Orchard near Olalla. The first two were the boxes he'd set out; the third was a medium-sized wooden container with a weathered brass fastener and hinges. It looked more decorative than functional, the kind of thing one might pick up at an import store. It was about ten inches tall and a foot wide.

He picked it up. It had something inside. Not expecting much of a treasure, Ken Saterlee figured someone had dropped off the box to take advantage of his FREE sign.

He opened the box and nearly vomited. Twenty minutes later, detectives from the Kitsap County Sheriff's Office were on the scene.

Inside the box was a human head.

Medical Examiner Birdy Waterman had hoped that the head would show up in her basement office sooner rather than later. She rescheduled the autopsy of a car-crash victim the minute she heard the missing piece of the Marissa Cassava case would be arriving. When it did, she took the box that the deputy coroner had ferried into the autopsy suite and set it on the smaller of the two stainless steel tables.

She was alone: her assistant was out with a bad sprain, and homicide detectives Kendall Stark and Josh Anderson were still combing the scene around Willock Road in search of anything they could turn up to help with the investigation. That morning, Dr. Waterman wore her hair up, twisting her thick black locks into a French braid. She planned on meeting a man she had once dated for drinks right after work. He was in Seattle on business. Birdy always considered him one of the good ones, one of the men she wished she'd tried harder to find a way to share her life with. But she hadn't back then. It was probably too late now. She'd never know. Judging by the hour, the head on the table would eat up the rest of the day and then some.

There would be no dinner that night with an old friend.

With nimble gloved fingertips, she opened the lid on the box. The reporting deputy had been correct when he said that it was an "antique-looking" container, not a real antique by any means. She fully expected that when she flipped it over it would say, MADE IN INDONESIA or MADE IN CHINA.

She looked down. "Hello, Marissa," she said. "What in the world did he do to you?"

Gently, she lifted the head and set it on the table. The woman's brown eyes were staring upward, open, blank in their gaze. Her hair had broken off in patches on the side of her head. The pathologist rotated the head almost sweetly, the way a person might pick up a small animal. Not wanting to hurt it. The eyes looked right at her.

Dr. Waterman ran her light over the face, looking for signs of trauma, fibers, fingerprints, anything that might help tell the story of the Kitsap Cutter's third victim. She swabbed the mouth for semen and other biologicals.

Everything looked so clean. So pristine. She wondered how the head could have stayed so preserved, so perfect. Her answer came when she used her temperature probe to record the temperature of the head. It was a routine task in any autopsy, although usually the coroner took the liver temp to determine how long the victim had been dead.

"Forty-four degrees," she said to herself, recording the information on a chart. The temperature outside exceeded that by five degrees.

Next, she took a closer look at the neck, paying particular attention to the condition of the vertebra. The head had been removed from the body with surgical precision. A clean slice that matched perfectly with the body that she'd processed the previous year.

She had hoped to find some tool marks cut into the bone that might indicate what had been used for the decapitation. Serrated blade? Hunting knife? A piece of evidence that might point to the killer had eluded her when she examined the body.

Again, nothing. So very clean.

A butcher? A skilled hunter? A doctor? she wondered. *Or someone just quick, strong, and maybe lucky enough to sever the head from the body in a clean, swift hack?*

The tissue where the head had been severed was clean, like a piece of washed meat. No blood. No fluids whatsoever. It was dry, the way human flesh can sometimes resemble beef jerky.

Birdy Waterman knew the head had been stored somewhere, cared for, maybe even used in some ritualistic manner. It had been a trophy, but ultimately it was discarded with some junk.

She lifted the covering over Marissa Cassava's body—frozen since its recovery at Anderson Point—and reunited it with her head. It took her back to the reservation when she and her friends would swap Barbie doll heads, ditching the blonde for the one with the dark hair, the one that somewhat resembled them. She inched up the fabric, thinking about the young woman with a baby waiting at home, and how someone, *something*, undeniably evil had done this to her.

Her mask on, goggles in place, she turned on the Stryker saw she used to cut into the skull. Despite the saw's superb air filter, bone dust blew through the air and onto the pathologist's protective gear. To some, the noise was the most hideous sound imaginable, but to Dr. Waterman it was the sound of getting to the truth.

Inside the cranium, blood sparkled like tiny shards of rubies. Still frozen.

As she wrapped things up, she returned her attention to the wooden box. She flipped it over and smiled: A WAL-MART EXCLUSIVE MADE IN CHINA.

She pulled off her gloves and washed up. A quick phone call later, and the homicide detectives were on their way.

Chapter Thirty-nine

January 15, 3:25 p.m.
Port Orchard

Kendall Stark and Josh Anderson stood in the morgue, looking at the reassembled head and body as Birdy Waterman rolled back a sheet. They'd come directly from Willock Road, Kendall's shoes still muddy from an unfortunate slip in a ditch.

"I know you've seen a lot of things come across your autopsy table, but really, Birdy, this has to be one for the ages," she said. "It makes me sick."

"Yeah, remind me not to eat dinner," Josh said.

Kendall looked at Josh. "I'll remind you that this is someone's daughter."

Dr. Waterman couldn't let the moment pass without her own retort. "And *I'll* remind you that the victims' support group is doing another round of sensitivity training, Detective. You might want to get in on it."

"I'm just saying what comes to me."

"That's the problem," the pathologist said.

The forensic pathologist led the detectives toward the body on the table.

She pulled on a pair of gloves. "I'm disgusted and intrigued at the same time. Usually I'm merely heartbroken and disgusted. No one who comes to see me comes for a social visit," she said.

Kendall nodded. Point made. She braced herself as the sheet was pulled back to reveal the sum of what had been Marissa Cassava. The open eyes were so unnerving that Kendall immediately understood why people take the time to shut them when someone dies.

"Do you know if she was alive when she was—"

"If you're asking me if she was alive during decapitation, I can tell you she wasn't."

Kendall nodded. "Thank you. I know I should be desensitized to some things but, really, this was the most brutal thing I could imagine."

"You don't want to be desensitized, Detective. Your emotions are a gift. Your feelings are all about compassion. That's why you're so good with victims."

"The living ones, you mean."

"Yes, of course."

Josh looked at the face. "What more can you tell us about her?"

The pathologist allowed her eyes to wander over the detectives as she started to talk. "A couple of things. The head was kept below freezing. I did a temp check, and then when I examined the brain, I found ice crystals."

It took Kendall a second to wrap her mind around that. The obvious seemed incomprehensible, beyond evil.

"So you're thinking the killer kept the head in the freezer?" Josh asked. "This isn't like some cannibal move, is it?"

"No, not exactly. I mean, if it was a 'cannibal move,' as you call it, then I expect he would have eaten it."

Kendall didn't understand. "Then why did he freeze it?"

"Just a guess here, but it's been written about in the literature. He kept it for one of two reasons. One, he thought of it as a trophy."

Josh piped up. "Jeffrey Dahmer kept some body parts that he didn't eat because he wanted to be close to the victim."

"The other reason, Birdy?" Kendall asked

Birdy took a second to search for the right words.

"This is very troubling, but when I swabbed her mouth for biologicals, semen specifically, I drew a blank. Nothing in the pockets of the mouth that usually hold such things. But when I went in as deep as I could go down her throat, I found the presence of semen. I think that whoever kept the head used it as some kind of grotesque sex toy."

Kendall's mind lurched at the hideous possibility that the killer had used the open mouth of his dead victim for sex. *Did he hold the head? Did someone else hold it? Did he thrust his hips to create enough friction to ejaculate, or did he lift the head up and down?*

It turned her stomach.

"This makes me sick," she finally said.

"You're not alone."

"Thank you," Kendall said, appreciating that Birdy Waterman didn't disrespect her for her feelings but instead thought they made her a better investigator. She knew that later when she discussed Birdy's findings with Josh, she'd have to describe everything in a detached, cool manner. If Josh made some disgusting joke, she'd have to slough it off.

"Are you going to release the body for burial?" Kendall asked.

Birdy nodded slightly as she scanned the report she'd compiled. "I have a few more tests, but I expect to be done tonight."

"DNA?"

"Off to the state crime lab."

"What can I tell her mother?"

"Tell her what you feel is best. She doesn't need to know

about the sex-toy aspect right now. If—*when*—we catch the perp, she'll need to know then."

"Agreed."

Kendall looked at Josh. Her eyes were cool, and there was no trace of emotion on her face.

"Josh, can you keep your mouth shut on this? I mean, can you keep it out of the paper?"

Josh jabbed a finger at Kendall. "I'm getting tired of you putting the blame on me! There's no way that I've leaked anything. My private life is just that, my *private* life."

Only once did Serenity truly cross the line, and she knew that by telling Josh the truth, she'd risk everything. By then it was more than her credibility as a news reporter. She could live with that. But she'd also fallen a little for Josh. He had an oversized ego and a kind of obnoxious charm when he was "on," but when it was just the two of them, he seemed genuine. A decent guy. Certainly a bit of a father figure, but not so much that it felt creepy to be attracted to him.

"Look," Josh said, "people are talking about us, and I'm not sure where we stand."

"'Where we stand'?" she asked. "I don't get your meaning. At least, I'm hoping that I'm reading too much into the remark."

Josh shook his head. "No. No, I didn't mean that. We're casual, right?"

"As casual as I can be without being easy," she said.

"Right. I think," he said, letting a smile come to his face. "The problem isn't us but what Kendall and the others are saying."

"What? That I'm sleeping with you to get a break on the Cutter?"

"Basically."

"That's funny. That's really funny, Josh. You know that's not what this is about."

He stared at her. "I know. I just had to say it. I just can't have you put anything in the paper about the case that comes from me. Okay?"

"Nothing will come from you," Serenity said. "Promise."

After they'd made love and he drifted off to sleep, Serenity slipped out of bed, put on one of Josh's robes, and quietly made her way to his home office down the hallway. A rope light tucked behind the crown molding guided her steps with a wash of faint blue light. Josh had insisted that the lighting feature was some wonderful upgrade, but Serenity thought it was cheesy, like something in a sandwich shop or around a movie theater food concession. He'd mentioned earlier in the evening that he'd brought home some case files, including Dr. Waterman's autopsy report.

Her eyes immediately went to the toxicology report. Four flecks of red lead-based paint had been found in the dead woman's vagina.

Pigment is consistent with paint produced in the
U.S. in the 1940s, pre-awareness of the dangers of lead
toxicity. Paint fragments show a 20-degree curve
consistent with adherence to a dowel.

Serenity felt a flush of fear from the realization that the most evil of men actually had whispered in her ear. The caller had known what he was talking about. He'd told Serenity that he'd used "Grandma's rolling pin" as a sex toy. The idea of it disgusted her, but the gleeful manner in which the caller recounted the story made her hang on every word. Words alone, she knew, didn't always convey the message.

. . . *and she loved it. I called her my sweet pie-hole. She was a hot one . . . too bad she didn't last as long as she could have. I thought she had a lot more fun in her . . .*

"Serenity," Josh called from the bedroom. His voice was sleepy and sexy, but it shook her nevertheless. "Don't make me come and get you," he said.

Serenity shut the file folder and shoved it back into Josh's black leather briefcase.

Two days later, the *Lighthouse* published its latest scoop, this time in the form of a Tad Stevens op-ed piece:

The Unthinkable: Vic Raped by Foreign Object

The editorial was over the top in the righteous indignation that newspapers sometimes employ, when in reality they are courting eyeballs on their inky pages; if they didn't want to inflict further injury to the victims' families, they wouldn't publish the salacious details. Stevens attributed the detail about rape with a foreign object to insiders handling the investigation, a vague reference that left Sheriff Jim McCray and his investigative team scurrying once more to plug the leak.

Stevens ended the piece with a clarion call for justice: "Someone out there is doing unspeakable evil and he must be stopped. If you have any leads, call this paper or the Sheriff's Office."

The Sheriff's Office seemed like an afterthought.

The afternoon that the editorial ran in the paper, Serenity Hutchins took another phone call. Serenity was standing in line at a sandwich shop on Bay Street when she answered PRIVATE CALLER.

"Your publisher really laid it on the line," the caller said. "Big, tough, pointy-nosed nerd calling for justice."

It was the same strange voice.

"Turn yourself in," she said, for the first time conceding—at least to him—that someone's life was worth more than a shot at the big time.

"I enjoy what I'm doing," he said. "Why would I stop now?"

"Because what you're doing is . . ." her words trailed off. Serenity wanted to say *evil* or *deplorable* or something that really drove the point home, but those adjectives felt insufficient.

"You're at a loss for words," he said.

"No, I'm not."

"I can't think of a single reason to stop killing," he said. "Canoe?"

The phone went dead.

"Salami grinder?" the man behind the sandwich prep counter said.

She nodded. Her bones felt chilled. She wondered if she had heard the voice of the killer correctly.

Did he say "Can you?" or "Canoe?"

PART FOUR
Carol

*Have you ever felt the ice of a blade as it plays
in the wetness between your legs? I have.*

—FROM A VOICE MESSAGE LEFT FOR SERENITY

Chapter Forty

If there is a neighborhood of distinction in South Kitsap, most would consider it to be McCormick Woods, on the eastern edge of Port Orchard. It was an enormous development of rambling acreage surrounding a golf course and dotted with an eclectic mix of custom homes that showcased dreams, sometimes at the expense of good taste. Look here: a Mediterranean villa. Over there: a Craftsman-style monstrosity. Next door: a block-stretching rambler built for older people who disdain stairs.

The Godding place was an Italian-styled affair with stucco and archways that were meant to inspire oohs and aahs from the architecturally challenged folks who drove by, wishing they'd be able to get a peek at the interior.

Unfortunately, the grandeur of the house's exterior was a cover-up for the heartbreak that resided there.

In fact, Carol Godding's birthday present from her husband the previous year was her abandonment. Dan Godding, a former Kitsap County Commissioner, left Carol, the house, the dog, and everything they owned when he drained the couple's liquid assets and moved to central Florida with his high school sweetheart. A plucky woman, Carol sucked it up (as her ex likely knew she would), kept current on the mortgage, and started to sell off everything that reminded her of Dan. She'd worked her way through most of the items in the garage: tools, a decrepit Porsche that Dan was going to restore, and a golf cart. Next on her hit list were the sporting goods—hers *and* his. That week she listed on Craigslist a canoe that had been a favorite of hers. Dan had refused to take the classes at the South Kitsap High School pool. He just didn't see the purpose of paddling when he could use a powerboat.

Later, when hurt turned to anger, Carol saw that as a watershed moment. How could she love a man who thought the loud noise of a powerboat was preferable to quietly gliding through the water in a canoe?

She downloaded a photo showing her canoeing on the protected waters of Sinclair Inlet, not far from McCormick Woods. In the photograph she looked younger than her years in a chartreuse polar fleece vest and hat, smiling from ear to ear as she held up her paddle as if to say "I did it!"

Sam Castile was among the first of a half dozen callers.

"Saw your ad," he said. "Is the canoe still available?"

"I think so. I had some lookers earlier today. Said they'd be back."

"My son and I are in the area. Would it be convenient if we came by?"

"Now?'

"I can be there in ten minutes."

Carol looked at the time. She'd been planning on making a Sunday Costco run before the day got away from her. But she wanted to get rid of that canoe. As much as she loved it, she was determined to downsize everything from her old life, sell the house, and get out of the neighborhood, where she had never wanted to live in the first place.

She gave him the address.

"I'll be waiting. What's your name?"

"Rick Davis," he said. "See you in a few."

The human body is a cocoon of skin. No matter the color, the condition, the age, the membrane that stretches over the bony frame of a person's skeleton and musculature is the key to understanding the demise of so many. A knife. A box cutter. The shattered neck of a beer bottle. All had been deployed by those who seek to do harm. Kendall had seen the evil that men—and even an occasional woman—do with the sharp edge of a tool meant to slice the cocoon that holds a person together. Skin was so fragile, like a tissue paper cover on a drum; it could be punctured by the prick of a sharp tool.

She twirled through the autopsy photos on the CD that Dr. Waterman had burned and sent over. In total, there were more than 400 images, all gruesome and tragic as they told the story of what happened. Skye's skin was chalky white. The gash that severed her carotid artery was more than an inch wide, the tissue pushing out like the screaming lips of a clown, red, full. On her back in the vicinity of her shoulder blades were two large puncture wounds, narrow at the top like a pair of inverted keyholes. The young woman had been hung like a deer carcass and left to bleed out. The county's forensic pathologist indicated that the killer had done a thorough job. She'd had lost around two pints of blood in her body—one fifth of the volume of a woman of her weight.

Wounds postmortem [Dr. Waterman had written in her notes]. *The wound on the left is a quarter-inch larger, shows some hesitation. Serrated blade. The wound on the right is crisper, cleaner. It is possible that*

*perpetrator of these postmortem injuries gained
confidence as he gained experience. There is one bit
of caution here. The angle of the second cut is about
twenty degrees different than the first. This kind of
differential suggests the possibility that the same
person did not make both cuts.*

Kendall looked at the photograph that Dr. Waterman had
referenced with that last point. The angle change was not
visible in the photo. An idea rolled around in her thoughts.
Was there a pair of killers? There was a kind of timidness
suggested by one of the perpetrators. There was also the idea
that Marissa's face had been enhanced, likely in death, with
makeup.

Was one a woman?

Like all who vanish, Carol Godding had no idea that it was
the day of her disappearance. When she laid her clothes on
her freshly made bed, she was unsure if the brown slacks
really could be worn with the foggy-blue top that the sales-
woman at the Tacoma Mall Nordstrom had insisted was "to
die for." It just didn't look right, and she was unsure if the
old trick of trying to tie the outfit together with accessories
was really going to work. She put on blue jeans and a sweater
instead, facing the mirror over the antique pecan-wood bu-
reau that had belonged to her grandmother. She set a couple
of necklaces out and held them to her throat one at a time.
The first, a chunky gold link that was supposed to be Italian
in design, had been purchased by her mother from QVC.

Not working for me, she said to herself, setting the chain
down. She held up a strand of blue and brown beads that had
a far more inspiring origin. She'd purchased them herself the
summer before when she traveled to Peru with her best
friend, Connie.

Former best friend, she thought, fastening the lobster-claw clasp and refusing to revisit the incident that had shredded their bond. Over a man, no less. She gave herself one more look in the mirror and shook her head.

This is as good as I'm going to get with this ensemble.

"I see you beat me to it," Gary Wyatt said, watching the man and his young son try to hoist the yellow canoe into the back of his long-bed pickup.

Sam Castile spun around and slapped on a quick smile.

"Yeah, your loss," he said. "Early bird, all that stuff."

Gary, a sandy-haired grandfather of six, shrugged as he lumbered over to the rear of the truck.

"Can I give you a hand?" he said, his eyes lingering on the prize that he'd missed out on.

Max Castile stepped back so the older man could help.

"Sure. Bought a bunch of other stuff too."

The inside of the canoe was covered with a brown plastic tarp. Gary bent at his knees and started to lift.

"Jesus, did you buy some bricks or what?"

Sam laughed. "Something like that. Some old cinder blocks she had out back."

"Oh. She said she was selling as much of her ex-husband's stuff as she could. Wonder what else she has left."

The canoe was now in the back of the truck, and Sam ran a nylon rope from hooks on either side of the tailgate through a steel loop on the end of the boat.

"She's gone," he said. "Took off for church or something. Took the money and ran."

"Just my luck," Gary said.

Sam turned to his son. "Ready to go, buddy?"

Max, who hadn't said a word, nodded like a bobblehead.

"Thanks for the help. Nice to know there are still good people in Port Orchard."

"No worries. Have fun with the canoe."

Sam waved as he pulled away slowly, watching Gary as he went back to his car.

It was Carol Godding's sixty-two-year-old *Kitsap Sun* paperboy who noticed that something was wrong. Three days worth of *Sun*s crammed the bright blue plastic paper tube affixed below Carol's mailbox. He remembered how she'd mentioned she was heading to Southern California for a few weeks and figured he'd got the dates wrong. He pulled out the newspapers and put them in the backseat of his car. Next he called her number and left a message.

"Ms. Godding, call me when you get back to town. I'll start up the paper lickety-split."

Several days passed, and no one else noticed she was gone. The Goddings had not fostered ideal relations with their neighbors. Dan had waged war with the people on both sides over a wall of prolific Leyland cypresses that he'd planted to create some privacy but ultimately blocked others' views of the golf course.

Carol had apologized for the less-than-neighborly attitude of her husband and tried to make amends. But by then battle lines had been drawn, and she was considered to be a bitch married to an asshole. It was a stigma that, despite her kind and outgoing nature, she couldn't shake. When she volunteered at the community garage sale to raise money for the Port Orchard food bank, she got the cold shoulder from the women in charge. As a result, no one cared enough about Carol to notice if something was amiss.

There were no second chances in McCormick Woods.

Kirsten Potts was called "The Enforcer" or "The Landscaping Nazi" behind her back. Kirsten didn't care. In fact, when she first heard of the moniker she only feigned indignation.

To her, backbiting and fear brought results. She lived in Mc-Cormick Woods because she liked the orderliness of a neighborhood with strict covenants. She wasn't really supposed to patrol the streets of the development, looking for bushes that needed to be trimmed or lawns that needed to be mowed. She'd been told several times by the homeowners association president that they were "not to seek out infractions like a police force but to wait for neighbors to bring things to our attention."

Kristen didn't care. She routinely drove around McCormick Woods with a camera, a ruler, and a wary eye. She'd been watching the Godding place for the past week. The Goddings had been on her radar for years after the Leyland cypress brouhaha, but they'd kept the place in tiptop condition. Lawn edged. Pines trimmed poodle perfect. The fountain in front never foamy. She'd heard gossip about the Goddings from the committee after Carol started writing the homeowners' dues from a new account. Dan's car was gone too.

The yard was looking shaggier and shaggier, and Kirsten Potts decided action was the order of the day. She rang the bell; no answer. She knocked as loudly as her tight little fist could pound.

She leaned close to the sidelight next to the door, but the house was quiet. She went around to the garage, noticing the sorry state of the lawn.

Jeesh! Talk about letting a place go to seed! she thought.

Kirsten Potts didn't consider herself a snoop. Snoops almost never do. She felt an urge to try the side door to the garage. She turned the knob and pushed it open. When she stepped inside, she immediately knew something terrible had happened there.

She opened her phone and called 911.

Chapter Forty-one

Kendall Stark ate alone at a small café in downtown Port Orchard. She'd brought a salad Steven had made the night before but had left it in the car. Now it was a soggy mess. The café was no great shakes, but it gave her a moment to think. She watched a woman across the room cut her daughter's hamburger into small pieces while she talked on a cell phone. The girl was about fifteen and obviously impaired. She sat hunched over her plate while her mother did her duty.

Poor girl. Maybe cerebral palsy? Kendall was unsure. But what struck her was how the mother just went on and on with her phone conversation, cutting the food as if her child were not present. She was grateful for Cody, happy that despite her son's problems they were connected. They had a bond. He might not be the son of her dreams, but she'd learned to love every minute they shared. The realization had come slowly.

Her phone vibrated. She set down her fork and answered

a call from Josh. It soon became clear that the apple pie she had ordered, which the waitress had said was the best in the county, was going to go uneaten.

"I'm way up north in Kingston," he said. "We've got a deputy out at McCormick Woods on a call, Kendall, but since you're not far, can you check it out?"

She took down an address in McCormick Woods.

Kendall Stark surveyed the interior of the Godding garage. There was a pegboard with outlines of various tools, most of which were missing. Carol's car, a dark blue Lexus, was in perfect condition. In the space next to the car was what had caught Kirsten Potts's attention. In the middle of the concrete floor was Carol's dog, a Doberman named Dolly.

Someone had taken hedge loppers and sheared off the dog's head.

A pool of dried blood fanned out over the concrete floor. The dog's decomposing head was separated from its body by about four feet. A rope apparently had been used to choke the dog before it was decapitated. Kendall recorded the scene with pictures and measurements. She sketched out what she was seeing and phoned Animal Control to come get the dog.

A few neighbors had gathered in the driveway, a self-satisfied Kirsten Potts in the center of the group. They seemed to seize the moment to do some neighborhood kibitzing. One woman brought up the subject of the new menu at Mary Mac's, the clubhouse restaurant, and how it didn't offer enough vegetarian options.

"Honestly," said the woman, whose earlobes were stretched into pendulums of flesh by a pair of too-heavy earrings, "the management there seems more focused on cutesy golf-inspired names for their menu items than what they serve there. A Par Four Omelet—come on!"

Kirsten didn't appreciate that the conversation was being diverted from her, so she ignored the vegetarian complaint.

"I was worried about the condition of her yard," she told a woman in black stretch pants and a red plaid jacket. "I never thought their dog was much of a problem."

Kendall approached the group, and they fell silent.

"Here comes the detective," Kirsten said.

"Does anyone know how we can reach Ms. Godding?" she asked. "Do you know where she works?"

Plaid Jacket shrugged. "I heard that she looked for a job after her husband left her. Couldn't find anything in her field, whatever it was. I didn't know her well."

A truck from animal control pulled up, and the group watched two men go inside the garage.

"She was selling a lot of stuff online," said Kirsten, proving herself to be the neighborhood know-it-all.

A retired commander from the Navy who lived next door spoke up.

"She told me that she was going to visit friends or relatives down south. She wasn't too explicit, and I didn't ask. She traveled a lot."

Kendall took down the man's name and phone number.

"So the consensus here is that Ms. Godding is on vacation."

Kirsten piped up. "If you're leaving for more than three days, you're required to alert the HOA."

"Her ex never followed the rules, either," Big Earrings said.

The animal control officers emerged a moment later carrying the dog's corpse in a thick plastic wrapping.

Kendall made sure the garage door was locked. She noticed a large water bowl on the patio. It was elevated in a metal frame, a glossy white ceramic dish decorated with coal-black paw prints and Dolly's name. Wind chimes in the shape of silvery dog bones spun on a chain from the eaves. That dog was loved, Kendall thought. If Carol Godding was going out of town for more than three hours, she likely wouldn't have left Dolly alone. She got in her car and drove back to the office, leaving a group of deputies to cordon off the site.

Josh had been working the case from another angle, and Kendall needed to know what he had found out.

Carol Godding had been dumped by her husband, and by all accounts she'd gotten over it—at least, as much as any woman can when the man she loves with all her heart drops the bomb. Until that moment Carol had fooled herself into thinking that she was happy. She was middle-aged and facing the prospect of starting over.

Kendall's examination of the Godding residence pretty much told the story. The refrigerator was stocked with flavored waters and diet salad dressings. The guest bedroom had been heaped with things that her husband had left behind: engineering books, workout clothes, and CDs by rock bands that hadn't been relevant for two decades. The front room was mostly empty of furniture, which had been replaced by a dozen cardboard boxes that held housewares, linens, and books. The boxes weren't completely full.

When Josh told Kendall that he'd learned from the neighbors that Carol had participated in the McCormick Woods neighborhood garage sale, the state of the home's disarray made sense.

"Did you see the stack of garage sale signs by the back door?"

Kendall nodded.

"She was on the committee for last week's big sale. Her job was to put up and take down the signage. One of the neighbors asked for them, and I didn't see any harm, so I let her take them."

"I thought the neighbors didn't care for Carol."

"Her husband. They hated *him*."

"I see."

"Seriously, I don't think the woman who asked for the

signs cared much about anything other than getting the signs back. She's having her own sale next door on Saturday. She's worried that our missing-persons case will bring out the lookie loos."

Kendall shook her head. "Kill me before I ever move into one of those subdivisions. Promise me, okay?"

Josh grinned. "Deal."

Steven Stark had used the afternoon to split wood from a cherished madrona that had died two summers before. Madronas were red-barked trees native to the Northwest that were striking in form and color. Anyone who had one growing in his yard felt lucky. The Starks had only one, and Kendall had cried when it started to die limb by limb, all of its characteristic waxy green leaves turning bronze. The wood had cured, making it easier to split. Easier, but not easy: Madronas are a dense hardwood, known to bend a penny nail.

Sweat bloomed under Steven's arms and ran from his temples as he hoisted and swung a sharpened ax into the heart of each piece of wood. Cody sat on the swing in the backyard not really watching his father but seemingly captivated by thoughts in his head that he'd never be able to share.

"Hi, you two," Kendall said, emerging from inside the house. She was wearing dark gray slacks with a blouse of sea-foam green that she had put on that morning. Despite the long day, she looked lovely. Her cropped blond hair caught the late-afternoon light, almost making it glow. She kissed Cody and gave his swing a gentle push before planting a kiss on Steven's sweaty lips.

"You taste like salt," she said.

Steven smiled at her. Their eyes locked.

"You taste like honey." He set the ax down. Behind him was a mountain of evidence that he'd been hard at work.

"Long day," he said. "For you too."

Kendall sat down on the swing next to their son. "An incident out at McCormick Woods today." She looked at Cody; his gaze was fixed on a small flock of Canada geese overhead. She wouldn't give any details.

"I'm worried," was all she could say.

Steven knew what that meant. Kendall could be completely poker-faced during an interrogation, but not with those she loved. She had a face that invited those who loved her to see the need for comfort. Later that night, with Cody asleep, she would tell her husband about the dead dog and the missing woman.

She'd even use the words that had been the invention of the *Lighthouse* news staff:

Has the Cutter struck again?

Ultimately she dismissed it. Carol was not a young woman. She didn't have anything in common with the others. On the surface, she was a professional woman of some means. Skye was a free-spirit wannabe; Celesta was a food service worker and brush picker; Marissa was a prostitute.

There was very little reason to carry on without his daughter, and Cullen Hornbeck had considered becoming one of those tragic statistics that make the TV news now and then: the one that sadly reminds the world that it is too painful for many parents to outlive their children, that when the rhythm of life is disrupted to such a degree, only death, it seems, can salve the wounds.

Skye had been dead and buried for months, and there was no getting over it. When Cullen logged on to his computer to compose a suicide note, he ran through some of the old e-mails that she had sent him. His heart ached with the loss and memory of his beautiful little girl.

He hadn't told anyone they had argued the day before she left. Skye had told him in no uncertain terms that her life was her own and that her college degree would always be there for her, like a savings plan for rainy day.

"But I won't always be young, Dad. I want to do something other than what you and Mom see for me. I don't know what it is, but I'll know it when I see it."

He had told her she was ungrateful. The next day she was gone.

As he rolled though his e-mails, he noticed that his spam filter was full. He opened the file and, one by one, started deleting the unwanted offers of sex, larger breasts, and a bigger penis. Near the list's end was a two-meg file—too large for the settings of his free e-mail account.

It was from Skye, sent the day *after* she disappeared.

He clicked on it.

The message was brief.

> Dad, Don't worry about me. Don't be mad. I'm going to do what you always told me you wanted me to do: be myself. I'll call you tomorrow.
> Love, S

The e-mail included a large, uncompressed photograph. Cullen clicked on the image, and slowly the pixels found focus and a picture filled his computer screen. It showed Skye standing on the deck of a Washington State Ferry, the cloud-laden Seattle skyline in the background. She had a big smile on her face and a backpack slung over her shoulder. She was wearing a red hoodie, halfway unzipped. Around her neck was the sterling silver yin-and-yang necklace that her mother had made for her when she graduated from high school. Not only did the sight of his daughter looking at the lens with a smile on her face bring tears to his eyes, it brought him newfound resolve. There would be time to be together in heaven. But not yet.

He forwarded the e-mail to the two women who seemed to care most about his daughter's fate; neither woman was Skye's mother.

Cullen tapped out a short note:

Just found this. . . . She made it to Bremerton. . . . Please find
my daughter's killer. She said she'd call me "tomorrow"—
there was no tomorrow for Skye.—CB

Kendall Stark opened Cullen Hornbeck's e-mail on an office
computer and deliberated on the photograph while Josh looked
over her shoulder.

"She was a beautiful girl," Josh said, as if such a remark
had anything to do with the reason they were viewing the
last known image of the Cutter's second victim.

"Notice something?" Kendall asked.

"One thing jumps out, for sure." He pointed to the name
of the vessel, visible on a flotation device in the foreground.
It was familiar to most native western Washingtonians. "She
was on the *Walla Walla*, which means she made it to Bremerton."

Kendall nodded. "Also, look: she's not wearing the green
blouse she had on when we found her body in Little Clam
Bay. That can only mean she either changed her outfit that
day—not likely—or she was picked up by someone after she
got off the boat."

Josh processed what Kendall had said. "Not only that," he
said. "She promised to call her dad the next day, which we
know she never did. Look at the time stamp on the photo. It
was Sunday."

It was not a night for eighties music. Her cat, Mr. Smith, at
her feet and the sounds of a Seattle classical music station
filling the apartment, Serenity Hutchins went about the task
of checking her e-mail before calling it a night. She resisted the
urge to Twitter, or log on to Facebook. Those were extras after
a long day. E-mail, however, was just part of staying connected
with those friends and family members who really mattered.

She had twenty messages in her in-box, but skipped the others in favor of Cullen Hornbeck's. She talked to him at least once a week, and for a while, early on in the case, they had traded e-mails daily. But their contact had dwindled, and it pained her.

The picture of Skye on the ferry appeared, and she felt a lump in her throat. Skye was such a beautiful girl, and if Cullen was correct, this image had to have been taken not long— hours, maybe—before she died. She wanted to write back with a request to publish the photograph in the paper. She stopped herself. Partly because it was opportunistic and she knew it. But there was another reason. The pendant around the dead girl's neck jolted her a little.

She'd seen someone wearing one just like it.

She clicked on the zoom feature and expanded her view. Around Skye's neck was a silver charm. It was a familiar design, the ancient Chinese symbol of the connection between opposing forces. Good and evil. Light and dark. Laughter and tears. And while its design was common, its construction was unique.

It was silver and black, with the silver part hammered with a hundred tiny dents. Both of the swirls were accented by a diamond.

Chapter Forty-two

February 4, 9:40 p.m.
Bremerton

Pillow talk was always the surest way to get a good scoop. As Serenity Hutchins lay next to Josh Anderson, it crossed her mind that she was using him as much as he was using her. Her youth, her figure, and the pleasure that he gained from being with her were undeniable. He kept saying so. As the light crept across his features while he stared into her eyes, she noticed that he was pleading in a way. It was gross. It was demeaning.

And yet, there she was.

"You feel like going out to eat?" he asked, rolling closer to her on the bed. "Or we could see what's in the fridge. I'm a pretty good cook, babe."

"Sounds good," she lied.

Josh propped his head up on her pillow. She could feel his foot caress her.

"Which?"

"Let's stay in."

Serenity knew that what she had been doing was wrong. It was wrong on every level imaginable. She could hear the girls at the paper whisper about how she "slept with her source." Charlie Keller would probably say something inane like "you gotta do what you gotta do," as if there could be some excuse for her behavior. She didn't want the people she knew in town to see her out with Josh Anderson and make judgments about her.

Even though they would be correct.

"Let me cook for you," she said. "You've had a tough day."

"They're all tough," he said, planting his feet on the floor and reaching for a robe slung on the back of a chair.

"What happened over at McCormick Woods this afternoon?"

He looked at her, sizing her up a little, wondering if she only cared about what he could tell her. Not about him. Deep down he knew the answer, and for a beat he felt deflated. It was no longer about how handsome he was, how sexy he was, how charming he could be. A pretty young woman like Serenity Hutchins, he figured, was either looking for money or a father figure. With his string of bad marriages and poor financial decisions, money was not the reason she was attracted to him. As for being a father figure, he knew that she had some unresolved family issues. His own relationship with his son was likely the best measure that he was hardly a paragon of fatherhood.

It was about what he could tell her.

The sex was good, and whatever she was really doing there in his bed seemed a fair tradeoff. She made him feel younger, virile. She made him think that he could still catch the eye of a pretty girl, even when she was clearly using him.

"You're asking about Godding, correct?"

Serenity tucked a towel around her lithe body, her breasts compressed by the fabric. "I never got the name. I just heard there was something strange going on in Kitsap's version of Stepford."

"Whatever I tell you will be in the paper, right?"

"You know the rules. You tell me. I write it."

They walked into the kitchen of his Bremerton view condo and swung open the door of his stainless-steel refrigerator. The interior held an array of Styrofoam takeout boxes: Chinese, Italian, and something so far gone that it could be either.

"I hate leftovers," he said, scanning the shelves. "Always bring 'em home, but never eat 'em."

She wrapped her arms around him from behind and leaned over so she could see past him.

"Eggs are good. I make a pretty good omelet. Cheese in there?"

He nodded and fished around in the refrigerator.

"So while I whisk, you tell me what's going on at McCormick Woods."

Josh sat down at the kitchen bar. "We're not really sure," he said. "Kendall went out there on the call. One of the neighbors, a real busybody, wanted to give the resident in question the 'what for' for not maintaining her yard and made, as you reporters like to write, a 'grisly discovery.'"

Serenity turned on the blue flame of the range. A pat of butter hit the skillet and started to melt.

"Yes, we do love *grisly*."

The pan started to smoke a little, and she lowered the flame.

"What did she find? I mean, if it was the homeowner, you'd have sent out a press release."

Josh nodded. "A dead dog."

"A dog."

"Not just. Even worse. A decapitated dog."

Serenity poured the yellow egg mixture into the hot pan. "You're kidding? That's awful. What happened?"

"We don't know. Some freak, I guess. Maybe the dog barked

too much and another McCormick resident decided to shut Rover up permanently."

As the eggs began to set up, she sprinkled from a pouch of pre-shredded Tillamook cheddar. "What did the owner say?"

"Can't find her."

"How come?"

"Kendall's on it. The woman was supposedly going to California or somewhere to visit friends. Apparently she never made it."

Serenity ran a spatula along the inside edge of the skillet. "Did she live alone?"

"Divorced."

She folded the omelet and slid it onto a sage-green Fiestaware plate. "What's the woman's name again?"

Josh popped some semi-stale bread into a toaster. "Carol Godding."

"This isn't some satanic animal mutilation like those horses in Enumclaw a few years back, is it?"

Josh took a bite and murmured his approval. "No. Just a nut job from the neighborhood. People in neighborhoods like that would rather poison a dog than confront the person next door about his barking all day. That's my guess."

The next morning, Serenity Hutchins moved her latest article to a folder on the server so that Charlie Keller could edit it. There wasn't much to it. Serenity knew that sometimes the story that leads to another is as important as a bylined feature above the fold.

Dog Mutilated in McCormick Woods

Kitsap County sheriff's detectives were called out to investigate the mutilation of a family pet on Wednesday in the McCormick Woods neighborhood.

"It was the vilest thing I've ever seen," said the woman who made the grisly discovery. "The dog—a Doberman, I think—was in the garage. Blood was everywhere. It made me sick."

Calls to the owner's phone have gone unanswered. The owner, neighbors say, is on vacation.

Brandi Jones was in tears as she read the article in the *Lighthouse* while she waited for her brother, Nate, to finish his swimming lessons the following afternoon. The Jones family lived two doors down from the Goddings. Whenever the Goddings were out of town, she took care of Dolly. She was probably the only one who really knew Carol and what a wonderful person she was.

Brandi wasn't sure who to call, the reporter who'd written the story or the Sheriff's Office.

She called 911 and was patched through to Kendall Stark. Brandi began sobbing again before she could even get her name out.

"I'm sorry," she said. "I'm so sorry. I just called to tell you that I babysit Dolly when Carol is away."

Kendall didn't have to ask the distraught girl to explain what she was referring to. The names Dolly and Carol were fresh on her mind.

"I'm sorry about what happened," Kendall said.

Heaving with emotion, the girl was unable to speak. Kendall waited patiently for her to regain her composure.

"Take your time. We're in no hurry," Kendall said. "Slow down."

Brandi's sobs finally subsided and she took a deep breath.

"I'm worried about Carol," she said.

"We understand she's on vacation. We're trying to track her down."

The girl started to cry again. Each word was like a fist to her throat.

"That's just it. She's *not* on vacation. I'm scheduled to take care of Dolly *next* week."

"Are you sure?"

"Yes. My mom put it on the calendar. There's no way she would have put it there if it wasn't correct. My mom's like that. . . . Something happened to Carol. I just know it."

Kendall made a few notes and took down Brandi's information, promising to let her know if she tracked down Carol Godding.

"Detective Stark," Brandi said, "Carol really loved Dolly. She really loved her dog."

Kendall thought of the dog toys and the food dishes she'd seen.

"I'm sure she did," she said, her mind beginning to race. *Celesta, Skye, Marissa, and now Carol.*

The Fun House was a dump in most ways, but Melody found herself spending more and more time there. Sam had told her that as long as she "watered the bitch" and "fed her some table scraps," so she'd be in good condition when he got home from work, he didn't care what Melody did.

She looked at her watch and knew she had about a half hour before Max came home from school and she'd have no more time for herself. She sat in the red-plastic-covered recliner and turned on the TV.

A moan came from the back bedroom, but she turned the sound up.

Seattle Now was on, and she enjoyed the soap opera updates provided by a perky woman with a chatty style that made her enjoy the plot points on the shows she didn't even watch.

A louder moan from the room . . .

"Shut up!" Melody called out. "You want me to shut you up? Don't make me!"

The host started previewing the next day's show, and an electric charge went through Melody's body.

Oh God, it's happening! People are talking on TV about us.

Melody heard a ping and looked at her laptop. As quickly as she could, she clicked on the space to enter her bid on the online auction site. She was going after a pair of Depression-glass salt and pepper shakers that she considered especially lovely. She no longer knew why she collected such things, but it was an old habit. She had filled the log home's kitchen with old eggbeaters, ceramic juicers, rolling pins, and salt and pepper shakers, and other kitchenware. Sam had his collection, and she had hers.

She looked at the photo on the screen.

I'm going to get you, she thought. *I don't know what I'll do with you or where I'll put you, but I'm going to get you.*

Her smile faded at the sound of more moaning.

"Goddamn you! I'm trying to get things done, and you won't shut up!"

Chapter Forty-three

Even in the fog of her fear, Carol Godding's first thought was about Dolly. Had she let the dog out? Why had she barked so loudly? Had it been all night? Dogs weren't against the rules at McCormick Woods, although the Welcome to the HOA newsletter highlighted how Basenjis were "ideal, quiet companions" and "the dogs of choice" for a quiet neighborhood. Carol hadn't heard of Basenjis before coming to McCormick Woods, and she asked her husband about them.

"Barkless dogs," Dan had said, rolling his eyes upward as he signed the homeowners association contract, which held the Goddings to the strictest standards of yard maintenance, house color, and noise level—even stipulating that the driveway "must be free of all vehicles excepted for visitors."

As her consciousness stirred, Carol thought that she'd overslept and that if she didn't haul herself out of bed right away, then she'd screw up her entire day.

Got to wake up. Got to get out of bed. Now!

She couldn't move. It was as if she were being held immobile in a straitjacket. She opened her eyes, but she could see nothing.

Where am I?

She tried to wriggle; she tried to speak. Nothing worked.

Have I had a stroke? Am I paralyzed?

She twisted once more, moving her frame an inch or two. She wasn't paralyzed; She was bound. Her mouth was sealed shut.

She spun through the events of the day moment by moment. The skirt. The beads from Peru. The recollection that Connie had been a double-crossing, man-stealing whore. A conversation about cutting through the slate waters of Sinclair Inlet in her canoe.

Nothing after that.

She turned her head slightly, her face pressed against cold plastic. As awareness came, so did a deep shudder. It rolled through her constricted body like a wave trying to break over an earthen dam. A slight crack. She shivered. Tears came to her eyes.

The little boy. The man who'd come for the canoe. *And nothing after that.*

Her eyes, blurry with tears, adjusted to the darkness. She was not outside. She hadn't fallen in her garage in some freak accident. She hadn't been rushed to the hospital. *She'd been taken.* She could feel the chill of a draft pour over her body, and for the first time she noticed that she was no longer wearing her blue jeans and sweater. Her panties and bra were missing too. The bands around her wrists and ankles and the tape over her mouth were all she had on. She knew what that meant, and if she could have screamed just then, she would have let out the kind of bloodcurdling shriek that would wake the dead in a cemetery a county away. But she couldn't. All she could do was squirm, wait, and pray.

* * *

Carol saw a fleck of light, but she didn't know if it was coming from the floor or the ceiling . . . from heaven or hell.

The slit of light widened, then narrowed. She could feel hot, damp hands on her. She was on her back, and the hands swung her legs up into the air. She could say nothing, although in her mind she was screaming at the top of her lungs.

"Keep your legs loose, okay?" he said.

For the first time she could feel the air against her naked vagina. She tensed.

"That's it. Fight me. I like it when one of my girls fights me."

One of your girls?

She noticed then that her eyes were partially taped shut too.

"You belong to me," he said. "I'll do whatever I want to you and then toss you away like a used Kleenex."

Unable to scream or cry out, Carol tightened her body once more. She felt him push himself inside her, and her revulsion was so great, she nearly vomited.

"Tighten, bitch."

He was growling at her, commanding her to be his bitch. He was saying something about her being put on this earth to serve him. With each word, each grinding thrust of his pelvis against hers, she cried. Through the slightest opening under her taped eyes, she could see the light widen again.

Then she heard another voice. "How's our bitch doing today?"

It was the voice of a woman.

She felt someone touch her on the inner thigh.

"Nice skin. Soft, creamy. The way you like it, babe. The way I like it too. I want to play too. Let me play with our new toy."

The words coming from the woman confused Carol.

New toy.

Chapter Forty-four

The lights went up, and the affable host of *Seattle Now,* Jerry Porter, forty and holding, peered into the camera. He had a kind of manufactured intensity: dark eyes and tawny powdered skin that in the age of high def looked more coated than the naturally smooth, youthful glow he and his makeup artist had tried so hard to project. His jacket was Nordstrom navy and his tie a red and yellow argyle. It was a preppy look that had been his trademark since he first landed in Seattle on his way to a top-ten market.

A trip that never found its final destination.

"We have a shocking story today." He paused, pretending to correct himself on the script that he'd written—"a *horrifying* story today. If you've been watching this station or reading the paper, then you know across Puget Sound from here in sleepy Kitsap County at least three women have been brutally murdered by a man who has come to be nicknamed the 'Cutter.' "

In rapid succession a series of photographs filled the TV screen. First the now-familiar image of Celesta Delgado at her high school graduation; next, a photograph of Skye Hornbeck taken a few months before she went missing—judging by her quilted attire, during a ski trip; finally, a photograph of an almost unrecognizable Marissa Cassava looking oddly demure, long before heavy eyeliner and piercings masked a sweet charm that probably no one apart from her mother had known.

The host continued as the camera panned away to reveal two men and two women sitting in a row of swivel-based dinette chairs that had been welded by the stage crew to keep from turning.

"At least three women have been brutally murdered in Kitsap County, and family members want to know why the killer is still at large. I'm Jerry Porter, and this is *Seattle Now*."

Cullen Hornbeck, Tulio Pena, Donna Solomon, and Serenity Hutchins blinked away the lights.

In her office, Kendall reached for her phone and dialed Josh's number. She hadn't seen him all day.

"Are you watching this?" she asked.

"Yeah, if you mean *Seattle Now*, never miss it." His tone was deadpan. He didn't tell Kendall that he was in the show's green room waiting for Serenity.

"Did you know Serenity was going to be on it?" she asked.

"She might have mentioned it."

Annoyed to be the last to know, Kendall snapped her phone shut and turned her attention back to the TV screen.

"I don't like to speak ill of the investigators," Cullen Hornbeck said, the focus solely on him. Although the camera purportedly added ten pounds, Kendall thought that Skye's father actually looked as if he'd shrunk since the last time she saw him. "I know they are doing the best they can," he went on, a bit of the Canadian accent filtering through, "but it isn't good enough."

Next, the camera turned to Donna Solomon, who was nodding in obvious agreement. Almost aggressively so.

"Look," she said, "my daughter was no saint, but what that maniac did to her shouldn't go unpunished."

Jerry Porter got out of his chair and walked behind the four guests, resting his hand on Tulio Pena's slightly trembling shoulder.

"Your fiancée was the first victim," the host said, "and the Sheriff's Office just dismissed her case out of hand, correct?"

Tulio could not speak right then. The lights caught his glistening tears. In the awkward silence, the producers—in a surprisingly kind move—aired a second photo of Celesta. Under her name: VICTIM ONE. For the next couple of minutes, the host talked to each of the family members on the stage, reciting the details of the victims' lives and what was known of their gruesome deaths.

"The Sheriff's Office should be ashamed of how they done Celesta," he said. "If they had caught her killer, then Skye and Marissa would still be alive."

Kendall could feel her blood pressure rise, but she took a deep breath and tried to reason her way out of her anger. She'd done the best she could. There was no reason in the beginning of the case to think a serial killer was on the loose. There is no pattern to discern when there is only a single body. It is hard to make a case for a serial murderer when there are two dead, unless the cause of death and the victims' profiles are a clear match.

"When we return, we'll talk to the journalist who has been on top of the case from the very beginning. She'll reveal information that she's held tight to the vest. Stay close. You won't want to miss it."

Kendall dialed Josh's number, but this time it went to voice mail.

Damn him! she thought.

She fumed through four commercials, wishing that she

wasn't watching the show live and could fast-forward to the information that Serenity Hutchins was about to reveal.

When the show resumed, Serenity had been reseated next to the host. She wore a celery green suit jacket with khakis and open-toed shoes. She looked older on TV than she did stomping around the courthouse. Jerry Porter started to cover some of the story's background and how Serenity had been reporting the case for the small-town paper, but in the middle of his introduction he abruptly stopped.

"Just a moment," he said, tilting his head slightly as he listened to his earpiece. "We have a caller."

Serenity didn't say anything, though she appeared a little unnerved.

"Go ahead," Jerry said.

"Hello, Serenity," the familiar voice began, its odd cadence and timbre filling the studio and sending a chill down her spine.

"Yes," she said, looking at the host.

"You know who this is," the voice said. "This is your friend calling to say how lovely you look on TV today."

Serenity locked eyes with the host. "Jerry, this isn't what we discussed."

"Hey, don't look at me," Jerry shot back, clearly enjoying live TV. "He called in. He's the guy, isn't he?"

Serenity reached for the tiny microphone that a production assistant/intern had clipped to her lapel. Livid at being blindsided, she said to Jerry, "If this is the guy, he's doing this for attention." She stood to leave, but the host motioned her to sit down.

The family members who thought they were there to tell their stories sat in stunned silence.

"Let's hear him out," Jerry said, his face lit up with the excitement of the call and the idea that it was frazzling the young reporter.

This makes for Emmy TV, he thought.

"Serenity, I'm surprised you didn't correct the producers

and that insufferable host," the caller said. "You know that there have been more than three victims."

Serenity slid back into her seat, frozen, her mic dangling.

"What do you mean?" Jerry Porter asked, looking out into the studio audience as the phantom voice came from a wall-mounted speaker. The dozen or so tourists were perched on the edges of their seats. The Cutter had been news outside of his own area, as serial killers always are.

"Serenity will have to tell you. I tell her all my secrets," he said.

"I don't know what he's talking about," she said, glaring at Jerry.

"Oh, but you do," the caller said.

"I thought there were three victims," Jerry said, his eyebrows lifting as he looked questioningly back at the young reporter.

"There are," she answered, bewildered. "At least, as of this morning, there were."

"Caller, are you there?" Jerry asked, looking straight in the camera.

A short pause followed, and once more the voice crackled into the air-conditioned chill of the studio. "I'm here. I'm surprised that the reporter didn't fill you in. I'm guessing she likes to keep details to herself."

Josh Anderson stood in front of the monitor in the Seattle TV station's green room, flirting with a pretty brunette production assistant named Ellen, who was doing her best to concentrate on what she was doing: wiping the counter where someone's guest had splashed coffee. She wasn't interested in the Kitsap County detective, but what was unfolding on TV got her attention.

"Wow!" she said, turning her attention to the monitor. "I didn't know they were going to drop this kind of bomb on the show."

The Kitsap County detective, his phone buzzing with another call from Kendall Stark, looked at the young woman gaping at the TV screen and shook his head.

"I didn't, either," he said.

The TV was a distraction on her day off. Jamie Lyndon had cocooned herself in a fluffy eiderdown most of the morning and, although she would never admit it, well into the afternoon. She surfed the channels, letting the various programs take her mind off the CENCOM office, where she fielded desperate call after desperate call.

She clicked on *Seattle Now* just as a caller was speaking to the young woman reporter.

The voice was mechanical, strange, and unforgettable.

Without a beat, she threw off the covers and dialed the direct line for the investigative unit of the Kitsap County Sheriff's Office. She got Kendall Stark's voice mail.

"Detective Stark, Jamie Lyndon, CENCOM operator. I'm at home watching TV, and I hear this voice. The same voice of the creep who called in to say he was the Kitsap Cutter. I'm sure of it. Call me back."

Serenity scurried down the TV station's corridor, her heels smacking against the high gloss of a polished tile floor like machine-gun fire. Josh Anderson was right behind her. He implored her to slow down, but she kept going.

"What was that all about?" he called out.

"I don't know," she said, not turning around.

He grabbed her by the shoulder, but she twisted away and kept moving.

"Don't do this, Josh. I don't want to go into this."

"Who was that on the phone?"

"It was *him*," she said.

"What do you mean *him*?"

"I don't *know* who he is. He's the guy that's been calling me." Serenity stopped and spun around. Her arms were wrapped tightly around her torso, as if holding her frame could slow the pounding of her heart. Her eyes were filled with terror, not tears. Serenity fought the urge to fall apart. Too much was at stake.

Josh was so enraged he didn't care that his voice carried into the sales and production offices that lined the corridor. "Why didn't you tell me?"

"Because I wasn't sure if he was the real deal or just a creep," she countered. "But he *is*. I know he is."

"What makes you say that?"

"He told me who was next."

Josh's anger turned to confusion. "What are you talking about?"

"Carol Godding."

Josh shrugged it off. "She doesn't fit the profile," he said, slightly annoyed that they were having this conversation. "She's too old—the others were in their twenties. Kendall and I went over that ground, believe me."

Serenity's eyes pleaded. "It doesn't matter. He told me that he was going to 'change it up' and go for someone older. He told me that he likes to break the rules, Josh."

"'The rules'?"

"Yes, as if there are goddamn rules for serial killing."

PART FIVE
Paige

I'm glad you brought the crown.
Sharp edges. I can have some fun with those.

—FROM A WITNESS INTERVIEW TRANSCRIPT

Chapter Forty-five

March 16, 8 a.m.
Port Orchard

While the minivan idled, Paige Wilson looked in the hand-held mirror and glowered. This was not the style she was going for. Teal eye shadow and an overly intense smear of slightly orange blush just above her cheekbones had been painted with a practiced hand, to be sure. There could be no faulting the skill of its application—if you liked *that* kind of look. There was no way out of it, and Paige knew it. She was seventeen, but the heavy hand of her "queen mother's" Max Factor makeup made her look more like a TV hooker or someone's washed-out mother looking for a third husband at the Bethel Saloon.

"When you are up on the float," Maggie Thompson said in her deep smoker's voice, "you have to use everything you've got to project a positive image."

"Yeah, but I'm not going up on a float." Paige climbed out of the minivan in the lot of the Port Orchard *Lighthouse*. "I'm giving an interview."

"Oh, honey, every time someone is looking at you, you're on a float."

Maggie was overstuffed in a turquoise velour tracksuit that had never seen the track. She'd been serving as the queen mother for Port Orchard's Fathoms o' Fun pageant for as long as anyone could remember. She was a pleasant but pushy woman in her sixties who knew that managing young beauty queens was akin to herding cats: damn near impossible.

Paige was an ash blonde with sparkling green eyes who had won the competition with a stirring rendition of the Dolly Parton sentimental charmer redone to utter bombast by Whitney Houston: "I Will Always Love You." Paige missed most of the notes, of course, but she had the hand gestures down pat, the kind of big motions that made her look every bit a TV pop star wannabe.

Clutch fist. Raise arms. Hold out palms. Make a pushing motion.

Besides, her competition was a girl who demonstrated batik on a T-shirt and another who read a haiku dressed in a kimono. Batik and haiku were the runners-up, relegated to the back of the float and a mere $100 in scholarship money. Paige was crowned the winner, picking up a $1,000 scholarship and a rhinestone-studded tiara that she loathed, as it pinched the top of her head and nearly made her cry.

"I know it hurts a little," Queen Mother Maggie had said, "but behind every beauty there is a little pain. Think of a rose. Thorns hurt, don't they?"

When *Lighthouse* reporter Serenity Hutchins wrote a front-page article about Paige being crowned the previous summer, she headlined the article: FATHOM'S QUEEN TURNS A NEW 'PAIGE.'

In the months of following her coronation, Paige and her court did the obligatory store openings, posed with Navy sailors in Bremerton, huddled on a parade float that showcased Port Orchard and its place as one of Kitsap County's most pleasant towns. Paige gamely did whatever Maggie and the creepy float driver requested. She thought that by being the best Fathoms

Queen ever there would be some kind of a reward, that a glimmer of something good would present itself and lead to greater opportunities.

Anywhere but here, she thought. *Anywhere but Port Orchard.*

Despite the possible renewed activity of the Cutter that spring, Charlie Keller insisted that Serenity do the traditional follow-up story on the beauty queen and what she had learned in her yearlong "reign" representing Port Orchard and the festival.

So there she was. Paige Wilson, that damned torture device of a crown on her head, sash ("warm iron, never hot . . . the rayon will melt") in place, and wearing a Target tea-length dress that her queen mother had insisted on, knew that she had to turn on the charm for the reporter. She had to tell Serenity just what she wanted to hear. Anything that approximated the truth was never to pass her lips.

She imagined how the interview would go if she could just tell it like it really was.

The guy who drives the float tried to have sex with one of my princesses.

The queen mother is a complete control freak. No wonder her kids are either in jail or never talk to her.

The lousy thousand bucks wasn't worth all the aggravation they put me through!

Serenity approached and smiled at her by the front desk. The interior dialogue stopped.

"You look so pretty," the reporter said.

The pageant automaton kicked in: "Thank you. It is a total honor to be here. I'm having quite a year and am so excited to tell you all about it."

Serenity led Paige into an interview room and offered her coffee.

"We're not allowed to," she said. "Water would be great!"

Serenity smiled. "All right . . . let's talk about your work with the South Kitsap Food Bank."

Neither woman wanted to be there just then, but they both had their jobs to do.

And so did one of the *Lighthouse*'s most devoted readers.

The Fun House smelled of Clorox, sweat, and strawberries. Melody Castile was on her knees, scrubbing the floors of the mobile home while Sam Castile messed with some leather gear that he'd ordered from a bondage catalog he found on the Internet. While Max was off with his Aunt Serenity for a day at the Point Defiance Zoo in Tacoma, the Castiles focused on some housekeeping and role-playing.

Just another Saturday afternoon.

"What do you think of this, bitch?" Sam asked, planting his feet in front of Melody. He was naked except for a black leather jockstrap with a detail of silver studs across the pouch that formed the outline of a human skull. He folded his arms across his chest and flexed. His eyes glared at her.

Melody stopped scrubbing and looked up.

"Mmmm," she said. "Love it. I *want* it."

"I found something *I* want," Sam said, stepping back and going toward the dining table next to the front door.

Melody felt a distinct coolness of her husband's dismissal. It stung a little, but she didn't say anything. She waited for Sam to continue.

"I'm thinking of something younger," he said.

Melody nodded and went back to her cleaning, now running her sponge over the surface of the chest freezer. "Sounds like fun."

Actually, it sounded like more trouble.

Sam walked back toward her, carrying a copy of the *Lighthouse*. "Let's go get *her*," he said, tapping his finger on the front page.

Melody acknowledged the black-and-white photograph of a young woman pushing several cans of tuna across a counter to an unkempt old man in a torn windbreaker.

"Pretty," Melody said. She smiled.

Sam rubbed his hands over his hairy chest, letting his fingertips linger on his nipples.

"Yeah. And I hope stupid too. Hot and stupid. That's how we like them, right?"

The article was headlined:

Fathom's Queen Helped Feed the Hungry

"Yes," Melody said. "That's how we like them."

Max Castile went into his father's office to hunt for the video game that he'd been promised if he made his bed every single day for a full week, which he had. The room wasn't necessarily off-limits—at least no key was required to get inside. The office was set up with three computers, a brand-new Sony DVR, a TV, a library of unmarked videos and DVR cases, and a jumble of wires that led from one machine to the next. His dad was at the shipyard, and his mother was out in the yard, digging a ditch alongside the old vegetable garden. Max had been helping her but made an excuse to go inside to use the bathroom.

Really, all he wanted was that video game disk.

He ran his eyes over his father's cache of equipment, most of which he'd already seen. Only one item looked unfamiliar: a headset connected to a small metal box. A decal on the box indicated a brand name. Max picked it up. He tried to sound out what the headset and box were all about.

DigiALTAVOICE.

The word was hard to sound out, and Max set the device down again next to his father's computer.

"Max, I need you to turn on the water," his mom called from the yard.

He saw the disk he wanted and grabbed it.

"Okay, Mom!"

Chapter Forty-six

March 21, noon
Key Peninsula

Melody Castile drank some wine and stared and let the warmth of the alcohol take her back in time. A face stared dead-eyed back at her. It was the visage of a toy, merely the representation of a woman. A doll. She applied some mascara to the eyelashes and quickly learned to use the gentlest of motions. Too much of an upsweep and the lashes would slip from the lids and stick on to the tiny bristles of the little round brush. The face was cold and firm, and she worked slowly to make sure that the blush looked all right.

This is like playing dolls, she thought, feeling a smile creep over her lips. It surprised her a little. What she was doing to please her husband was not something that could easily be explained. It was her way of giving him a gift, a "pretty joy," as she called it. She fiddled with the woman's mouth, inserting a six-inch section of broom handle that she'd sawed off expressly for that purpose. She worked the jaw, slightly stiff and very cold.

"You have no idea how much fun you are. How good you are. You're my baby's little whore. Do me proud," she said, stepping back to regard her handiwork. "My, my, you really *are* a pretty thing, if I do say so. And I do."

Melody gathered her things from her worktable and straightened up the mattress in the Fun House bedroom.

This is going to be so good, she thought. *He's going to be so pleased.*

She sipped more wine and imagined a conversation that she was all but certain would take place. Someday. She wasn't sure exactly when, but someday.

"Tell me about the head, Melody."

"You want to know about that, don't you? Everybody does. I don't really see what the big deal is. It's just a head."

"What did you do with the head?"

"You already know."

"Yes, but I want to hear from you."

"I'm sure you would. I'm sure you would like to know every juicy detail. Maybe you'll want to write a book someday. Say some shit about me or Samuel. Get some money."

"This isn't about a book. Or money. It's about the truth."

"So you say. Okay, I'll play along. I'll accept that you want the truth for some sick, twisted reason."

"Whatever you say. Just tell me."

"It was just for fun. Just something to do. I'm sure you'll try to pin all sorts of meaning to it. But you know meaning is what boring people come up with to explain why their lives really don't suck. Why they are better than everyone else."

"The head. Tell me about it."

"I'm getting there. We just thought it would be fun. I painted her up like a little doll, and she gave Sam a blow job whenever he wanted. I'd hold the head and work it up and down on him until he came. I know it sounds nasty, but we had fun."

"Tell me about the makeup."

"I did it for him. And I will tell you, it wasn't easy. He's pretty picky. I had to get it just so. You have no idea how many times he made me haul that head back to the worktable and redo it."

She started to laugh.

"You think this is amusing."

"Don't you?"

"Not really. How did you keep it? Preserve it?"

"You know we kept it in the freezer. I defrosted her by running warm water over her and painted her up and gave my man what he wanted. He always would say, 'Shut up and suck,' and, of course, she didn't say much at all."

"How often did he have sex with the head?"

"I don't know. Ten times. He even took it into the shower a couple of times and played with it in there. Everything gets boring after a while. Even certain kinds of sex."

Melody downed more wine and tried to think her way through all that she was doing and what was likely to come.

"You don't understand him, and you never will," she said aloud, her eyes seemingly incapable of landing on any single place. She tried to focus on her face in the mirror, but the commands in her head seemed to distract her. "You don't understand how it was."

She smiled. She tightened her fists, balled up like weapons. She relaxed.

"Not everyone is the same," she began again. "Not everyone feels the same needs. Sometimes a man's needs are outside the norms. But that doesn't make them wrong, you know."

She tilted her head. She imagined right then that she'd be able to pull out some charm, something that would sway the listener when the time came to tell her story.

Whenever that was . . . it had to be done right.

*   *   *

Sam Castile let out staccato laughter as a puffed-up journalist on the Discovery Channel prattled on about how serial killers like to relive their crimes by amassing souvenirs of items that belonged to their victims.

"They frequently get aroused by touching—fondling, if you will—the reminders of their kill," the man said.

Sam turned to his wife as they snuggled in bed. "What a moron."

"I know what you mean," Melody said. Her affect was blank, but she tried to imbue her words with a touch of indignation.

"You're my lioness," he said. "I bring things to you sometimes, just for love."

She touched the silver chain that hung heavy around her neck. It was all that he allowed her to wear. She knew then that love had nothing to do with their relationship. It was parasitic all the way around. She preyed on him. He preyed on her. Together, they were a force to seek out others who could be drawn, albeit unwillingly, into their game.

"My fantasies are not about an object but the intangible," he said hotly into her ear. "You know what turns me on. What makes me hard."

She knew, of course. Fear turned him on.

Yet, he did keep some things from those who didn't win the game or who bored him. Or displeased *her*. High up in the garage rafters was a bright yellow canoe, its floor stained with blood. In the kitchen drawer, under the mess of things for which there was no defined storage place, was a cell phone with numbers, starting with the 604 area code, captured in its speed-dial directory.

Chapter Forty-seven

March 26, 8:15 p.m.
Key Peninsula

His father was out in his shop and his mother was preoccupied with something in the computer room. Their warning, threatening as it had been, had done little to stop Max Castile's desire to ferret out the source of the noise he'd heard coming from the mobile home. He lingered in the doorway of the main house, looking at his mother as she clicked through Web pages and answered e-mail. A glass of Chablis sat next to her mouse. It seemed as if after every download she took a sip.

Max pulled the door closer to its frame and returned to the kitchen, where he retrieved the flashlight from the drawer and padded across the lawn. He moved as silently as he could not wanting to stir a leaf or snap a twig. He did not turn on the flashlight. He planned to use that once he got inside. He'd seen where his folks had kept a spare key, in the hollow of a plastic "rock" that had been set there for that purpose.

He fumbled for the rock in the dark, finding it after a couple of tries.

The key went into the lock, and he turned the handle.

The foul air hit him hard. *It smells like a dirty diaper,* he thought.

He passed the light over the dinette table and shone it around the small kitchen. The place was so clean, he wondered about the source of the odor.

With the flashlight directed at the floor, he went to the bedroom. He passed the beam over the mattress.

It was not a dog or other animal: it was the naked body of a girl.

What is she doing here?

Her eyes fluttered a little.

"Hey, lady," Max said. "Who are you?"

"Help me."

Adrenaline surged through Max's body, and he dropped the flashlight. It hit the floor and spun in a near complete revolution, casting a spray of illumination over the mattress, where the woman whimpered in a ragged, hushed voice.

Max picked up the flashlight and crawled close to her.

Duct tape had fastened her ankles and wrist to the exposed metal frame of the interior of the mattress. She'd been gagged with some cloth, but it had slipped enough to allow her to speak.

"Hurry," she said. "Before he comes back."

"Who are you, anyway? What are you doing here?"

"My name is Carol. Please . . . please get me out of here."

Max sat mute for a moment. She hadn't explained what she was doing there, but he didn't press her. He knew that this was not some computer game; it was real.

"How?" he asked, knowing to keep his voice low.

"Over there."

He followed her gaze to the wooden chair next to the wall. The chair was facing the wall, leaving its rails like a cage.

Protected by the wooden slats was a box of tools: a box cutter, screwdriver, electric drill, and spools of duct tape.

"There's a knife in there," Carol said, struggling to use her eyes to indicate where Max should go. "Shine the light. You'll see it."

The box was wooden, with hinges that had the patina of age. Max remembered when he and his mother had bought several such boxes when they'd gone shopping in Port Orchard some months back.

The beam met the shiny glint of a utility knife, and Max lurched for it as if it might move on its own to elude him.

"Please," she begged again, tears streaming from her eyes now.

Max was unsure why his own eyes had misted, but they had. It made what he had to do all the more difficult. As he bent at her bound feet, he winced as he sliced.

She let out a cry, and he was afraid he'd cut her. She wriggled her feet, bloody and bruised.

"It's okay," she said, her voice a rasp. "My hands next."

"Max!"

Jolted by his name, Max turned around. It was his mother's voice.

"I have to go," he said.

"You have to get me out of here. Cut my wrists," Carol said.

He looked at her.

"Max! Max!"

In the flash of awareness of what he had to do, what had to be right, Max Castile sawed on the tape.

"Thank you. Thank you," Carol said. "Thank you . . . Max."

The boy said nothing in response. He dropped the blade and ran for the door. He didn't look back, but Carol, battered, nude, and scared to death, was right behind him.

He didn't remember picking it up, but Max had the flashlight back in his hand. The beam stabbed over the cedars and firs.

"Max, there you are. Where have you been?"

Melody was in the middle of the yard.

"Just looking for the raccoon that was eating the dog food," he said, his words choppy with fear and the breathlessness of what he'd just done.

"What have you done?" Melody screamed at her son. In the light coming flooding the grassy space of the yard from the kitchen window, she could easily see a smear of blood on her terror-filled boy's T-shirt.

She knew.

Melody looked over at the Fun House. Then she saw the white figure of Carol Godding stagger into the woods.

"Sam!" she screamed in the direction of the garage. "Sam, get your ass over here. We've got a problem!"

She looked down at her son and grabbed him by the arm so hard, Max thought she would pull it from its socket. "You," she said, "get to your room. Shut up! Say nothing about whatever you think you just saw. This is a grown-up game, and you had no goddamn business playing over in the mobile!"

As angry as she was, Melody Castile knew better than to call it the Fun House.

Max studied his mother's face and wondered what kind of game could be so cruel.

Chapter Forty-eight

March 27, 8:30 p.m.
Key Peninsula

It took Carol Godding a moment to orient herself in the darkness of the forest. She had no idea where she was or where she should go. She only knew what direction Max had gone when the woman's voice had summoned him, and knew that that was *not* where she should go. She shivered as she tried to gather her wits. *Where?* The moonlight illuminated a narrow slit of water on the forest floor, a small creek. She followed it, trying not to make a sound, but her lungs heaved with each step. A woman who had never been on a Washington beach without flip-flops because the rocky shoreline was too jagged, Carol did her very best to ignore the pain in the soles of her bleeding feet and pressed on as fast as she could.

Where am I? God, please help me!

A dog or coyote howled somewhere far away, and Carol froze for a split second. She had no idea which way to turn. She looked up through the fir trees that surrounded her; the sky was indigo, the moon nearly three quarters full. She wished that the boy who had found her on that mattress had given her the flashlight. Had she managed to escape, only to wander aimlessly in the darkness of the forest?

She fought down a wave of panic. Only one direction made sense: *forward*. Away from where she came.

She was sure that her captors were searching for her.

The white-blue spectrum of light confused Carol, burning her eyes as it bore down on her. She was weak. Terrified. Disoriented. She'd had nothing but strawberry gelatin since her capture, and she couldn't think clearly enough to comprehend what she was seeing. A light from God? Had the moon crashed into the roadway?

As the headlights of the car came closer and the sound of the engine and tires on asphalt grew louder, a wave of recognition broke over Carol, and she started to wave frantically. She no longer cared about modesty; the fact that she was naked meant nothing to her now. She just wanted the car to stop and take her away from there.

"Help! Please! Help!" she said, her voice growing in volume with each word. "Help me!"

The car slowed, and then swerved slightly to avoid her. The taillights went bright red, and the driver pulled over to the side of roadway, forty yards from where Carol stood motionless for a second, her eyes still blinded by the brightness.

A plume of exhaust pulsed as Carol ran toward the car.

Gravel flew as the driver accelerated.

"Don't leave! Don't go!" she cried out, tears flowing down her cheeks.

The car disappeared over the hill. Help had vanished.

Carol was crying, wondering if what was happening to her was real or a terrifying dream. She dropped to her knees on the roadway, gravel digging into her skin as she cried out for help.

Why didn't that car stop? Why didn't the driver save me?

A beat later, she heard the squeal of brakes. The driver had turned around and was coming toward her. *Thank God!* She was going to be saved. The headlights were trained on her then, and she squinted, shivering and crying. She was going to be saved. The car stopped, and she blinked in the intensity of its high beams.

Chapter Forty-nine

March 27, midnight
Port Orchard

On Saturday night, while her parents were at the Clearwater Casino in Poulsbo, Paige was stuck babysitting her younger brother in the Wilsons' home on Beach Drive in Port Orchard. Foamy water curled and smacked against a stone bulkhead as she watched a ferry go to Bremerton. It wasn't the last boat of the night, but she was sure it was full of people who'd been out partying in Seattle. They were the lucky ones. They understood that the world was a bigger place than Kitsap County.

Paige turned off the floodlights that illuminated the thin edge of the shore. Whenever her parents went out to gamble, it was a sure bet they'd be home very, very late. If she didn't have to watch her little brother, Kerry, she could slip away and party with the rest of her friends. It didn't seem fair. She'd done everything right. Good grades. No drugs. And a beauty queen to boot. Yet, as she lay on the couch with HBO flickering over the flat-screen TV, she couldn't help but wonder if she'd end up stuck in Port Zero for the rest of her life.

She popped on her Facebook account and posted some comments on her friend's "wall."

Watching the brat again! I hate him! I hate this town! LOL!

Later, her phone pinged with a text message from a number she did not recognize.

YOU EVER DO ANY MODELING? HAVE A LEGIT AGENCY. WOULD LIKE TO TALK.

Paige answered with the speed of a practiced teenage two-thumbed texter.

U R GROSS.

He answered, CALL ME.
I M NOT STUPID, she texted back.

YOUR LOSS. BYE.

The HBO special she was watching about life in a house of prostitution concluded, and Paige went off to bed. As she pulled up the slippery satin duvet, she heard the ping of her cell phone once more.

It was a new text from the supposed modeling agent:

DIDN'T MEAN TO BUG YOU.

She texted:

OK. NO BIGGIE.
STILL THINK YOU COULD BE A MODEL. GOOD LUCK TO YOU.

Paige slipped under the covers. It was after 1 A.M., and the house was deadly quiet. She'd checked on Kerry, and he was asleep, butt up in the air. The cat was out for the night. The dishwasher had cycled. It was the same as any other Friday night. She wondered if every other Friday night for the rest of her life would be the same. Sure, she'd get older. She'd go out on her own. She figured that her Fathoms scholarship would get her nothing more than a quarter at Olympic Community College in Bremerton. The only way out of the town was either to get pregnant by a boy whose family had money or something totally unexpected taking place.

She picked up her cell phone and pushed the call feature for the number of the man who had offered her what she hoped was her golden opportunity.

A ticket out of town.

Paige didn't tell anyone about the contact with the agent. She didn't want to hear anyone say that the Fathoms o' Fun crown had caused brain damage. She remembered what a boy at South Kitsap had posted on Facebook when she won the pageant:

Paige Wilson is a Port Orchard "10," but that's a Seattle "4"!

She would prove them wrong. All of them.

Melody Castile looked one last time at the home page that she and her husband had put up with images of young, pretty women they'd pirated from the Internet. She knew it was as easy to erase as it had been to create. A gallery of women with pearly smiles, streaked hair, and big dreams had been search-and-click-easy to find. It was a hidden site, the kind that could only be found if a link was provided. No search engines picked it up. Password protected and accessed by approved readers, it was a phantom Web site. A trap.

Melody hit the delete button, and Dantastic Models was no more.

Although no one knew it, neither was Paige Wilson.

The Poplars Motel was a few blocks south of the Kitsap Mall in Silverdale. If there had been any poplars at one time, they'd been replaced by a rotating assortment of the kinds of businesses that populate strip malls off major thoroughfares: teriyaki huts, copy centers, bridal boutiques, and the like. Paige Wilson had heard of casting calls taking place in motel and hotel rooms, so she thought nothing of the request to meet at one. She'd talked to the woman who ran Dan Prendergast's agency, Mercedes, and she indicated that Dan was based in Oxnard, California, and would be in the Kitsap area only for two days.

"Dan saw your photo on the *Lighthouse* Web site," she said. "Always looking for fresh faces."

"I was a little concerned," she said, "but I went to your site and saw that he represented a lot of different girls."

"Oh, yes. One of our girls might be on *America's Next Top Model* next season," she said.

Mercedes asked if she'd be coming with her parents or a chaperone. "No worries if you do," Mercedes said. "Just, sometimes they get in the way. Good intentions can ruin things. Not everyone understands the process. No nudity, of course, but some of the shots will be slightly provocative. Wholesome but sexy."

Paige understood where Mercedes was coming from. She felt Queen Mother Maggie Thompson would put a halt to things before they got started, saying that modeling was not in keeping with the Fathoms image. Her parents, on the other hand, would tell her to get her head out of the clouds and focus on reality.

Maybe a job at Wal-Mart?

"Bring your laptop," Mercedes said. "That way we can download some test shots right away."

Paige played the conversation over in her head Sunday afternoon as she pulled her red beater Datsun into the parking lot of the Poplars. There was no risk. Mercedes sounded so nice. At the worst, she'd get some test shots that she could upload on her Facebook when she got home.

"Paige?" a voice called out as she emerged from her car.

"Yes?"

"I'm Mercedes. Dan's running late. He's at Red Robin having lunch. We're supposed to go meet him there."

Paige started for her car.

"We can take mine," Mercedes said. "We're coming back here anyway to take test photos."

Paige looked admiringly at the silver yin-and-yang necklace that hung from Mercedes's neck.

"It's special, isn't it?" Mercedes smiled.

Paige reached over and touched it. "I'm a silver girl too," she said.

"My husband bought it for me. Handmade. I just love the things he does for me."

"You're lucky," Paige said.

"We all are," she said, not meaning a word of it. "Lucky as can be."

Paige Wilson craned her slender neck. "Hey, I think you missed the entrance to the Red Robin," she said.

"Oh, dear," Mercedes said. "I'll turn around up ahead."

Paige shrugged. "No problem."

The car pulled into an office park that had been built to resemble the feed silos of a farm and circled around the empty buildings.

Paige crinkled her nose. "What's that smell?"

"Just a second," Mercedes said.

From behind the passenger seat, a hairy hand with a chloroform-soaked cloth came at her.

There was no struggle.

With the exception of Midnight Cassava, there hadn't been much of a struggle with any of them. Celesta had fought a little. Skye had fallen into darkness with the second breath. Midnight had put up a tough-chick fight by the elevator. That had been messy. Carol had slumped like a sack of flour to her garage floor. And now Paige Wilson looked like she'd fallen asleep after a long car trip.

Melody turned in her husband's direction as he returned the cloth he'd used to subdue Paige to a Ziploc bag. He was grinning, and she knew she'd pleased him. Still, she had to ask anyway. His approval meant everything.

"Are we good, babe?"

"Always. Let's go back to her car. You can drive it home. I'll take her."

Kendall Stark smoothed out the wrinkles in the pale blue blanket that enveloped Cody as she tucked him in. The blanket's edges were frayed, and she noticed how Steven had repaired it with iron-on batting tape. She wondered when he'd done that. She wondered if the case that was ripping her apart had stolen other small moments of family life that she'd never even known about. All she could think about was the Cutter. Her mind was swirling with the thoughts of the case, the missteps she'd made, the anguish she'd been unable to lessen. As her son's sleepy eyes began to shut, she thought about his innocence—and the innocence of those who'd died at the hands of the serial killer. He was unaware of the evil of the world. That was, she thought, a beautiful thing.

The one gift that autism had given him. The only gift.

With Cody asleep, Kendall kissed his warm forehead and headed toward the door. The evenings always went like that. Her phone buzzed, and she ignored it.

* * *

Serenity snapped her phone shut. In a way, she was relieved that Detective Stark hadn't answered. She'd make up an excuse if Detective Stark asked her later why she'd called. In the split second it took for her to push her speed-dial and get the detective's voice mail, she'd begrudgingly found herself sliding down a slippery slope.

She'd never forgive herself for doing so.

The odd voice who'd called her moments before had said only sixteen words:

I'm going to pick up your little beauty queen and take her for a test ride.

It was a threat. And a chillingly specific one at that.

Chapter Fifty

March 29, 7 p.m.
Port Orchard

Deana Wilson was fuming in her granite slab kitchen. She
and Brent, her land-use-planner husband, had dinner plans at
the Boat Shed in Bremerton, and Paige was nowhere to be
found. Deana had received a text message from her daughter
the day before, indicating she'd be spending Sunday with a
girlfriend, then going off to school the next morning.

At forty-two, Deana was a gorgeous woman with a sophisticated bob haircut and teeth so white, they glowed in the
dark. Her beauty had been passed on to her daughter. Thank-
fully, for Paige, not her self-centered tendencies.

You can be so thoughtless, Paige! Deana thought as she
paced the cream and sand living room. *You should have been
home hours ago!*

She called a number of Paige's girlfriends, but no one had
a clue where the teenager was. Next she took a seat on a
kitchen bar stool, looked out at the rippling wake of a pass-

ing ferry, and dialed Maggie Thompson. Deana told her that Paige hadn't come home from school and how she'd repeatedly tried her cell, but there had been no answer.

"I'm sorry, Maggie, I've checked the calendar, and I don't see any Fathoms event for today."

"We have one scheduled for Olalla Elementary a week from Monday," Maggie said. "That's up next. Nothing today."

"I have that one marked down," Deana said, looking at the Currier & Ives calendar that hung by the corn-yellow wall phone that Brent had never got around to taking out when the family went cellular. Deana made a mental note to remind him to take care of it. A phone was not a kitchen accessory unless it was a charming antique. A corn-yellow wall-mounted Princess phone missed that mark by a mile.

"Did you try Danica and Taylor-Marie?" Maggie said, referring to the two Fathoms princesses. Danica Moses had been the batik artist, and Taylor-Marie Ferguson had read the haikus.

"Yes, I called them first. They have no idea where she is." For the first time Deana let a tone of worry enter the conversation. "Maggie, they told me that they didn't see her in school today."

"Don't fret. I'm sure she's all right. I've worked with a lot of these girls, and they can get pretty touchy. It isn't easy being a queen, you know."

It was a not-so-sly reference to the fact that Maggie had once held the title herself.

"I know," Deana said. "But honestly, that girl can be so insensitive. She's so selfish." She paused. "You know what I mean."

Maggie sighed into the phone. "Yes, I do. Not as bad as 2003, but our Queen Paige is giving us a moment or two."

Deana Wilson thanked Maggie and hung up.

Queen or not, when she gets home, Paige is going to get it, she thought.

An hour later Brent came home and immediately dialed the Port Orchard Police.

"You know something, Deana?" Brent said, while shaking his head as they waited to give a description of their missing daughter. "If she's run away, I'm going to blame you."

"Me?"

"Yeah, you."

Brent couldn't stop himself. "If there's a more self-centered mother on the planet, I haven't seen any evidence of it. Just so you know."

Deana averted her gaze.

A twinge of shame with a capsule dose of reality?

She didn't say a word.

Kendall carried her phone away from the sofa where she, Steven, and Cody had been curled up, munching buttered popcorn and watching a DVD. She hated the intrusion of a phone call, but it was urgent and it was Josh.

"Heads up on a missing girl," he said.

She slowly let the air leak out of her lungs as she got up and walked to the privacy of the kitchen. "Oh no. Tell me."

"This year's Fathoms queen, Paige Wilson. Parents don't know if she ran away or what. Port Orchard Police are working it but want an assist."

"When?"

"Yesterday."

"Sunday," she said.

"Right. That's what *I* thought."

"Nothing for us tonight. But tomorrow, first thing, we can give the Port Orchard guys a hand."

Kendall went back to the TV, and Cody took his place in her lap.

"Everything all right?" Steven asked, knowing by the look on her face it wasn't.

"We don't know. Might be looking at another victim."

Steven showed his concern by patting her hand.

"Jesus, babe," he said softly.

She nodded and put her fingers to her lips. She didn't want to talk about it just then. It was all she *could* think about, though. Whatever was showing on the TV was invisible to her.

If Paige Wilson had been taken by the Cutter, her nightmare had only just begun.

It beckoned. The tiny tear in the aluminum foil over the window was an invitation to do what he'd been told *never* to do. It took about thirty seconds to decide to once more break one of the biggest family rules. Max Castile wasn't tall enough to see through that window without a boost, but he was smart enough to roll the wagon his father had him use to haul wood next to the mobile so he could step up to see what was making those noises.

To see for sure what he imagined was going on inside the mobile.

Max climbed up onto the wagon. It teetered as its wheels sank into the damp soil. He squinted. Getting a good look wasn't easy. It was frustrating. It was like trying to line a thread through the eye of a tiny needle. He moved his head from left to right to try to capture what it was. He could make out his father's beefy frame, naked save for a black hood over his head. Tattoos from his tour with the Navy, an anchor and a dagger that curled around his shoulder, were shiny with sweat. Seeing his dad like that seemed so wrong; he averted his eyes for a second. He could make out another leg, also naked, but he could not see who it belonged to.

"No," came a muffled whimper.

Max just stared, his eyes glued to the fragments of flesh he could see move in and out of the view through the slit in the foil.

They looked like the menacing figures on the magazines he'd seen in the Navy footlocker.

Max twisted his neck and pressed his face against the glass, looking at the figure on the mattress. His heart rate quickened as the boy processed what he was seeing. He climbed off the wagon and went toward the house.

Chapter Fifty-one

It was slightly foggy when Kendall Stark showed up at Maggie Thompson's two-story wood frame house on Baby Doll Road, up Mile Hill Road from downtown Port Orchard. The queen mother had been in the middle of a quilting project when she answered the door. She carried strips of aqua and green pieces of fabric in her slightly nicotine-stained fingers.

"The piece I'm working on for my grandson is called 'Under the Sea,' " she said, leading Kendall into a living room cluttered with fabric, batting, and a large tracing that laid out the scheme she was following, a quilt depicting King Neptune and various sea creatures in gaudy hues.

"Pretty," Kendall said, gently scooting aside a stack of rumpled material to take a seat on a tan leather recliner.

Maggie grinned, her teeth a buttery yellow. "I won a rosette last year at the fair, so I'm pretty good at this."

"I can see that," Kendall said, indicating the gold and blue ribbon hanging above the jumbled fireplace mantel. Before

Maggie could launch into quilting tips, Kendall quickly turned to the reason she'd called for an interview appointment.

"Did Paige say anything to you that will help us find out where she's gone?"

"At first I figured she just skipped school and went to Seattle for the day. A lot of these kids around here do. They complain about how boring Port Orchard is and how there's nothing to do. Boring here, you know. Pepsi?"

"No thanks," Kendall said as Maggie popped open a can of diet soda. "If she was bored, did she say where she'd go?"

Maggie shook her head. "Look, I've been doing this Fathoms gig for years, and one thing I've learned is, you can't trust these girls one iota. Over the years they've gotten more and more deceptive. They say they care about the homeless, the environment, and what have you. All they care about is getting some money and being able to brag they were a beauty queen."

Maggie Thompson was on a roll, and Kendall just leaned back and let the woman go on.

"Paige was a phony. I guess they all are. I honestly don't know why I bother carting them around, getting them to look classy, when they're just some backwater girls with no ambition. Not like Shelly Monroe."

Kendall knew Shelly Monroe. She was the Fathoms Queen in the late 1970s and used it as a springboard to a semi-successful television career. She'd been a weather girl in Seattle for a few years before landing a long-running gig on a game show on which she rolled oversized fuzzy dice. She had even written an autobiography called *Double or Nothing: My Life in the Wacky World of Game Shows.*

"Not everyone is a Shelly," Kendall said.

"I get that. But honestly, the girls of the last ten years or so seem to think that everything should be handed to them. They want this. They want that. Their constant requests are so tiring, and there's no end to them. Can you tell I'm a little burned out?"

Kendall nodded in agreement. "Yes," she said, steering the subject back to the reason she was there. "Let's talk about Paige. Had she said anything at all to you to indicate a problem? Boyfriend troubles? Something she was planning on doing? Anything at all?"

Maggie sipped her soda and thought for a moment. "I heard her talking to Danica, one of the other girls, about how she wanted to do some modeling. I think she signed up for an agency online. . . ."

Danica Moses was still bitter that she'd been first runner-up in the pageant and made no bones about it when Kendall found her at her job at the Wendy's restaurant in the Wal-Mart parking lot on Bethel Avenue. She was a pretty girl with brown eyes and long cinnamon hair that she wore in braids she'd twirled together herself. She wore a blue polo shirt with the word TRAINEE embroidered over the left breast in flamboyant script.

She sat with Kendall in a booth near the salad bar.

"I took my duties seriously," she said. "Paige didn't. That's the truth. She didn't care about winning the title, and I'm glad that she showed her true colors by skipping out."

"You don't seem to like her much, Danica."

Danica looked over at her boss, an Indian with piercing dark eyes that reminded her that, despite the police interest, she was still on the clock.

"Don't get me started. She just thought she was better than this town, that's all." Danica looked around. "Do you think she was even that pretty?"

Kendall wasn't there to discuss whether there should be a do-over of the Fathoms Queen pageant. "Pretty enough to win, I guess."

Danica made a face. It wasn't the answer she was hoping for. "Well, I love this town," she said, catching another glimpse of her boss. "I love this restaurant. I would have served my time as Fathoms Queen before doing anything to harm the good name of Port Orchard."

Serve her time? Was being a beauty queen like being a prisoner?

"Maggie Thompson told me that you and Paige talked about a modeling opportunity."

Danica's face went scarlet. "It wasn't like that. I wasn't interested in being a model. I want to go to college and get a nursing degree. I actually care about people. Paige was all about the easy way out of Port Orchard. She found some modeling agency on the Internet. I saw it on her laptop. I asked her about it. She didn't say much."

Danica seemed antsy, as if she had to use the restroom or get back to work. Kendall figured the latter. The boss was drumming his knuckles on the gleaming countertop.

"Well, then, what did she say?"

"Not much. Like I said," Danica went on, "she bragged a little like she always did. She thought that she was so much better than the rest of us because she won first place. She picked out an ugly crown, if you ask me."

Kendall hadn't. "Did she say she was going off to meet anyone?"

"No, she didn't. I expect she wouldn't tell me that anyway. You know, in case things didn't work out. I don't think she trusted me."

On her way back to the office, Kendall ate a hamburger she'd ordered off the Wendy's dollar menu. It wasn't that great, but it certainly wasn't overpriced. If Paige Wilson had gone off to Seattle to meet with a modeling agent, she'd come home soon enough. There was no way to check her laptop to determine which Web site Danica had seen when the two girls were talking about Paige's modeling plans.

Kendall learned from Josh that Paige Wilson's laptop was

missing, along with her cell phone and car. Skye's cell phone had been missing too. She wondered if there was some connection.

Or if she was merely grasping at straws.

Chapter Fifty-two

March 31, 1 p.m.
Vashon Island, Washington

The water was corduroy as bands of blue and gray etched the surface of Colvos Passage, the mile-wide stretch of Puget Sound that separates Kitsap County from Vashon Island. The island's western side is a sparse mix of beachfront cottages and farmhouses facing an equally rural southern Kitsap County. Robert Carmichael and his sister, Leah, were bored out of their minds as they took a break from their grandparents' place up the hill from Lisabeula, a park that had once been a campsite for Scouts and Native Americans long before Scouting was anyone's idea of fun. The teens hiked down the steep road along a creek to the five-acre park. Fifteen-year-old Robert was hoping to get a glimpse of a pod of whales, as he had during the dull visit the year before. Leah, almost fourteen, didn't care what they did. Their grandmother had been on Leah's case for text messaging when she should be "engaging" with human beings.

Grandma didn't get it.

They followed a trail to a madrona tree that had slipped down the hillside, its red bark rubbed off, leaving a green and brown indentation where others had tied a rope swing. During a hot summer's high tide, it was the perfect setup for swinging and jumping into the water. The tide was out, and the wind coming down from the south brought a brisk chill. March was a far cry from summer weather.

Robert grabbed the rope, stepped up on the big knot at its base, and gripped another knot above his shoulders.

"Watch this," he said, looking over at his sister, who was frustrated with her Sidekick.

"There's no signal here. This sucks," she said.

"So what? Engage with *people*, remember," Robert said as he started to move over the beach toward the water.

"If you were a *person*, I might."

Robert kept going as his sister dug her feet into the rocky beach, a disinterested gaze on her face that she'd perfected. He caught a glimpse of something red next to a silvery and gray remnant of a fir.

"Over by that driftwood," he said, "someone left a backpack. Check it out."

"Last time we found a dead harbor seal here," Leah said. "Anything would be a step up from that stinky thing."

She got up, put her phone in her back pocket, and walked over to the log. She bent at the knees to get a closer look.

"Hey, it's a purse. It's been out in the water. Not as gross as a dead seal, but not so great, either."

Robert jumped off the rope swing and landed with a thud, his feet digging two deep holes in the gritty beach.

"Let me see. Could be some money in it."

"If there is any, you better split it with me."

Robert shot his sister a dirty look. "If there is any money, we're going to give it back to the owner, stupid."

"I hate you, Mr. Perfect. Whatever." Her eyes widened all of a sudden. "That's a Dooney," she said as her brother picked up the soggy red leather purse.

"A what?"

"Dooney & Bourke." Leah squatted next to Robert, who hadn't a clue as to what she was saying. "An expensive purse. Too bad it's ruined."

He undid the clasp and dumped the contents of the purse onto a flat space atop the driftwood. A makeup brush; a lipstick; a pair of sunglasses; a set of car keys on a circular key fob with the DB logotype on it; a soggy packet of tissues; a tampon that had done what it was supposed to do—absorb liquid; a hairbrush; a tin of Altoids; a Mont Blanc pen; and a wallet that matched the red leather of the purse.

Leah didn't bother telling her brother that the pen was expensive too.

"Not much here," Robert said, opening the soggy wallet. "No money."

Leah started to put her earbuds back in place. "That sucks too."

From behind a clear plastic shield, fogged from the elements, the teenage boy retrieved a driver's license. Although the photo had flaked off, the name was still legible: CAROL GODDING.

"Let's head back to Grandma's," Robert said. He scooped up the contents of the soggy purse and put everything back inside.

Leah scrunched her nose in an exaggerated manner. "You're bringing that?"

Robert shrugged as they started up the hill. "You said it was expensive."

"When it wasn't waterlogged. Now it's a piece of crap. But if you're going to keep it, can I have the pen?"

Melody rubbed the interior of the freezer with a rag soaked in diluted bleach. There had been so much to do to get the place ready for the new girl—the new toy. She could hear her husband laugh as the girl in the next room begged for her life

She hated the sounds the playthings made. It wasn't because she felt sorry for them; it was more out of embarrassment. She knew that no amount of pleading or begging could set any of them free.

Not until Sam had done what he wanted.

Not until she'd done what Sam commanded her to do.

The freezer gleamed, and she noticed that she had missed a spot of blood. She wiped it again. Gone . . . then back.

She noticed for the first time that her knuckles were bleeding.

"Damn you, bitch!" she called out. "You made me bleed. Daddy! She made me bleed!"

The moaning in the other room stopped.

Good, Melody thought. *She shut up. Good girl.*

The freezer sparkling clean, Melody set down her cloth and took a pair of brand-new steak knives from the Fun House's kitchen drawer. She hooked her fingers through a spool of fence wire and started toward the bedroom door.

Sam summoned her from another room.

"Coming!" she called out.

Elizabeth Carmichael studied the kids' find. A concerned look pinched her normally tranquil face as she considered the sodden purse, the pen, and the wallet her grandchildren had found on the beach near her Vashon Island home.

"Did you see anything else down there?" she asked.

"There's nothing to see, Grandma. Just some water and seagulls. Real exciting." Leah wanted nothing more than to have her grandmother send her to her room so she could listen to music and text her friends at home in Seattle's North End.

"Leah, this is serious. We need to call the police about this," Elizabeth Carmichael said, going for her kitchen telephone. "I've heard this woman's name on the news."

Before she shrugged it all off and plugged her iPod earbuds back in, Leah couldn't resist getting one more comment in. "Can't we just take it to a lost and found somewhere on the island? You must have a lost and found around here somewhere."

"We have no such thing," Elizabeth said as she dialed the number for the King County Sheriff's Office, which served the island with a small station and a couple of patrol cars.

"My grandchildren unearthed something on the beach at Lisabeula," she said. "I think it belonged to that woman missing from Port Orchard. She was on the news. Carol Godding."

After her grandmother hung up, Leah eyed the pen one more time.

"You're not keeping that," Robert said. "Get real, Leah. This stuff belonged to a woman who might have been killed by the Kitsap Cutter."

Robert Carmichael watched the news too.

Kendall stood on the rocky shore and looked west across Colvos Passage to Kitsap County. A dog barked. Gulls swooped down into the wake of a green and white Foss tugboat towing a two-block-long boom of peeled logs toward Olympia or Tacoma. A deckhand tossed a cigarette into the water. Kendall had never been on that side of Vashon Island before. The view of the southern- and easternmost part of the county was somewhat deceptive. Million-dollar residences that aspired to look like Nantucket or Martha's Vineyard shored up the frontage along the passage. Those were the homes of the people of means; seldom were they visited by the likes of her and her badge.

A young King County deputy with a buzz cut pointed to the location where Robert Carmichael had indicated he'd found the purse.

"See that fan of roots?" he asked Kendall, pointing to a mighty old fir that had succumbed to the crumbling cliffs on one side of the passage or the other.

She nodded.

"Near the base of that."

Kendall sighed. There was no chance that there was any more evidence. The tide was high. Everything that might have been a clue was submerged.

The deputy handed her the Dooney, sealed in a large clear-plastic bag.

"Anyhow, I hope this helps," he said.

"Of course I do too," she said, knowing Carol Godding was more than merely missing. In all likelihood she was, indeed, victim four.

The day after the quarreling brother and sister found Carol Godding's purse, a Native American fishing crew dropped their nets in Colvos Passage near Olalla Bay, about a mile south of Lisabeula. The water, rippled shiny like corroded shellac on an old tabletop, accepted the weighted nets, and the men on the boat took a moment to kick back and pass the time. Fishing was always about waiting; and in the case of Native Americans, it was also about putting up with the glares and hostile looks of the fisherman on the causeway bridge who cannot match the catch of a net dropped into the blue. At about 4 P.M., it was time to reel in the curtain of nets.

"Pretty heavy," one of the younger men said as the winch strained to lift a load of salmon.

"Maybe you snagged a deadhead," another said.

"Not that bad," the first fisherman shot back. "Just a good haul."

Yet, it wasn't a good haul. As the net broke the rippled surface of the passage, first a hand appeared, then the arm, and finally, the remainder of a nude and battered body.

Carol Godding had risen to the surface.

Chapter Fifty-three

April 2, 9 a.m.
Port Orchard

The nude corpse on Birdy Waterman's stainless-steel table was not like the others who had been defiled by the Cutter. In fact, even those who profile such things would have discounted Carol Godding as a possible victim of the same man who had murdered Celesta, Skye, and Midnight. At forty-five, Carol was no ingénue. She might have been a lovely woman in life, but the waters of Puget Sound, the knotted fury of the fishermen's nets, and, of course, what the killer had done to her had stolen that all away. However, the forensic pathologist also noticed two small scars behind Carol's ears, indications that she had likely had a face-lift. There were also several tiny and recent scars running along her abdomen, the telltale signs of a tumescent liposuction procedure.

Birdy knew that Carol had recently gotten divorced. Birdy had never married herself, but she understood the reaction to aging. The need to halt it all before it was too late. Some women didn't see themselves for the greatness they held but as a package, a vessel, that had been coveted by men. Carol Godding had likely spent the last few months of her life pulling out all the stops to get herself back in the game before a ruthless killer stopped her.

Birdy noted how Carol's wrists and ankles were striated by wounds exactly like those of the other victims. She hated to use the gimmicky name for the perpetrator, but in seeing the teasing injuries made by a blade on Carol's torso, Birdy had to admit that the Kitsap Cutter had struck again.

She took out the camera and started documenting the body as found. There was an indignity to the process, and Birdy knew it. A woman like the one on the table had been consumed with how she looked, how she was progressing in her personal makeover.

The one that would put her life back on track.

"You're late," Birdy said as the Kitsap County detectives entered the room.

"You started early," Josh said.

"Reset your watch. I started on time."

"Sorry, Doctor," Kendall said, setting down her things and disappearing into the changing room. She kept talking through the cracked doorway. "We got held up by some media calls. Word is out about Ms. Godding being victim four."

Birdy looked up from the body.

"Word is about right, I'd say," she said.

As Kendall emerged in her pale green scrubs, Josh went to change. Again the door was kept open.

"This gal's no spring chicken," he called out. "What would a sexual sadist want with her?"

The two women looked at each other and shook their heads.

"This isn't necessarily about sex but about the feeling that the killer gets from the pain that he's causing," Kendall said.

She also wanted to say something about how the victim on the table was younger than Josh was, by about six years, and he still considered himself hot stuff.

Yet, she didn't.

As the three hovered over Carol's remains, there was an unplanned moment of silence. Each took in what could not be ignored. The body had been pierced by a knife a total of fourteen times. The wounds had not been deep, no more than a quarter inch at best.

The stabbing had been part of the game.

"Did she bleed to death?" Kendall finally asked.

Birdy stopped taking pictures. "No. Look here." She tilted the head slightly as she opened Carol's blue eyes.

"Patriotic, this gal. Red, white, and blue," Josh said, clever and cruel at the same time.

Neither woman commented on Josh's second inappropriate comment of the hour.

"Petechial hemorrhaging," Birdy said. "I expect the hyoid has been crushed too. This victim was manually strangled. No ligature marks." The pathologist pointed at some bruising on the neck. "Look, you can see the fingertips here."

"Looks like dirt," Josh said.

Kendall peered at the skin. "I see them."

Josh took a step closer. "Yeah, I guess so. But if she was strangled, that doesn't fit the MO of the killer."

"She was raped, wasn't she?" Kendall said.

The pathologist made a nod of resignation. "I've swabbed. This perpetrator is careful, smart."

She reached for her scalpel to do what the killer had done. The blade of her knife was not so different from the one that had tortured Carol Godding. Birdy performed a zipper pull, opening up the battered body.

Dr. Waterman fixed her eyes on Josh. "Just so you know," she said, "if I see any of this report in the paper tomorrow, I'll go to the sheriff and have you bounced off this case for good. You understand?"

Josh Anderson's face went a little pink. "Look, Birdy, I've never compromised a case. *Ever.* I resent what you're implying."

"I'm not implying anything, Detective. I'm stating a fact. That's what I'll do."

"Look," he said. "I've never compromised a case for any reason, and you know that." He looked at Kendall, maybe for support. She stayed mute.

"Josh, I end up with the result of what these maniacs do," Dr. Waterman said. She looked over at Carol. "We have a serial killer working in our own backyard, and some of the things that have been in the paper could compromise what I think we both want: an end to this."

"You know something, Doctor," Josh said, dispensing with familiarity, "you couldn't be more wrong."

"I hope so," she said. "I actually don't mind being wrong now and then. I learn from it." She was thinking of Celesta just then and how the early discounting of her disappearance as an abduction had delayed an effective investigation. She wished she could turn back the clock for all of them— Celesta, Skye, Marissa, Carol, and in all likelihood Paige.

With the skill that comes with practice, Birdy rolled Carol's body over so that she could view the wounds on her back. She'd been sliced in four places, not deeply but teasingly shallow. She noted the locations on the body chart that accompanied every autopsy. It was a bald, alien-like figure that reduced the person to nothing more than an outline.

Carol's skin was slightly gray, with the exception of the wound areas and some postmortem bruising on her shoulder blades. There, a couple of shiny specks glinted. Birdy looked closer.

Something was adhering to Carol's back.

In the arsenal of equipment in her Rubbermaid tote, Birdy found a UV light. Turning it on, she ran the bluish beam over the body. Tiny particles pulsed under the glow.

What were they?

Painstakingly, the forensic pathologist collected each minute fleck, fifteen in total. They looked like pieces of fiberglass.

* * *

Kendall and Josh walked across the parking lot without speaking. Kendall couldn't take her mind off the victim, and Josh couldn't stop brooding over the lashing that Dr. Waterman had given him over his relationship with Serenity Hutchins.

Josh broke the silence. "She's a good reporter," he said.

"No one's *that* good, Josh. Birdy is right. If you're not blabbing case facts to her directly, then she's digging into your stuff when you're not around."

"She'd never do that."

Kendall lingered by the door. She wasn't ready to go inside without telling Josh what everyone in the Sheriff's Office was already saying.

"This is the biggest case we've ever had, and you've compromised it. Get it together, Josh. Someone out there is torturing and killing innocent victims. Your ego is of no consequence in the grand scheme of things."

He didn't reply. He knew she was right.

Josh Anderson dialed Serenity the first chance he had. She was at her desk, working on an article. The newsroom was mostly silent, and she almost resisted answering. Personal calls were allowed, of course, but things hadn't been going well with Josh lately.

"I need to talk to you," he said.

"I'm in the middle of something," she said.

"This is serious, Serenity. Meet me."

She looked at her computer screen and let out a sigh. "I guess so. Tonight?"

"No. Now."

"Now?"

"I'll be there in five minutes. See you out front."

* * *

"Where are we going?" Serenity asked after getting into Josh's idling BMW in the customer parking spot in front of the *Lighthouse* editorial and advertising offices.

"Nowhere. We just need to talk. But not here and not on the phone."

He drove down Mile Hill and pulled into the mostly empty parking lot at the South Kitsap Mall behind the A&W.

He turned off the engine and turned to Serenity.

"Where in the world are you getting the information that you've been putting into the paper?"

"I've told you," she said, coolly. "I have my sources."

"I know. Who?"

"I can't—or, rather, I won't—say."

"Damn it, Serenity. I got ripped a new one by Dr. Waterman today at the Godding autopsy. She thinks—*everyone* thinks—that I'm your goddamn source."

"You know you're not."

"It doesn't matter. Perception is everything. So tell me: Who is your source?"

Serenity looked out the window. She paused, considering. "I can't say. Not for sure. But I think the guy who's been calling me is the Kitsap Cutter. I mean, I really do think he is, Josh."

"Jesus, are you sure?"

She looked back at him; this time her eyes flooded with tears. "I am. I really am. It scares the hell out of me too."

Josh leaned closer and put his hand on her shoulder. "Who is it?"

"I don't know. All I know is that he's not finished. He told me that much. He says he won't stop until he's caught."

To the right of her desk, Kendall had hung photographs of the Kitsap Cutter's victims. While the brutality that each had endured indicated a specific type of sexually sadistic serial killer, the women themselves were a diverse bunch. They weren't a collection of "throwaways," as some media people characterize a victim like Midnight Cassava. Carol was an accomplished professional woman; Skye, a recent college graduate.

Kendall wondered if there was some similarity in their backgrounds that had attracted the Cutter to them, or if their selection had been completely random. She looked at Paige's photo and retrieved her file. Why her? What had made her stand out? She read the article in the paper about her being crowned Fathoms o' Fun Queen and how she was going to use her achievement to feed the homeless and embark on a career in the entertainment industry.

Her eyes wandered over Celesta Delgado, victim one, and then to her file. She studied the witness statements and Dr. Waterman's autopsy report. Her hands had been expertly removed. Was the killer a butcher? Chef? An ardent hunter? She perused the article Serenity Hutchins had written when the partially clad body was found in Mason County. She recalled what she had learned about brush picking and saw the photo that had been published the previous summer showing Celesta as the hostess at the grand opening for the remodeled Azteca.

Victim two, Marissa, had also been profiled by the *Lighthouse* reporter, although less sympathetically than Celesta. Marissa's mother had conceded that her daughter had had a "troubled" past, including arrests and convictions for prostitution and check kiting. Her head had been removed and the two parts of her body discarded in two different places, at two different times. The head in the box was meant to shock, which it did. She was found nude.

Skye Hornbeck, victim three, had been an adventure seeker—the opposite of Celesta, who had merely aspired to a cozy middle-class life with her future husband. Skye had been strangled and stabbed and was missing a necklace, but there was no way to tell if the other victims had had any personal effects taken by the killer.

Celesta's engagement ring was presumably somewhere with her hand.

Marissa couldn't hang on to any jewelry, hence the wrist tattoo of her daughter's name.

All had been dumped in water. The killer surely had a boat. But so did a hundred thousand other people in the Seattle Tacoma area. Finding the right boat was like finding a needle stuck in the muddy bottom of Puget Sound.

Impossible.

There was no way she could stop herself. There was a kind of rush that came with reporting the news of a serial killer's latest victims. Serenity Hutchins knew that some kind of evil being had anointed her to be the messenger of his deeds. The afternoon that Carol Godding's body was snagged in the fishermen's nets, she posted an entry on the *Lighthouse* news blog—there was no waiting for the print edition.

The posting was headlined:

CAROL GODDING'S BODY FOUND
IS PAIGE WILSON THE KILLER'S NEXT VICTIM?

She wrote that while the Kitsap County Sheriff's Office had not made an official statement that the missing beauty queen was a victim of the Kitsap Cutter, she had it on "good authority" that they suspected as much.

A source close to the investigation indicated that Wilson is the fifth victim, and there likely will be others.

She didn't say that the source was the killer himself.

Sam Castile read the blog and grinned.

"'Close to the case?' She has no idea just how close she is," he said to himself.

Chapter Fifty-four

April 2, 8:35 p.m.
Key Peninsula

Kendall looked at the map pinned to her office wall. A casual visitor would not have understood the meaning of the red dots marking Little Clam Bay, Anderson Point, Lisabeula, and the Mary E. Theler Wetlands.

She and Josh had canvassed marinas all over Kitsap County and Gig Harbor in Pierce County. Each of those was marked with a gold star. The detectives knew that the person dumping the bodies was doing it from a boat. A lot of good that did them. Puget Sound was often referred to as the "Boating Capital of the United States."

"You look intense," Josh said after sauntering into her office, looking as if he were on vacation or about to climb onto a bar stool.

Without a care in the world.

Kendall was stressed and made no attempt to hide it. "Why wouldn't I be, Josh? There's a maniac out there, and everyone from the FBI to the Seattle PD thinks we don't know what we're doing."

"We're doing the best we can," he said.

"Not good enough." Kendall let it go. She didn't want to get into it with Josh just now. It seemed that he'd let his personal life cloud his occasional good sense, and it irritated her. "Look, the killer is a boater. We know that. He has to moor his boat somewhere around here."

"He could trailer it and launch it from a boat-ramp too."

Kendall disagreed: "I don't see how he'd have time to haul it in and out, dump a body, and get back to whatever rock he lives under."

Josh sat down with his long legs stretched out. "People like that always find the time," he said.

Again the noise beckoned. Max Castile thought he'd heard a small animal bawl from behind the mobile home, shrouded from view by a stand of native cedar and a hedge of black bamboo his parents had planted. He'd been admonished to stay away from the mobile "for safety reasons," and he was the kind of obedient child who knew that when his parents said something, they meant business. From his bedroom window, Max could see into the detached garage. His father was crouched over his workbench, silhouetted by the fluorescent tubes that hung overhead on a pair of galvanized chains. As he looked into the garage, Max imagined that he had become a character in a video game and that his dad was some kind of metallic scorpion that he could take out with a blast of his laser. Sometimes he wanted to do just that. He tiptoed past the master bedroom, where his mother had fallen asleep holding a novel in her lap. The book rested in her hand as if she were about to turn the page.

The boy decided to go through the kitchen to get a flashlight. If his mom caught him there, he'd say something about needing a glass of water or being scared. Something she'd believe. The light was in the utility drawer next to the fridge. He slid it open slowly, quietly. Max fished out the flashlight and started to follow the noise across the darkened yard. It faded in the wind, and he stopped to listen.

Where is it coming from? What is it?

Nothing.

He picked up a large stick and waited for the noise again.

"Pleee-eee-se!"

Just as he thought: it was coming from the direction of the old mobile home.

Max checked behind him. No one was watching. His father had never bothered to skirt the trailer, so he crouched down low and looked to see if there was something caught under the structure.

"Pleee-eee-se!"

It was coming from *inside* the mobile home.

As Max reached for the door handle, a hand pulled at his shoulder and nearly knocked him to the ground.

"What are you doing here?"

Max spun around and faced his mother. Melody Castile's eyes were fierce with anger. It was a mom's usual look of disapproval multiplied by a thousand.

Max blinked back tears.

"Mom, I thought I heard something."

She gripped his shoulders and shook him. "What did your dad and I tell you? This place is not for you!"

"I'm sorry. I just thought . . ."

Without another word, she yanked her son back toward the house.

Paige Wilson had heard shards of the confrontation between mother and son as she lay on the mattress in her own filth. The duct tape that had been applied to her mouth had slipped off, allowing her to call out for help. As she rolled her head back on the mattress, Paige felt the familiar pressure of the bobby pins that held her crown to her head.

How had all of this happened? she wondered, retracing the text messages, the promises of a modeling contract, the meeting in the parking lot at the Poplars . . . and finally the smelly cloth going over her face before falling into darkness.

She tried to burn into her memory the last thing she had seen: a Department of Defense parking decal, silver and blue, with a beginning sequence of identifiers: D7D. She'd seen the familiar stickers her whole life. Whoever owned the car had been employed at the shipyard or maybe the submarine base at Bangor. Rental cars don't come with DOD decals.

Whoever had her was not some modeling agent and his assistant from California. Lying on that mattress, in the middle of nowhere, she knew she was a long way from *Top Model*. A long way from anywhere at all.

She whimpered helplessly in the dark and tried to come to grips with her situation and think of how to get out of there.

Paige had been a virgin before she was captured and violated. She had told her friends otherwise, as if bragging about having had sex made her seem adult. She didn't want to be called "the Virgin Queen," so she'd made up a lie about a boyfriend at a prep school in Tacoma. Paige had been all talk. She'd let the float driver fondle her breasts once, but that was the sole extent of her experience with men.

Now she was cut, bleeding, and all but certain she was going to die.

After returning to the house and putting Max in his room for the rest of the night, Melody went to the garage, where Sam was washing out the inside of Paige Wilson's car. He wore gloves and used a chamois that she'd purchased from a late-night TV pitchman. They'd laughed at how the pitchman could tout the uses they'd devised for his product. Certainly it could soak up soda pop from the floor, but it also did a good job obliterating fingerprints.

Sam stopped what he was doing. "What's with you?"

"What's with me? That's a good one."

"Are we playing games here, Mel? Because if we are, I'm missing something."

Melody was tense, her arms folded across her chest, her hair matted against her sweating forehead.

"Max almost went into the Fun House. That little bitch we picked up was making some noise. You need to make her quiet."

Her tone was indignant—she expected him to do something. *Now*.

"Oh, *I* need to?" Sam set down his dripping chamois. His eyes were ice, and the veins in his neck plumped with blood. "What's the matter with you? *You* go shut her up. For good."

"I don't do that," she said.

He jabbed a finger at her.

"You do as I *tell* you. That's our deal, babe."

Bernardo Reardon, the detective with the Mason County Sheriff's Office who'd met with Kendall and Josh when Celesta's body was a heap of waterlogged flesh the previous March, looked down at the report submitted by the state crime lab in Olympia. It had been among a batch of documents found in the trunk of a fired lab worker's car.

It was unremarkable except for one small notation.

Trace analysis recovered distinct particles of marine fiberglass and sealant used by U.S. boat manufacturers prior to 1980.

He got Kendall on the phone in her office and told her what he knew.

"Basically, whoever dumped the body had an older boat," he said. "All have been water dump sites, so I guess that's no real news."

Kendall thumbed through Birdy's autopsy report on Carol Godding.

"Godding also had particles recovered from her shoulder blades," she said.

"Maybe they'll match."

Kendall was thinking about the age of the boat.

"Almost thirty years old," she said. "Can't be too many of those around here."

"I was thinking the same thing," Bernardo said. "I mean, a boat that old is not exactly a classic, you know, like a Chris-Craft."

"Old, but not a classic," she repeated.

Serenity allowed the thought to come to her, though she'd resisted it before. Sam Castile had a boat. An old one. Sam had a proclivity for bizarre, controlling behavior. Even Melody had said so. Serenity recalled the clues she'd seen at the log house when she and her parents had visited there. Something was strange. She'd recalled how Josh had asked her about the rolling pin and how she'd dismissed it out of hand.

Her heart pounding, she called her sister.

No answer.

"I'm sorry for bugging you about this, Melody. Don't take it the wrong way. But I'm worried about Sam. He might be involved in something. Something bad."

She thought better of leaving such a message and waited for the prompt so she could erase it. It felt good to have it out of her system. But no such prompt came.

Sam Castile held his wife's phone to his ear and stared at her.

"We're going to need to take care of the little bitch," he said. "You hate Serenity."

"Yes, I hate her," she repeated.

"She's always had everything that you wanted."

"Don't remind me."

"I need to remind you, bitch, because you're so goddamn stupid, you wouldn't know how to do *anything* if I didn't tell you how."

It soothed her a little when he treated her like she was nothing.

"Your parents never understood you the way I do," he said, turning around to measure her reaction. "They underestimated what you are and who you are."

"I know. I know."

He started toward the Fun House. "Taking care of her will not only stop her from asking stupid questions, it will be payback for everyone for what they did to you. Best of all, we'll have a hot time doing it."

He didn't seem to care that in killing Serenity he was breaking one of his rules. Rules, he knew, were never meant for him.

Chapter Fifty-five

April 3, 2:10 p.m.
Olympia, Washington

Police in Olympia, an hour to the south and east of Kitsap County, found Paige Wilson's red Datsun abandoned in front of a mystery bookshop in the historic downtown section of Washington's capital city. A traffic enforcement officer named Jerry had chalked it earlier in the day, but it wasn't until the bookstore was closing that evening that someone noticed that the car wasn't going anywhere. Police ran the tags and notified Kitsap County when they learned it was registered to a Brent Wilson and that there was a missing person hit out on the car. It belonged to a missing beauty queen, Paige Wilson, seventeen.

Early the next morning, Kendall Stark drove down Beach Drive to the Wilsons' place to let them know their daughter's vehicle had been recovered—and, more importantly, that there was no trace of Paige.

Deana Wilson was in the driveway when Kendall pulled n. She wore a pale blue bathrobe, and her hair was wet from the shower. She'd read the news blog and contacted everyone she could think of—the reporter, the editor, the sheriff—to see if it was really true.

"We can't reveal our sources," the *Lighthouse* editor had said.

"We don't know where they got their information. We don't have any information confirming your daughter was abducted by anyone," was the canned response from the Sheriff's Office.

Kendall had called to say she was coming by. The wary look in Deana's reddened eyes indicated that she already knew the detective had not brought good news.

"I put our son on the bus a few minutes ago," she said,. "I found myself just standing here, waiting, not wanting to go back into the house until you got here."

Her face was pale, and her features, without makeup, seemed to recede into the anguish that consumed her.

"Let's go inside," Kendall said.

Deana nodded and led Kendall across a pathway of cedar rounds to the front door.

"You found her," Deana said, without looking at Kendall. They walked to the kitchen, where her husband sat framed by the view of Puget Sound and the gray mottled trunks of a grove of alders.

"No, no," Kendall said, acknowledging Brent Wilson. "We found her car."

Brent, a man who almost never betrayed any emotion about anything, started to cry upon hearing the news.

"This is not good," Deana said, gripping her husband's hand on the kitchen table, where they'd seated themselves.

"We don't know what it means," Kendall said, trying not to offer false hope but not wanting to lie to the couple, who were already fearing the worst possible outcome.

"I know," Brent said, pulling away from his wife. He'd composed himself by then. "It means that she's gone. It means that she's dead."

Before Kendall could say a word, Deana let go of her husband's hand and pushed away from the table.

"We've read the papers. We know that there's some kind of freak out there."

"That's an enormous leap, Ms. Wilson," Kendall said.

Deana gulped. "Then where is she?"

Kendall told her the truth. "We don't know."

"Please find her," Deana said.

Kendall nodded. "We're doing everything we can."

After leaving the Wilsons', Kendall returned a call that Josh had made to her while she was inside delivering the news. He told her he'd received word from the state crime lab in Olympia. They'd expedited the forensic exam.

"We've got a whole lot of nothing on the car," he said. "The interior is devoid of any prints, any blood, anything at all."

"Not even a trace of Paige?"

"Right. They found one thing and one thing only. On the steering wheel they picked up some latex particles."

"Gloves?"

"You got it."

Kendall braked to a stop to allow a family of Canada geese to walk across Beach Drive to the water. "That tells us plenty, doesn't it, Josh?"

"Yeah—that the perpetrator is careful."

"We knew that. It also tells us the worst possible news. If we'd thought for one second that Paige might have run away, that's out the window. No teenager is going to wipe her car, vacuum it out, and wear gloves while she's doing it."

"Nope," he said. "No teenager's going to vacuum her car—period."

The geese safely out of the way, Kendall drove the winding road past the veterans' home and toward downtown Port Orchard.

"You know it, and I know it, Josh. Paige Wilson is the fifth victim."

"Probably, Kendall."

"We have to find her before we're too late."

Josh let out a sigh. "We both know that if time hasn't already run out, it will."

Kendall first broached the subject of a pattern to the killings with Steven after Cody had been put to bed that Friday night. The dates associated with the case nagged at her. She sat on the edge of their bed with an eighteen-month cat calendar that she'd purchased for her mother but had never given her because it would only remind her that she didn't know what day of the week it was most of the time.

She marked the dates that the Cutter's victims had vanished, or were believed to have vanished. Every one had been on the far left of the calendar—a Sunday.

"Don't ask me," Steven said. "I'm an ad salesman, and I'll buy just about anything."

She smiled at him and knew that he was right about that.

On Saturday morning she went looking for Josh, whom she knew would be in the office. Despite the fact that he now had a girlfriend, he did not have much of a life. She found him once more by the coffeepot in the break room.

"Josh, there is a pattern here," she said, pulling him aside.

He poured an avalanche of dry creamer into his cup and followed her.

"How so?"

"Sundays. All of the vics disappeared on a Sunday."

She held out a sheet with the dates highlighted.

March 29 (Celesta)
April 26 (Marissa)
September 26 (Skye)
January 31 (Carol)

He looked interested but unconvinced. "I thought that Skye disappeared on a Saturday," he said.

Kendall nodded. "Right. But maybe she wasn't actually captured by the killer until Sunday. His day."

"Are you thinking something religious here?"

"No. There's nothing that this creep has said to anyone, left at any scene, to suggest he's a religiously motivated killer. I'm wondering if it's simply because it's convenient for him to capture his vics on weekends."

"Because he's not working."

Kendall set down her calendar notes.

"I've thought that through. I'm thinking that Sunday is the day he captures them, but he really needs Mondays off. Monday is the day he gets himself together for the workweek. Since his killing has been intermittent, I'd say he doesn't get every Monday off."

"I hate Mondays," Josh said.

If she was correct, Kendall knew that she could add another name to the list: Paige. She went missing on Sunday too.

Chapter Fifty-six

April 5, 4 p.m.
Key Peninsula

It was Saturday afternoon, and an Almond Joy was calling
her name from the newsroom's vending machine. Serenity
Hutchins was poking around her desk for some spare change
when she answered her sister's call.

"I need you," Melody said, in tears. "Can you come over?"

Serenity looked around. The newsroom was quiet. She
was working on a background piece about Paige Wilson, the
missing teenager.

"Now isn't the best time," she said.

"It's about me and Max," Melody said. "Something terrible has happened. I need you."

Serenity stopped searching for quarters. She had never been
close to her sister, but she adored Max. Melody sounded
completely out of sorts.

"What's going on?" she asked.

"This isn't the kind of thing I can talk about on the phone."

"Well, give me an idea. I'm on deadline here."

"I'm terrified, and I need my sister."

The despair in Melody's voice moved something in Serenity's heart. She longed for a genuine connection with her sister.

"I'll be there in an hour."

"Don't tell anyone," Melody said.

The Castiles' gate had been left opened. *Strange*, Serenity thought, but a nice change from the usual inconvenience nevertheless. She loathed the damn gate, the faux cameras, and the motion detection lights that her brother-in-law had installed at the entrance to the property. She drove up the curving, rutted gravel driveway and parked in front of the garage.

Melody, dressed in dirty blue jeans and a cream-colored sweater, met her by her car door.

"Serenity, thanks for coming," she said, each word an anxious gulp. "I really needed you, and you're here."

Serenity got out the car and embraced her sister. Melody had never been much of a hugger. Now, however, Serenity could feel her sister's arms pulse as they wrapped around her shoulders. When she pulled back to look into Melody's face, Serenity expected it to be wrought with emotion.

Yet Melody's eyes were devoid of expression.

"What is it?" Serenity asked. "Where is Max?"

"He's in the house," Melody said. Her body was shaking and she made crying sounds, but nothing came from her eyes. Not a single teardrop.

"Where's Sam?" Serenity looked around the yard, then turned to her sister again. "What's going on? What did you want to talk to me about?"

"Serenity," Melody said, "I want out of this marriage. . . . I'm worried about Max. His father, you know, isn't quite right."

No argument there, but Serenity didn't say so.

"I don't know what to do," Melody went on.

"You get a lawyer, that's what you do. What happened?"

"I'll show you," Melody said. "Let's go inside. I think I know what happened."

Serenity expected her sister to lead her to the front door of the house, but instead Melody started in the direction of the mobile home.

"What's in there?"

"I think that's where it happened to him. I think Max was abused."

Serenity felt her pulse quicken as they went down the moist dirt pathway through a stand of black bamboo.

"Oh, God! Are you sure?"

"I'm not sure. But I think you can help."

"I'll do what I can, of course."

They walked down the moist dirt pathway.

Melody put her hand on Serenity's shoulder, pushing gently as they went up the steps. "I found something. I'll show you." She opened the Fun House door so Serenity could go inside ahead of her. The interior was dark. Serenity noticed right away that the front windows had been covered with aluminum foil.

"I saw this done once in a pot-growing operation in Kingston," she said.

A hand reached from the darkness and pressed a smelly cloth over her nose and mouth.

Chapter Fifty-seven

Kendall Stark hung up the phone and turned to Josh Anderson. He'd assumed it was a media call into the Sheriff's Office about the possibility of the Kitsap Cutter's fifth victim, Paige Wilson. Kendall had used words like "off covering the beat" and "big story that needs care."

She looked hard at him. "That was Charlie Keller," she said. "He's worried about your girlfriend."

"What about her?" Josh asked, popping a starlight peppermint into his mouth.

"Says she didn't show up for work this a.m. He even went to her apartment. No one's there."

He crunched the candy. "She's a big girl."

"When did you see her last?"

"I don't know. Saturday morning, I guess. Hey, we're not exclusive."

Kendall shook her head. "Not that you seem to care, but

I'm guessing that she'd rather be dead than have her editor write 'Is Paige Wilson Victim Five?' "

"You're right about that," he said. "She's all about the big story."

"Keller says she said something about going out to her sister's place."

"Her sister is a piece of work. Good. Glad to know that she's helping her."

"Aren't you worried?"

"Kendall, what's the big deal?"

"The big deal is that a woman who links all of our victims has gone AWOL. I'm guessing, Josh, you'd care more about her if you hadn't slept with her."

Josh's face went a reddish shade. Kendall's words had stung. "I care," he said. "We had a bit of an argument on Friday. I just figured she was cooling off over the weekend."

The little boy with the dark, knowing eyes watched quietly as other children in the classroom took out well-worn crayons and started to follow the instructions of Sally Marshall, their teacher. Inside, he seethed.

"I want you to think about your favorite things," she said.

"Like our dog?" another boy asked.

No one who saw Ms. Marshall would think she was anything but an elementary school teacher. A plain brunette, she never failed to wear the kind of cutesy attire that would appeal to small children. That Monday morning she wore a pair of iron-creased jeans, a white blouse with a Peter Pan collar, and a vest with an appliquéd tic-tac-toe board. The *X*'s and *O*'s were attached with Velcro.

"A picture of your puppy would be wonderful, Patrick, but how about a picture of your dog and you together?"

"I'm not a good drawer of people," he said.

"Do your best. That's what we all should do." She hovered over a few of the kids before moving to the next row.

The kids up front—Patrick, Jared, Ashton, Sonata, Mimi, and Gabrielle—were her favorites, and the other kids knew it.

Throughout the classroom, little hands began to draw. Some rendered images of family vacations. Mickey Mouse, or the approximation of some happy little rodent, appeared on at least two. Some girls drew rainbows and horses.

"After we finish," the teacher went on, "we'll have one of the class moms take them to laminating, and that way we can use them as placemats." She stopped at Madison Foster's desk. The little girl was drawing the picture of a house with a pointed roof, a brick chimney, and a row of fir trees.

"Maddie, that's lovely. Where is that place?"

Maddie, a sullen girl with missing front teeth and a slept-on ponytail, looked up, her hand still moving the black crayon as she colored a curlicue of smoke.

"Ms. Marshall! That's my house!"

The teacher put her hand on Maddie's shoulder. "Oh, of course it is!"

The truth was far from the depiction on the paper. Maddie lived with her mother and four brothers in a single-wide mobile home at the end of a long driveway from the main road. Half the time there was no heat, and for sure there was no chimney. No row of fir trees. Just a front yard littered with appliances, a Frigidaire graveyard.

The teacher heard one of the boys in the back laughing, and she turned around. Jeremy Wagner was standing next to Max Castile's desk and pointing.

"What's that? You're gonna be in trouble, Max. Here comes the teacher."

Max looked up and threw his crayons to the floor, sending them rolling down the aisle. He flipped over his paper.

"Max, what in the world?" Ms. Marshall put her hand on her hips. "Why did you do that?"

Max didn't say anything, but Jeremy jumped right in.

"Ms. Marshall, Max drew a gross picture!"

"Max, may I see your paper?" she asked.

"No," he said. "You can't. I don't want to get in trouble."

"Let me see it."

Max, a boy never given too much emotion, started to cry. His tears only seemed to fuel Jeremy's rant and the growing interest of other kids in the classroom.

"Max's in trouble! Max's gonna get a talking-to. Nasty picture. Nasty!"

Sally Marshall tugged at the corner of Max's paper and eased it off his desk. She flipped it over and let out a gasp.

Slumped in a small, steel-framed, plastic-upholstered chair across from the receptionist's impeccably buffed counter, the boy with tousled hair, brown eyes, and the shrunken countenance of a kid in trouble just stared at a map of the states. It was decorated with a border of presidential portraits that ended with William Jefferson Clinton. All matted fur and cheap yellow marble eyes, the school mascot, a stuffed lynx, gave him the evil eye.

It was not as good as the hunting trophies his dad had hung in the log house. Not near as convincingly alive.

He wasn't sure what the principal and Ms. Marshall were saying, but he knew it was all about him.

And the voice, from the principal, was harsh, despite the attempt to keep his words low. "We need to reach his parents."

"I've tried."

"Obviously, Sally," the principal said, "you've neglected to update the boy's contact information with their cell numbers. People change their numbers about once a year. We'll need to call the authorities. State law."

"I know," Ms. Marshall said, her voice now brittle. "I understand protocol."

She emerged from the principal's office and knelt low in front of Max.

"Honey, we've tried to reach your mom and dad, but no one's home. Do you know where they are?"

The boy shrugged. "I dunno. My dad's off on Mondays."

"Do you know if they have a cell phone?"

He shook his head. "They have cell phones, but I don't know the number."

Composed now, the teacher spoke directly into Max's eyes.

"Since we can't reach your parents, we have to call the police to come in. They have people who might be able to help you."

"What did I do? I didn't mean it."

She held out her hand. "I know. Let's go and wait in the nurse's office until the officers get here."

"Is it because of what I colored?"

The teacher nodded. "That's right. They'll need to ask you a few questions about what you colored."

The call came into the Sheriff's Office at 1:03 P.M. A dispatcher logged the time and routed it to the investigative unit. Josh Anderson, who had made three calls to Serenity since the morning, looked at the blinking red light and swallowed a piece of black licorice that had made his front teeth the same color.

He picked up, but it wasn't her.

Kendall watched as he scribbled a few illegible notes on a desk pad. As he always did. She'd seen him unfold an eighteen-inch paper and fight through his chicken scratches to come up with the answer a prosecutor sought. No BlackBerry notes. Not even a steno pad. Josh Anderson was too young to be so old-school.

She looked at the pad.

Max Castile, 8, sexual abuse. The words were circled for emphasis. She noticed another name on the paper: *Trey Vedder, Port Orchard Marina.*

"Josh, what's going on?" she asked.

He looked up. "Teacher and principal reported a disturbing drawing. It falls under guidelines. They report, and we follow up."

"What did he draw?"

Josh reached for his jacket. "Don't know yet. Reporting teacher said was that it was sexual. I believe her exact words were 'horrifically sexual.' One thing you should know, Kendall . . ."

"What's that?"

Josh looked worried. "The boy in question is Serenity's nephew. A nice kid. I met him once." He picked up his car keys and started for the hallway.

"Where are you going now?" she asked.

"I'll follow up on the call that came in from the marina. Kid says he's seen something 'freaky' down there. You handle the sex case. You handle those better than I would anyway, conflict of interest or not."

Chapter Fifty-eight

April 6, 10:50 a.m.
Key Peninsula

Kendall Stark caught her breath when she laid eyes on Max's drawing on top of Principal Al Judson's desk. Judson was a stoop-shouldered man of about fifty-five with sparse white hair. He had the sour demeanor of a man with indigestion or one who longed for any other job than the one he held.

"You can see our concern," he said.

"I do," she said, meeting his gaze before looking back down at the paper.

It was a mostly black-and-white rendering, although there were splashes of red in three places. Max, who was left-handed, had smudged some of the imagery. It showed a woman supine on what Kendall figured was a bed. The drawing, with its mix of perspective, had a kind of surreal look. Next to the woman, at the foot of the bed, was a man standing. He was holding a knife. Like the woman, he was nude. Between his legs was a depiction of a penis.

There were splashes of blood on the blade and at the point where the female figure's two legs converged.

"What's with her arms?" she asked. "It looks like they're tied above her head."

"Sick, isn't it?" Principal Judson said.

"If it is what we think it is," Kendall said.

"Maybe it's from a video game," the principal said. "I know they have an Xbox, because the boy traded games and got in trouble for it."

Kendall nodded at the possibility, although she'd never known an Xbox game to have such abhorrent imagery. She wondered if Cody had seen such things.

"Or maybe some porn he saw when an adult carelessly left the TV on," Al Judson said.

"That's more than porn," Kendall said, her expression grim. "But I know there has to be an explanation."

There was another detail that eluded the detective for a moment because it was so faint, as if it had been erased or smudged away.

The woman on the bed wore a crown.

Kendall said nothing more as she took the paper and rolled it into a tube. She put it inside a glassine bag and marked her initials, the date, and the Castile surname. She made her way toward Max in the nurse's office.

Max looked on the verge of tears when he saw that she was carrying the drawing. His teacher had her hand on his shoulder.

"Everything will be all right," she said.

He didn't say anything.

Kendall patted the paper-covered examination table. "I need you to sit up here so we can see eye to eye. Okay?"

The little boy hopped up on the table, tearing the paper covering and looking embarrassed about the ripping sound.

"I didn't do anything," he said.

"Max," Kendall said, "where did you get the idea for this drawing?"

Max looked away.

She didn't want to lead him with questions designed to get a response that she could later use in court. Inside, she hoped that what Max Castile had drawn had absolutely no basis in reality. At least, not at his house. Maybe some kid had brought some filthy photo from home and he had drawn the image from memory.

"Who is the man?" she asked.

"I don't know."

Kendall wasn't getting anywhere.

She decided to press a little, "Is this something you've seen?"

"I don't know." He started to cry, and she lifted him off the table and held him.

"It's okay," she said softy. "We'll take care of this. We've left messages for your mom and dad. We'll all figure this out."

Kendall went back into the principal's office to call Child Protective Services. While she waited to be connected to a caseworker, she thought of the antique rolling pin that had been used as a device of torture and how the name Castile had come up in the case before. She knew that something evil had been going on in the Castile home, and the innocent little boy in the principal's office had seen it.

Chapter Fifty-nine

April 6, 11:15 a.m.
Port Orchard

The headline on the front page of the *Lighthouse,* left on the dock by a boater, piqued Trey Vedder's interest, which was unusual. The teen almost never read a newspaper or cracked open a book. The closest he ever came to a piece of paper was when he sat on the toilet or when he picked up trash around the marina. But then, as he sat smoking on a bench overlooking the marina, the headline of this particular piece of newsprint beckoned to him:

Marine Fiberglass Clue in Cutter Case?

The article, by Serenity Hutchins, related the news first announced by the Mason County Sheriff's Office, then confirmed by Kitsap County's coroner:

> Particles found on two of the victims indicate they'd been aboard a watercraft, most likely

pre-1979, when composite materials were altered because of government regulations. . . .

Trey dialed the Sheriff's Office and, as instructed, waited.
A half hour later, he stood and nodded in the direction of a
well-dressed man who parked his BMW in front of the marina. It was Josh Anderson, wearing charcoal pants and an
Eddie Bauer pullover. The investigator hurried in the young
man's direction.

"You Trey?" he said.

The teen stood. "That's me."

"You see something we should know about?"

Trey pointed to the article with a motor oil–stained finger.

"I don't know if this is anything, but there's one guy that
kind of creeps me out. Follow me."

The pair started walking down the ramp to the slips
where a hodgepodge of boats—sloops and power, new and
old—were moored. Barn swallows that had started nests in
the covered moorage skimmed the glass of Sinclair Inlet.
The air was heavy with the smells of diesel, creosote, and
briny water.

Trey told the detective how he'd observed what he thought
was strange behavior with a particular boat owner.

"He lied to me big-time last year. Said he was fishing
when I knew he hadn't been."

Josh sized up the kid. He looked as if he'd skipped his
weekly shave, the beginnings of goatee shadowing his chin.

"You mean poaching?" he asked.

Trey shook his head. "I mean lying."

"I'm listening."

Trey took a deep breath and started talking about the encounter with the bucket of bloody water, how the boat's
owner had taken the craft out the day before Carol Godding's
body was found in Colvos Passage and the same day Marissa
Cassava's headless body was recovered near Anderson Point.

He checked the marina log against the dates in the newspaper article.

"I checked the harbormaster's log on that," he added. "He fueled up those days too. It's right there in the log."

There are lots of people who would like to help the police solve crimes; many are devotees of *CSI* and other series about forensics. Josh wondered if Trey was one of those people. Statistically, he was way too young. But with the way those kids at Sedgewick Junior High had put Skye Hornbeck's photo on the Internet, there was no telling what young people would do for attention.

"I was working the night before that lady was found. You can check my time card."

The kid hadn't told him anything significant yet, and he was already planning a stint on the witness stand. "No need for that right now," Josh said.

"Okay. But you *can*. Anyway, I was working that night and the skipper of that boat—" He stopped and pointed at the old cabin cruiser. "That's the guy's boat. The *Saltshaker*."

The old Sea Ray wasn't exactly a thing of beauty. Its hull was dingy, and the canvas covering over the stern was tattered and cracked.

"Anyway, he and his wife, and his boy were hauling something heavy—you know all wrapped up."

"Yes," Josh said, now prodding.

Trey shifted his attention back at the detective. "It looked like a body. You know, all wrapped up in a brown plastic tarp."

Josh reached for a cigarette as they stood on the pier next to a NO SMOKING sign.

The teenager played with the zipper of his hoodie. "I asked Sam if I could help. I mean, they *were* struggling. He refused help. When they came back, the tarp was folded up and they carried it off. I thought maybe they tossed some trash into the Sound. You'd be surprised how many do that."

"I guess I would be," Josh said, his interest swelling.

"I read the article today in the paper about the fiberglass. Fits that old piece of crap," he said, looking once more at the boat.

You're quite a detective, kiddo, Josh thought, but didn't say so. "What's this Sam's last name?"

"Castile," Trey said. "His wife is Melody. She's kind of a bitch too. But nicer than he is, that's for sure. I felt sorry for their kid."

Josh felt adrenaline course through his lean body. *Castile. Melody Castile. Serenity's sister and her husband.*

Without taking his eyes off the boat, he reached for his phone.

"Kendall, you know how to get to the Castiles' place on the peninsula?"

"On my way now."

"Castiles have a boat. Kid here at the marina puts Sam Castile in the water when our vics went missing."

Kendall turned her SUV sharply, nearly missing her exit on to the highway. "The Cutter doesn't work alone," she said.

"The wife's part of it."

"I'm afraid so. And, Josh, I'm afraid we'll find Serenity there, too. I hope we're not too late."

Serenity, bound on a mattress, could feel the presence of another naked body next to her. It was a girl, a familiar face. Her blond hair was matted with blood. Her eyes were slits, *fluttering* slits.

It was Paige Wilson, and she was alive.

"Melody!" Serenity called out.

No answer.

She turned toward Paige and tried to nudge her with her shoulder.

"Are you okay?"

It was a stupid question, but in the moment, it was the best she could do.

"Paige, are you okay?"

Paige murmured something unintelligible.

Alive.

Serenity could not tell if it was dark or light outside. She could not be certain how long she'd been unconscious. Her wrists hurt. Her feet felt like they'd been weighted down with something.

"My pretty bitch," came the voice from the foot of the mattress.

It was low, husky, and horrifyingly familiar.

"I'm going to enjoy you. And you're going to enjoy me."

She knew it was Sam.

"Melody, get me out of here. Your husband is a goddamn freak!"

There was no answer from Melody.

"It's just you and me," he said. "You're the one I've been waiting for."

He touched her inner thigh, and she screamed.

"I like a fighter. Carol was a fighter. Skye and the others, not so much."

Serenity didn't seek clarification. She knew who he was talking about. She started to speak to her sister, but she felt herself slipping into darkness. She fought it, but her strength failed her. As blackness came, she heard the sound of an electric drill pulse and saw the glint of a rhinestone tiara.

"She'll have that crown on when they find her," Sam said. She heard him fish for something in a box next to the mattress.

"I need two molly bolts, goddamn it," he said. "Who has been messing with my stuff?"

Chapter Sixty

April 6, 2:40 p.m.
Key Peninsula

Kendall and Josh parked the SUV and BMW on the road outside the gate. They'd arrived at the location in the woods within moments of each other.

"The video cam is a phony," Josh said, getting out if his BMW. "Serenity told me that Sam Castile is one of those guys who's more into looks than reality. Wants the world to see him as some big deal instead of just an average guy."

"Let's leave the cars here," she said.

The pair walked quietly along the bracken-fern-fringed driveway toward the log-built home. The scene was eerily quiet with the kind of heavy, oppressive stillness that comes in the spring when the Northwest's cool marine air loses out to the season.

"Her car's not here," Josh said, looking around.

Kendall crept up to the glass panes of the garage door and peered inside.

"Oh," she said in a whisper, "yes it is."

The missing reporter's familiar car was parked inside. Up in the rafters, Kendall caught a sliver of yellow.

Carol Godding's canoe.

Inside the Fun House, a muted alarm had sounded.

Melody Castile peered out the window of the back bedroom, where she'd been reading a magazine. Sam had been firm in his demand that she should just sit and wait. He'd call her to the mattress when he was good and ready. No matter what she heard, the only command that she should heed would be *his* words to join *him*.

She looked through a hole scratched in the foil covering the window. She craned her neck. It was like peering through the scope of a rifle: She could see only what was directly ahead. There were no peripheral cues. She caught only a fleeting glimpse of the sheriff's detectives and hurried down the hallway. She opened the door to the darkened room, where she found an oily and sweaty Sam next to her sister, now gagged with an athletic sock.

"Sam, someone's here. The police, maybe—I don't know. But someone's here."

The smell of the sex, oil, and sweat nearly made her vomit. For a second she felt a twinge of sorrow for Serenity.

But only for a second.

"Jesus, bitch!" Sam said, looking at her, then at Serenity and Paige. "Finish her!" He stood up, his penis erect and protruding from a leather getup, part jockstrap and part chaps, designed for the wearer's pleasure alone.

"No," she said.

"Prove your love to me, bitch."

Melody hesitated, then took a step backward. "No, she's my sister."

"She's a loser. You're a loser. Deal with it. Do as I say! I'll do the beauty queen."

Melody stood frozen, no reaction on her face.

"Do you hear me?" He balled up a fist as if to strike her.
Not again. Not anymore.

There were three things she could do: She could run. She could fight him. She could do as she was told.

Serenity's eyes were submerged in tears. She twisted her wrists and her feet, but she could hardly move. She was trapped. Her sister—*her only sister*—was standing over her with a box cutter in her hand.

"Cut me a piece of her," he said.

"I . . . I . . ." Melody pushed the lever that extended the blade and dropped to her knees.

Chapter Sixty-one

April 6, 3 p.m.
Key Peninsula

There was a dark prescience, A sense of foreboding that frequently came with the job. Kendall had felt the fear of what
they might find on the Castile property the instant she stepped
out of her car. Guns drawn, she and Josh circled the rooms
of the house in the woods. It looked so mundane. Hunting
and fishing paraphernalia hung on the peeled-wood logs of
the walls, but the rest of the décor seemed bland and so average. Like an average family lived there.

By then both investigators knew that Sam, Melody, and
little Max were far from average.

They heard a crash coming from the mobile home on the
side of the property, and they followed each other outside
Smoke streamed from a window.

"Calling for a fire unit," Kendall said, making the notifi
cation.

"There's no way any responders are getting out here,"

Josh said, going for the garden hose. "Probably should let the dump burn," he said.

Kendall went up the steps toward the door, which was ajar.

"Help me! Help me!"

The smoke roiled at her, and Kendall got down on her knees. She turned and called to Josh over her shoulder, "Someone's trapped inside! I'm going in!"

Josh dropped the hose and ran in the direction of the mobile.

"Help!"

The voice belonged to Serenity.

As she made her way inside, Kendall heard the back door of the mobile slam against its cheap aluminum frame.

"Josh! Go around the back! Castile is making a run for it!"

Kendall began to cough from the smoke, but she crawled deeper into the mobile. Accelerant of some kind had been used to set the fire. The fumes were from gasoline or turpentine. She'd recalled the workbench she'd seen while peering into the garage: rows of paint, bales of wire, nails, cleaning solutions . . . She put her hand over her mouth and nose to stifle her choking, but the smoke was already inside her lungs. She was sure that if she started hacking, she'd have to stop, and whoever was trapped would surely die.

Where was the fire unit?

"We're in here!"

This time the voice was not familiar.

Crawling on the floor under the blanket of black, acrid smoke, Kendall propelled herself in the direction of the back bedroom. In the dim light, she made out the figure of a woman frantically trying to free another from bondage.

"Dear God," she said, "are you all right?"

"Please, get us out of here!" Serenity screamed.

Melody, whose face appeared bloodied, shouted, "Get all of us out of here!"

For the first time, Kendall noticed that Serenity was not alone on that mattress. The body of Paige Wilson, curled in a ball, was next to her.

"Oh, God," she said. "Paige! Can you hear me?"

Kendall helped Melody undo the straps that pinned Serenity to the mattress. Finally free, the reporter got on her hands and knees, then pulled herself up and stood. Her mouth moved, but nothing came out at first—it just opened and closed without emitting a sound. Her body was red with blood, but she had not been cut. Dried tears streaked her cheeks.

Kendall, tears rolling down her cheeks, hooked her hands under Paige's arms and started to drag her.

"Help me!" she said to Melody, who stood still in the thickening smoke.

"Oh, yes," she said, grabbing Paige as Serenity stumbled in front of them.

The four made it outside, heaving and coughing, their eyes stinging from the fumes. Kendall removed her jacket and put it over Paige, checking her pulse.

Good.

She felt the teenager's rib cage rise and fall with her breath.

Alive.

Paige's eyes fluttered, and she moaned. Her face was scratched, her body red and sore from the ordeal, the terror of which, Kendall knew, would never, ever leave her.

On either side of her forehead two X's had been inked with a Sharpie.

They watched the conflagration blow out the mobile windows as it sent a toxic black tower roaring into the tree tops. Kendall retrieved a blanket from a porch swing and wrapped it around Serenity's shoulders. The reporter still had not said a word.

Her sister was another matter.

"I'm so sorry," she said. "I had no idea Sam would this. I had no idea about any of this! I thought it was some kind of game."

Kendall looked up from where she knelt beside Paige.

"A game? What kind of game leaves four women dead?"

Melody was making crying sounds, but no tears dripped. "Look, you have to believe me. I had no idea what Sam was doing."

Serenity, clearly in shock, had barely said a word as she stood shivering. Her eyes, now alert, darted in the direction of her sister. Melody loosened her grip on something she was holding, and it fell on the gravel driveway.

Skye's yin and yang necklace.

"How could you," Serenity finally said.

Melody took a step back, away from the other women. "How could I what? You have no idea what I've done."

"I hate you, Melody."

Melody looked over at the burning mobile.

"Get in line," she said.

Kendall drew her gun once more. "Don't even think about running. Get down. On the dirt. *Now.*"

The wheels turned as Melody weighed the detective's order.

"Down, now!"

She dropped to her knees, her expression grim. But cool, given the circumstances, oddly so.

Serenity reached for the necklace, the glimmer of the hammered silver turned black by the flames, and it swung like a pendulum.

Paige opened her eyes and let out a scream that mixed with the sound of sirens through the smoke. And although there were a hundred questions swirling through Kendall Stark's mind, two thoughts pushed their way to the forefront.

Where is Josh? Did he stop Sam Castile?

Josh had never lost sight of Sam, now clad in a T-shirt and faded blue jeans and scrambling over the forest deadfall toward the road, a couple hundred yards away. Josh had drawn his weapon, and when he yelled at the man to freeze, Sam Castile did something remarkable.

Sam stopped and put his hands up in the air.

"So you got me," he said. "Big deal."

"Big deal for you," Josh said, a little out of breath, adrenaline pumping through his veins. "Drop to your knees."

"That sounds like something I'd say," Sam said, a smile breaking over his sweaty face.

As he ran his hands over Sam's frame to ensure that he carried no weaponry, Josh recited the Miranda rights.

"Wonder if your little girlfriend made it out okay." Although the words were uttered with sarcasm, Sam's gape held no emotion. His eyes were as lifeless as buttons, unblinking, unfeeling. "She's a hot little thing."

Josh cuffed him with plastic restraints that he'd pulled from his coat pocket. "I wonder if you're going to be on the receiving end of the needle at Walla Walla."

"You and I are not so different, you know," Sam said.

Josh tried to let the remark pass as if he hadn't even heard it, but it was hard to do. Just the idea that he was anything like the piece of scum he'd just picked up made him even angrier. He didn't ask all the questions he wanted to. He worried that Kendall might not have made it into the mobile in time to save Serenity.

"We both like using a young thing now and then, right?" Sam said with a wink.

Josh thought about it for only a second before he punched Sam in the gut, sending him to the ground.

"I'll have your badge for that," Sam said, choking for air.

The detective relaxed his fist. "Oh, I don't think so, pal. It'll be your word against mine, and I have a pretty good idea who they'll believe."

Melody stood mute, barely looking at anyone as the responders arrived—more visitors in that hour than in the decade she'd lived there. Smoke and steam spun high above the trees as local firefighters emptied their sole water tank. Paramedics hovered over Paige and Serenity, who were placed in the back of the ambulance. Paige was given oxygen, but Serenity refused it. She was bloodied and bruised, but her expression was resolute.

"I can drive myself home," she said.

Kendall patted her hand. "No, you can't. Not after what you've been though."

"I want to talk to my sister."

"She's in custody, Serenity."

"I want to know what has been going on here."

"There's time for that. But not now," Kendall said.

The ambulance doors shut, and the red and white vehicle began to pull away as Josh returned to the driveway. Sam and Melody Castile were on their way to booking. Josh looked the worse for the wear, his slacks torn by blackberry vines, his face bleeding from minor scratches from vegetation incurred during the pursuit.

"She's going to be okay," Kendall said, following his eyes to Serenity.

"She's tough, isn't she?" he said, trying to reel in his emotions.

"She is."

The pair stood for a minute before heading back to their vehicles and the mountain of paperwork that faced them at the office.

"They did this together," Kendall said. "Sam and Melody."

"She'll say she was abused."

"They always do. And maybe she was. But honestly, her own sister?"

Josh thought of the Paul Bernardo and Karla Homolka case in Canada. He didn't bring it up because he knew the outcome and it chilled him. Karla and Bernardo had raped and murdered Karla's sister, Tammy. Karla testified against Bernardo and eventually found her way to freedom. The idea of a man and woman joining forces to commit debased acts was hardly unheard-of: Fred and Rosemary West had raped and murdered as many as a dozen girls—including their own daughter—in Great Britain from the 1960s to the 1980s.

But this was close to home.

"I feel sorry for the little boy," Josh said.

"I'm not without hope there. He sent us here with his drawing," Kendall pointed out. "He knew what he was doing."

"I wonder what will happen to him?"

"He's got family," she said.

Chapter Sixty-two

They were on opposite sides of the glass partition separating good from evil, the yin and yang of the justice system. Others were facing each other through the transparent wall as well. Some were husbands talking to wives whom they still stood by; some were fathers trying to understand the error of their ways as they spoke with delinquent daughters. The glass was an inch thick, a good insulator of sound. So despite the fact that one could look into the other's eyes and talk, they had to use a telephone. Intimacy was reduced, but safety ensured. That pretty much summed up the way visitors' row at the Kitsap County Jail had been designed. Only once had the glass been damaged: when an angry inmate used the receiver instead of words to make a point, leaving a spiderweb of fissures.

Serenity studied her sister as she reached for the phone.
"You doing all right?"

Melody's eyes were cold. Colder than usual. "What kind of a question is that? I'm not doing all right at all."

"Melody, I can see that. Tell me what is going on."

"Is this for the paper?"

"This is for *me*."

"I'm not speaking to anyone without a lawyer. I'm not stupid, Serenity. I mean, I'm not going to be stupid anymore."

"Melody, please."

Although Melody looked directly at Serenity, there appeared to be nothing warm and alive behind her eyes. Not even a glimmer of the sister she thought she knew.

"Everybody does what they have to do to survive," she said. "Let's leave it at that."

"What about Celesta, Skye, Marissa, Carol . . . Paige?"

Melody's eyes looked increasingly distant, no longer holding any trace of recognition. She was like an empty vessel, devoid of emotion, love. It was as if her soul had been replaced by something cold, mechanical.

"You know the beginning and the ending, Serenity."

"I think so. I guess so."

"You want to know the middle, don't you?"

Serenity nodded.

"Everybody does."

"Tell me," Serenity said, her eyes welling with tears. She knew that the woman on the other side of the glass was no longer her sister. She was an imposter. A shape-shifter. A thief of all of her memories.

"What do you want to know?"

"I wouldn't know where to begin."

Serenity bolstered herself on the counter and gripped the phone. "You didn't, you *couldn't* have been a participant in this. Not really?"

Melody's eyes flickered for a second, and Serenity wondered if her sister had come back. In that flash of recognition, she allowed herself to believe that Melody had found a core of humanity stirring somewhere deep inside herself.

The wheels of memory seemed to whirl behind Melody's eyes, but she remained quiet.

"The bitch has escaped!"

Melody Castile could barely contain her rage. She was mad at her son, at herself, at Sam, but mostly angry that Carol Godding had disappeared into the woods. None of the others that had been their playthings had ever dared to try to escape. No one left the Fun House alive. But this woman, the divorcee from Port Orchard, had done the impossible.

"You take the car," Sam said. "Go up the road to the culvert. That's the only way she can get out of here. I'll follow on foot. I'll get her and take care of her."

Melody ran into the house, grabbed the car keys, and bolted back outside as Sam vanished with a Maglite behind the Fun House. In a second, Melody was behind the wheel of the silver Jeep. She cursed the damned gate as she spun the car around the driveway, then got back out of the vehicle to unlock and fling open the annoying barrier. There was no need to go back and lock it. She didn't expect that she'd be gone that long.

Within five minutes, her headlights caught the image of the ghostly white figure of a woman on the side of the road. Melody tried to identify what she was seeing.

Was it a doll? A mannequin? Or was it someone's little girl? A girl like she'd once been . . .

She swerved around the woman, as if to allow a hitch-iker extra room.

For safety, always give those walking on the shoulder at least a fifteen-foot cushion, came to her mind.

Melody thought of what her father had said when he taught her how to drive. She remembered how her face had stung when he slapped her for knocking over the road cones used to practice parallel parking.

She pressed the ball of her foot against the accelerator and circled back. The car skidded on the gravel and stopped; Melody swung the driver's-side door open as fast as she could, as if slowing down for even a moment would break the momentum of what she was bent on doing.

She lunged for Carol, who'd slumped onto her bloody knees.

"Get up," Melody said.

"You," Carol said, crying. "Why *you*?"

"Because," she said. "If not you, then it will be me."

Carol's face was smeared in dirt and blood, making the whites of her eyes look larger in the darkness. Wide, full of terror.

"Please! I won't tell anyone!"

Melody stiffened and drew back. She turned in the direction of the woods, behind the cowering woman.

Branches cracked, and Sam emerged. His face was a mask of rage. Melody snapped back into the moment and grabbed Carol by the hair.

"For you, babe," she said, summoning her nerve.

Sam said nothing as he bathed Carol's body in the glow of his flashlight. She had dissolved into a shivering mass of blood-streaked flesh.

"Good girl," he said to his wife. "Now finish her."

Melody pulled on Carol's hair, lifting her bowed head.

"Don't hurt me. Please let me go! You don't want to do this!"

Sam played the light over Carol's terrified face.

"I can't," Melody said.

"You can, and you will." He produced a hunting knife from his pants pocket and handed it to her. "Finish her!"

"No, I won't. I can't, Sam. You do it. I'll help you, but can't do it myself."

Sam arched his brow and shrugged. It was as if Melody's reluctance, her passivity, warranted some kind of show of strength.

He grabbed Carol by the neck and strangled her. Still alive, she slumped into the gravel.

"She's ready. Do it," he said.

A moment later the blade was buried in Carol's neck and blood pulsed from the gash, sending a fountain of red into the beam of the headlights.

Serenity looked into Melody's empty eyes. She tried to summon some kind of conviction that what her sister was saying was true. Melody had told Serenity a sanitized version of what had transpired, leaving out the Fun House. Leaving out the fury in which she drove to find Carol.

Leaving out the fact that she'd seen her on the side of the road.

"Then what happened?" Serenity asked.

Melody broke their mutual gaze.

"I'm not sure," she said. "I never saw her. I only did what Sam wanted me to do. I looked for her, but there was nothing else. Nothing at all."

Behind the glass shield, Melody was about to hang up the phone when a glimmer of alertness came to her eyes.

"I can't say that I'm sorry," she said. "I know that you want me to. But I did what I did for a good reason. At least, I thought so at the time."

"How could you, Melody? How could you have gone along with him?"

The semblance of understanding had vanished.

"Who said it was Sam's idea?" Her eyes now had no spark. "Besides, you played a role in this thing too."

Serenity was struck mute, her mouth half open in incomprehension.

"You knew there were other victims," Melody said. "And you knew ahead of time."

"I don't know what you're talking about."

"Yes, you do. I told you."

"You never told me anything. Your sick husband called and bragged about what he'd done."

"Funny, that's not how I remember it, Serenity. I was the one who called you when you did that story about Paige Wilson and the food bank."

Of course Serenity remembered the call.

I'm going to pick up your little beauty queen and take her for a test ride, the caller had said.

"You *never* called me."

Melody clipped the phone between her chin and shoulder and ran her hands over her hair.

"You know what I'm talking about, don't you? You could have warned her. You could have stopped it, but you were too busy screwing that detective of yours and trying to find a way to use this story to launch yourself out of Port Zero."

"That's a lie," Serenity said, eyes glistening.

Melody smiled at her sister, set down the phone, and turned away.

Serenity pounded her fist on the glass, and Melody spun around.

"Don't say a word," she mouthed. "Don't ever say a word."

Melody shrugged but wore a satisfied look on her face.

Serenity watched her sister follow an officer in a blue uniform down the corridor that led to the jail's cellblock. Her orange flip-flops could be heard through the glass. In a moment Melody was gone.

Gone forever.

Josh Anderson and Kendall Stark were waiting outside the jail's visitor reception door when Serenity emerged from he

visit with her sister. She wore jeans, a cardigan, and no
makeup. She was still very pretty. Bandages concealed the
wounds on her wrists.

It was obvious that the encounter with her sister had shaken
her.

"Well?" Josh asked.

Serenity dabbed at her eyes. "Nothing. She told me nothing."

The time for tears had long since passed. She knew then
that she'd unwittingly played a role in the selection of some
victims. Most had been featured in the pages of the *Lighthouse*.

"You don't look like you're okay," Kendall said, putting
her hand gently on Serenity's shoulder.

She looked at her and nodded. "I'm fine. I just wish she
would have told me something," she said.

The three walked across the parking lot toward the back
entrance of the courthouse. It had stopped raining, and the
air was filled with the scent of motor oil and wet asphalt. A
seagull circled overhead. Jurors dismissed from a case filed
past. One, a heavyset woman in a crocheted sweater and capri
pants, glanced in their direction, wondering if they were
somehow connected to the same trial. The woman carried a
paperback novel about a serial killer to pass the time. She
wondered if she'd see the three in court and hear their story.
She nodded in their direction, and Kendall smiled back.

"How's Max?" Kendall said.

"Better than I'd be," Serenity said, as if what had happened to her in the Fun House was inconsequential.

Josh held the door open, and the two women went inside.

"You're holding up pretty good," he said. His tone was a
little longing, and he knew it. But it didn't matter.

"Considering. I guess so," Serenity said, not allowing herself to be affected by Josh's emotions. She couldn't go there
yet. Too much had happened. Too much still needed to be

done. "I'm going to petition the court to let me take Max. He's a good kid. I'm all the family he's got."

"Raising a child isn't easy," Kendall said, speaking from her heart and from the experience of having a child with special needs. A psychologically damaged child like Max Castile would come with a load of baggage.

"He's got no one else but me," Serenity said.

Epilogue

I can't be blamed for any of this.
It isn't fair and anyone with half a brain knows it. I'm
a victim too.

—FROM A LETTER MAILED FROM KITSAP COUNTY JAIL

Late summer
Port Orchard

Serenity Hutchins woke up in the blackness of a mild summer night. She heard a noise coming from the kitchen of her Mariner's Glen apartment. She opened her phone to see the time; it was almost 2 A.M. She'd had a hard time sleeping since the ordeal in the Fun House, and she'd made plans to pack up and move to Seattle. A call from Kendall Stark that afternoon that Sam Castille had been beaten to death in a prison holding cell had brought an unsettling mix of relief, anger, and sadness. *Just like Dahmer*, she thought.

She slipped her arms through the sleeves of a kimono that had belonged to her mother and navigated past boxes, rolls of tape, and a deluge of things she was either going to throw away or give to charity. Cautiously, she followed the noise down the hallway into the kitchen.

Her feet slipped a little on the wet floor.

Serenity flipped the switch on the ceiling light, and a drip of blood caught her eye. It was also smeared on the cheap cabinetry surrounding the sink. Her heart raced.

"Max!" she called out, running back down the hall toward the second bedroom.

Her nephew was sitting upright in bed.

She turned on the sailboat lamp on the bed stand. "Honey, are you all right? What happened?"

Max blinked away the bright light. "I'm okay," he said.

She put her arms around him and held him.

"Did you cut yourself?"

He shook his head.

"I saw some blood in the kitchen." She pulled his hands out from under the covers.

Clean. Good. He's okay.

The next morning, the kitchen was clean. No blood anywhere. Serenity dismissed what she thought she'd seen. It had been a reaction to the stress of all she'd endured. The conselor she was seeing had told her it would take time to heal. To start over.

When she called for Mr. Smith to come to his full food dish, the cat was nowhere to be found. She called for her cat over and over, but no answer. Also missing was the box cutter that she'd set out on the dining table with other moving supplies. Its bloody tip wiped clean, the blade was wrapped up in a towel under the bathroom sink.

ACKNOWLEDGMENTS

The author would like to thank David Chesanow, Jessica Wolfe, Tina Marie Brewer, Bunny Kuhlman, Jim Thomsen, and Charles Turner for their help in getting this book ready for readers.

To best-in-the-business editor Michaela Hamilton, literary agent Susan Raihofer, and film agent Joel Gotler: I greatly value all that each of you do on my behalf. Also, much appreciation to Kensington's tireless Doug Mendini, who might have the most important job of all: seeing that my books get into the hands of booksellers across America and Canada.

I'd like to give a shout out to the reference librarians at the Peninsula Library in Gig Harbor for being so accommodating and giving me a home away from home—Joy, Adam, Beverly, and Lynn, you are the best.

While this is a work of fiction, I do want to acknowledge the time taken and the tours given by various Kitsap law enforcement offices. Thank you to Sheriff Steve Boyer, Detective Lt. Earl Smith, Corrections Sgt. Steve Lawson, and Deputy Scott Wilson of the Kitsap County Sheriff's Office. Thanks also to Kitsap County Coroner Greg Sandstrom for the tour of the old coroner's office.

Last, but surely not least, I'd like to acknowledge my beautiful and smart daughters, Morgan and Marta, and the love of my life, Claudia.

TURN THE PAGE FOR AN EXCITING PREVIEW OF
GREGG OLSEN'S NEXT EXPLOSIVE THRILLER

COMING FROM PINNACLE IN 2011

She knew setting the stage was as crucial as it was easy. All one had to do was think like a CSI or a cop. Maybe a little like a nosy mother-in-law. She'd had a few of those to contend with, too. Ultimately, she knew that no detail was too frivolous. Even the mundane had to be considered, very carefully. The point of setting the stage was to ensure that she was in the final act.

The act that had her getting everything she ever wanted.

The plasma over the fireplace was playing Bill O'Reilly's Fox TV show. Her husband loved the anchorman's take on politics, business, and culture. He even drank from a "Culture Warrior" mug.

She considered the newsman an insufferable blowhard.

She felt the chill of the air conditioner as she stood nude behind the sofa.

"Babe, how about a piece of that pie," he said, his eyes fixed on the screen.

She exhaled, fired, and pulled the gun from his head. Blood spurted like a stomped-on catsup package. Specks of red freckled her glove-covered arm. There was likely more blood than she could see with the naked eye, but that was fine. She knew how to handle it. She'd planned for it. He gurgled a little, but it wasn't the sound of a man fighting for his life. That was over. It was the sound of air and gas oozing from his trachea. He slumped over. She made her way to the shower, already running. She pulled off the glove and set it inside a trash can lined with plastic. The water was ice cold by then. Even for her, it had taken considerable effort to summon the nerve to do what she had wanted to do. She hated cold.

Gunfire was messy.

Blowback is hell.

Spatter matters.

And only time will tell.

It was a kind of verse that she'd conjured that moment, and she allowed a smile to cross her lips as the icy water poured over her. She looked down at her legs, long, lovely. Flawless.

But not for long.

The water had gone from crimson, to pink, to clear, swirling down the drain between her painted toes. She turned off the shower and reached for a towel. As she patted her face dry she caught a glimpse of herself in the mirror.

Still lovely. Still rich. Even more so at that very moment than she'd ever been in her life.

She poked her arms through the sleeves of a sheer white nightgown and let the filmy fabric tumble down her body. This was part of setting the stage. Her augmented breasts—not freakishly so, just enough to arouse a man when she needed to—would protrude only slightly. She'd act modest and embarrassed, but if the cops on the scene were under fifty, they'd be looking where they shouldn't.

A distraction. One of many.

She poured a plastic cup of bleach down the shower drain and ran the water while she counted to ten.

Grabbing the waste can liner with the glove and the empty plastic bleach cup nestled inside, she hurried back into the living room and surveyed the scene. Exactly seven minute had passed since she pulled the trigger propelling the slug into her unsuspecting . . . pie-waiting . . . TV watching . . . husband. It was important for her to get on with it. The pool of blood around his head would began to congeal and her story would not seem so plausible. She knocked the contents atop the coffee table to the floor. Using her hip, she pushed over a potted button fern. Black soil scattered over an Oriental rug. A drawer in a sideboard was pulled to the floor. Knives fell like gleaming pixie sticks.

It looked like a struggle. Not much of one, but one that could have taken place in the moments that she'd later describe.

Next, she put on a second rubber kitchen glove—the long kind that ran from fingertips to elbow—and picked up the gun. She was grateful for all the things that money could buy just then. Pilates. Yoga. Tai chi. She'd taken all those courses with the other rich bitches. They never accepted her, but that didn't matter. She wasn't there to get to know them. She was there to limber up. She bent down and twisted her shoulder as she pointed the gun at her leg and fired.

She didn't cry out.

Instead, she bit her lip and started toward the door. She was no longer concerned about blood and where it fell. In the throes of her imagined escape, there could be blood anywhere. *His or hers.* She left the door open, and started to pick up the pace by the koi pond that had been the labor of love, apparently, of the previous owners. She didn't love anything or anyone. Except, of course, a brimming bank account. She bent down, her nightgown now more red than white. She'd missed her femoral artery, of course. But she hadn't expected that much blood.

Good thing the neighbor's still home, she thought, looking through the open wrought-iron gate to the property next door, a beam of light slashing a through the coiffed foliage.

She slipped the gun into the plastic bag, dropped in a three-pound lead weight, and deposited it into the koi pond.

Each time she moved her leg she let out a yelp. Then a scream. Finally she turned on the tears.

One notch at a time.

Colton Fulton couldn't sleep and was watching TV. He wasn't sure if it was the crab cakes or the fight he'd had with his daughter. He was queasy and uneasy all at the same time. He scrolled through the satellite guide. Nothing was on. Nothing good, anyway. It was a muggy night, the kind with thick, choking air and without even a twitchy breeze to vibrate the feathery tops of the Pampas grass that divided his home from the neighbors.

Oh, the neighbors. He'd heard them arguing earlier in the evening. They'd barely moved in and they seemed to never miss the opportunity to seize the attention of everyone within earshot and eyesight. New car. New landscaping. New this. *New that.* Colton had been alone for more than a year and knew that his days of keeping up with anyone were long gone. At 55, and divorced, Colton Fulton was going to have to make do with the residual trappings of the life he'd once known. Before the asshole with the Porsche scooped up his wife and left him in the dust. She's been the proverbial trophy wife, with tits that stood like Twin Peaks when she was on her back.

The best money could buy. That he could buy.

Colton's time had passed. Not those two next door. They were on the way up. Up and more up.

He hoisted himself up from the couch and went to the kitchen, where he poured himself a glass of wine, dropping an ice cube into the slightly amber liquid. He didn't care if ice cubes in wine was some big faux pas. Hell, it was Chablis out of a box, for Christ's sake. Bored and tired, he flipped through television shows recorded earlier in the week before settling on an Oprah broadcast that celebrated all the things he'd need to do to have his "best life."

"My best life was five, no, ten years ago," he thought.

Another sip. A guzzle. And he hoped that sleep would come right then and there on the couch that he and Teri had picked out together. When he was carefree. When he was climbing the corporate ladder with the vigor and grit of a man who knew that he'd have the world in his hands. Always. Forever.

And just like that his pity party for one was over.

He thought he heard a sound at the door. His ex-wife's cat Darcy scooted under the dining table in the other room. How he hated that damn cat. Colton looked at his mantel clock and determined that he must have misheard. It was after eleven, too late for a visitor. He turned up the volume. A moment later, the unmistakable sound of a fist bumping the pane glass center of the front door.

"Who'd be over at this hour?" he muttered to himself as he went toward the door.

He turned on the overhead light and let out a gasp.

The glass inset was smeared in blood.

"God, what's happened?" he asked, moving closer to get a better view. In that instant when reality is suppressed for a more plausible, a more acceptable scenario, he allowed himself to think that a bird might have lost its way in the dark, hitting the widow and splattering is blood. Yet, at once, he knew that there was too much blood for that.

The bloody smear looked like a big red octopus.

Or the shape of a human hand.

Without considering any risk to his personal safety, the now underemployed sales executive turned the lock and swung open the door.

Wilting on the front steps was a female figure, a woman in her nightgown. It must have been a white nightgown, but now it was bloodred. The woman's hair was wet. She was lying there, making the kind of guttural sounds that people do as they fight for their last breath.

"Good God," Colton said, dropping to his knees. "What happened?"

The woman, curled in a defensive ball, lifted her damp head. Her hands were smeared with blood.

"Help," she said.

He knew her. He'd seen her going in and out of the big brick Tudor across the street. He couldn't remember her name.

"I need an ambulance," she said.

"Of course you do. I'll call for one now."

"Not for me," she said. "My husband. He's been shot, too. We've both been shot. He needs help. Oh dear God. Help me. Help him!"

"What happened?"

"A man got in. Our security system is down. He got in the house to rob us. He shot us. He shot my husband."

Colton paced. It was all happening so fast. He was slightly drunk from the cheap wine and he knew it. He wasn't sure right then if he should go for his phone—charging in the kitchen—or get something to help stop the bleeding.

"Are you going to call for help? I need help, too!" the woman said, struggling to her feet.

He made no attempt to keep her from coming in but slammed the door shut behind her and turned the deadbolt. The SOB who'd shot his neighbor was out there. His ex-wife had a thing against guns, so he no longer had any in the house. She'd taken everything from him. Everything but the cat, the mortgage, and the damned leather sofa.

"Yeah, dialing now."

The woman who had staggered from the front door to the sofa was crying loudly, loud enough to be heard by the 911 dispatcher.

Setting the stage. That's right.

He knelt next to her as he gave his address to the dispatcher. He looked in to her fearful eyes. "It's my neighbor . . . Ms. . . ."

"Connelly," she said, "Rachel Connelly. My husband . . my husband *is* Alex Connelly."

Jesus, of course. Alex Connelly, the bigwig at Charles Schwab. He was rich, successful, and now, dead.

If there was something to be grateful for, it was that he was alive. *It wasn't much,* Colton thought, *but it was better than the sap next door.*

Riley O'Neal stared at the blank face of her computer screen. French roast coffee perfumed the confines of her open con- cept home office. She watched her Siamese fighting fish, Rusty, blow bubbles on the surface of the brandy snifter that was his home. It was just before 6 A.M., and she had time to pol- ish a chapter of the true crime book that she'd been working on—with renewed vigor—since the *Seattle P-I* shuttered its newsroom after more than a century of being the "news- paperman's newspaper."

Her cell phone rang. Her eyes darted to the tiny screen, but she did not recognize the number. It was too early for a source to call. Neither was it a number for one of the other reporters who regularly called to commiserate about their futures in a post–newspaper employment world. The area code was 630, which was unfamiliar. A beat later, the caller tried a second time.

It must be urgent, she thought. She clapped the phone to her ear.

"Hello?"

"Riley?"

The voice was a whisper.

"This is Riley O'Neal," she said.

"Riley, this is your sister."

Riley no longer needed the early morning jolt of a mud- thick French roast. The words were a cattle prod in her heart.

"Rae?"

Silence.

"Rae? Is that you?"

"I'm in the hospital. I've been hurt. I need you."

"Where?"

"In the leg. I've been shot."

"Oh my, but no, *where* are you?

"Mercy."

Riley felt her adrenaline pulse. She needed more information. She had no idea in which city her sister had resided. They were twins, but they hadn't spoken in seven years.

"Chicago," Rachel said. "Please come."

"What happened?"

"An intruder. I was shot. My husband was killed."

Husband? Riley had no idea that Rachel had married. Again.

"Will you come? I need your help."

"What kind of help?"

Again, an awkward silence, the kind that invites the person waiting to hear to press the phone tighter to her ear.

"They're whispering about me . . . I think they think I did this," she said.

"I'll be there," Riley said, coming to her sister's aid.

Once more.

She hung up and looked across the room at a photograph of two little girls posing in ballet tights on a balance beam. Their hair was blond, eyes blue. Everything about them was the same, but in reverse. Like looking into a mirror. Riley's hair parted naturally on the left side of her face, Rachel's on the right. Riley's upper left lip had a mole, Rachel had hers— on the right side—removed when she was 14. Their mother dressed them alike until junior high. No one could tell them apart. They were so close. *So identical.*

Yet they were not the same. Not by a mile.

The SENSATIONAL
true story of a minister who
used his faith for evil

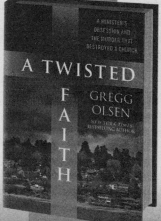

Follow Nick Hacheney, a philandering minister who used his faith as a tool for seduction and manipulation to engage in numerous affairs with members of his congregation, all while plotting and carrying out the brutal murder of his wife.

From one of the foremost names in true crime, a gripping and truly unforgettable story of a man whose charisma and desire rocked an entire community.

A MINISTER'S OBSESSION AND THE MURDER THAT DESTROYED A CHURCH

A TWISTED FAITH

GREGG OLSEN

NEW YORK TIMES BESTSELLING AUTHOR

Available April 2010

ST. MARTIN'S PRESS   www.stmartins.com

GREAT BOOKS,
GREAT SAVINGS!

When You Visit Our Website:
www.kensingtonbooks.com

You Can Save Money Off The Retail Price
Of Any Book You Purchase!

- **All Your Favorite Kensington Authors**
- **New Releases & Timeless Classics**
- **Overnight Shipping Available**
- **eBooks Available For Many Titles**
- **All Major Credit Cards Accepted**

Visit Us Today To Start Saving!
www.kensingtonbooks.com

All Orders Are Subject To Availability.
Shipping and Handling Charges Apply.
Offers and Prices Subject To Change Without Notice.

More Books From Your Favorite Thriller Authors

Necessary Evil by David Dun	0-7860-1398-2	$6.99US/$8.99CAN
The Hanged Man by T.J. MacGregor	0-7860-0646-3	$5.99US/$7.50CAN
The Seventh Sense by T.J. MacGregor	0-7860-1083-5	$6.99US/$8.99CAN
Vanished by T.J. MacGregor	0-7860-1162-9	$6.99US/$8.99CAN
The Other Extreme by T.J. MacGregor	0-7860-1322-2	$6.99US/$8.99CAN
Dark of the Moon by P.J. Parrish	0-7860-1054-1	$6.99US/$8.99CAN
Dead of Winter by P.J. Parrish	0-7860-1189-0	$6.99US/$8.99CAN
All the Way Home by Wendy Corsi Staub	0-7860-1092-4	$6.99US/$8.99CAN
Fade to Black by Wendy Corsi Staub	0-7860-1488-1	$6.99US/$9.99CAN
The Last to Know by Wendy Corsi Staub	0-7860-1196-3	$6.99US/$8.99CAN

Available Wherever Books Are Sold!

Visit our website at **www.kensingtonbooks.com**

More Nail-Biting Suspense From
Kevin O'Brien

__Only Son   1-57566-211-6 $5.99US/$7.99CAN

__The Next to Die 0-7860-1237-4 $6.99US/$8.99CAN

__Make Them Cry 0-7860-1451-2 $6.99US/$9.99CAN

__Watch Them Die 0-7860-1452-0 $6.99US/$9.99CAN

__Left for Dead   0-7860-1661-2 $6.99US/$9.99CAN

__The Last Victim 0-7860-1662-0 $6.99US/$9.99CAN

Available Wherever Books Are Sold!

Visit our website at **www.kensingtonbooks.com**

More Thrilling Suspense From

T.J. MacGregor

—Total Silence by T.J. MacGregor	**0-7860-1558-6**	**$6.99**US/**$9.99**CAN
—The Seventh Sense by T.J. MacGregor	**0-7860-1083-5**	**$6.99**US/**$8.99**CAN
—Category Five by T.J. MacGregor	**0-7860-1680-9**	**$6.99**US/**$9.99**CAN
—The Other Extreme by T.J. MacGregor	**0-7860-1322-2**	**$6.99**US/**$8.99**CAN
—Out of Sight by T.J. MacGregor	**0-7860-1323-0**	**$6.99**US/**$9.99**CAN
—Black Water by T.J. MacGregor	**0-7860-1557-8**	**$6.99**US/**$9.99**CAN

Available Wherever Books Are Sold!

Visit our website at **www.kensingtonbooks.com**